*From Deputy Sheriff to Federal Judge . . . and the Lessons Learned Along the Way*

by Henry E. Hudson

Published and distributed by Loft Press, Inc.
P.O. Box 150, Fort Valley, VA 22652
www.loftpress.com



ISBN 1-893846-69-2
First printing September 2007

Designed and typeset by AAH Graphics, Inc., Fort Valley, Virginia
www.aahgraphics.com

# FOREWORD

Maybe it's just me, but it seems that my most lucid moments occur during morning runs. This book is the product of just such an experience, along the oceanfront in Kauai, Hawaii.

Despite my share of controversy, public life has blessed me with many opportunities for adventure and personal fulfillment. Many of the cases prosecuted by me or at my direction dominated the national news. For me, there has been no greater honor than public service. On reflection that morning, I concluded it was a story worth telling.

The task of researching and developing the necessary details far exceeded my expectations. Fortunately, I was able to recruit a cadre of friends and neighbors to help.

Aside from my wife Tara, who persuaded me to radically revise the first two chapters, the comments of my neighbors, Ginger Joyner and Lori Gillespie, were invaluable, along with lots of input from others. I also appreciate the thoughtful suggestions offered by my superb secretary, Robin Belcher, my resourceful former law clerk, Hana Brilliant, and my always effervescent court reporter, Krista Liscio.

A special note of thanks to the guys at the Department of Justice, David Margolis, Ken Melson and Bob Trono, who reviewed the manuscript to insure that I was not giving away any national secrets. I am also eternally grateful to my publisher, Stephen R. Hunter, of Loft Press and my excellent editor, Ann Hunter. Without their guidance and commitment, this book may never have progressed beyond a rough draft.

# IN THIS BOOK

# Prologue

Lots of law school graduates hope to be trial lawyers, meaning one who actually goes to court and argues cases. But typically only a few have an interest in making a career of putting away criminals. I'm sure it comes as no surprise that most gravitate toward the civil side of trial practice—personal injury, employment, business or labor law, or perhaps patent litigation. That's where the money is! Those who launch their careers as prosecutors are driven by a variety of motives. Some feel a serious calling, others a quest for adventure. Still others simply want to hone their trial skills and enhance their resume in preparation for pursuing more lucrative areas of practice. I do not fault those who choose to make the big money. Private practice, both civil and criminal, is prestigious, challenging, and personally rewarding. Life is intense, but cushy at the large firms.

As the cost of living spirals and the price of college tuition escalates, financial pressure often forces even the most devoted prosecutors into the private sector, at about double their government salary. Prosecutors with a successful track record are usually a hot commodity in the private world. Some adjust well, others don't. Good prosecutors who stay the course are a special breed. Some relish the excitement of pursuing the bad guys. Others love reading their name in the morning paper. Some feel a patriotic spirit. And for others its an insatiable quest for law and order. But all share a few common traits—a willingness to make personal sacrifices, a passion to correct injustice and the courage to hold those who violate the law accountable.

Many decisions are tough. Some are praised, others are scorned. Few citizens take lightly having their behavior corrected. Of course, the conduct of their neighbor is a different story. In a way, prosecutors are truly the people's lawyer. They feel an unparalleled sense of accomplishment by putting away a violent thug, dope dealer, or sexual predator. They have no expectation of receiving a bonus or monetary award, only a victim's heartfelt expression of appreciation. Or perhaps a simple note of thanks from a civic association for a job well done. It's a feeling of gratification that some who choose other paths in life may never understand. It is to that special breed of lawyers that this book is dedicated.

# 1
# Carolyn Hamm

Her casual style and unkempt looks were deceiving. On first impression, she appeared shy and retiring; neither of her next door neighbors had ever met her. But her personality came alive among her close circle of friends. She enjoyed sports but her real passion was architecture. She loved old buildings so much that she built her highly specialized law practice around their preservation.

A statuesque, well-educated lady in her early thirties, Carolyn Hamm was single and enjoyed an active social life. When she failed to report for work on the morning of January 25, 1985, at a prestigious District of Columbia law firm, her secretary began calling her home every fifteen minutes. It was a little strange that no one answered.

Her partners were taken aback when she missed her 10:00 a.m. appointment. It was out of character. As time passed, panic began to set in. Finally, her secretary called Hamm's best friend. Did she know anything? They had played squash together two nights previously, but she had not heard from her since. The friend was not concerned—she suspected that Hamm was probably running a few errands in preparation for her eagerly awaited vacation to Peru.

Carolyn Hamm would run no errands, that day or ever. Her nude body was hanging from a water pipe in the basement of her house. She had a noose around her neck. Her hands were tied behind her back. Strangely, no injuries, bruises or bodily fluids were visible. The scene was so bizarre that at first the police suspected some type of erotic suicide, but a broken rear window seemed to dispel that theory. The possibilities were endless, but a determination of the cause of death would have to await the arrival of the Deputy Chief Medical Examiner, Dr. James Beyer.

Meanwhile, I toured the house with Sergeant Frank Hawkins, head of the Arlington County Police Robbery Homicide Unit. As commonwealth's attorney, putting all the pieces together in a court of law was my job—that's what the people had elected me to do.

Snow had been falling earlier that morning when Carolyn Hamm's best friend finally decided to placate Hamm's secretary by checking on the missing lawyer. As she approached Hamm's small two-story white residence in South Arlington, nothing appeared to be amiss. Hamm's old blue Plymouth compact was parked in the driveway. Describing the experience to me later, she said the first thing that drew her attention was the front door. It appeared to be slightly open, with snow blowing inside. She parked her car, traipsed through the snow and peered inside the door, calling Hamm's name several times. No answer.

The young lady's attention was then diverted by a car pulling into the driveway across the street. She haled Hamm's neighbor as he got out of his car and asked if he would accompany her into the house. They pushed the door open and again called Carolyn's name, but heard no movement. As they entered, she found that Hamm's house was in its typical state of disarray. Hamm was far more engaged in her field of architectural law than in housekeeping.

After advancing several slow cautious steps, her friend noticed Hamm's purse, contents scattered, on the floor just inside the doorway. They checked the dining room and kitchen, also messy as usual. A partially consumed bottle of Heineken's beer sat open on the drain board and a camera sat idle on the dining room table. Strange. Hamm wasn't a drinker. Hamm's terry cloth robe was heaped in a pile in the living room. They next headed upstairs, stepping over mounds of books, magazines and letters. All the drawers in Hamm's bedroom were open, with items strewn on the floor. The room was disheveled even by Hamm's standards, but not suspicious. At least not at that point.

Hamm's friend then walked into the bathroom. She observed the gym clothes Hamm had worn two nights previously when they played squash. They were laying on the floor as though someone had just stepped out of them. The next object she saw riveted her attention: Hamm's prescription glasses with thick lens were sitting on the counter top. She knew Hamm could not function without them. Where in the hell could she be?

Now deeply concerned, they descended the stairs and retraced their path back through the kitchen area. Her friend knew that Hamm's greatest fear was someone breaking into her house. She had mentioned it in passing just the preceding week.

With some trepidation, they headed down the dark stairwell. It was bone chillingly cold. A roll of carpet lay partially unwound, a strand of heavy cord beside it. The frayed end suggested that a section had been sliced off. A long-bladed knife was lying next to the carpet. Cautiously, they looked around the corner into the adjacent room. After regaining their composure, they rushed to the phone and dialed 911.

I had seen lots of dead bodies. As commonwealth's attorney, I inspected every homicide scene with the assigned detective and often attended the autopsies. In my prior life as a volunteer firefighter and emergency medical technician, I'd experienced plenty of blood and gore. But this case was unsettling. There were no obvious suspects. It appeared to be the work of a ritualistic killer. Why the noose, when the killer could have just stabbed her with the knife?

Hamm's nude body was lying on the cement floor when she was discovered. The rope attached to the noose around her neck extended over a water pipe and through a window leading into the garage. The other end of the rope was attached to the front bumper of Hamm's other car, which was parked in the garage.

The medical examiner spent almost an hour examining the body before it was transported to the morgue. Based on the appearance of the body, Dr. Beyer estimated that Hamm had been dead almost two days—in other words—since about the time she arrived home from her squash game on Monday, January 23, and that the fluid stains on her body were suggestive of sexual assault. The image of her killer lying in wait when she entered the dark house on a cold snowy night spawned goose bumps on even the most battle-tested cops at the scene.

As I watched Dr. Beyer patiently inspect every inch of her body, I periodically glanced at Hamm's face and into her open eyes. They evoked a haunting image. What was the last thing those eyes saw before the ligature shut off her flow of oxygen?

As I began to refocus, I knew I had seen her somewhere before. But where? Later that day, after learning more about her background and the unique nature of her law practice, it came to me. Carolyn Hamm had visited my booth at the Arlington County Fair the preceding August. I had been campaigning for reelection. Unlike most people, who reluctantly snatched a piece of literature and kept on walking, Hamm stopped to sound out my position on a number of things, including historical covenants. After a pleasant ten-minute chat where I informed her that my office didn't handle covenant enforcement, she walked off.

Carolyn Hamm had attractive physical features, but she was a large-framed woman. That posed a puzzling question. How could a person acting alone have subdued an athletic lady of her size, defiled her, and left her hanging from a water pipe? Hamm's body had no defensive wounds, indicating that she had probably put up minimal resistance. But the idea that she had submitted to such abuse was unfathomable. That is why there was some early suspicion that it could have been some form of auto-erotic suicide. But that was physically impossible. Hamm could not find her way to the basement without her glasses, much less rig the noose—not to mention tying her hands behind her back. This was clearly a homicide, and the possibility was overwhelming that he, or they, would strike again.

Carolyn Hamm's modest home was located at 4291 23rd Street South, about three blocks from Wakefield High School. I knew the area well. My wife and I, as well as my brother-in-law and sister-in-law, had graduated from Wakefield almost twenty years earlier. It was a quiet residential area, relatively crime free, but two other burglaries had been reported in the general vicinity in the preceding weeks. In both cases, the residents were young females who lived alone. Both houses had been entered through a basement window. In one case, the intruder left before the occupant returned home. However, he left a number of sexually explicit magazines in her bedroom and a length of cord cut from her venetian blinds. Hamm's hands had also been bound with a piece of cord that appeared to be cut from the blinds.

In the other case, the perpetrator was laying in wait in an unlit house when the young lady who lived there arrived home. The assailant accosted her from behind with a knife and forced her to have intercourse. Fearful for her life at that point, she screamed and pummeled him with her fists. He eventually fled, but only after slashing her several times with the knife, leaving irreparable scars.

Crime scene investigators scoured Hamm's house for fingerprints, bodily fluids, and trace evidence. Debra Davis of the Arlington County Police forensic unit even brought in a laser scanner that highlights trace materials such as hairs and fibers. Unfortunately, the house was so untidy that it was difficult to microscopically sort material of evidentiary value from the dirt and debris. Processing of the crime scene yielded nothing of immediate value, with the possible exception of semen stains on Hamm's pink robe. Without any knowledge of her personal life, we could not even speculate as to their origin.

An old adage among homicide investigators says that if no suspect is developed within two weeks, the chances of solving a homicide are drastically reduced. The detectives assigned to this case, Bob Carrig and Chuck Shelton, were beginning to get that feeling when they finally received their first lead of potential value.

The neighbor who discovered Hamm's body called Detective Shelton to report that his sister had observed a young man walking in front of Hamm's house on the night it was believed she was murdered. I interviewed the lady. She told me that sometime after 8:00 p.m. that evening, she pulled up in front of her mother's home, located across the street from the murder scene. A young man whom she recognized was walking in her direction. He passed within several feet of her car. She had known him for fifteen years. At a hearing in the Arlington County General District Court, she testified that she may have even waved to him. She positively identified the young man as David Vasquez, a former neighbor. She described Vasquez as kind of a "pervert," someone who made her uncomfortable. According to her, while employed at Wakefield High School as a janitor, he was rumored to have stolen gym clothes from the girls' locker room. She also reported once seeing Vasquez stare at Hamm while she was sunbathing in her back yard. And there was more.

Almost simultaneously, Shelton received a tip from the police officer who routinely patrolled Hamm's neighborhood. The officer advised that a long-time resident of the area, whom he knew well, suspected that a "weird young man" named David, in his mid-thirties, might be involved. He said that David, a former custodian at Wakefield High School, had often been seen standing and staring at young girls. Through more detailed interviews we learned that this neighbor was a retired Army Colonel and CIA intelligence analyst.

In a surprising revelation, the Colonel later told Detective Shelton and me that he had encountered the young man, whom he later identified as David Vasquez, standing on a street corner the day after Hamm's body was found, watching the police process the house. The Colonel said that he had known Vasquez for years and characterized as him as "mentally slow."

I used the Colonel as a witness at the Vasquez preliminary hearing. He was unshakable on cross-examination. Was he sure it was Vasquez? "Heck yes," he responded—they had even exchanged greetings that day.

While canvassing the neighborhood for additional leads, detectives learned that Vasquez had previously lived just a few blocks from Hamm. The couple with whom he formerly resided was stunned that David might be a suspect, but was fully cooperative with Shelton and Carrig, and allowed them to search David's room, which still contained some of his property. Most noteworthy were a number of pornographic and detective-type magazines. Of particular interest were those containing photographs depicting young women in bondage being subjected to physical torture and hanging. The imagery appeared consistent with the evolving profile of the suspected perpetrator. During their interview of the couple, the detectives also learned that Vasquez had relocated to his mother's home in Manassas, Virginia. To the best of the couple's knowledge, Vasquez was working at McDonald's in Manassas.

On another front, to assist in developing a working suspect profile, detectives from the sex crimes unit sought the aid of the FBI Behavioral Science Unit at Quantico, Virginia. Using all the information gathered to that date, the behavioral scientists created a composite of the potential personality traits, psychological makeup, background, and lifestyle characteristics suggested by the crime scene. Although the development of such a profile is not an exact science, it is a useful tool in the absence of other concrete leads. The FBI has an amazing track record for accuracy. The confidential results of their work became a significant factor as the case unraveled.

Armed with the information that had surfaced to that point, Shelton and Carrig proceeded to the Manassas McDonald's to interview David Vasquez. The Colonel had understated David's mental capacity. Later tests determined that he had an IQ of about seventy, considered by psychologists to be at the lower end of the dull normal range. Despite being chronologically in his mid-thirties, Vasquez had the appearance and mannerisms of a teenager. The detectives politely informed him that they needed his help investigating an incident that had occurred in his old neighborhood in Arlington County. They assured him that he was not in trouble, but wanted to discuss the incident with him at the Prince William County Police Department, located several blocks down the street.

En route, they chatted casually with Vasquez. At police headquarters he was escorted to an interview room in the Criminal Investigation Section. Employing a common interview technique, Shelton and Carrig spent the first half hour engaging Vasquez in small talk in order to build rapport. They confirmed that he lived in Manassas with his mother, had minimal education, marginal social skills, and had never driven an automobile.

Carrig then began pressing Vasquez about his whereabouts on the night Hamm was murdered. He played the bad cop, Shelton, the good cop, roles they had honed to perfection. Vasquez at first denied any knowledge of the incident. He recalled having gone bowling that day in the Manassas area after getting off work at McDonald's, but he could not remember with whom. He claimed that he went straight home after leaving the bowling alley and remained there for the rest of the night. He said that his mother could confirm it.

The detectives had several immediate concerns about Vasquez that didn't seem to fit. He didn't have a car or driver's license, and had no way of getting to South Arlington that night, a distance of more than thirty miles. Besides, Vasquez was small in stature and weighed considerably less than Hamm. The detectives' first impression was that Vasquez was not capable of committing the crime. He was too mentally fragile and physically frail. He also appeared too meek to sexually overpower Carolyn Hamm. Could he have hooked up with someone else that night and just tagged along?

The detectives might have cut the interview short if it had not been for one statement that sparked their interest. Vasquez claimed that he had not been to Arlington County in months. The two witnesses, the neighbor and the Colonel who saw him on South 23rd Street around the date of the murder, could have been off by a day or so, but hardly that far off the mark. The detectives turned up the heat and continued to press him, suggesting that based on the eye-witness accounts, he must be lying. Vasquez remained steadfast in his denial.

Finally, Shelton took a different, more manipulative tack. He told Vasquez that his fingerprints had been found in the house. Although considered by some to be a hardball tactic, the use of such deception is both legal and widely accepted as an interview strategy. Vasquez was clearly jolted and visibly shaken, but still he would not budge.

Finally, the relentless pressure proved to be overpowering. Totally perplexed, and with his will to resist spent, Vasquez, in an obvious attempt to move the conversation past that point, hesitatingly conceded that maybe he could have been on South 23rd Street visiting someone, but he didn't know who.

The interview then took a strange turn. Through aggressive questioning, high decibel at times, the detectives were able to disgorge an equivocal admission from Vasquez that he might, in an almost metaphysical sense, have raped and murdered Hamm. The unusual twist was that Vasquez maintained that, if he did it, he must have done it in his imagination because his body was not physically there. It couldn't have been because he said that he had no way to get there.

Vasquez then elaborated on his dream by explaining that Hamm had invited him into the house to help move furniture. He said he might have raped her on the living room floor after tying her hands behind her back, but that he did it at her request. Why did he tie her hands, Carrig asked? Vasquez replied that Hamm was into bondage. He just wanted to please her. Vasquez then astoundingly explained that despite his protests, she begged him to kill her. Carrig, sensing that he was finally getting somewhere, asked Vasquez to describe how he killed her. Vasquez pondered a moment, and responded with a question, "With a knife?"

Disappointed with the answer, Carrig shot back, "You hung her."

Increasingly malleable, Vasquez gave Carrig a blank stare and replied in a conciliatory tone, "Okay, I hung her."

The interview continued for several hours. With each question, Vasquez retreated farther from his earlier admissions. Finally the conversation looped full circle, with Vasquez flatly denying even having been in South Arlington in months. Frustrated, Shelton and Carrig stepped out of the room to assess the situation and to contact their supervisor for advice. The consensus was to bring Vasquez to the Arlington County Police Department for a more formal interview. They also wanted the home turf advantage. Vasquez agreed to go voluntarily, provided he could first call his mother and tell her where he was going.

Despite the limited evidentiary value of the murky first statement, the detectives believed they were on the right track. At that point it was the only track. From a legal perspective, they also knew that potential problems lay ahead. Although they had informed Vasquez that he was not under arrest, circumstances changed as the discussion progressed. It began as a consensual conversation, but once Vasquez admitted that he might have killed Hamm, even in his imagination, it is doubtful that he would have been free to leave. At that point, the setting legally evolved into a custodial interrogation, altering the rules of engagement and requiring Miranda warnings and a waiver of rights. So far, Vasquez had not been advised of his rights. But who could have foreseen this unorthodox turn of events? And this was just the beginning.

Vasquez was taken to an interview room at Arlington County Police headquarters. En route, Carrig gave Vasquez a cigar to smoke and kept the conversation light. Again, no one told him he was under arrest. He had not even been handcuffed during the drive from Manassas. Unable to predict what might occur next, Shelton was cautious, advised Vasquez of his Miranda rights, and asked him to sign a waiver of rights form. Vasquez complied without hesitation.

The conversation that ensued was much the same as the first, including the nonsensical detachment of body and spirit. Vasquez continued to describe how in his mind he had raped and murdered Hamm, but he was inexorable in his insistence that he could not have been physically present in Arlington that day. The detectives used every known interrogation technique, including walking Vasquez through the details of the crime scene. Although intended to refresh his recollection, this, in retrospect, proved to be a mistake. The best method of authenticating a confession is eliciting the suspect's knowledge of unpublicized details that only the perpetrator would know. Supplying Vasquez with these particulars during the interview deprived us of the benefit of this time-honored test of reliability and cast a perpetual cloud over the case.

Finally, the detectives gave up for the day. It was now early evening, and they headed straight to my office with their boss, Sergeant Frank Hawkins, in tow. After briefing me on the interview, we kicked the situation around for well over an hour. Despite the shortcomings of the confession, we uniformly concluded that Vasquez could not be released. What if he struck again? The decision was further complicated by our recognition that Vasquez did not appear to have the mental or physical strength to have pulled this off. Carrig at that point reminded me that there had been two sets of footprints in the snow leading to Hamm's broken basement window. The pieces began to fit. If two people were involved, Vasquez must have been the accomplice. Of course, that also meant that we still had a homicidal maniac on the street.

There were still many unanswered questions, but a decision had to be made immediately. As always, I erred on the side of caution. He just seemed to know too much. I told Carrig and Shelton to charge Vasquez with murder.

Chuck Shelton, a veteran homicide investigator, knew from experience that once Vasquez had court-appointed counsel there would be no further interviews. The lawyers would advise him to keep his mouth shut. One of the most prominent criminal lawyers in America has a large stuffed fish with a lure in its mouth hanging on the wall of his office. He tells his clients that the fish and the client have a lot in common. If they had both kept their mouths shut, they would not be in his office that day.

Early the following morning, Shelton brought Vasquez back down from the jail to the detective bureau in a final attempt to get a comprehensible confession. Again, Shelton meticulously read Vasquez his rights and had him sign a waiver form. The run-up conversation ascended slowly, but suddenly took a dramatic turn.

Before Shelton could frame his first substantive question, Vasquez revealed that he had terrible dreams about killing Carolyn Hamm. Abruptly, and without the slightest prompting, Vasquez's entire personality transformed radically. No longer was he the timid stumbling soft-spoken wimp. A deep, resonant panting voice emanated from his mouth. He spoke clearly and confidently. Chilled by the transformation, Shelton grabbed a tape recorder to capture what appeared to be a cathartic moment.

For fifteen minutes, Vasquez narrated with precise detail how he broke into Hamm's house through the rear window, waited until she arrived home, undressed her in the living room, forced her upstairs into the bedroom, raped her, brought her downstairs, cut a piece of cord from the blinds and tied her hands, took her to the basement, sliced a section from the rope binding the carpet, and strung her up on the water pipe.

Shelton shut the recorder off and gasped for breath. He desperately needed a cold beer. He hurriedly returned Vasquez to jail and headed to my office.

In the days that followed, Shelton took samples of Vasquez's head and pubic hairs for forensic comparison with hairs recovered from the crime scene. The state laboratory was able to match the characteristics of his hairs with several of those collected in Hamm's house. The results were helpful but hardly a smoking gun. In those days—before DNA testing—the most you could scientifically achieve was a finding that the known and unknown hair follicles had the same physical features when examined under a dual lens microscope. This enabled the forensic scientist to testify that the individual from whom the known sample was taken was one of several million people with the same hair characteristics. It would add flavor to the final argument, but certainly not insure a conviction.

On the other hand, the semen samples recovered from the scene did not match Vasquez's blood type. This was of little concern, because we never believed that Vasquez was acting alone or that he was the main actor. In searching Vasquez's former bedroom in South Arlington, we had found "peep" photos, surreptitiously taken of young girls. Also, some people in the old neighborhood said he had a tendency to stand around and stare at young ladies for uncomfortably long periods. I thought, and the detectives did too, that Vasquez was just a tag along who wanted to watch the other guy. Admittedly, our unscientific opinion did not exactly square with his confession.

Our next order of business was to try to cut an immediate deal with Vasquez to turn in the other guy, who was still at large and could strike again. His attorneys replied that their client knew nothing.

The next move, justified by the dramatic shift in his personality during the third interview, was to have Vasquez examined by a psychiatrist to determine if he was competent to stand trial and if he had been insane when the crime was committed. Our lay suspicion was that he suffered from split personality. Secondarily, we hoped that the psychiatric examination might serve as a reality check and inspire him to cooperate in identifying the second man. Much to our astonishment, the physician found Vasquez to be of sound mind. He also concluded that Vasquez was close to mildly mentally retarded. The court immediately set a date for a preliminary hearing, something we had hoped to avoid by offering Vasquez a sweet plea deal in exchange for testifying against his more malicious confederate. Now we had to show our cards.

In the interim we uncovered no additional evidence. I therefore put on a very lean case at the preliminary hearing—the friend who discovered the body, the neighbors who saw Vasquez on South 23rd Street, and Detective Shelton to recount the confession. A preliminary hearing is a very abbreviated proceeding. It is conducted by a court one level below the circuit court, or trial court. A preliminary hearing is designed to insure that there is probable cause to hold a defendant who has been arrested on a felony charge pending action by the grand jury. Despite a spirited challenge by Vasquez's lawyers that the confession was involuntary and not admissible into evidence, the general district court judge had no problem finding that we had proven the requisite probable cause. Not wishing to venture into a hornet's nest, the judge declined to opine on the legal soundness of the confession.

The following week the grand jury indicted Vasquez for capital murder, robbery, burglary and other related felonies. At his arraignment several days later, I formally announced, in his presence, that I would be seeking the death penalty. As intended, Vasquez reacted with visible trepidation. We still wanted the name of the other guy and I needed his help.

The linchpin of our case was the confession—without it we had no case against Vasquez. So when his lawyers filed a motion to exclude the confession as evidence at trial, we went into high gear preparing for the hearing. I brought in one of my most capable assistants, Liam O'Grady, to help with the hearing and the inevitable trial. I had no doubt that, for me, this was a career-defining case, and it drew intense media coverage.

The hearing on the motion to suppress the three confessions took three days—a high stakes proceeding. The confession was the infrastructure of our case. If we were to lose, the embarrassment would be monumental, particularly to the police department. In essence, Vasquez's attorneys argued that the statements were made involuntarily and in violation of his Miranda rights. Detective Chuck Shelton absorbed some tough blows on cross-examination in attempting to justify his hardball tactics, particularly given Vasquez's limited mental capacity. The issues were close in this trial judge's nightmare. The bottom line could be the release of a vicious murderer back into the community. Judge William L. Winston informed counsel that he would notify us when he reached a decision—maybe the toughest in his career.

O'Grady and I heard nothing for almost a month. Then, on the Friday afternoon immediately preceding our Monday morning trial date, we received the court's opinion. Judge Winston threw out the first two statements, which had marginal value, but upheld the admissibility of the third, more detailed and chilling, cathartic confession.

As we awaited the court's ruling, we continued to press for a plea and cooperation against the second man. No such luck! Vasquez continued to stonewall, despite his attorneys' encouragement to cough up the second guy, if he was involved, and avoid the death penalty.

Although savaged by the press, we were satisfied with the decision. Frankly, we dreaded the thought of explaining the first two statements to the jury. We would love to have had them totally suppressed, where they could fade into oblivion. Unfortunately, it was likely that the first two statements would come into evidence anyway. The defense would have to introduce them in order to discredit the reliability of the third. Ultimately, it would be a wash, with neither side gaining any benefit.

As the trial date approached, the attorneys turned up the pressure on their client. One week before trial, Vasquez's attorneys—he had two court-appointed lawyers because he was charged with a capital offense—came by my office to deliver some last minute medical reports. They expressed a sincere hope that if their client was in fact guilty he would have a change of heart. He was apparently horrified by the possibility of receiving the death penalty.

Although death was a sentencing option set by the legislature for capital murder, we did not intend to zealously press for it in his case. I was convinced that Vasquez had been present when Hamm was murdered, but I still did not believe he was the actual killer. However, we were mindful that if the jury formed its impression of Vasquez strictly on the third confession—which had the attributes of a cold-blooded killer—there was a realistic possibility that he was destined for death row. The clock ticked away. The trial was set for Monday morning, and O'Grady and I were as ready as our evidence would allow.

Around noon on Thursday, Vasquez's lawyers informed O'Grady that Vasquez had been undergoing, at his own initiative, sodium ambytol (truth serum) interrogation by a psychiatrist they had retained. No one from my office or the police department was involved, and we were not privy to the results. We remained guardedly optimistic that Vasquez would change his mind.

On Saturday morning, forty-eight hours before trial, O'Grady and I were in the office early, walking through the evidence one final time with Detectives Carrig and Shelton. About 11:00 a.m. we heard knocking on the door. It was Vasquez's attorneys. They reported that the final sodium ambytol procedure had been horrifying, but the attorney-client privilege would not permit them to disclose the details. Most importantly, Vasquez would plead to non-capital murder and robbery if we would limit his sentencing exposure. They added that they were unable to provide any information about any other person who might have been involved and implored us not to press them further.

O'Grady and I huddled with the detectives for about ten minutes and proposed a specific sentencing recommendation of thirty years to serve. We thought that was about what Vasquez's involvement was worth, based on the information at hand. No one believed that Vasquez had killed Hamm with his own hands, but why was he taking the fall for the second guy?

The lawyers agreed without hesitation to the proposed sentencing recommendation, and I knew Judge Winston would accept the recommendation, too. Vasquez's attorneys left to confer with their client and returned in less than a half hour. To our astonishment, they took the deal without any counteroffer. O'Grady and I had been prepared to go lower, if necessary to clinch the deal.

When I called Judge Winston at home to inform him that the trial was off, the sigh of relief was palpable.

On Monday morning, Vasquez entered his plea and was sentenced to thirty years in the penitentiary. The police department, the judge, and I all thought it was an excellent disposition, given the inherent difficulties with the case. The *Arlington Journal* newspaper did not agree. It criticized the police department for the tactics used to induce the confessions and derided me for intimidating Vasquez, a poor mentally challenged guy, into pleading guilty to murder on such paltry evidence. I promptly uncapped my pen and fired off a response that read in part:

> The decisions made daily in the criminal justice system are tough and at times gut-wrenching. Lawyers, prosecutors and police officers are called upon to make decisions in the heat of the day which others casually review in the coolness of the evening.
>
> The decision to accept Mr. Vasquez's plea of guilty was based on all the evidence available after an exhaustive investigation. And it is important to remember that if every case prosecuted were required to be free of all doubt, few people would ever be convicted of a criminal offense.
>
> The law measures the quantum of doubt on a scale of reasonableness. On the morning David Vasquez pled guilty to murder, his own lawyers, the police and I were convinced that a jury would find him guilty beyond a reasonable doubt. Given that much, what would the informed conscience of the community—indeed, what would your editorial page—have said had I simply dismissed the charges and released David Vasquez back to the streets?

Several years passed before I heard anything further on the Vasquez case. In late 1988, I received a telephone call from Helen Fahey, who had served as one of my assistants and had succeeded me as commonwealth's attorney of Arlington County. She told me they now knew who killed Carolyn Hamm. My curiosity was piqued and my heart pounded with anticipation. Okay, who did it?

She calmly said it was too complicated to explain over the telephone. Could I come to the Arlington County Police Department for a briefing? Within minutes, I left the United States Attorney's Office and headed up the George Washington Parkway to Arlington County.

Several thoughts crossed my mind as I ascended the hill to the Arlington Courthouse. If Vasquez was the killer, would I be criticized for recommending a sentence that was too light? If he was not, what should I have done differently?

I couldn't help thinking back over the past twenty years, to the beginnings of my political career, here in this same courthouse. Things seemed to be going so well. Would this be the end?

## II

# Lawman, or Man of the Law?

I was about three weeks shy of my twenty-second birthday when the sheriff presented me with a silver star in a leather case. P.J. Snoots, with whom I had frequently worked as a volunteer fireman and emergency medical technician, was a sergeant with the sheriff's office. He pulled a few strings and got me a job as a deputy sheriff.

My only prior experience with the sheriff's office had been a rescue call I had taken one evening as an EMT. An infamous serial burglar had tied a strand of ripped bed sheets together and attempted to escape from the jail by removing the bars from a window and lowering himself to the ground—a distance of about five stories. It raised quite a stir when the sheets broke and he fell about seventy feet into a large bush. Fortunately, the bush cushioned his impact and no bones were broken. But his screams could be heard for a quarter mile when he was anally impaled by a seven-inch branch and damn near bled to death.

My indoctrination period as a deputy was short. Sheriff J. Elwood Clements and I hit it off immediately. The usual rookie assignment was working midnights in the jail, which was not air conditioned in those days and reeked of assorted foul odors. However, I was placed in the circuit court as a trainee bailiff, a plum job that set my compass bearings for all that followed in life.

I rotated daily among the four circuit court judges, opening court, escorting jurors, guarding inmates, serving witness summons, and providing court security. Most valuable was the opportunity to sit in court and watch trials every day and discuss the cases with the judge—a unique and priceless experience; an insider's view.

I began making contacts that would shape my career. I also met Bob Holmes, another summer deputy, who continues to be one of my close friends. In later life as lawyers we would handle many cases together. He would also support me in the riskiest venture of my life.

In the afternoons, when court concluded, Bob and I would often serve court papers together around the county. We worked in plain clothes and drove a marked sheriff's car dubbed Unit 55, equipped with siren and red lights—great fun for two twenty-two-year-olds. We loved showing our badges and acting important. Occasionally, someone would actually take us seriously.

Even though Bob and I were dealing with some pretty rough characters, we had received no formal training except for a few minutes of daily instruction from experienced deputies. But all that changed about three weeks later when we were ordered to attend a basic training class. It was held at the crack of dawn on a sprawling farm in Nelson County, Virginia. After herding all the cattle out of the field, we received instruction in handling firearms, making arrests, cuffing detainees, serving papers, and handling prisoners. It was a full day. After I mowed down an entire row of beer cans, I was declared qualified with my snub-nosed .38-caliber Smith & Wesson revolver.

I was then considered fully trained—armed and, frankly, dangerous. In time, deputies on the career track were sent to a regional academy for more extensive training. Shortly after I left the sheriff's office, Virginia law imposed formal training standards for all law enforcement officers.

The next week I received my permanent assignment, the Juvenile and Domestic Relations Court. I was the bailiff for the Honorable Andrew B. Ferrari, a wonderful fellow who served as a patient mentor as I wrestled with some tough decisions in life. His generous recommendation was an asset to my law school application. The judge pretty much allowed me to run the docket, under his direction. I called the cases in the hallway and ushered the parties into court. The judge, who relished the good guy role, entrusted me with the task of diplomatically chewing out lawyers who showed up late, or pled for more time to prepare their case—a skill that would serve me well when I became a circuit court judge.

I also escorted all juvenile prisoners, in restraints, from the holding facility to and from Court, often through public hallways. Many of the teenagers we were dealing with were more ruthless and hardened than the adults being tried in circuit court. Some of these youngsters had committed brutal rapes, multiple robberies or vicious assaults. Almost without exception these punks were already on probation for some other serious offense. In time, many of them would graduate to the adult system. In some neighborhoods, scraps with the law were a badge of honor and a rite of passage.

Twelve years later, as the newly elected commonwealth's attorney of Arlington County, I determined that ninety percent of the violent juvenile crime was being committed by about two percent of the juvenile offenders. Chief of police Smokey Stover and I implemented a controversial program to prosecute these hardcore hoodlums as adult offenders and to send the truly incorrigible ones to prison. Juvenile court officials gasped in astonishment and shuddered in disbelief. They described the policy as "draconian," and called me callous and insensitive. But the citizens and the press saw it differently.

My opinion of the juvenile justice system was shaped in large part by my days as a juvenile court bailiff. Most young people hauled into juvenile court profit from probation and counseling. Many simply need more structure than their parents are willing or able to provide. In some instances parents are the obstacle that frustrates the goals of the court. Parents should be supportive of their children, but they must also have the courage to acknowledge their wrongdoing and take swift corrective action. Encouraging kids to rationalize their misbehavior by relying on legal technicalities sometimes promotes, rather than resolves, behavioral problems.

The only drawback to working juvenile court was the unpredictability of the docket. On some days all our assigned cases settled, and the docket was completed in less than an hour. I would dash to the office and grab court papers to serve before a supervisor caught wind of it and assigned me to do something less desirable. But despite my best efforts to lay low, I was frequently intercepted by the chief deputy and directed to report to the transportation supervisor. Normally that meant moving prisoners.

Soon it was fall and Bob Holmes had headed off to law school, while I remained with the sheriff's office for another year. I enjoyed law enforcement work, but yearned for something more challenging. Urban and suburban sheriff's offices in Virginia primarily handle court security, running the jail, and serving court papers. The police department handled the rest.

I, therefore, decided to apply for a special agent position with the U.S. Bureau of Narcotics and Dangerous Drugs, the predecessor to the Drug Enforcement Administration (DEA). I was excited by the idea of working undercover and busting drug dealers. Later, when I learned that the vacancies were in New York City, Chicago, and Los Angeles, my interest dissipated.

Ferrying prisoners soon lost its appeal. There were three basic categories of prisoner transportation assignments in the sheriff's office. The most dreaded was driving people committed by the court to a state mental facility. Most were taken to Western State Hospital in Staunton, just west of the Blue Ridge Mountains, an eight-hour round trip. The drive was bearable, assuming that the person being transported was controllable. Most were calm and polite, but some went kicking and screaming, requiring restraints the entire trip. For some reason it was standard operating procedure to drive the sheriff's office vehicle twenty-five miles an hour over the speed limit the entire way. The Virginia State Police were tolerant in those days. Now, a deputy traveling that fast on a routine transport might be cited for reckless driving.

The worst part of the trip to Western State Hospital was dinner. I usually rode with Karl McCormick, a retired captain with the District of Columbia Police Department, my supervisor. I drove under his direction—every trip was reminiscent of my high school driver training class. We had a wonderful relationship, and he taught me a great deal about law enforcement, but Karl had an insatiable appetite. On the return trip, we would always stop for dinner at the Howard Johnson's in Harrisonburg, where Karl could enjoy their all-you-can-eat specials. Maybe it was my imagination, but I swear the wait staff would stop and stare when he entered. He was a legend. They all knew him. Karl would eat for hours, often four or five servings. I loved the guy, but I was embarrassed and just wanted to leave.

Another miserable task was taking inmates to the doctor, or dentist. Imagine hauling a shackled prisoner into a physician's office. People in the waiting room were terrified. Nurses were apprehensive and greeted you with conspicuous disdain. Doctors were cold and dismissive. There was no small talk. That's why most larger detention facilities today have physicians on contract to perform on-site services.

The most tolerable transport assignment was taking prisoners "down state," to the penitentiary or a correctional facility. It was a quick turn around; you'd be back in a few hours, because we usually traveled at eighty miles an hour. I visited every correctional facility in Virginia. There weren't that many in those days; the real proliferation of prisons in Virginia occurred in the 1990s.

In 1994, when I served as a member of Governor George Allen's Commission to Abolish Parole and Reform Sentencing in Virginia, one of our recommendations was the establishment of more work-oriented correctional facilities to perform public works type projects, such as painting buildings or cleaning roads. The intent was not only to allow inmates to earn a minimum wage, but also to provide some benefit to the community. The idea was nixed in the General Assembly, in large measure because of the strident objection of labor unions. They claimed inmate work forces displaced other minimum wage workers.

Life at the Virginia State Penitentiary was tough. An imposing brick rectangle of high weathered walls, tattooed with fermenting moss and mildew, and topped with razor wire, it had a haunting institutional appearance. It was located in the heart of the City of Richmond on the corner of Belvidere and Spring Streets. Parts of the decaying structure were reportedly designed and built by Thomas Jefferson. The complex consisted of several housing blocks or buildings, a disciplinary block for problem inmates, a medical unit, a mess hall and a metal shop, all situated around a large courtyard. The administration building was at the far end of the yard.

A recreation field on the east side of the yard included a baseball diamond and a basketball court, with a weight-lifting area annexed on the south side. But most inmates used their exercise time to stand in the yard in small groups, talking and smoking. I always wondered what they could be talking about, day after day, year after year.

I didn't mind transporting inmates to the state pen, but I dreaded going into the bowels of the institution, even for the ten or fifteen minutes required for a drop off. It was far more unsettling behind the walls, because there you sensed the complete lack of personal freedom. It was stark and chilling. The atmosphere was always tense. The correctional staff rarely smiled, even at other law enforcement officers. You always suspected someone was watching you, and they were.

The turnover rate among staff was tremendous, approaching twenty-five percent a year. The facility lacked many of the modern security features used to control an inmate population. Ten minutes inside the receiving area was enough to convince me to stay on the straight and narrow. But the time came when I did get a real close look at life on the inside.

We used to joke in the sheriff's office that it was harder to get a prisoner into the penitentiary than a son or daughter into college. Because of limited capacity, placement of prisoners with the state correctional system was competitive. To conserve precious space, the state would compensate local sheriffs for holding state prisoners, inmates sentenced to serve hard time of one year or more in state prison. But local jails were busting at the seams, too. Many were under court-ordered population caps. Eventually a group of politically powerful sheriffs filed a lawsuit against the Virginia Department of Corrections to force it to take prisoners sentenced to the penitentiary. The settlement provided some relief, but tension continued.

One day after we finished court, the chief deputy yelled for me to come into his office. In his Marine Corps–honed command voice, he informed me that some inmate in the jail claimed to have persistent abdominal pain. "Get him up to Arlington Hospital" for examination, he barked. That sixty-plus-year-old inmate was serving time for passing bad checks, and like about half the jail population, waiting to be accepted by the state pen. A likeable chap who had spent much of his adult life behind bars, he was a polite and cooperative trustee, with no history of violent behavior. Since no one else was available, the chief instructed me to handle it alone.

We were about six blocks from the courthouse when the chief radioed that I should change my destination to the penitentiary hospital. Since the inmate was technically a state prisoner, they had decided to conduct the examination and testing there in Richmond. I was ordered to deliver him by 1:00 p.m. It was about 11:45 a.m., so I put the pedal to the metal. We made it with a minute or two to spare.

When I presented the inmate at the receiving window and explained that he had an appointment at the medical unit at 1:00 p.m., I received the typical warm greeting. The expressionless correctional officer, wearing a sweat-stained uniform and dark glasses, slammed the window and walked away. I felt like an unwanted door-to-door salesman.

The beefy officer sauntered over to a desk, made a phone call, conferred with another fellow, and returned to the window about five minutes later. Then he told me that I would have to check my weapon. Wait a minute, I smiled, and explained that that wouldn't be necessary. I'd just come back and get him later.

I must have hit a sensitive nerve, because the stone-faced guard launched into a withering lecture. At a drill instructor's pitch he informed me that the man was my prisoner and that I would be responsible for him during the examination. "Is that clear?"

I handed the officer my revolver and braced for what awaited me, thinking, "If that's how they treat me, how do they treat inmates?"

Fortunately, the receiving area was cooled by several large fans. We stood along the cement wall for about ten minutes. There was no place to sit. The inmate was obviously uncomfortable. The receiving officer was unconcerned. We were now about twenty minutes late for the appointment. Eventually the large metal gate opened. The receiving officer directed us to the next stage of the entry process, a chamber with a front and rear gate, operated by a guard in a protective cage. The rear gate led to the interior of the institution. Here, all persons entering the facility were searched for weapons and contraband. After a burly sergeant patted us down and announced, "okay," another gate swung open, leading into the yard.

The sergeant pointed to a paint-starved building at the far end of the yard and told me to follow a correctional officer to the front door. I was warned to stay on the sidewalk and avoid contact with inmates. Sounded like a plan to me.

We were escorted out into the yard by a female correctional officer. She looked about twenty-five years old and weighed about one hundred twenty pounds on a five-foot seven-inch frame. Several hundred inmates roamed the yard in small groups, smoking. She told us to follow closely behind her, which provided little comfort, but we complied. She cleared our path by waving inmates out of our way and appeared to be in complete control. She sure had a take-no-shit personality. Still, if someone broke bad, I would waste no time hauling ass back to the receiving gate.

As always, I was working in plain clothes—a cheap shirt, clip-on tie, and blue blazer with khaki slacks. Nothing I'd miss if it were destroyed. We took about ten steps into the yard and every inmate stopped as if frozen in place, and stared at us. It was frightening as hell. And then it happened.

I heard someone yell, "Hudson, what the hell are you doing here?" I turned and saw Frankie Altizer, a high school classmate, being dragged to the disciplinary block by two guards. I tepidly waved and kept walking. We continued to pace toward the front door, and still the inmates stared, motionless. I wondered what I was getting myself into. Little did I know.

We entered the medical building and were directed to a waiting area where we joined a half dozen other inmates. None looked seriously ill or particularly dangerous. In time, a male orderly escorted us to the examination area. The physician, who spoke with a Hispanic accent, was refreshingly courteous and seemed genuinely concerned. I sat in a folding metal chair while the doctor examined my charge. Finally, the doctor said that the inmate might require more testing and left the room. Meanwhile, prisoners were moving about in the hallway. Several even peered into the room. Correctional officers were posted in various locations. I was gradually acclimating myself.

In about a half hour, a nurse stepped in and told me that the doctor needed to "observe him for a while." I sure wished I'd brought a book to read. I sat there for what seemed like another hour. She returned and told me that the inmate was being "admitted for observation; he may have appendicitis." I asked when someone would be available to escort me out; I needed to get home. She paused for a moment, then said that a correctional supervisor would be with me in a minute. It was now pushing 4:00 p.m. My mother normally served dinner at 6:30 p.m. I was getting impatient, and hungry.

In time, a sergeant walked in and reiterated that the doctor did not want the inmate moved without his approval. And, since the inmate had not been formally received into the state system, he was my prisoner. As long as he was at the hospital facility, I'd have to stay with him. I had two options: Remove the prisoner against the doctor's orders, or sit patiently. No way were they going to let me dump this inmate—who had been sentenced to the penitentiary—into the state system.

I asked how long the observation period would last and the sergeant said that the doctor would decide whether to operate the next morning. I quietly had a panic attack. I was not about to spend the night in this place.

The sergeant was mildly amused. No doubt he found my trepidation entertaining. I called the sheriff, who negotiated a deal with the Department of Corrections. The sheriff would hold several state prisoners at the Arlington County Jail for an extended period in exchange for the penitentiary's accepting custody of the sick inmate and releasing the hostage—me. I stepped out of the front gate onto a dark street at 7:30 p.m., never to return. The old penitentiary was razed twenty-five years later. Ethyl corporate headquarters now occupies that corner.

As summer approached, I explored other law enforcement job opportunities. I had received my bachelor's degree in international studies and had taken a couple of graduate courses. The foreign service did not appeal to me.

I was now engaged to Tara Lydon, and I needed to make some serious plans. I enjoyed working in the sheriff's office, but unless you were the heir apparent to the sheriff's job, the position had no future. The salary of a deputy was forty-eight hundred dollars a year. Tara made more as a clerk with the Department of Defense.

Since then, I have always respected sheriffs and their deputies. With low pay and limited resources, they protect the front lines in law enforcement. They often work alone in rural areas with no other officer nearby to back them up. As my friend and former colleague at WWRC radio and host of "War Stories" on the Fox News Channel, Ollie North, is fond of saying, "Theirs is a story that deserves to be told."

Sheriff J. Elwood Clements was a powerful figure in Arlington County politics. He was part of what is today an extinct species—Byrd Democrats. Byrd Democrats were conservative followers of the late U.S. Senator Harry F. Byrd, Sr., a legendary Virginia political figure. For decades, Senator Byrd maintained an inexorable grip on local Virginia politics. During that era, elected Republicans at the local level in Virginia were as rare as the condor. Today, with shifting political tides, most adherents to the Byrd philosophy vote Republican.

Working around politicians is contagious. I quickly got sucked in and became involved in Democratic politics, distributing literature and working the polls. Although I later migrated to the Republican camp, I met a lot of life-long friends in the Democratic party, many of whom stood by me when I decided to run for public office as a Republican.

It began to seem that being a prosecutor might be my calling. I enjoyed the courtroom, particularly dealing with lawyers and police officers, and I was fascinated with the power of the law. As I would later espouse from the political stump, " The prosecutor is the people's lawyer," a mantra that became my personal creed.

Scoring well on the Law School Aptitude Test, I was confronted with two issues: How would I support a wife while attending law school?. How could I get into the fall term at school when it was already June? This is where my contacts at the Courthouse really paid off.

Angie Iandolo was a local lawyer who practiced in the Arlington courts. His wife, Bonnie, was the Director of Admissions at American University School of Law. Thanks to Angie's good offices, Bonnie smuggled me into the fall evening class so I could work during the day and attend class at night. It sounded like a tough grind, but I had no other option. In time it would prove to be a stroke of luck.

Tara and I were married on August 28, 1970, at the Arlington Methodist Church, where my family attended when I was a child. Her brother Lance, who had been one of my best friends in high school, was my best man, I had been his two years earlier. Tara and I honeymooned in Puerto Rico. It was a disaster. We returned after two days. The streets wreaked of the stench of garbage, and the people were conspicuously unfriendly. We decided to try Miami. Being the off-season, we figured we'd have the place to ourselves. The travel agent assured us that no reservations were needed. We arrived in Miami on the opening day of the National Psychiatric Association convention. No rooms were available. We decided to laugh rather than cry, returned to Northern Virginia, and settled into our one-bedroom apartment. Life appeared on track, but I needed a job. Fortunately, my mother and father agreed to cover most of my law school tuition.

III

# HITTIN' THE BOOKS

A little eccentric, H. Bruce Green was exactly the way you would envision a southern politician—complete with tattered hat. His attention to protocol and decorum was impeccable. Reelected Clerk of the Arlington County Circuit Court five times, he had served for almost forty years when I met him. His father had served before him. A small, trim courtly gentleman who always wore a rumpled suit, white shirt and wide smile, Bruce Green made a habit of speaking to everyone and never uttered an unkind word about anyone. He was so formal, they said he cut his grass in a coat and tie and never stepped on a elevator until every voter was inside.

Landing a job as one of his courtroom deputies was a real badge of distinction in those days. Dozens of prominent lawyers and judges began their careers right there, and for this they were forever indebted. I am proud to be a member of that select group. On the chess board of life, it was my third most important move. The first was marrying Tara. The second was to be running for office ten years downstream.

A former Grand Master of the Masons in Virginia, Bruce Green was a stalwart of the Byrd machine. His family enjoyed a close personal relationship with both generations of the Byrd dynasty. A man of legendary political influence, Mr. Green had faced no political opposition in more than thirty years. Every aspiring politician sought his endorsement and wise counsel. A young man could not help being impressed with his mastery of interpersonal skills.

I took quick note of how effectively his courteous demeanor could defuse an adversary or calm an outraged citizen. Learning to disarm the disgruntled without conceding the point at issue proved to be a valuable lesson in psychology. Developing an understanding of human behavior is critical to success in the political world.

I always loved Bruce Green's political commentary. At his urging, I joined the Masonic Lodge and advanced to Master Mason—a passport into a circle of influential Arlingtonians.

Being selected as a deputy clerk of court was a classic instance of being in the right place at the right time. Mr. Green usually hired a night law student for one of his courtroom deputy positions. A vacancy occurred when Bill Artz passed the bar. I immediately tracked down Mr. Green, affectionately called "Boss" by his male employees. He hired me on the spot at the generous annual salary of fifty-five hundred dollars. Thank goodness Tara was earning seven thousand at the Department of Defense. We rented a small apartment and I began law school at American University as Tara completed her undergraduate studies at George Mason. I attended class four nights a week, Tara, three. The little time we spent together was quality time.

As a deputy clerk of court I sat up front in the courtroom, at a desk about ten feet from the judge. I was responsible for maintaining court records, preserving exhibits, and preparing orders reflecting each court proceeding. The assignments varied: some days civil cases, others criminal.

I developed a close relationship with each of the four circuit court judges. Aside from the statutory duties, the deputy clerk is also a kind of informal aide to the court. This provided almost unlimited access and extensive face time. Because of the bond and trust that developed, the judges would often share their personal views of a case and the lawyer's performance. They patiently spent countless hours explaining legal principles and, essentially, teaching me how to be a lawyer.

No law school class could provide the type of individual training I received from the judges of that court. It is too bad that law schools prefer professors with academic credentials over those with practical experience. When I eventually took the bar examination in 1974, ten of the twenty essay questions on Virginia law involved esoteric Virginia procedures I learned working in the clerk's office.

Sitting in court everyday was like attending a legal laboratory. Some lawyers were masterful, others simply buffoons. I took copious notes on trial strategy, tactics, and cross-examination techniques. I still use those experiences to illustrate trial techniques to young lawyers. One particularly stands out in my mind.

The defendant was on trial for burglary and rape. The victim, a female Marine sergeant living alone, was awakened during the night by a man in her bedroom. After placing his hand over her mouth and striking her with his fist, he sexually assaulted her. At trial, the prosecutor routinely asked the sergeant if she could identify her assailant in the courtroom. She stared at the defendant for several seconds, then explained that she was a deeply religious woman who took her oath seriously. She could not in good conscience swear that the person sitting at the defense table was her attacker.

Aware that his case was lost, the prosecutor sat down without asking any additional questions.

The defense lawyer could not resist the temptation of taking a victory lap. With great ceremony, he stood up and asked his client to do likewise. In a voice resonant with confidence, he directed his client to turn to both sides and sit down. He concluded the stunt by asking the witness to take a good look at his client and, "please take as much time as you need." Allowing a moment or two for the intrigue to ferment, the lawyer next inquired, "Ma'am, you can't say for sure that this is the man who raped you, is that right?"

The sergeant sat there for a full minute and then said, "After having a chance to see him from that angle, there's no doubt in my mind that's the guy who raped me."

The defendant was convicted and got over a hundred years to serve. Of course, he was still eligible for parole after serving just twelve years. Moral to the story? Never cross-examine a witness whose testimony supports your side of the case.

The jury never heard the epilogue to the story. About a month after breaking into the sergeant's apartment and defiling her, the thug broke into the same unit a second time, again in the early predawn hours. Unbeknown to the intruder, the sergeant had moved. The new occupant, a District of Columbia police officer, greeted the intruder with two blasts of a shotgun. The wounds left substantial facial disfigurement. Maybe that's why the sergeant couldn't identify him at first.

Law school was also a period for self-evaluation and periodic recalibration of my personal compass. Now I knew that I wanted to be a prosecutor, and either seek public office or serve in a high-level law enforcement capacity. My personal deficiencies were polish and self-confidence. To shore up these deficiencies I began carefully noting the strong traits of people I admired, particularly judges and other public officials.

Judge William L. Winston taught me to use common sense in approaching legal issues. A stickler on trial preparation, Winston held lawyers to a high standard. He was once so incensed by the quality of the prosecution that he actually acquitted a defendant who had entered a guilty plea.

Judge, later Justice, Charles S. Russell instilled the importance of principled reasoning, grounding decisions in well-articulated findings and conclusions. He could hand down an extemporaneous oral decision from the bench with the grammatical precision, case citations, and sparkling language of a carefully crafted memorandum.

On the other hand, in my attempt to emulate these men I so admired, I also picked up a couple of their habits, such as writing with a fountain pen—I now own more than a dozen—and smoking cigars. I still smoke one a week. Okay, sometimes two.

When I began my clerkship, Walter T. McCarthy was the chief judge. He had been on the Arlington Circuit Court for almost forty years. He was about twenty-five years older than his fellow judges, who always addressed him as Judge McCarthy. A courteous and friendly gentleman, McCarthy had a stone-faced, almost callous, demeanor on the bench. Nothing moved him; he was virtually unflappable.

My supervisor, Bennie Taylor, an irascible retired D.C. Police detective sergeant was an interesting guy. When a lawyer filed a ridiculous request, he enjoyed making a copy, stamping it with a huge BULLSHIT stamp, and sending it back to the attorney. Most recipients found it humorous. He also kept a running list of the dumbest lawyers. He called it the "top ten." Lawyers with the distinction of staying on the "top ten" for a full year were enshrined in the hall of fame.

Bennie once told me a story about Judge McCarthy that has been confirmed by several other reliable sources. They say it's true. I'll never forget it.

## Who You Callin' a . . . ?

A young man was on trial in front of Judge McCarthy for statutory rape. Although the evidence was weak, the victim's mother, a pastor, would accept nothing short of full vindication of her daughter's cherished chastity. Both the defendant and the victim were black, and both were from prominent families. The courtroom was packed. The community was in an uproar. Judge McCarthy calmly sifted through the evidence.

The defendant's family hired the neighborhood lawyer, Johnny Alsander (not his real name), to represent their son. Mr. Alsander was a soft-spoken deliberative gentleman just over five feet tall. He practiced very little criminal law, but he knew the stakes were high in this case.

The thermometer hovered at ninety on the appointed trial date. The crowd that filled the sixth floor courtroom was tense and vocal. The prosecution had three witnesses: the victim, the investigating detective and the victim's mother, who insisted on testifying. The defense had nine witnesses, all young men from the victim's neighborhood sworn and escorted to the witness room.

The prosecution's case took less than an hour. Mr. Alsander's cross-examination of the victim required less than five minutes. The prosecution rested and the storm struck. After the defense called five young men, two from the victim's congregation, who described under oath their sexual encounters with the victim, the court declined to hear further evidence on the point. Alsander confidently rested his case without even calling the defendant to the stand.

In rebuttal, the prosecution called the victim's mother. The witness room door swung open suddenly. Sporting a wide-brimmed hat with a dark black veil, the Reverend emerged and proceeded with ceremonial cadence to the witness stand. After the oath was administered, she plopped her two hundred and fifty pound frame into the chair and cleared her voice.

To maximize witness control, the prosecution framed its questions narrowly. Unfortunately, the Reverend's reply was uniformly unresponsive and heavily spiced with extraneous editorial comments concerning her daughter's honor and righteousness. Despite his best effort to the contrary, the prosecutor knew he had opened the door to potentially ugly cross-examination.

Alsander began his examination with a series of softball questions. Then the viper struck. The diminutive lawyer shuffled through a mound of papers as though in search of a smoking gun document. He then adjusted his glasses and raised his head slowly.

"Reverend, are you familiar with your daughter's reputation?"

The question drew a pointed stare from the matronly witness.

"I mean among the men folks," the attorney added.

The Reverend turned toward the judge and with harnessed emotion inquired, "Your honor, am I supposed to answer that question?"

Judge McCarthy pondered a bit as he rocked in his overstuffed chair and stroked his thick mane of white hair. "There's no objection, I don't see why not."

The Reverend turned her head toward defense counsel and pushed the veil away from her face, revealing a countenance engulfed with anger.

"Lawyer Alsander, you little sawed-off-son-of-a-bitch, who the hell you think you callin' a whore."

After about thirty seconds of silence, and without cracking so much as a faint smile, the court inquired, "Any follow up questions Mr. Alsander?"

The most enduring lessons that I learned during my days as a courtroom clerk were from Judge Charles H. Duff, who succeeded Judge McCarthy. Judge

Duff was the quintessential Virginia gentlemen. He was never flustered and always disarmingly polite in the courtroom. He treated everyone, from distinguished members of the bar to devious criminals, with dignity and respect. Litigants responded in kind. His philosophy of governance could be summarized as, "the more power the people give you, the more responsibility you have to use it discretely." I will never forget that maxim, which I have frequently passed on to others.

I had the pleasure of serving as Judge Duff's courtroom clerk on one of the first days he handled the domestic relations docket, an assignment dreaded by every circuit court judge. It was a Friday afternoon. The issue before the court was custody of the divorcing couple's poodle. The contest was vicious. Each side called multiple witnesses to attest to its superiority as the dog's custodian. The wife was emotional. The husband determined. He even called a pricey expert witness, a veterinarian, I believe, to bolster his case. Judge Duff sat straight-faced and patient.

In the end, the judge awarded custody of the poodle to the doggie dad. The wife was devastated. Several weeks later, the couple was back in Judge Duff's court fighting over something else. At the end of the hearing, the judge, in his ever-pleasant manner, inquired how the dog was doing. The husband matter-of-factly announced that he had given the dog away. His sole objective had been to deprive his wife of her beloved pet. Speechless, Duff shook his head and walked off the bench. As he descended the stairway, he turned to me in disgust and uttered the only words of profanity I ever heard from his lips. I, too, would learn as a circuit court judge that, too often, custody battles are at core disputes over objects—often—living beings. Fortunately in that instance, it was a dog rather than a child.

My hope on finishing law school was to obtain a job as an assistant commonwealth's attorney, and I took advantage of every opportunity to ingratiate myself with the county prosecutor, William E. Hassan. As his nickname, "Wild Bill" implies, he was a character. A short raspy Irishman in his early sixties, with a irascible personality, Hassan spent ten years as a Secret Service agent before attending law school. He would scream at criminal defense lawyers so loudly you could hear him in the public hallway. Once, on election day, he even got into a fist fight with a lawyer in public. It didn't affect the outcome; people, even lawyers, loved him. Once he calmed down they generally got what they wanted. Behind the pugnacious veneer, he was a very compassionate guy who gave many young lawbreakers a second and, even sometimes, a third chance.

Hassan's temper was legendary. It was frequently sparked by audacious questioning of his authority. One morning, Hassan walked into the back of traffic court. Wild Bill rarely appeared in the lower courts except to pass through and let his presence be known. He had a staff of nine assistants who prosecuted the cases in the county courts, now known as general district courts. On this day Hassan called a motorcycle officer aside and informed him that he intended to nolle prosse[1] or drop a traffic ticket issued by the officer. The officer apparently protested strenuously. The high voltage prosecutor was outraged.

Hassan pranced to the front of the courtroom and asked the judge to call the case, which the court did as a courtesy. Hassan moved to nolle prosse the case. The court without hesitation granted the routine motion. As Hassan turned to walk away, he noticed the frustrated officer shaking his head. Hassan swirled around, with almost a hundred citizens in the crowded courtroom, and yelled, "and furthermore, all Officer Davis's cases are nolle prossed." The court just stared at the politically powerful prosecutor. The officer, half in shock, mumbled something. Hassan turned and announced as he walked toward the door that he might nolle prosse every ticket the officer wrote for the rest of his career. True story; I was there.

Not every judge allowed Wild Bill to get away with his infamous antics, but he always seemed to get the last word. They say that he had pulled a similar stunt in front of Judge Paul D. Brown about fifteen years earlier. Brown sat patiently while the bombastic prosecutor vented about a decision Brown had made. The judge then politely informed Hassan that his conduct was outrageous and that he was in contempt of court. Brown ordered him to pay a fine of five dollars. Hassan whipped out his wallet and walked toward the judge's bench. He slowly and methodically slammed five individual one dollar bills on the bench as he screamed, "and this doesn't begin to express the contempt I have for this court." Hassan then turned and walked out of the courtroom. Brown was reportedly too speechless to jail him.

Despite his occasional temper tantrums, Bill Hassan was highly respected within the legal community. He was an accomplished trial lawyer who had prosecuted a number of high visibility cases in his lengthy career. I took advantage of every opportunity to remind him that I wanted to serve as an assistant commonwealth's attorney when I finished law school. He, too, had completed law school at night. He always seemed receptive, and told me to come see him

[1] A colloquialism for nolle prosequi.

when I was nearing graduation. Unfortunately, complications from diabetes forced him into retirement before that day came.

Since Hassan retired before his term expired, the chief judge of the circuit court was empowered by state law to appoint his successor. A number of lawyers were in contention. My future plans hinged on the decision.

# IV

# Assistant Commonwealth's Attorney

Three and a half years of law school at night was a real drag. I enjoyed the people, many of whom are still my friends. I had no academic aspirations beyond simply graduating. Because of my accelerated schedule, I finished one semester early, which gave me plenty of time to study for the bar. Fortunately I passed it the first time. For me, the Virginia law and procedures portion was challenging, but not difficult. On the other hand, the multistate portion was next to impossible. Each question had two potentially correct answers, but one was the preferred answer. Because the multistate exam is a product of academia, the gold standard often represents the prevailing view among law professors, as opposed to practicing lawyers. There is a significant difference in these perspectives, since many, if not most, law professors have never practiced law. At any rate, in May 1974 I received a green postcard from the Virginia Board of Bar Examiners announcing that I had passed.

By then, Judge Winston had selected an interim commonwealth's attorney, Claude M. Hilton. Claude was an alumnus of the clerk's office. He was about six years my senior, with a superb legal reputation. He was a former assistant commonwealth's attorney with a general law practice right across from the courthouse. Luckily, I knew him well. He agreed to hire me as an assistant commonwealth's attorney. I started the following Monday at an annual salary of twelve thousand dollars.

Tara and I now had a combined income exceeding twenty thousand dollars a year. We decided to buy a small rambler in Fairfax County for fifty-two thousand dollars.

I arrived in the office at 8:00 a.m. my first day as a prosecutor. The office manager, Ann, whom I knew well from Bill Hassan's days, handed me a stack of pink traffic summons. She said, "take traffic." There were no further instructions. My career as a prosecutor was launched. Having spent six years as a court clerk and bailiff, I really needed no direction. It was basic. I was a little nervous, but things went fine. Traffic cases normally turn on the facts as opposed to the law. Acquittals are rare in traffic court. Most defendants are not represented by counsel. Almost without exception, when a defendant appears with a lawyer some type of deal is cut, reducing the speed or sending the driver to traffic school. In those days, even first offender drunk driving cases were commonly reduced to reckless driving after the defendant completed the Alcohol Safety Action Program. In due course, that practice would change.

After a couple of weeks in traffic court, I advanced to the criminal side of what was then known as the county court. Unlike the traffic docket, which routinely exceeded a hundred cases, the criminal docket was more manageable in size. Typically, about twenty cases were set for trial each day, along with a couple of felony cases set for preliminary hearing, and a host of bond motions, probation violations, requests for continuance and other assorted matters. Of the twenty cases marked for trial, most were disposed of on guilty pleas. On average, I would try six cases a day. They varied from assault and battery and concealed weapons to trespassing and shoplifting. The formidable task was trial preparation.

In the lower courts in those days, most business was conducted in the hallway. The prosecutor would stand outside the courtroom and lawyers would line up to discuss a proposed deal, sometimes twenty at a time. The assistant commonwealth's attorney would then consult with the arresting officer or victim and come back with a counter offer. The process would continue until a meeting of the minds was reached. If not, we'd try the case.

With rare exceptions, you had no contact with the witnesses or the case file prior to court. You would learn your court assignment that morning, and were fortunate to have ten minutes to prepare each case. Sometimes, when the judge was in a hurry, there was no time to even meet the witnesses, much less hear their stories. On more than one occasion, I called a witness to the stand and began my direct examination by asking, "Please give us your name and explain why you're here today." At times it was embarrassing, but it had been the way of doing things in Arlington for decades. It provided unparalleled training. You learned to think on your feet—evaluate a case quickly and devise a trial strategy. Most important, you honed your witness-examination skills, particularly cross-examining witnesses without the benefit of advanced preparation—a dying art.

Years later, when I was elected commonwealth's attorney, I assigned my assistants to court one month in advance, so citizens could contact them to discuss their cases before trial. The size of the docket had tripled by then. I also established a victim/witness assistance unit, comprised mainly of senior citizens who volunteered their time. The victim/witness unit called each victim and subpoenaed witnesses before trial to discuss their case and explain where to park, when to arrive and where to report. It would also elicit a summary of what each witness knew about the case. These notes were made a part of the office file. This made the prosecutor's job much more manageable. It was at least a place to start.

In my first six months of working for Claude Hilton as an assistant commonwealth's attorney, trying cases was only a part of my portfolio of responsibilities. My principal mission was getting Claude elected to a full term of office. Like everyone else in the Arlington County Courthouse, we considered ourselves to be Democrats, Byrd Democrats. For all practical purposes, Republicans were extinct. Unfortunately, we had serious if not formidable competition for the Democratic nomination from William S. Burroughs. While Claude had the power of incumbency, Bill Burroughs was a mainstream party activist. Claude and I were newcomers on the party periphery, and our campaign staff had little depth. By default, I was managing the campaign. We were up against the party machine. As soon as I finished court each day, we headed out to campaign. It was a classic grass roots operation, knock on doors, distribute literature, and put up posters—an old fashioned all volunteer operation. I usually got home around 10:00 p.m.

In time, I earned the privilege of trying more complex felony cases. As the junior member of the staff, I was usually assigned the burglary, theft, and drug cases. The stuff no one else wanted. Most cases resulted in guilty pleas with specific sentencing recommendations. Only about one out of every twenty-five cases actually went to trial. I vividly remember my first jury trial. Chauncey McDonald was charged with possession of a Schedule VI substance, tetracycline, in an unlabeled vial, a misdemeanor. Virginia law required drugs in that lesser category to be carried in a properly labeled vial.

McDonald was a person of interest to the Arlington County Police, someone constantly on the other side of the law. They badly wanted a conviction. Otherwise, I doubt he would have even been charged with such a seemingly insignificant offense. But I didn't make the charging decisions, I just tried the cases Claude assigned me.

The trial began on a bad note. As Judge Duff read the charge against McDonald to the jury, he looked at me with a flummoxed expression, and audibly mumbled, "Tetracycline, that's what my doctor prescribes for my face." A trivial case got even tougher. The prosecution's case took less than two hours. I called the officer who had discovered the vial on McDonald, Detective Cindy Brown, to establish the chain of custody, and a state forensic chemist to testify that the substance in the vial was tetracycline, a Schedule VI drug. The defense called no witnesses. His final argument focused on the frivolous nature of the charge and the waste of tax dollars associated with trial—the argument had some merit in this case.

In final argument, I hammered away at the jury that the General Assembly of Virginia, their elected representatives, had passed the law and it was their sworn duty as a jury to follow it. The jury began deliberations shortly after lunch. They deliberated a full day, returning their verdict in the late afternoon of the second day. They found McDonald guilty and recommended a fine of one dollar. McDonald, who lived life in the fast lane, died several months later. Not a momentous victory, but my mother was proud.

Meanwhile, the campaign cranked on. Claude Hilton had unshakeable confidence, constantly reassuring me that all the key people were on his side. If so, they kept a low profile. Burroughs's support was palpable. He carpet bombed the county with brochures and mail outs. He dropped three pieces of literature for every one of ours. All the Democratic worker bees were pounding the pavement for Burroughs. At that point, I realized that we were swimming against a strong tide. Claude was unfazed.

In those days no one spent money on polling. The budget for a local campaign was around ten thousand dollars. The time-tested support indicator was bumper stickers. Political pundits counted the number of bumper stickers on cars during the last two weeks of the campaign. It was unscientific, but surprisingly accurate. The bumper sticker index reflected the need for a quick bump to pull this one out. So we put together a power piece—a mail out that compared Hilton's strengths against those of Burroughs. Unfortunately, the printing wasn't ready until three days before the election. We worked late into the evening labeling and bundling the brochures. A friend and I rushed the bags of mail to the bulk mail office at the regional post office in Merrifield, Virginia.

We arrived fifteen minutes before closing. They refused to accept it. We argued that the mailing was time sensitive and that the campaign could be decided by this mail-out. The man on duty essentially ordered us to take the mail bags and get out. I asked to speak to someone at a higher level. He blew me off and said there was no way it was going that night. I was desperate and remembered that a part-time bailiff in the sheriff's office, Ray Tubbs, was a retired high level official with the postal service. After several tries, I got Tubbs. Ray was an ardent Hilton supporter. I explained the situation. He told me to wait for him in the convenience store parking lot where I was standing.

Almost an hour later Tubbs pulled into the parking lot with another gentleman in the car. It was now about 11:00 p.m. My thoughts during the preceding hour had been almost totally consumed by ideas about postelection employment. Tubbs waved for us to follow him. We pulled up at the rear entrance of the post office, where trucks were being loaded. Staying a careful ten feet behind, I followed them inside. Tubbs's companion turned out to be the regional director of the U.S. Postal Service. Need I say more? The brochure was delivered in the next day's mail.

At about this time, I made local headlines with my first high publicity case. The owner of a local canine security firm was charged with cruelty to animals. Allegedly, the firm was not housing its crew of German shepherds in proper sanitary facilities. For some reason, the local newspapers gave the case front page coverage. At trial, I called five witnesses, including a veterinarian who testified as an expert. I cited cases and argued passionately. At the close of the prosecution evidence the court dismissed the case, almost without explanation. I was flabbergasted. I had an excellent relationship with the judge, so I went back into chambers to find out what had gone wrong.

The normally mild-mannered judge sported an angry crimson face. Before I could utter a sound, he blurted, "Damn dogs crap on my lawn." End of matter.

I arrived at the courthouse early on election night. The polls closed at 7:00 p.m. Most precincts had reported by 8:00 p.m. Hilton had an elaborate victory celebration planned. I stood at the rear door of the courthouse awaiting his arrival. At about 8:30 p.m., he and his wife pulled into the parking lot. He was smiling as he got out of the car. I wondered if he knew something I didn't. As he ascended the stairs with the self-confidence of a young soap opera star receiving an Emmy, I broke the news: "We lost." The results weren't even close. We lost thirty-seven of thirty-nine precincts. I headed directly home to plot my job-search strategy.

The next week, after visiting several local law firms, most of which offered a minimum salary and a small percentage of what I brought in, I decided to take my chances with Bill Burroughs. It turned out to be a wise decision.

In the interim, I was trying increasingly more complex cases at a steady clip. Although I made my fair share of mistakes, I was developing a respectable record. I did not try to cultivate a private practice on the side. Tara still attended George Mason University at night, so I had the flexibility to work late. I spent my time visiting crime scenes, getting involved in the investigations, and helping the police draft search warrant affidavits. Before long, many of the significant cases were coming my way.

During my early years as a prosecutor I was narrow minded and at times offensively self-righteous. It may have been ambition, or immaturity, but I had not yet learned that there are usually two sides to every story. This is typical. Many prosecutors undergo a process of judgmental maturation. In time, even hard chargers learn to understand that defendants are human beings, someone's son or daughter. That must be factored into the equation as you attempt to sort the good from the bad. I learned this lesson from one of the most aggressive prosecutors who ever lived. He had remarkable grasp of human behavior. During my career, I've learned to appreciate the value of human psychology as a professional tool. Understanding people is central to the art of cross-examination. Logic and common sense are integral elements of legal advocacy.

As a young court bailiff, I always enjoyed watching Justin W. Williams in action. He was the most mismatched person I ever met. He'd wear bright yellow trousers with a tattered red sport coat. He drove an ancient yellow Volkswagen convertible so filled with litter and old newspapers that it would accommodate no passengers. A humble guy, he was notoriously eccentric, but uniformly loved and respected. His signature was the wooden box of three by five cards that he brought to court for every trial. It contained a card outlining every court decision even remotely relevant to the case. His knowledge and memory of the law were unassailable. He was a walking computer and remarkably effective.

Williams was also well known for over-trying every case. He never called just one witness to prove a point—no matter how tangential—when three were available. This drove the judges crazy. His over preparation, however, had one major advantage: He rarely made a mistake.

While Williams's eccentricities were always topical, his judgment and the respect he commanded from criminal defense lawyers always impressed me. Police officers always wanted him to prosecute their cases. And ironically, criminal defense lawyers always breathed a sigh of relief when they learned that Justin was assigned to prosecute their clients. He believed in full disclosure of the prosecution's case. He realized that there were two sides to every story. The truth of this maxim will become even more apparent later, when I explain my investigation of a soldier allegedly castrated by three bikers in a local bar.

Few people had a greater impact on my life than Justin Williams. We spoke almost daily in the courthouse hallways. Many people encouraged me to become a prosecutor, but Justin convinced me. He explained that the prosecutor is the real quarterback of law enforcement, the one who calls the signals and scores the points. Police officers do the blocking and tackling. On reflection, the analogy fit. But most of all, he taught me the importance of distinguishing between good people who exercise poor judgment and bad people who are truly evil. Rarely in the spectrum of human conduct is good or evil absolute. In later years Justin and I worked together as colleagues, successfully prosecuting the Arlington heroin connection, uprooting the tentacles of the Sicilian Mafia in Northern Virginia and seizing Hillbilly Haynie's oceanfront playboy mansion, purchased with proceeds from his international hashish importation syndicate.

Williams left the Office of the Commonwealth's Attorney in 1969 to become an assistant United States attorney. Shortly thereafter, he married his first wife. Philosophically, they were polar extremes. An unexpected encounter at their house on North Brandywine Street in Arlington almost sent their relationship into a tailspin. Mrs. Williams returned home unexpectedly one afternoon. As she walked upstairs to the bedroom, she heard movement. Several steps from the bedroom door, she heard a female voice say softly, "Justin." She looked into the room and observed a young woman standing next to the dresser. Fuming, she asked her what the hell she was doing there. The woman, unflustered, calmly replied that she was "waiting for Justin." Justin's wife stomped out of the house. The woman proceeded to pilfer every valuable item in sight, including William's Department of Justice credentials (that's how she knew his name) and revolver.

The police were not called until later that evening when Williams returned home and convinced his wife that they had been the victim of a burglary. There were no immediate suspects. The police prepared a composite sketch of the perpetrator and created a wanted poster containing a description of the missing property. The flyer was circulated in the community. Several days later, a neighbor on Brandywine Street called the Arlington Police to report that her niece might be the person depicted on the flyer. The neighbor had discovered a revolver concealed in her vacuum cleaner. Further, she said that her niece had been recently released from jail and that she resembled the sketch.

Kathleen Clancy was arrested and brought to Arlington County, but only after passing dozens of checks on William's account. I personally prosecuted the case. With his approval and in order to spare Justin any embarrassment, I negotiated a plea bargain. Clancy pled guilty to burglary and other related charges and received a sentence of about two years. But the story doesn't end there.

Despite being a little rough around the edges, Clancy was rather charming and attractive, and extremely manipulative. She was able to inveigle the trust of the jail staff, ordinarily tough people to con. The sheriff's office made no attempt to send her down state. When the Department of Corrections eventually designated her to a state facility and informed the sheriff's office that they would pick her up on an appointed date, one of the deputies agreed to drive her to the women's prison at Goochland, Virginia. It was not unusual for the sheriff to transport a designated inmate to a state facility, particularly to expedite removal from the local jail. But that was not the case here. The circumstances with Clancy were clearly out of the ordinary.

En route to rural Goochland County, located about thirty-five miles west of Richmond, Clancy persuaded the female deputy to stop at a restaurant for lunch. As the story was later told, Clancy was unshackled and the two sat down at a table to dine, in flagrant violation of sheriff's office policy. The ensuing events are unclear. However, one thing is certain. Clancy was arrested several months later near the Canadian border with the deputy's credentials in her possession. Not only that: Somehow she had used the credentials to charge food and motel rooms along her path of flight. The sheriff received a bill for more than two thousand dollars. Heads rolled.

* * *

The day finally came when Bill Burroughs was sworn in as commonwealth's attorney. He was a capable lawyer who had served as an assistant under Bill Hassan. No one doubted his legal skills, but some questioned whether he was the right person for the job. Even though I had managed his opponent's campaign, I became the point of contact during the transition. He and I bonded quickly. Regrettably, our relationship would culminate in a bloody political duel.

The central issue in Bill's successful campaign was drug enforcement, particularly in the schools. The group within the Arlington County Police Department responsible for conducting drug investigations was called the Special Unit. They also handled gambling, prostitution, and related vice cases. It was the premier unit within the department, and membership was a ticket to upward mobility. Special Unit investigations were an intriguing blend of intelligence gathering and calculated pursuit, enshrouded in a veil of secrecy. All its members were hand picked by the supervising lieutenant, William K. "Smokey" Stover. Stover was as tough as boot leather and ruled the unit by sheer intimidation. No indiscretions were tolerated. He loved to say that his detectives were "as pure as the driven snow." One detective was bounced back to the street for a single act of marital infidelity. The men and women assigned to the Special Unit were bright and tireless, but in actuality, they were a pretty wild crowd. Their track record, however, was legendary. Stover would tolerate no less.

Stover was such an imposing figure that he always got his way. So when he asked to have his own prosecutor assigned to the Special Unit, Burroughs complied. I had known Stover since my days as firefighter and was always anxious to be of assistance to him in the clerk's office. I was flattered when he convinced Burroughs to assign me to his unit, since I had been practicing law for less than a year. The assignment proved to be another career-defining moment, because I became a recognized expert on the prosecution of narcotics and vice cases.

As a result, in 1985, I was asked by President Ronald Reagan to chair a national commission on pornography, commonly referred to as the "Meese Commission"—even though Attorney General Ed Meese had nothing to do with the establishment of the commission. It was created at the president's direction by Attorney General William French Smith. That commission was greeted with a tidal wave of controversy—perhaps more than any other in the 1980s—and I was destined to be pummeled by verbal rocks. The formation of the commission sparked a literal avalanche of criticism from every major newspaper around the country that perceived our mission as a direct assault on the First Amendment—an act of moral aggression. As chairman, I absorbed the worst of it. Newspaper editors depicted me as a young lawyer "who cut his teeth trying pornography cases." Actually, I never tried a pornography case, but it was my experience with the Special Unit that led to this persistent tag.

To fully appreciate the long-range implications of my early years as a vice and narcotics prosecutor, it's important to understand the political landscape of Arlington County. It was and still is a community composed of self-described proud, progressive thinkers. Along with its neighbor to the south, the City of Alexandria, the region's population enjoys the distinction of being the most liberal area of Virginia. Arlington is composed primarily of well educated, free spirited Democrats. Most Republican candidates running for statewide office do not even bother to campaign in Arlington.

The majority of Arlingtonians undoubtedly harbored an absolutist viewpoint on the First Amendment—adults should be able to read and publish whatever they choose, without government interference. The limits of this philosophy, however, were tested when the first adult bookstore sprouted up in a commercial shopping strip near a residential community. Within months, several similar stores were opened. Public anger was fomented to near riot proportions. These folks were passionate advocates of the unfettered right to publish whatever a person wished, as long as it wasn't done in their neighborhood. Burroughs demanded immediate action.

Contrary to public opinion, investigating pornography establishments is not a task relished by any police officer, even a vice investigator. Most such stores have a gritty aura and tend to draw an unsavory clientele. There is also a provable correlation between criminal activity and the presence of these shops in a defined geographic area.

The credit for devising the strategy to close the adult bookstores in Arlington County belongs to Bill Burroughs. He painstakingly researched the law. We sent an undercover officer into each of the stores to purchase the raunchiest material on display. These materials were submitted to the court, which found their visual depictions to be obscene, and a search warrant for each store was issued. Carefully following the law, the detectives serving the warrants seized only a representative copy of each publication that appeared to meet the standard for obscenity. This approach foreclosed any allegations of prior restraint. Burroughs then filed a lawsuit against each of the seized publications and had them judicially declared obscene. The game plan was to employ the court's obscenity findings as the "community standard." Fortunately, Burroughs's persistence was more than the bookstore owners could handle. They closed and relocated outside of Arlington.

## Massage Parlors

The next community scourge proved more difficult to conquer and considerably more controversial. While we were attempting to dismantle the adult bookstores, a half dozen massage parlors opened in Arlington. Informants indicated that these parlors were actually houses of prostitution operating under the guise of health clubs. But, tactically, they were difficult to crack. Smokey Stover appropriately refused to allow a police officer to engage in sexual activity in his official capacity. In order to obtain a conviction for prostitution, Arlington judges required more than sexual banter; a simple verbal offer and acceptance was not enough in their view. The prosecution had to prove an "act in furtherance of prostitution." This affirmative act would necessitate the officer compromising himself, which Stover would not tolerate.

The masseuses, or massage technicians as they preferred to be called, as a precaution against arrest, routinely required patrons to disrobe before negotiating illicit sex acts. Obviously, they were well counseled on the law. Masseuses never undressed first, because that could be construed as an "act in furtherance of prostitution." Alternatively, they would rub the patron's genitals, knowing that only a cop would protest. The fact that these practices offended Stover's strict standards of conduct for officers was well known within the industry. The masseuses capitalized on the restrictive police policy and for more than a year successfully insulated the parlors from vice squad infiltration.

The best source of information concerning the inner workings of the parlors came from disgruntled patrons who had their money or credit cards stolen during acts of sexual indulgence. Detectives also interviewed patrons or "Johns" exiting the parlors. The method of operation in the parlors was simple and unsophisticated. Johns would usually request a full body massage and pay the initial fee at the reception area. This money, which varied from seventy-five to one hundred twenty-five dollars, went to the house, or owner. The John would then enter the massage room and being told to undress, might undress entirely, or might remain in his undershorts.

The masseuses were all scantily clad, and most had no formal massage training. Some had prior convictions for prostitution or larceny. The masseuse began by administering a haphazardly applied rubdown, always deliberately brushing against the patron's genitals. She would then ask if the patron wanted any "extras." Regular customers understood the lingo. They would graphically describe their requests and a price would be negotiated. In fairness, not all masseuses would engage in intercourse or oral sex, but many were eager to do so for the right price.

The approach to more introverted or less experienced patrons varied. If the masseuse had not dealt with the John previously, she would engage in sexually suggestive dialogue calculated to elicit a request for a high dollar sex act. If this proved unsuccessful, she would offer the patron what was commonly referred to as a "local," generally understood to be a lubricated hand ejaculation. Each masseuse negotiated her own price, but the going rate was about forty dollars for a "local." Without exception, all masseuses offered this service. For most, it was their principle source of income. Some of the more anatomically gifted masseuses offered more erotic versions, by allowing men to ejaculate between their breasts. One masseuse we later interviewed said that she was making more than two hundred thousand dollars a year giving breast massages. If you saw her you would understand why.

Without a wiretap, drug and vice investigations are developed through the cultivation of evidence from three sources. First is the gathering of informant information. In this case, none of the Johns we interviewed would willingly testify, and those who might had minimal credibility. Most patrons, many of whom were married with families, agreed to talk to police only with an assurance that their sexual escapade would remain confidential. The second source of evidence is undercover infiltration. This would have been the preferred approach, but for ethical reasons, it was not feasible in this case.

The third common technique is the use of search warrants. The real art of drug and vice investigation is engineering legally sound affidavits demonstrating probable cause for a search warrant. We thought we had sufficient probable cause that illicit sex acts were occurring in the parlors, but this was not a case where a successful prosecution could be built around the type of physical evidence a search warrant can best yield. We seriously doubted that the masseuses were maintaining any written records of illegal sex acts. To confirm this suspicion, we attempted to use a "trash pull."

This involves surreptitiously picking up the target location trash after it is put out for collection. Once trash is placed in a public area for collection, it loses its legal privacy and there are no search and seizure issues. Even a trash pull proved challenging in this case, because most parlors were open all night. This eliminated the normal cover of darkness. Absconding with someone's trash in broad daylight tends to draw suspicious glances.

Nevertheless, several trash pulls proved successful. Wearing rubber gloves, detectives were able to cull numerous used condoms from the mound of refuse. This would provide useful corroborative evidence, but it was clearly insufficient to convince an objective jury that these massage parlors were houses of prostitution. We expected to attract a lot of public attention; we couldn't go forward with a weak case. Frustration was building. Suddenly the solution appeared, unexpectedly, at our fishing club's annual gala.

### The Hookers

The "Hookers" began with six members and evolved into a group of twenty-five cops and prosecutors. Twice a year we traveled to the Outer Banks of North Carolina or the Eastern Shore of Virginia to fish, drink beer, and smoke cigars. I was elected president of the Hookers, for life. And although we occasionally caught fish, we never allowed that to interfere with cigar smoking or beer drinking.

Each year the Hookers hosted the Hookers Ball. Over time the event progressed from a small group of revelers to a mob scene with close to four hundred attendees. The ball was essentially a dance with a huge buffet and unlimited beer and wine. It became the courthouse social event of the year. So what did the Hookers Ball have to do with investigating massage parlors? Connections. Net working of the most productive kind.

Several Special Unit detectives were members of the Hookers. In jest, one of the detectives teased a self-proclaimed sexually promiscuous sheriff's office investigator about "sending him in undercover in the massage parlors." No one appeared to take the suggestion seriously. However, the following Monday morning he appeared in my office and volunteered for the assignment. Initially, there was a great deal of skepticism about a sworn law enforcement officer being paid by the public to have sex. It took some convincing, but eventually, Stover and Burroughs signed off on it, since it did not involve an Arlington County Police Officer. The sheriff, surprisingly, had no objection, provided that the identity of the investigator was protected and that his activities fell short of actual intercourse. Our investigation went into overdrive.

Within two months, the investigator had received "locals" from multiple masseuses in each of the operating parlors. The investigator explained his experiences to the grand jury, which promptly handed down indictments for operating a public nuisance against each parlor owner. Search warrants were served at each business location, but few masseuses were arrested, as most were anxious to testify against their employer in exchange for immunity from prosecution.

There were two kinds of women working in the parlors: those who worked to survive and those who were simply greedy. The former were drug addicts or single mothers desperate for money. The latter were attractive women able to earn a six-figure salary masturbating men. And some of those women actually enjoyed the male attention they received as a masseuse. In the final analysis, the masseuses were more valuable as witnesses than as defendants. With their testimony, the parlor operators had no choice but to enter guilty pleas and get out of town. That's exactly what happened. Years later they were back—as outcall escort services. Unfortunately, the appetite for vice is boundless.

As an epilogue to the massage parlor story, in the fall of 1983, I was campaigning for reelection as Commonwealth's Attorney of Arlington County. The criminal defense lawyers and the liberal wing of the Democratic party wanted me out. On one particular evening, my opponent and I were debating in front of the Arlington Civic Federation, a group historically controlled by Democratic activists. My opponent clearly had the home field advantage. Attempting to capitalize on the leftward tilt of the crowd, he passionately pounded on me for wasting public money and trampling on individual rights by investigating adult bookstores and massage parlors. Unsure of the crowd's reaction, and convinced that I had few supporters in the group, I decided to stand my ground. I responded by explaining that unlike my opponent, I was a life-long Arlingtonian and I was proud that

Arlington County was the only jurisdiction in the Washington, D.C., area with no adult bookstores and no massage parlors.

It took a full minute for the crowd to compose itself. It's hard to say which was more embarrassing to my opponent, the standing ovation or the shouts of "keep it up." The issue never surfaced again during the campaign.

Pursuing vice cases was a small part of my portfolio of responsibility as attorney for the Special Unit. Most of my time was spent investigating and prosecuting drug cases. Our principle target was heroin, which was becoming increasingly prevalent in the black communities of Arlington. Many of the purse snatchings and most of the armed robberies in the county were committed by heroin addicts. Black leaders in the community protested that no attention was being given to problems in their neighborhood.

The inaction was not the result of inattention. It was nearly impossible to infiltrate the Arlington heroin market. Most of it was being sold on the street to local users. Traffickers were extremely circumspect about their contacts. There was only a handful of black officers in the police department, and they were well known in the community. The idea of using a white officer to make undercover buys in a black neighborhood was ridiculous. The common technique of using a paid confidential informant to make a controlled buy, a purchase under the supervision of a detective, proved impossible. Potential informants who lived in the neighborhood feared retribution and had no safe sanctuary. Dealers shunned people they knew had been arrested for fear they had been "flipped" by police and might be trying to "work off" the charge by jamming someone else. They also kept an arm's length from strangers in the neighborhood. Penetrating this crowd would be a challenge. But that's the thrill of this type of work.

V

# Bustin' Drug Traffickers

Lt. Smokey Stover came up with a brilliant plan—negotiate an officer exchange with the D.C. Metropolitan Police Department, which had hundreds of black police officers experienced in buying drugs undercover. They found the perfect guy for this assignment. He was a young officer about twenty-two years old, tall, nice looking and very outgoing, with but a single character flaw.

Rather than use an informant to directly facilitate a drug buy, the Special Unit used a paid informant to introduce the clandestine officer to other men at the neighborhood watering hole. The crafty young officer took it from there. Within weeks he had made undercover heroin buys from all the major players. It turned out that he had also helped himself to many of the young ladies in the neighborhood. These indiscretions did not affect the integrity of our investigation, but they surfaced during an internal affairs investigation conducted later by the D.C. Police Department, totally unrelated to the case. It seems the young woman with whom the officer was living would periodically learn of his secret trysts. Infuriated, she would mail his police-issued service revolver to police headquarters with a note that she had found it on the street in D.C. Because mishandling a service weapon is a serious violation of police regulations, this would spawn an internal police investigation. Apparently she did this at least three times. For whatever reason, shortly after our drug investigation ended, the officer left the D.C Police and slipped into oblivion. As far as I know, he has not been heard from since.

The undercover investigation proved to be a monumental success. The grand jury returned close to a hundred indictments. Almost every major heroin trafficker in the area was ensnared, most on multiple counts. I insisted on handling every case. Burroughs had no objection. The indictments were only the first step of the master plan. The coordinating detective, David Weaver, and I had our sights trained on the main supplier, Garcine Black. A regional distributor, Black was based in the City of Alexandria, immediately south of Arlington. The Alexandria City Police had been pursuing Black for years to no avail. He was well disciplined and rarely had contact with street-level drug dealers. His immediate associates insulated themselves by using long-established intermediaries between themselves and street level pushers. Neither Black nor his inner circle of associates used narcotics. This is typical of drug kingpins seeking to build a successful business enterprise. People with a habit tend to pilfer the product.

Black maintained a tight grip on his organization. Within the black community in Northern Virginia, he muscled out all the competition. The organization had one element of vulnerability, his personal stable of women. Black attempted to identify as many attractive female heroin addicts or potential addicts as possible, of all races, ages, and backgrounds. After supplying them with enough heroin to ensure their chemical enslavement, he would abruptly cut off their supply, barring any of his dealers from furnishing heroin to them. When they were desperate, he would force them to deal with him directly, but he would refuse to sell them their heroin. Instead, they had to perform sexual services for his friends in exchange for drugs. Some of them had respectable jobs and families. Most were too intimidated to cooperate with the police, but over time some resolved to break way. These women proved to be a valuable source of intelligence, but not enough to bring down Black.

Black instructed all his dealers who had been busted in our investigation to hang tough. He knew we'd try to leverage the charges for cooperation. He was right. Although a few caved and agreed to testify, most insisted on going to trial, which became labor intensive. I conducted about thirty jury trials over the ensuing six months. It was great experience for me, but Detective Weaver and I were exhausted. Even after being convicted and sentenced to five to fifteen years in prison, these defendants were slow to crack. Weaver and I decided to use a different approach.

The crime of conspiracy to commit a felony had been on the books in Virginia for decades. In essence, it prohibited two or more people from agreeing to violate the law. Unlike the law of many other states, the law of Virginia did not even require proof of an overt act. In other words, to be convicted, all the prosecution had to prove was that more than one person had agreed to commit a crime, even if they took no action to carry out the plan. It was a potent law enforcement weapon. Before 1976, no one in Northern Virginia and few people statewide had ever been prosecuted for conspiracy under state law.

On the other hand, federal prosecutors routinely employed the conspiracy statute to disrupt large-scale drug trafficking syndicates. After concluding that all routes of entry into the Black organization were dead ends, Detective Weaver and I decided to confer with our old friend, Assistant United States Attorney Justin W. Williams. With our continuing assistance and active participation, Justin agreed to adopt the Garcine Black case for federal prosecution. He arranged for Special Agent Ernie Staples of the United States Drug Enforcement Administration to coordinate the investigation from the federal side. His first task was to give us a full-day tutorial on building a historical conspiracy case. I used the technique I learned from Staples with considerable success for the next fifteen years.

A historical conspiracy is a prosecution based on events that occurred in the past. It flows backwards from the date it is discovered by law enforcement. In contrast, a contemporary conspiracy starts from the day of law enforcement infiltration and progresses forward. Contemporary conspiracies require either a confidential informant or an undercover agent on the inside. Because we didn't have that, our options were limited, and we had to work backwards.

Weaver, Staples, and I began meeting with the attorneys for each of the defendants convicted in the Arlington drug bust. The presence of a federal agent and the threat of federal prosecution upped the ante substantially. With Williams's concurrence we agreed, in exchange for cooperation, to give each defendant immunity from federal prosecution for conspiracy along with a letter to the Virginia Parole Board recommending early release on parole. In those days most defendants were eligible for parole after serving as little as a sixth of their sentence. Unless the defendant was disruptive during his incarceration, our letter virtually assured parole first time up. This was an attractive offer.

There were several reasons why most defendants took the deal. First, at that point they had usually experienced a taste of the penitentiary, and couldn't handle it. Life was much tougher there than in the local jail. Even the bad boys began to break. Second, no one wanted to face a federal prosecution and the possibility of ten to fifteen years of additional hard time. Lastly, we convinced them that there was no possibility of retaliation, since Black would serve all his time in a federal rather than a state facility.

We began detailed debriefings of each defendant, identifying major transactions and developing corroboration. Most had undergone a dramatic change in attitude. The dynamics had shifted. Weaned from heroin and stripped of their bravado, they welcomed contact with the outside world. We were literally their ticket to freedom—and we never let them forget it. Establishing this type of dependant relationship is a classic element of the interrogation process.

It took almost six months to craft the blueprint for a tight conspiracy case. Historical conspiracies are fraught with proof problems because they are constructed with the testimony of cooperating coconspirators who will receive a reduced sentence for their testimony. A prominent criminal defense attorney once referred to such evidence as "a pack of perjurers bathing in a sea of immunity." It is therefore imperative that prosecutors build the conspiracy around events provable by multiple witnesses or for which there is documentary corroboration. For example, if a witness was prepared to testify that an event occurred at a motel on an approximate date, we would try to obtain room rental or credit card records to bolster the testimony.

To make sure that none of our witnesses got cold feet and backed out at the last minute, we called each cooperating defendant before a federal grand jury to recount the salient parts of their debriefings. Their testimony was recorded by a court reporter and later transcribed. Under the controlling law at that time, if the witness balked at trial, the transcript could be used as evidence. This is no longer legal unless the implicated person has been given a chance to cross-examine the witness.

When we were done, an indictment was prepared and presented to the federal grand jury. Garcine Black and his inner circle of confederates were indicted. Williams arranged to have the indictment sealed from public inspection and to have warrants issued for the arrest of all those who had been indicted. As I learned from Special Agent Staples, service of the arrest warrants was a prime opportunity to gather evidence, and required strategic planning.

Arrest provides a unique opportunity to search the arrestee, his or her vehicle and, under some circumstances, home. The element of surprise is critical. You want to catch the defendant "dirty"—holding drugs or other evidence. If he knows you are coming, that is unlikely. Timing is critical. With the number of witnesses we presented to the grand jury, an eventual leak was inevitable. With all this in the mix, we began plotting the bust of Garcine Black.

Although our case against Black was relatively strong, with almost a dozen cooperating coconspirators, seizing drugs directly from him at the time of his arrest would clinch his conviction. In drug prosecutor jargon, this is called "putting dope on the table." We had earlier undercover buys of small quantities of heroin from several of the coconspirators, who would testify that they had received it from one of Black's indicted lieutenants. However, to achieve maximum impact we needed a large enough quantity to portray Black as the big time dealer we believed him to be. But this was tricky because Black rarely touched the stuff himself.

American prisons are full of men neutered by jilted lovers. When cops want information, they seek it from vengeful ex-lovers. In Black's case, it was one of his stable of love slaves who flipped him.

### Smoking out the Big Guy

It was pushing 2:00 a.m. when we positioned ourselves about a hundred yards from the Pentagon Motel. I was riding with Sergeant Ed Cheslock of the Special Unit. Weaver and Staples secreted themselves in the motel parking lot, along with numerous other Arlington and Alexandria drug investigators. Since Weaver and Staples were the principle investigators, they would make the collar.

If you looked up "flea bag hotel" in a dictionary, you'd find a description of the old Pentagon Motel. It was located somewhat off the beaten path on South Clark Street, in an industrial area of Arlington County just outside of Crystal City.[2] There were only a few cars in the lot at night. Most business was conducted during the day. I couldn't imagine anyone actually spending the night there, and few people did. Average stay? About two hours.

We had received word that Black was meeting with his Alexandria wholesalers that night, so we waited patiently. After an hour or so, his girlfriend's distinctive yellow Volkswagen appeared. We were amazed that there were no countersurveillance tactics, like driving around the block several times, to smoke out police observers. Black looked calm and confident as he walked toward the stairway in the cool night air. Using binoculars, we could see shades moving in a window about halfway down the corridor.

This is when timing becomes critical and movement becomes a careful calculation between the coefficients of time and patience. A dozen detectives were anxiously poised and ready, but if we acted prematurely, we ran the risk of striking before the dope was in open view—or better yet—in the hand of the target. This type of miscalculation could enable Black to claim he had been unaware of its presence, perhaps hindering a successful prosecution.

The minutes ticked by until finally, at about 2:30 a.m. Black, taking his time, entered the room. Sergeant Cheslock checked his watch and conferred by radio with the Alexandria vice narcotics commander. Each had an equal interest in the case, and it was their informant that dropped the dime. About five minutes later, Cheslock directed the arrest team to move in. Emerging from the motel, Weaver and Staples appeared first, with Black in tow. Predictably, he was clean.

[2] The old Pentagon Motel has long since been sold and refurbished. It currently enjoys a fine reputation under its new ownership.

The other occupant of the room had several ounces of heroin in his pocket. There was nothing in open view except a small amount on a night stand.

Following his arrest, Black was polite and cooperative, but refused to give any information. The other occupant of the room, a known Black associate with mid-level status in the organization, got an offer he couldn't refuse. At first, he declined to say anything. However, the detectives explained that without his assistance in the investigation, they would be forced to reveal that he was the snitch who had set Black up. This, of course, was not true, but it turned out to be sufficient leverage to ensure his full cooperation. If the detectives had put this information on the street, the consequences could have been harsh. Drug enforcement is challenging, but it's also dirty and dangerous. I loved it.

Within days after Black's arrest, the other coconspirators were taken into custody. All defendants were arraigned and the case was set for trial in United States District Court in Alexandria before Judge Oren R. Lewis. Unlike most courts, the U.S. District Court in the Eastern District of Virginia, known nationally as the "rocket docket," prides itself in moving cases quickly. Criminal cases are set for trial four to six weeks from the date of arraignment. They move like grain through a goose. The case against Black and his eight coconspirators was set for trial five weeks after arraignment. There were about twenty-five government witnesses to be interviewed, discovery to be provided, and lots of legal research necessary to prepare for trial.

Although I volunteered to assist, my job was essentially complete at that point. The case was in Justin Williams's hands. I felt relieved. No matter what happened, our end of the investigation was an undisputed success. Bill Burroughs and United States Attorney William B. Cummings called a press conference to announce that Black and his group were out of business. Press coverage was excellent.

My respite was brief. The following morning Williams called with a suggestion. If Burroughs agreed, the United States attorney would try to get permission from the Department of Justice to appoint me as a special assistant United States attorney. Although common today, this was an unusual practice in 1976. This designation would allow me to participate fully in the federal trial. Burroughs enthusiastically endorsed the idea. Weaver, Staples, and I spent the next five weeks interviewing witnesses and preparing the factual portion of the case. After conducting more than thirty jury trials involving drug trafficking in state court, I was becoming an expert. This was another skill that would soon pay dividends. We worked about fifteen hours a day, but no one complained.

In the weeks that followed, the field of defendants was winnowed down to six. The others pled guilty and agreed to testify. Deals at this late stage are risky. Plea agreements are always conditioned on truthful testimony, but sometimes these guys retain their loyalty to the kingpin for fear of retaliation. They spin the prosecutor during trial by giving vague evasive answers, "failing" to remember, or even committing perjury. Prosecutors are not allowed to place witnesses before the grand jury to preserve testimony after an indictment is returned. Therefore, safeguards are limited. Each testifying defendant is thoroughly debriefed before the plea agreement is finalized. This so called proffer could be used to cross-examine and "impeach" a government witness who reneged on his agreement, but it couldn't be placed before the jury as substantive evidence as grand jury testimony could in those days. Therefore, the testimony of late pleading defendants had to be used with care and caution.

In the final run-up before trial, an unexpected event occurred. Garcine Black decided to plead guilty to possession of heroin with the intent to distribute. The government agreed to recommend a sentence of fifteen years. Although modest by today's standards, in 1976 that was a hefty sentence. The agreement did not require him to cooperate with the prosecution, which he refused to do, but at that point we didn't need his help anyway. The most attractive part of the deal was its anticipated effect on the other defendants remaining in the case. Normally, when the king falls, the pawns follow. No one budged.

The trial began on a Monday morning. It was scheduled for three days. In most federal courts, a case of similar complexity would take three weeks. But not before Judge "Roarin' Oren" Lewis. A gruff jurist in his early eighties, Judge Lewis moved cases at lightening speed. He had minimal regard for legal niceties and his decisions were frequently reversed by the court of appeals.

Years later as an assistant United States attorney, I was in front of Judge Lewis on a motion to dismiss an indictment. Defense counsel, who was from out of town, asked if Judge Lewis had read his brief. Lewis responded that in twenty-six years as a United States District Judge he had never read a brief, and asked why he should start now.

Lewis was unpredictable and extremely intimidating. He frequently asked questions of witnesses and made comments that drew stern criticism from the appellate court. But as a federal judge, he had been appointed for life and he really didn't give a damn.

From the moment Judge Lewis took the bench, he incessantly pushed the case. After we'd asked a witness a half dozen questions, Lewis would invariably inquire if we had further questions of the witness. Williams and I put on thirty witnesses in two days, along with opening statements by six lawyers. The trial was proceeding smoothly. The bomb dropped the third morning.

When court convened on Wednesday morning, before the jury was brought in, Williams proudly paced to the podium and announced that the government rested its case. The defense lawyers each moved for dismissal based on inadequate proof of their client's guilt, a routine motion necessary to preserve the defendant's right of appeal. It was promptly denied by Judge Lewis. The defendants then announced that they did not intend to put on any evidence and rested their cases. When Williams then stood to inform the court that the government had no objection to the defendants' proposed jury instructions, the judge cut him off in mid-sentence.

"What about this Black fella—that's all I've heard about—isn't either side callin' him as a witness?—he pled guilty already," Lewis bellowed.

The lawyers all looked at each other and responded in the negative.

"Alright then, I'm callin' Mr. Black as the court's witness."

Jaws dropped. Williams asked if Black's attorney should be notified.

Lewis shook his head and repeated, "He's already pled guilty. Why's he need a lawyer?"

No one had any idea what Black was going to say. He had never given a statement to anyone. Having already pled guilty, he could have taken the rap and exonerated all the other the defendants. Given the strength of our case, this was unlikely. However, of greater concern was the effect of all this on appeal. Everyone assumed a federal judge had the authority to call witnesses, but no one had ever known of its happening. Lewis then called a recess and directed the U.S. Marshals to produce Garcine Black, who was in custody, in his courtroom in one hour.

When court resumed, the jury was seated and Black was brought into the courtroom. The lawyers sat patiently at counsel table. Lewis looked about the courtroom. "Mr. Hudson, go ahead with your questions," Lewis directed, after apparently selecting me at random.

I remarked to myself, "What questions?"

After conferring briefly with Williams, I walked to the podium. As is customary, I asked Black his name. I then inquired if he had pled guilty in this court to possession of heroin with the intent to distribute. He acknowledged that he had. I next asked if he had been in the business of selling heroin in Arlington County and the City of Alexandria. Again, he politely responded in the affirmative. I then pointed to the five defendants. "Were these five men selling your heroin?" Black paused before answering. I braced for the response.

Lewis yelled, "Were these your boys, yes or no?"

Black slowly shook his head affirmatively and softly replied, "Yes." The defendants neither objected nor asked any questions on cross-examination.

Following final arguments of counsel and jury instructions by the court, the jury deliberated only thirty-five minutes before returning its verdict. There were no surprises. All defendants were convicted.

Although my caseload in the Office of the Commonwealth's Attorney became a bit more diversified, I continued to concentrate on drug cases. Using the skills I had learned in the Black case, I shifted my focus from street dealers to suppliers. I also decided to master the deployment of a weapon new to Virginia in the war on drugs.

## Electronic Surveillance

The Virginia electronic surveillance statute was enacted in 1973. With one exception, the statute had remained dormant. At first glance, the statute appeared extraordinarily complex. No court in Virginia had ruled on its constitutionality or on the admissibility of the resulting evidence. In fact, no case had ever been tried in Virginia using wiretap evidence. The feds had been using wire intercepts for years, with incredible results. They are particularly effective in penetrating close-knit drug syndicates in which there is no undercover access. As a prerequisite to applying for wiretap authority, the applicant must describe in detail, and under oath, how other normal investigative techniques have been tried and failed.

Ironically, the only other wiretap authorized under the statute had been obtained in Arlington County during Claude Hilton's short stint as commonwealth's attorney. The tap lasted only two days; the subjects were busted with a half ton of marijuana, and quickly pled guilty. The legality of the wiretap was never challenged. Fortunately, the affidavit and supporting paperwork were still available from that case, an invaluable model for future cases.

Beth Axelrod was an attractive white woman in her mid-twenties, with waist-length black hair and a knock-out figure. She was in the business of selling heroin. Atypically, her clientele was exclusively young Caucasians. The stereotypical heroin junkie was an economically depressed African American. Axelrod operated out of an apartment on the outskirts of Rosslyn, a tony subdivision of Arlington County, across the river from the District of Columbia. Her customers appeared to be clean cut and employed, other anomalies.

Surveillance of the exterior of Axelrod's apartment by the Special Unit revealed nothing particularly suspicious. Except for a significant number of male suitors, she lived a quiet life. Detective P.W. Cope had interviewed a couple of informants who described Axelrod as a key heroin source—hard to believe from her outward appearance. However, Cope could find no one who had dealt with her directly, or even had direct access. Most could only provide a description—white, slim, busty, and long black hair. Could there be more than one woman fitting the description?

Because heroin is so destructive, particularly its addictive pharmacology, our objective was more global than just convicting Axelrod. It was equally critical to identify her supplier. Was there a new Virginia connection? After countless hours of strategy discussion, it became increasingly obvious that only a wiretap could crack the case. Besides, it sounded exciting.

Both the application process for wiretap authorization and its operation are labor-intensive exercises. The supporting affidavit, explaining probable cause to believe a drug trafficking crime is being committed, and that the target telephone is being used in furtherance of the illegal activity, must be exhaustively detailed. The affidavit must also demonstrate that all normal investigative techniques have been tried and failed or appear unlikely to succeed. Detective Cope did a masterful job of preparing a rough draft. I added the final gloss. Bill Burroughs signed the request as commonwealth's attorney in the jurisdiction where the tap would be conducted. Step one completed.

I then hand-carried the application and accompanying affidavit to the attorney general of Virginia, in Richmond. After sitting in his office for an hour while he reviewed the materials, I met with Attorney General Tony Troy and his staff. I fielded a few questions and General Troy signed the formal application. The following day, Detective Cope and I presented the application and affidavit to Judge Charles H. Duff of the Arlington County Circuit Court. Judge Duff read the papers, concluded that the necessary probable cause existed, and signed the order authorizing the interception of Axelrod's telephone communications.

Because Virginia law required that all electronic surveillance be conducted by the Virginia State Police, they became a partner in the investigation. Under the command of Sergeant Bob Martin, the state police within hours contacted the telephone company and, using a court-issued subpoena, obtained the circuit wiring diagram for Axelrod's telephone. They also rented a block of rooms at a remote motel to serve as the intercept site. Martin next contracted with the telephone company to install a separate hard line connection to the motel to accommodate the surveillance equipment.

These preparations required about forty-eight hours. When everything was in place, Investigator Jack Hall, using the circuit diagram, located the cables and pairs for Axelrod's telephone in the junction box in the basement of her apartment building and surreptitiously connected the hardline. The telephone company, which had been ordered by the court not to disclose anything concerning the investigation, refused as a matter of policy to be involved in the final hook-up process. A call was then placed to Axelrod's phone to test the system. When it rang, we were in business.

Although there were exciting moments, such as when Axelrod's suitors would call and press their seductive charm, many days passed without any incriminating conversations—"pertinent calls." Arlington drug detectives remained on standby twenty-four hours a day to conduct visual surveillance of any meeting or to photograph any activity that might help build a case.

As days passed tension increased. Could we have been mistaken? It takes time to grasp a target's pattern of activity and to unscramble any coded jargon, so to speak. In this case it took about two weeks. From the wiretap and corroborating surveillance, we were able to confirm our initial suspicion.

Several of the young men in Axelrod's life were also in the heroin business. We didn't know if their actions were motivated by sex or profit. We identified most of them using a dialed number decoder, a device that decoded or translated the outgoing signals on a touch-tone telephone and printed out the number dialed. Using a court subpoena either Detective Cope or his partner Detective Cindy Brown would obtain the subscriber information from the telephone company. This information, in turn, would be used to obtain listings from the Virginia Division of Motor Vehicles on all cars listed to that person or address. In this way, the investigators were able to piece together probable identities and get general descriptions from their drivers' licenses.

Surveillance would then be set up at the identified address and occupants matching the gender of the voice on the phone would be inconspicuously photographed. In those instances where a caller came to Axelrod's apartment, photographs would be taken and listings run on the tags of the vehicle. The pieces began to fall into place. We identified all the players. In time, the investigators could identify their voices on the intercept. Many conversations suggested drug dealing, for example, "Man that was great shit I got yesterday," but we had no actual heroin to display to the jury. No dope on the table. Maybe the detectives would get lucky when we took the coconspirators down. The arrests would be made, if possible, at a time when they would most likely be holding drugs. Search warrants for their residences would follow. The timing of the take-down was critical.

The law requires that the wiretap be terminated once all the investigative objectives recited in the authorizing court order are achieved. We still hadn't identified Axelrod's source. The state police, however, reminded us daily that the operation was costing about ten thousand dollars a week. Besides, most of the state police investigators lived in the Culpeper area and were tired of sitting around a motel room day after day. They were anxious to get home, so Detective Cope decided to "heat the wire up." It was a risky move. But after twenty years as a vice investigator, when Paul Cope spoke, people listened.

The investigators had intercepted a number of innocuous-sounding calls from a Hispanic male in the Crystal City area of South Arlington. His relationship to Axelrod was hard to pin down. One night Cope decided to put a surveillance unit on his address and, sure enough, one of Axelrod's boys showed up. He left again after just a few minutes and drove directly to her apartment. Of all the individuals involved in this narcotics syndicate, he seemed to be one of the least likely members. He was clean cut, well dressed, lived in a nice middle-class neighborhood in Fairfax County, and appeared to be employed. Not the stereotypical heroin pusher. He either had a hell of a habit himself, an insatiable greed, or the hots for Axelrod. Maybe all three.

With the help of his partner, Detective Brown, Cope conducted surveillance of the Crystal City location. The next intercepted conversation between Axelrod and the seemingly out-of-place-guy from Fairfax suggested that he was headed to her apartment. Paul Cope's instincts were good. Sure enough, the guy stopped in Crystal City first. After consulting with his supervisor Sergeant Ed Cheslock and with Sergeant Bob Martin of the state police, Cope gave the dicey direction to stop and arrest the guy before he arrived at Axelrod's apartment. Obviously, this tactic had the collateral effect of potentially compromising the wire. But the dice came up right. The man they arrested was carrying more than an ounce of heroin. He was terrified, just as Cope had planned.

Startled, dazed, and bewildered, the young man agreed to cooperate with the investigators. With my permission, Cope advised him that his assistance would be considered in deciding what charges to place against him. Under Cope's supervision, the guy in custody placed a telephone call to Axelrod and advised her that the package "felt light," and asked how much she had purchased. She responded, "an ounce." Fueled by fury, Axelrod immediately placed a high-pitched call to her source, now known to be Peter Tallamantes, and accused him of shorting her. Four-letter words began to fly. Tallamantes reminded her that she still owed him money from the "last time." She responded that the last stuff was "shit" and that it "did nothing" for her. She added that some of her people wanted their money back. There was more. Every available detective in the Special Unit squealed tires heading out for Rosslyn.

The exact timing of a take down is almost always uncertain. Everyone waits for the perfect moment. Investigators try to select the point most calculated to yield the best case. In a situation like this, planning for the take down begins weeks prior. Search warrant affidavits are a work in progress, prepared as the case evolves, with only the concluding paragraphs left open. As events unraveled that evening, Detective Brown and I put the finishing touches on a half dozen of them and prepared arrest warrants for the entire cast of characters. In less than an hour all warrants were sworn to before a magistrate, properly issued, and assigned to detectives for service. At evening's close, eight defendants were in custody and about two additional ounces of heroin had been seized.

Essentially, wiretap cases turn on pretrial motions. The defendants challenge the probable cause to justify the tap and question the investigators' compliance with statutorily mandated procedures. However, since this was the first litigated wiretap in Virginia, I was confronted with a full-scale assault on the constitutionality of the Virginia electronic surveillance statute. The Virginia Attorney General's Office sent several attorneys to Arlington to assist. The hearing required three days.

Prior to the hearing I did weeks of research. I also contacted federal prosecutors from organized crime strike forces around the country, who routinely ran wiretaps, for advice on handling the motions. The Virginia statute mirrored the federal wiretapping law, which had been upheld by numerous federal courts. Judge Charles S. Russell gave short shrift to the constitutional claims. With respect to the contention that Cope's affidavit was deficient in demonstrating probable cause that Axelrod's phone was being used in furtherance of drug trafficking, I employed a tactic learned from the federal strike force.

I pointed out to Judge Russell that his colleague on the Arlington Circuit Court, Judge Charles H. Duff, had reviewed the affidavit in detail and found the requisite probable cause to authorize the tap. In effect, it put the authorizing judge's discretion in approving the tap at issue, rather than the content of the affidavit. Judge Russell probably saw right through the ploy, but he denied the motions to throw out the electronic surveillance.

Once the Court ruled that the intercepted communications were admissible in evidence at trial, most defendants folded and pled guilty. Tallamantes was the only hold out. He proceeded to trial with a jury, which convicted him of conspiracy to distribute heroin. It was the first case tried in Virginia state courts using wiretap evidence.

In the ensuing months, we employed wiretaps in two other cases, with mixed results. I developed a reputation as the expert in Virginia on wiretapping. With my stock trading high, I applied for a position in the United States Attorney's Office. Unfortunately, they were looking for someone with experience handling white-collar crime cases. Someone skilled in sorting through mounds of documents and piecing together a provable case.

Years later, during my first week as the United States attorney, I learned the value of this talent. When I visited the Defense Procurement Fraud Unit in the basement of the building, I discovered the room awash in files, boxes, and documents. That was understandable; they had been investigating one of the nation's largest shipbuilding companies for more than five years. I asked the FBI agent in charge how things were progressing. In frustration, he tossed his glasses on the desk and said, "Henry, there's a crime here, we all know there's a crime here, but after five years of digging, I'll be damned if we can find it."

Although I didn't get the job in the U.S. Attorney's Office when I first applied, they assured me that my time would come. At that point I was somewhat type-cast as a drug prosecutor. To retain me, Burroughs promoted me to chief assistant and I officially became the number-two guy in the office. The relationship worked out smoothly until the next Mother's day.

## FOREMAN-SHOEMAKER

Midmorning on May 8, 1977, the bodies of Alan Foreman and Donna Shoemaker were found in the garage at 1201 North George Mason Drive, a single-family residence about two blocks from Arlington Hospital. The call to the Arlington police originally went out as a possible murder-suicide. Detective Kenneth J. Madden was the first investigator to arrive. He found their bullet-riddled bodies in the front seat of Foreman's Jaguar. A seasoned homicide investigator with a reputation as a quick study, Madden sized up the scene in minutes. Both Foreman and Shoemaker had been shot repeatedly in the head at point blank range. Madden radioed his supervisor, Sergeant Frank Hawkins, to report that no gun had been found at the scene and there was no indication of forced entry to the residence. It was obviously a double homicide. But no one suspected that it would evolve into one of the most notorious murder cases in Northern Virginia history.

Hawkins ordered all homicide investigators to the scene. Within forty-eight hours, relations between Burroughs and me began to chill.

# VI
# Storm Clouds

The *Washington Post* described the Foreman-Shoemaker homicide as a gangland-styled murder, both bodies riddled with bullets. The underlying story, the investigation, and resulting prosecution exemplify the maxim that real life can be more bizarre than fiction. No novelist could spin this tale. To begin with, why did the people and entities involved have such low kindling points?

During 1976, Bill Burroughs's relationship with the Arlington County Police Department deteriorated with each passing day, driven by a combustible combination of personality and philosophical conflicts. The police brass viewed Bill as naive, inflexible, and dictatorial. Simply put, the cops didn't consider him to be a team player. He clearly mistrusted them and frequently questioned their judgment. Consequently, when major crimes occurred, like homicides, I became the point of contact. They sought my advice and direction to the conscious, and sometimes conspicuous, exclusion of Burroughs. This began to grate on Bill. In retrospect, I don't blame him. He repeatedly warned me to tell the police to contact him. I disregarded his directions and occasionally stoked the discontent. Call me disloyal if you must, but I enjoyed calling the shots.

The slaying of Alan Foreman and Donna Shoemaker in a quiet residential neighborhood in North Arlington was a headline grabber. Every newspaper with Northern Virginia circulation led their local coverage on May 8, 1977, with the story. Consequently, Burroughs knew my purpose when I walked into his office the next morning. I could tell by the look on his face how our conversation was going to go. Before I could brief him on the status of the investigation, he coldly advised me that he was handling the matter personally. If he needed my help or input, he'd tell me. The message was clear, and I knew he was serious.

The events that followed could only be described as a legal disaster. The case culminated in the acquittal of the contract hit-man, the appointment of a special prosecutor, the request of the Arlington police for a state police investigation of Burroughs, and finally, an effort by Burroughs to impanel a special grand jury to investigate the Virginia attorney general.

As the investigation unraveled, the story underlying the murder changed as dramatically as the facets of a kaleidoscope. Burroughs originally indicted three people: Charles Silcox, Richard Lee Earman, and Joseph N. Martin. On the eve of the Silcox trial, Burroughs dismissed the charges for lack of evidence. This was appropriate; from all indications Silcox had no involvement in the actual conspiracy. Earman was prosecuted by Burroughs and acquitted of capital murder. During the trial, Burroughs dropped the charges against Martin, for reasons that were frankly astounding. Meanwhile, Burroughs befriended Martin and professed a sincere belief that he was innocent. The police disagreed, vehemently.

Subsequently, Earman publicly confessed to killing Foreman and Shoemaker, and pled guilty to conspiracy to commit murder. As part of the deal, Earman testified against Martin. To sweeten the deal, Burroughs agreed that Earman could spend a week in the Bahamas before beginning his ten-year prison sentence. There's more.

Bowing to surging pressure, Burroughs stepped aside and a special prosecutor was appointed by the court to prosecute Martin, who was ultimately convicted of first degree murder. And that's only half the story. The epilogue is even more inconceivable.

We learned about the events underlying the murders of Alan Foreman and Donna Shoemaker from the testimony of the triggerman, Richard Lee Earman, a high-school drop-out who sold real estate and gave tennis lessons. However, although Earman testified under oath, he was a master at manipulating the police by telling them what they wanted to hear. He made a career of it. Unfortunately, his rendition probably remains the best evidence available. He was the centerpiece of the prosecution's case against Martin. Here's how it all began:

The investigation focused on Earman after his dark green Mercury Cougar was identified by Foreman's neighbor as having been seen in the vicinity of Foreman's home shortly after she heard the sound of breaking glass and gunshots on the night Foreman and Shoemaker were murdered. In addition, while searching the crime scene, police found a note with Earman's name and address scribbled on it. Later, a waitress at Tramps Disco in Georgetown, the nightlife hub of Washington, D.C., picked Earman's photo out of a police photo spread. The waitress knew Alan Foreman and Donna Shoemaker. They frequented the disco three or four times per month. They had met there. She described Foreman as one of the most popular guys on the discotheque circuit. She said that Foreman had "an eye for women, a taste for elegant three-piece suits, and a thirst for Chivas Regal scotch."

Richard Earman was well known in police circles. He was a former member of the notorious Beltway burglars, a group responsible for more than five thousand residential burglaries. Earlier, he had pulled five years in the state pen.

According to Earman, the Foreman-Shoemaker murders were part of an elaborate insurance fraud scheme concocted by Martin. Joseph Martin, age thirty and a graduate of George Mason University, was a salesman with New York Life Insurance Company. Martin devised the scam to boost his sales commissions, necessary to support his high-roller lifestyle. He drove a Mercedes Benz sports car and was building an impressive addition on his home. Martin had apparently written about six hundred thousand dollars in bogus policies for which he was paying the premiums. He was always desperate for cash, but not as desperate as his friend Alan Foreman, age twenty-six.

Along with his other expensive play habits, Foreman had a drug problem. Friends told the Arlington Police that he was always looking for money. Several months before the murder, Martin loaned Foreman thirty-five hundred dollars for an alleged real estate deal. As collateral for the loan, Martin obtained a fifty-six thousand dollar life insurance policy insuring Foreman's life. Martin borrowed five hundred dollars of the money loaned to Foreman from Charles Silcox, another friend. To add an additional layer of intrigue, Martin was married to Silcox's former wife.

The original beneficiary on Foreman's life insurance policy was Sally Dixon, his mother. Unbeknown to Dixon, but with Foreman's approval, Martin subsequently changed the beneficiary on the policy to his friend, Charles Silcox. Silcox learned of the change seven days later. Silcox apparently had never met either of the victims, Foreman or Shoemaker. Silcox found none of this suspicious. He told the detectives, "It was none of my business." The police found the story a bit far fetched.

Silcox was the district manager of a group of retail outlets called the Northern Virginia Door Stores. Martin promised Silcox a one hundred percent return on his five hundred dollar loan to Foreman, and even agreed to pay the one hundred dollar monthly premium on the insurance policy. After Silcox passed a lie-detector test, both Burroughs and the police were finally convinced that he had no knowledge of the murder plot. But the story was hard to swallow.

Although they had met formally only about a month before Foreman's death, Earman worked with Foreman as a real estate agent at Town and Country Realty. Foreman had an enviable sales record and was a member of the million dollar sales club. However, his impressive salary was not enough to support his lavish lifestyle. Earman contended that he sought Foreman out for advice on how to enhance his success in the real estate business. That's possible, but women and drugs were the more likely draw.

Martin became acquainted with Earman on the party circuit. Both loved life in the fast lane. They frequently chased women and gambled in the Bahamas together. When Martin became delinquent in paying the premiums on the bogus policy, he devised a plan to kill Foreman and collect the proceeds of the insurance. He turned to Earman for advice. Aware of Earman's shady past, and the fact that he had previously served hard time, Martin called Earman in January of 1977 and said that he had something important to discuss. The next month, on a gambling junket to the Bahamas, Martin broached the subject of killing Foreman.

According to Earman, Martin explained that he had a friend who wanted Foreman knocked off for welshing on a debt. Martin offered Earman fifteen thousand dollars to "procure a hit-man." He left the details to Earman, who could negotiate the deal however he wished. During the next two months, Earman met with Martin frequently for lunch at restaurants in Tysons Corner, a busy shopping area in Fairfax County west of Arlington, to figure out the cleanest way to kill Foreman and cash in the policy. Martin urged Earman to make it look like an accident. They considered setting Foreman's house on fire and "different things like that."

Earman also warned Martin that it would be tough to take out Foreman without also killing his girlfriend Shoemaker. They were inseparable. Martin was indifferent at first, but later thought a double homicide would provide the perfect cover for the insurance heist.

Earman eventually told Martin that he had arranged for "two black guys" from Florida to knock off Foreman. Actually, Earman intended to do it himself. He explained later on the witness stand during the Martin trial that for him it was purely a business decision. He decided to kill Foreman and pocket the entire fifteen thousand dollars.

Although Earman had previously met Foreman, the contact had been brief. Inspired by the mystery novel, *The First Deadly Sin,* Earman decided to carry out the hit by posing as a house-hunting college professor from Colorado. Following the script of the novel, he originally intended to kill Foreman with a mountain climbing pick. He even purchased the pick, and considered hitting him on top of the head as the two were looking at a house. Employing this ruse, Earman arranged a meeting with Foreman. Earman attempted to dress for the role, wearing a disheveled suit, a straw hat, and sunglasses. When Foreman's mother showed up unexpectedly at the meeting, he abandoned the plan.

Suspecting his cover was blown, Earman called Foreman several days later and admitted his chicanery. He explained that he was awed with Foreman's remarkable success as a realtor and that he needed Foreman's advice on a real estate venture. After a get-acquainted meeting at Foreman's office, they arranged to party the following Friday night in Georgetown, at Foreman's favorite spot, Tramps.

Earman met Foreman at his North Arlington home that Friday evening as arranged. He had a .32-caliber revolver inconspicuously concealed in his belt. As expected, Shoemaker was there to tag along. According to Earman, they had "a few drinks and smoked a joint" of marijuana at Foreman's, then headed to Tramps in Foreman's Jaguar, where they drank steadily for several hours. Foreman was too drunk to drive when they left Tramps, so he turned his keys over to Shoemaker.

They returned to Foreman's house around 2:00 a.m. All three were "very drunk." Earman was seated in the rear seat of the Jag. After they pulled into the garage, Earman shot both Foreman and Shoemaker once in the head. To create the impression that the killings had occurred during a robbery, he took Foreman's wallet. Assuming that Foreman and Shoemaker were dead, he casually walked out of the garage and drove his car about two blocks to Arlington Hospital, also located on North George Mason Drive.

After sitting in his car in the hospital parking lot for twenty minutes or so, Earman began to wonder if the single shots had been enough. If either recovered, he was looking at a capital murder rap. He couldn't take the chance. Earman returned to Foreman's garage and emptied the revolver "into their faces." As a diversionary tactic, he next removed the cash and credit cards from Foreman's wallet. He drove to Washington, D.C., and tossed them onto a busy street, hoping they would be quickly recovered and steer the police in the wrong direction. He then headed home and went to sleep.

The next morning Earman telephoned Martin and reported that the two black guys he'd hired had done the job, and had "split" for Florida. Martin promised payment within a month, but both were busted for murder before Earman could get the fifteen thousand dollars.

Within weeks of the arrests, Burroughs began to complain about the quality of the investigation. Despite the development of a fairly persuasive circumstantial case, Burroughs continued to press for additional witness interviews. Some of the potential witnesses were clearly peripheral, but I thought that others might have information of value. The police department agreed to interview several people on Burroughs's list, but they refused to "waste" time on the others. At core, the dispute really turned on who was in charge of the investigation. Inevitably, the controversy was reported in the press. Tension rapidly escalated.

Earman's case was the first one set for trial. Conversation between Burroughs and the police was limited. One week before jury selection, Burroughs requested a postponement of the trial on the ground that further investigation was necessary. Sensing that the prosecution was unprepared for trial, probably a correct assumption, Earman's lawyer vehemently objected to the continuance motion. Unimpressed with Burroughs's explanation, the court denied the postponement request. On the morning of trial, July 25, 1977, Burroughs stunned the court, community, and police department by asking that the murder charges against Earman be dismissed without prejudice. Translated, this meant that Burroughs could recharge Earman with murder later. The court granted the motion and dismissed the charges. Just before the dismissal, Burroughs obtained an arrest warrant charging Earman with burglarizing Foreman's home with the intent to commit murder. This was intended to keep Earman on a short leash pending reindictment. The subsequent indictment, which included a capital murder count, was docketed for trial on September 19, 1977.

To tamp down the resulting media frenzy, Burroughs publicly explained that on the Sunday evening before trial he had received "significant new information" which he declined to reveal. He did disclose, however, that the newly discovered information could lead to additional persons being charged and a potential change in the prosecution's legal theory, or method of proof. Burroughs was successful in convincing Martin's lawyer to agree to postpone his case until after Earman was tried. At this point, chaos was palpable. Martin's lawyer decided to simply sit back and watch the prosecution self-destruct.

The next defendant scheduled for trial was Charles Silcox. His case was set for September 13, one week before Earman's trial on the second indictment. Silcox was the beneficiary on the Foreman life insurance policy. After he passed a polygraph test that seemed to confirm that he had no knowledge of the plan to kill Foreman, Burroughs dropped charges. Although some people questioned the decision, and Silcox's explanation was hard to digest, I believe Burroughs made the right tactical call. He concluded that Silcox was an innocent dupe. Logic aside, in the final analysis, the prosecution really had no case. Moreover, Silcox was far more valuable as a prosecution witness. Suspicion alone will not legally support a conviction, and if Silcox had been acquitted, which was a strong possibility, the leverage would have been lost. These are the tough calls prosecutors must make.

The following week, Burroughs proceeded to trial in the Earman case. The prosecution's evidence was a confusing mass of shifting theories and surprising turns. Burroughs devoted the first three days of the trial to proving that Martin was the central figure in crafting the conspiracy. Suddenly, Burroughs cast aside the story that Martin and Earman were acting in league and jolted the jury with a radical change of course. He announced that for reasons he declined to reveal, charges against Martin were being dropped. Burroughs asked the jury to disregard the first three days of evidence and to accept the twisted notion that Foreman and Shoemaker were murdered because of a soured drug transaction. And, according to Burroughs, on second thought, Martin was not involved.

Martin turned state's evidence and, along with Silcox, testified against Earman. Perplexed and floundering in confusion, the jury found Earman not guilty of all charges.

What prompted the fatal shift in course? Burroughs never retreated from his tactical decision to publicly exonerate Martin and revamp the factual theory underlying his case against Earman literally in mid-stream. Few prosecutors would be so bold and so blindly self-confident. Although Burroughs was a bit naive, easily puzzled, and totally overwhelmed, he was a bright lawyer who simply viewed the world differently from the police and most other prosecutors. As the old saying goes, he danced to a different drummer.

Bill Burroughs was a person of steadfast commitment, totally dedicated to achieving what he thought was right. He consulted with me on many decisions, but chose to chart his own course. While I disagreed with his conclusions, I respected the intensity of his deliberations.

When pressed, Burroughs later publicly explained that on the eve of the Earman trial, Joe Martin reportedly received an anonymous letter threatening his life. Keep in mind that Martin continued to profess his innocence, and that he was a world-class con artist. Burroughs never saw the alleged letter. Martin claimed he burned it. Martin also produced results from a private polygrapher reflecting that a lie-detector test had cleared him of involvement in the killings of Foreman and Shoemaker. Burroughs fell for it and was convinced that Martin was innocent. The police were livid. The press had a field day. Burroughs's political future began to list. But the drama was just beginning to unfold.

Ecstatic over beating the murder rap, Earman threw a party, which Martin, who had testified against him, attended. Thinking they had outwitted the police and prosecutor, they regaled in their victory and ridiculed Burroughs. Unbeknown to them, they were standing in the eye of the storm.

Joe Martin had cultivated a direct line of communication with Bill Burroughs, which eventually proved to be an Achilles heel to both. Burroughs was determined to solve the Foreman-Shoemaker case and was convinced that Martin was a valuable asset. Martin, on the other hand, just wanted to control and manipulate Burroughs in order to avoid prosecution.

In November, several weeks after Earman's acquittal, Martin contacted Burroughs and told him he "wanted to get something off his chest." Burroughs suspected that his much maligned strategy had paid off, and that a case-breaking revelation was imminent. Instead, Martin confided that he and Earman had recently committed three burglaries in Fairfax County. Two of the burglaries occurred on November 19, 1977, at the Rosslyn Tire Store and at Blocher Reprographics in the Merrifield section of Fairfax. At Burroughs's direction, I notified an investigator with the Fairfax County Police Department. The threat of being prosecuted on these charges increased pressure on Martin to cooperate in the homicide investigation.

Until I left the Office of the Commonwealth's Attorney in late December to become a federal prosecutor, I was actively assisting Burroughs in unraveling the resulting enigma. As misguided as it may have been, Burroughs's determination never wavered. Detective David G. Green, a relentlessly inquisitive homicide investigator, was put on the case. This eased some of the personality conflicts.

Green began his investigation at square one, retracing every step and reinterviewing every significant witness, including Martin and Earman. After six months of thoroughly reexamining every available morsel of evidence, Green reached the only logical and tenable conclusion: Martin and Earman had killed Foreman and Shoemaker.

Despite his best efforts, Green could not convince Burroughs of Martin's involvement. Green refused to allow the case to lose traction, significantly raising the decibel level of the debate. Smokey Stover, former head of the Special Unit, was now the chief of police. Stover thrived on bare knuckles controversy. As the two sides dug in, tension escalated to the point of open and public hostility. Burroughs's continued personal contacts with Martin, which the police persistently questioned, fueled the animosity. Burroughs categorically refused to acknowledge that Martin was a key suspect. At this point, Burroughs was conducting his own independent investigation.

Finally, Chief Stover went on the offensive. In April 1978 he sent a letter to the governor of Virginia formally asking for an investigation of Burroughs and seeking the appointment of a special prosecutor to oversee the prosecution of Martin. In the chief's opinion, Burroughs's judgment had been colored by his relationship with Martin, which Burroughs persistently defended as critical to solving the Foreman-Shoemaker case. As required by state law, the governor referred the complaint to Attorney General J. Marshall Coleman, a Republican. Again, in compliance with the law, Coleman immediately brought in the state police to investigate.

On a parallel front, the Arlington County Police submitted a formal request to the Arlington County Circuit Court seeking the impanelment of a special grand jury to investigate Burroughs's handling of the Foreman-Shoremaker case—a move unprecedented in Virginia history. However, the county manager, who as chief executive had oversight authority over the police department, nixed the request. Despite a stern rebuke from the county manager and searing press coverage, the controversy continued to fester.

Even though the state police were not anxious to intercede in a high visibility local law enforcement feud, they conducted a thorough investigation. I spent several hours recounting my involvement in the case and describing my discussions with Bill Burroughs. I had worked with both investigators heading the inquiry. They were well seasoned, unbiased and objective. I suggested that the case had been mishandled by Burroughs, that Martin was clearly implicated, and most importantly, that there was no corruption on the part of Burroughs. He had simply exercised poor judgment and was too intransigent to retreat. Ultimately, the state police and the attorney general concurred. On July 30, 1978, Attorney General Coleman announced that the inquiry had revealed "no criminal wrongdoing" on Burroughs's part.

Rather than letting the controversy die down, Burroughs decided to retaliate. He convinced the Arlington County sheriff that it was all a political conspiracy and persuaded him to assign two deputies to investigate the state police's handling of the inquiry. Burroughs demanded to know the specific allegations against him and in essence, who had said what. I felt sorry for the investigators because no one took them seriously and the investigation went nowhere. Along with most people, I politely declined to be interviewed.

In September, Detective Green coaxed Earman to tell his side of the story. He spent an entire day being debriefed by Burroughs and Green. Overcome by bravado and convinced he had beaten the rap, Earman vaingloriously admitted killing Foreman and Shoemaker. He was rewarded by an indictment charging him with conspiracy to commit murder. He cut an immediate deal to plead guilty to a lesser conspiracy charge and testify against Martin, who had testified against him earlier. Earman, sporting long blonde hair and a golden tan, also negotiated a week's vacation in the Bahamas before reporting to jail. The story did not play well in the local papers.

With Earman implicating Martin in the double homicide, corroborated by bits and pieces of probative evidence, Burroughs found it increasingly difficult to defend Martin's innocence. The police persisted in applying pressure from all angles, but Burroughs continued to ruminate. Even his defenders began losing confidence. The media continued to question his judgment.

Frustrated that his investigation of the Virginia State Police had reached a fruitless dead-end, Burroughs switched tactics. In February 1979, he formally requested the Arlington County Circuit Court to impanel a special investigative grand jury to investigate the Virginia attorney general and the state police. The court denied the request. The press portrayed the maneuver as an act of political desperation.

Key members of the Arlington Democratic party began searching for an alterative candidate for commonwealth's attorney. The election was one year away. I had lunch with several political operatives, but I declined the invitation. I was too engaged in my new job as an assistant United States attorney. But several months later a single phone call changed my mind—and sent my life in a new direction.

Meanwhile, as the heat intensified and diminishing prospects of reelection loomed, Burroughs finally relented and sought an indictment of Martin for murder. It was promptly returned by the grand jury. When the grand jury concluded its deliberations, Burroughs again requested that they convert into a special investigative grand jury, as allowed by law, to hear his complaints against the state police and attorney general. The grand jurors declined. Unrepentant, Burroughs would try two more times to have those who investigated him investigated. He continued to allege that the investigation had been politically motivated and publicly demanded that the attorney general disclose the specific complaint against him.

Much to his dismay, the feisty commonwealth's attorney eventually got his wish.

# VIII

# Palm Beach Hash Connection

While storm clouds continued to gather over the Arlington County Courthouse, I was totally immersed in my new role as a federal prosecutor. Despite entreaties from numerous elected officials in Arlington, both Democrats and Republicans, I eschewed the notion of running for public office. Although I had been on the periphery of several Democratic campaigns, I was not attracted to making a career of elected politics. I was earning more than thirty thousand dollars a year, almost achieving my early lifetime goal of forty thousand. Life was stable, secure, and fairly predictable. My wife Tara and I had purchased a home and a West Highland white terrier puppy. My fishing club had two major trips a year. I felt committed to the U.S. Attorney's Office for the long haul. And besides, I was preoccupied with chasing international drug smugglers.

### Assistant United States Attorney

My swearing in as an assistant United States attorney took place at 8:30 a.m. on December 21, 1977. By 10:00 a.m. that same day, I was standing in front of a United States magistrate judge, along with my good friend Justin Williams, for the preliminary hearing for eleven alleged drug smugglers. They had been arrested several weeks earlier at Dulles International Airport for importing eight hundred pounds of hashish into the United States from India. The media described the seizure as the largest ever recovered in the Washington, D.C., area.

The hashish arrived at Dulles on a Pan American commercial flight originating in New Delhi. The large brown chunks were concealed in forty-seven wooden crates, part of a sixty-seven-crate shipment of brass door knockers. Drug Enforcement Administration agents and U.S. Customs Service investigators had been alerted to the shipment by a cooperating customs broker. The agents removed the hashish and refilled the cartons with a comparable weight of sand.

The cartons were then stored in a bonded customs warehouse in Manassas, Virginia, under the surveillance of federal agents.

Several days later, two men arrived at the warehouse and loaded the supposed hashish into two nondescript trucks. Agents followed the trucks into Maryland to the parking lot of a Holiday Inn in Rockville, where they encountered two men, William S. Coury and Donald Haynie, who we later learned had arranged the deal. We didn't know that Donald David "Hillbilly" Haynie, who identified himself as a construction worker from Nashville, Tennessee, was one of the nation's largest hashish traffickers. In all, five people were arrested at that point, one of whom immediately agreed to cooperate.

Within minutes, DEA and customs agents burst into a room at the Dulles Holiday Inn and arrested four other people, including a professional gambler named George V. Carman who was carrying a metal suitcase containing one hundred twenty-five thousand dollars in U.S. currency. Agents also learned that the other three occupants of the room, a student and two restaurant workers, had arrived at Dulles Airport from Palm Beach, Florida, in a chartered Lear jet. Unsure of the pilots' involvement, the agents decided to take them into custody.

*The hashish and currency seized by federal agents at Dulles International Airport on December 3, 1977. (Courtesy of U.S. Department of Justice.)*

Their explanations were quickly confirmed and they were released. In time, their cooperation would prove invaluable.

The bust was arranged by a customs broker named Frank Bailey, who operated from an office at the Baltimore-Washington International Airport (BWI), in Maryland. As a "facilitator," Bailey was familiar with customs procedures and capable of moving commercial cargo through with minimal delay. In August 1977, Bailey was contacted by William Coury, an Atlanta customs broker, who described himself as a financial consultant. Coury casually inquired about customs drug interdiction at BWI. This made Bailey suspicious, particularly when he was asked about the use of drug detection dogs at regional airports.

Coury concluded the meeting by asking for Bailey's assistance in importing a shipment of goods from India. When Bailey probed further into the nature of the goods involved, Coury replied, "In certain situations people need to make a lot of money in a hurry."

Baily notified U.S. Customs of the suspicious proposition and they asked him to to allow events to play themselves out. The next day, Bailey received a telephone call from Atam P. Serin, a New Delhi customs broker, well known in international drug smuggling circles. Serin gave Bailey explicit instructions and arranged his flight to India.

Working with U.S. Customs, Bailey flew to India several days later and met Coury at the New Delhi International Hotel. They linked up with Serin and discussed the details of the proposed shipment, which was then revealed to be hashish. Bailey returned to the United States and fully briefed customs agents on what had transpired.

In October, Coury met with Bailey again, this time at Dulles International Airport, to review their plans for the hash shipment. Coury gave Bailey cash to rent a bonded warehouse in Northern Virginia. The law permits a licensed customs broker, such as Frank Bailey, to bring cargo subject to duty into the United States with limited border inspection. The cargo is then inspected by customs agents before release from the warehouse, which officially becomes its point of entry into the United States. In those days, it was commonly believed that cargo released from a bonded warehouse was subject to less scrutiny than cargo searched at the geographic border. That proved to be a risky assumption.

As soon as he got the heads up from Serin, Bailey tipped U.S. Customs agents that the shipment was en route on a Pan American airlines flight from New Delhi. Bailey said that the half ton of hashish would arrive at Dulles on December 3, 1977, concealed in containers of brass door knockers, and customs and DEA agents were lying in wait.

Prior to court, Justin Williams and I spent an hour kicking around strategy with the lead DEA agent assigned to the case, Dick Mangan. Unquestionably, this was a huge operation, but who were these guys and who were they working with? Obviously it was somebody big. At that point, the names Coury and Haynie meant nothing to us. In a typical drug deal of this size, the money men or financial backers are out of sight.

We had two options. We could prosecute what appeared on the surface to be a bunch of low-level bit players, or we could dismiss the charges for the time being and continue to investigate. The Speedy Trial Act limited the length of time they could be held without trial, so a general postponement wouldn't provide enough time. Besides, if these guys were part of a major drug syndicate, they'd want the earlier trial to eliminate any time for further investigation.

Our case was strong as to the two haulers, one of whom was a student and the other a caretaker of a cemetery, but weak as to the others. We figured that with some luck, we might recruit a couple of these mercenaries as sources of information. Those in the illicit drug business look out for themselves. In addition, DEA and Customs were convinced that all defendants could be easily relocated when the investigation was complete. The vote was unanimous—go for it. The gamble paid huge dividends, but the investigative odyssey took ten months and spanned the entire east coast.

The success of investigations of this dimension turns on the extent and effectiveness of law enforcement resources, particularly data bases. Although this was not a pioneer case, global conspiracies were the new prosecution frontier. Mangan was an expert in building conspiracy cases. He compiled a comprehensive list of all possible investigative leads, based on the identity of the guys arrested, their known associates, and the documents and records seized at the airport. The analysis would also entail tracing the money trail, and no one does that better than the IRS. I therefore recruited my brother-in-law, Lance Lydon, then a special agent with the IRS Criminal Investigations Division, to join the team. We also brought in another assistant United States attorney, Bob McDermott. Legal research was coordinated by a young law student from Georgetown University, Greta Van Susteren, now anchor of Fox News Channel's "On The Record."

We subpoenaed all corporate records pertaining to the known conspirators from the private Lear jet service used to ferry the three players to Dulles. The resulting documents revealed that Donald David Haynie was a regular customer, frequently chartering flights from Palm Beach to other locations around the country at a cost of seven hundred dollars an hour.

Meanwhile, other agents checked all available law enforcement networks for information concerning the men arrested in the Dulles motel room. One had been stopped attempting to board an aircraft six months earlier at the Palm Beach County Airport. He had been carrying a briefcase containing ninety-five thousand and twenty dollars in U.S. currency. When confronted by a narcotics investigator at the airport, he denied ownership of the briefcase that had been in his hand moments before. After presenting identification to the investigator, the guy simply turned and walked away. We were surprised to learn that this type of incident occurred all the time at the Palm Beach airport. The local police would just seize the cash for forfeiture and eventual public use.

As the agents continued to scour the intelligence data base for information, Justin Williams and I began approaching selected arrestees to cut deals for cooperation. Several of the lower-level laborer types were anxious to plead to a lesser offense, thereby reducing the time they would serve, and cooperate in the investigation. Most were merely "stash house" sitters, or resident managers of marijuana storage facilities. When debriefed, they gave us the collective picture of a national network, headed by Hillbilly Haynie, that smuggled tons of marijuana and hashish into the United States each year.

Bulk quantities of drugs were off-loaded from ships along the east coast into smaller vessels and taken to remote locations in the Florida Keys. Under the supervision of a man known as Armando, the marijuana and hash was transported by truck to houses in secluded residential areas of south Florida. It was stored in these stash houses until transferred to one of Haynie's wholesalers in Florida, Chicago, or Boston. Cooperating members of the drug syndicate recounted Haynie shipping as much as seven tons of marijuana to his wholesalers in a single day. Much of this information was confirmed by Chicago and Boston investigators who had seized large bulk quantities of marijuana linked directly to the Haynie network by local informants. We were onto something.

Although we still had a few more dots to connect, on September 8, 1978, Donald Haynie, William Coury, and ten others were indicted for conspiracy to import marijuana and hashish. In addition, Haynie was charged under the newly enacted "drug kingpin statute" for operating a continuing criminal enterprise. If convicted, Haynie faced a life sentence. The indictment described the conspiracy as spanning from January 1, 1977, up to the date of the indictment. It further alleged that the drug syndicate was responsible for importing more than twenty-seven thousand pounds of marijuana and over a half ton of hashish from India and South America. Based on the meticulous financial analysis conducted by my brother-in-law and his fellow IRS agents, the indictment disclosed that Haynie and his drug empire had grossed more than fifty-two million dollars.

As predicted, all twelve defendants were in custody within two weeks. Judge Albert V. Bryan, Jr., set the trial for November 27, 1978, in the federal court, Alexandria, Virginia, the "rocket docket." Defense attorneys were panic-stricken. Most defendants, including Haynie and Coury, were released on bond. Haynie's bond was subsequently revoked when he attempted to board a commercial aircraft using a ticket issued in a fictitious name. A number of lesser figures negotiated pleas and agreed to testify against Haynie—who from the outset vowed to go down with the ship. At his level, cooperation against his suppliers would result in a death warrant.

Even more inscrutable was George V. Carman, the money man, the professional gambler who had been arrested at Dulles Airport with the metal case containing one hundred twenty-five thousand dollars in U.S. currency. Loyal to a fault, Carman was every gangster's role model. All he'd give us was his name, rank, and serial number. We eventually dropped charges against him and gave him immunity from prosecution in exchange for revealing where he got the money. He refused. He wouldn't even give us his address. Judge Bryan entered, at our request, what is known as a compulsion order, directing him to testify or face jail for contempt. Carman wouldn't budge. He was held in contempt and ordered to remain in jail until he agreed to testify. One year later, he remained in the Alexandria city jail as defiant as ever.

The first significant figure in the conspiracy to come in out of the cold was William Simon Coury, the Atlanta customs broker. The circumstances under which Coury met Haynie added an interesting layer of drama to the story. Coury and Haynie shared an interest in Democratic politics. They met by chance encounter at the 1977 inauguration of President Jimmy Carter. They socialized several times during the inaugural festivities and spent the early morning hours hanging out at a club in Georgetown. Their association culminated in Haynie offering to invest fifty thousand dollars in Coury's business. Within days, one of Haynie's minions delivered a paper sack to Coury containing an eight-thousand-dollar cash down payment.

Coury had introduced himself to Frank Bailey as a financial consultant. That proved to be an apt description of his role in the Haynie organization. Soon after receiving the eight-thousand-dollar cash advance on the loan, Coury met with Haynie to discuss the terms of repayment. Coury explained that he anticipated a large settlement from an automobile accident, which could serve as collateral. But Haynie had other ideas. Haynie asked Coury if he had ever seen any hashish in his international travels, and suggested that the loan would be forgiven if Coury would help smuggle Nepalese Temple Balls, a potent form of hashish prepared by Nepalese mountain dwellers.

Unable to repay the loan, Coury, a middle-aged man who walked with a limp, was soon ensnared and found himself traveling around the world negotiating drug deals as Haynie's front man. He would also shuttle large sums of cash between Haynie's Palm Beach mansion and various wholesalers around the country as Haynie's bag man.

Haynie and his gorgeous, blonde model girlfriend resided in a leased oceanfront home in Palm Beach. The agents enjoyed conducting surveillance of the seaside mansion, and watching all the young ladies sunbathing nude on the sun deck. Immediately following Haynie's arrest, DEA and IRS agents received permission from the owner of the mansion, Dr. Richard Wright, to conduct a search of the interior.

Even though the house had been vacated just before Haynie's bond was revoked, the agents found traces of marijuana and documents corroborating his international travel. Dr. Wright, who had a strange relationship with Hillbilly Haynie, strenuously resisted testifying against him. However, as soon as her Ferrari was seized by the government, Haynie's girlfriend had no compunction about dumping all over him. She was a great witness.

As an aside, five years after the Haynie trial, I was traveling by air to the west coast for a meeting of the Pornography Commission. Fortuitously, Dr. Wright sat directly next to me. We recognized each other immediately. After an hour or so the ice was broken and he spoke. He explained that he had felt intimidated by the crowd that hung out with Haynie and hadn't wanted to get involved. Understandable! He later moved to another seat, at the far end of the plane.

Haynie and four of his associates proceeded to trial as scheduled on November 27, 1978, before a jury in federal district court. The other seven defendants indicted with them pled guilty and agreed to testify. Justin Williams, Bob McDermott, and I divided the trial fairly evenly. In all, we called thirty-eight witnesses, but it was the testimony of William Coury that buried them. As a central figure, he was able to finger every player.

The trial took an unprecedented nine days, a long time in the rocket docket, where cases that require months in other jurisdictions are tried in several days. The jury deliberated for a day and a half before convicting all defendants of assorted offenses relating to the conspiracy. Haynie was acquitted on the charge of conducting a continuing criminal enterprise. Why?

His attorney, Michael Kennedy, despite the judge's initial explicit direction to the contrary, repeatedly got away with mentioning in the jury's presence that the continuing criminal enterprise count carried a life sentence. The jury was not about to subject someone to life in prison for smuggling hash and marijuana, even in mega-ton quantities. Kennedy, who had previously represented Black Panther Huey P. Newton, was a true gentlemen and distinguished lawyer from New York City; one of the brightest lawyers I've ever come up against.

Over the years, I've learned something from every major trial, and this one was no exception. Michael Kennedy was a masterful cross-examiner. His wife, with whom he conferred frequently during the examination of witnesses, was an attorney with a background in psychology. She always sat directly behind him in the courtroom. He really did a number on William Coury, our flagship witness.

Kennedy was smooth as silk. Disarmingly polite and impeccably dressed, with an ever-present gold watch fob, Kennedy slowly led Coury through his dealings with Hillbilly. He next inquired about Coury's plea agreement and the potential penalties for all the charges we dropped in exchange for his testimony. The number was impressive, something like a hundred and fifty years. Then he zinged us. He asked if the United States had agreed not to charge him with operating a continuing criminal enterprise. Coury said yes. Kennedy was then able to ask Coury if he knew that the continuing criminal enterprise count carried a life sentence. Coury again said yes. Kennedy then emphasized that Coury was avoiding a possible life sentence by testifying against Haynie. It then became relevant to show motive, so Judge Bryan had to allow Coury to answer. Kennedy then repeatedly referred to it as the "life count" in his final argument to the jury. We knew we'd been hit by a torpedo—and there was more.

On direct examination, in order to portray Coury as a stable person and to enhance his credibility, Justin Williams asked him to "tell the jury a little about yourself." Coury proudly boasted that his family was his life's treasure. This seemingly innocuous tactic proved to be another mistake.

On cross-examination, Kennedy asked Coury to tell the jury how he explained his dealings with Haynie to his family—and to compound the humiliation, he went through each one individually. Obviously Coury had never told his family that he and Haynie were really international marijuana smugglers. In his final argument to the jury, Kennedy slowly and meticulously went through the exhaustive list of people to whom Coury had dissembled—his mother, his wife, his daughters, his business associates, his brother, and his pastor. Kennedy then turned to the jury and rhetorically asked, if Coury lied to all these people, who he claims are the most important people in his life, what makes you think he wouldn't lie to you? Damn good question! Williams and I squirmed in our seats. Another blast across the bow.

In January 1979, Judge Bryan sentenced Haynie to fifteen years in prison. The court also ordered that his assets, all of which were traceable to drug dealing, be forfeited to the United States. Coury was sentenced to three years. The lesser members of the conspiracy received sentences ranging from five years in prison to a few months in jail.

The financial information unearthed by my brother-in-law and his colleagues at IRS spawned a sequel investigation of another Haynie associate, his long-time lawyer. The agents were able to trace huge sums of currency, mostly cash, to the prominent Miami criminal lawyer. The paper trail suggested two shady explanations. Either the attorney was receiving fees that he failed to declare on his income tax return, or he was laundering drug proceeds. The attorney opted for the softer landing and pled guilty to tax charges.

It took us about two weeks to pack away two file cabinets worth of paperwork on the Haynie case. We still had appeals to argue and two fugitives who would be tried later if they were ever captured. One was the Indian customs broker, Atam P. Serin.

## An Essay on Politics

My attention gradually migrated back to the unfolding drama in Arlington County. During the interregnum, Joseph Martin was reindicted for the murders of Foreman and Shoemaker, with the cooperation of the triggerman, Richard Lee Earman. Burroughs continued his quest for information on the state police investigation. With election day only ten months away, I began receiving weekly invitations to lunch with Arlington Democrats seeking advice on an alternate candidate for commonwealth's attorney.

Although I publicly professed no interest in running, the thought became increasingly enticing. But I had a number of issues to weigh. Was I willing to give up my coveted job, which would probably be unavailable if I lost in November? Living on Tara's twelve thousand dollar salary as an editor with the Department of Defense would be tough. Could we make it? The thought of being unemployed for at least six months was unsettling. In addition, we would have to sell our new home in Fairfax County and move back into Arlington. Could we afford it? Tara and I concluded that the stakes were just too high.

Justin Williams and I promptly immersed ourselves in another headline-grabbing investigation, this time involving massage parlors in the City of Alexandria and an illegal bingo operation. Bingo? Not standard stuff for federal prosecutors, but this case allegedly involved political corruption and money laundering using offshore banks on a remote island in the Bahamas.

One evening in late March, Williams and I were updating United States Attorney Bill Cummings on our progress in the corruption probe. The massage-parlor-aspect of the case had become a hot topic in Alexandria. The local Olde Towne Alexandria newspaper gave the case daily coverage, salivating to publish the names of prominent folks caught with their pants down. Several years later I was pheasant hunting with the owner of that local scandal sheet. He told me that two types of people read his newspaper: those who enjoyed saying nasty things about other people, and those who wondered what nasty things other people were saying about them.

Cummings told Williams and me that the latest buzz at the Department of Justice was that Burroughs might be selected as U.S. attorney to replace him. We laughed and dismissed the rumor as ridiculous, but in politics you never know. Cummings, a Republican, had been selected by President Gerald Ford. Jimmy Carter, who was then president, had never asked for Cummings's resignation, as is the custom when a new president takes office.

I mulled the conversation over for fifteen or twenty minutes and finally decided to call Bill Burroughs at home and get the scoop first hand. Although Burroughs and I had moments of disagreement, particularly with respect to the Martin case, we enjoyed a good relationship. He was a pleasant guy to work for. Until the Foreman-Shoremaker homicide took command of the local headlines, most of the noteworthy cases handled by the office had been mine. I was also well aware that Burroughs's successor, if he left office before the end of his term, would be selected by the Arlington County Circuit Court judges. After serving as one of their courtroom clerks for four and a half years, and as a court bailiff for two years, I had a fairly close relationship with each of the judges. Although I was reluctant to cast the security of a great job to the wind to run for commonwealth's attorney, accepting the job on a court-appointed basis was a different proposition. It would be a risk-free move and an opportunity I couldn't pass up. It brought with it a considerable increase in salary and, even more, a tremendous rise in stature. Under Virginia law, the appointee would serve until the next general election and run as the incumbent. A safe bet.

My conversation with Burroughs was pleasant, but I could still detect the weight of the Martin investigation. He coyly declined to comment on his chances of being appointed United States attorney. Couched in terms of "what if," I asked him if he would be kind enough to drop a good word on my behalf with the judges if he got the job. Again, he demurred and finally replied that if a vacancy occurred, he would be supporting a friend of his then serving in the Virginia General Assembly. Although I ended the conversation politely, I was outraged. The person he had agreed to support, although a fine lawyer, in my view had no more interest in law enforcement than he did.

### We're Running

My anger was contagious. Tara, my Mom, and my Dad all shared my indignation. We talked over dinner that evening before making our decision. We were running against Burroughs, and I mean all of us. It was truly a family undertaking. I began making calls the next morning. I soon learned that even though I had a lot of support among Democrats, many of the party regulars had residual affection for Burroughs. Defeating him in a primary was iffy; I'd been there before—with my good friend Claude Hilton.

Hilton and I spent hours crafting a strategic plan. His advice was to run as an Independent with the endorsement of the Republican party. This would enable stalwart Democrats to cross party lines to vote for me and still be able to proudly tout that they had never voted for a Republican. Despite a shallow Republican base in Arlington County, there were three Independents on the Board of Supervisors elected with Republican backing. At Hilton's urging, I met with the Republican leaders, who offered money and people. They were hungry to knock off a Democratic incumbent, a rarity in Arlington. The resources they offered were too attractive to turn down.

Thanks to the generosity of my boss, Bill Cummings, a hard-core Republican, I spent several hours each day meeting with party officials. In possible violation of the Hatch Act, which made it illegal for federal employees to engage in partisan politics, I spoke to the Arlington County Republican Committee at its monthly meeting, and to several of the allied women's groups. The enthusiasm was inspiring. I was a new face with a penetrating message with universal appeal, "Isn't it time Arlington County had an effective commonwealth's attorney?" Anyone who read a daily newspaper in Northern Virginia knew exactly what I meant. We signed up more campaign workers than we needed, and recruited a battle-tested management team. I was even able to conscript my old partner in the sheriff's office, Bob Holmes, to serve as my treasurer. We were rolling, and it was only April.

In response to mounting pressure, I publicly stated that I would resign my job and formally announce my candidacy in May. But several tasks lay ahead of me before I left the federal prosecutor's office.

## Tricks of the Trade

Williams and I wrapped up the massage parlor investigation with about twenty-five convictions, mostly for interstate travel to facilitate prostitution and racketeering. The parlors in Alexandria operated much the same way they did in Arlington, except intercourse and oral sex were far more prevalent. Also, unlike Arlington, very few of the women employed there were single mothers simply trying to earn a living. Most were professional hookers who made big bucks. The most lucrative dimension of the business was the outcall service, which catered to higher-end customers such as traveling businessmen and diplomats.

Although some were generalists, most outcall masseuses had specialties. As reported in interviews published by local Alexandria newspapers, compensation among masseuses varied depending on their specialty. The highest paying "trick" was anal intercourse. The cost of this service varied from two hundred fifty dollars to, according to one woman, upwards of a thousand dollars, plus tip. The fee was driven by the quality of the goods. The woman who demanded and got top dollar turned three or four tricks a week. The rest of the time she spent working out to keep those buns tight and shapely. I never asked if they were insured.

Running a close second were women who performed various types of sado-masochistic routines using whips, chains, and dog collars. These leather-clad ladies were serious about their work and continuously upgraded their acts to stay ahead of the competition. They appeared to average between five hundred and a thousand dollars per session, and were busy seven days a week. Shorn of their specialized garb, few looked the part. But most of the women doing this type of stuff found it as sexually arousing as did their customers. Go figure!

In addition to the standard fare, the outcalls offered services to suit every fantasy and fetish, including oral sex, breast or foot masturbation, toe sucking, leg licking, and inanimate sexual object stimulation. They also offered a full range of services for gay clients and cross-dressers. Some men just wanted to talk dirty to a scantily clad woman. Others wanted to watch a woman defecate. The array of services was only limited by the human imagination. And the cost? About five hundred dollars a trick.

What's more unsettling is that the average patron could have been anyone's next door neighbor. There is no stereotypical pervert. Many seemingly respectable people are sexually stimulated by odd forms of degradation. But this stuff is tame compared to what I encountered as chairman of the Pornography Commission.

The most interesting hooker caught up in the investigation was a good-looking elementary school principal with a master's degree and a new Corvette.

Everyone thought she came from a wealthy family. The only wealthy family in her life was a prostitution syndicate. She was pulling down two thousand dollars every weekend, tax-free, of course.

Most of the massage-parlor employees pled guilty. Those in non-managerial positions received probation; supervisors got a month or two to serve. For many, the most severe penalty was paying tens of thousands of dollars in back taxes. All agreed to testify against the three owners and operators who hung tough and, against their attorneys' advice, insisted on a trial by jury. During the trial, the courtroom gallery was packed each day with reporters and spectators. The evidence was spicy and graphic as hooker after hooker described the tricks of her trade. Judge Lewis, a religious man who used no profanity, kept his eyes trained on the ceiling and periodically shouted, "I'll have no more of that talk in my courtroom." During one recess, Judge Lewis, who was over eighty years old, called me up to the bench and said, "Mr. Hudson, I always thought you were a nice young man—until now!"

The trial took a full week. The jury deliberated for four days before returning guilty verdicts on all three. Judge Lewis sentenced them to prison terms ranging from three to five years.

## Money-Laundering in the Bahamas

My attention then shifted to my last pending case. We had exhausted almost every lead in the bingo investigation. My brother-in-law Lance Lydon and a team of IRS special agents had combed thousands of documents and interviewed dozens of witnesses. If money was being skimmed and funneled to public officials, they couldn't find it. But several sources told us the money was being diverted to a small hotel on the island of Exuma in the Bahamas. Sure enough, the agents supposedly confirmed that one of the officials under suspicion had an interest in the Two Turtles Inn in Exuma.

Bill Cummings directed me to pack our crew and head to Exuma. I dutifully complied, but with one request. I asked Bill if Special Agent Jack Bartles of the FBI could come along. He had been the lead investigator on the prostitution investigation we'd just completed. There was a gas shortage on the island and we'd be traveling each day on foot. We needed extra help to complete the interviews and be home within two weeks. Jack had a rare sense of humor and literally kept everyone he worked with in stitches. The FBI agreed and we finalized preparations.

The Bahamian government distrusted the IRS—their most lucrative industry besides gambling was offshore banking. Therefore, the State Department assigned a handler to keep us on a short tether. To further keep tabs on our group, the Bahamian police detailed Detective Kirk Hutchinson to escort us everywhere. He was a tremendous asset.

Our first stop was Nassau. We had explicit instructions from the State Department to do nothing on Bahamian soil without the permission of the United States ambassador. We arrived at the U.S. Embassy at about 1:00 p.m. The ambassador, an insurance broker from Atlanta, Georgia, promptly disclosed that he was a personal friend of President Carter. As though we couldn't figure that out! He was reasonably cordial with me and Jack Bartles, but he informed my brother-in-law and his partner that he was uncomfortable with any IRS presence in the Bahamas. In the past, the Bahamian government had removed IRS agents from the islands for attempting to obtain records from offshore banks. The ambassador warned them that if they were walking down a street with a bank, they should cross over and walk on the other side. The subtext was, Don't interfere with the flow of offshore money—the economy depends on it.

The ambassador instructed the IRS agents to have no contact with any bank employee without his permission. Violations would result in immediate expulsion. I was directed to call him daily and brief him on who we intended to interview. As we prepared to depart, the ambassador lightened up a little. He seemed relieved with our assurance that we would follow his instructions. Of course, he had never worked with this crowd.

The following morning we linked up with Detective Kirk Hutchinson and grabbed a Bahamas Air flight, a time-worn DC-3, to Georgetown on the island of Exuma. Hutchinson and Bartles bonded immediately. The flight was crowded with women dragging screaming children, dogs, cats, and other assorted creatures. One lady had her pet bird, which sure as heck looked like a chicken to me. Predictably, Bartles brought cocktails for the entire group. We were on our third drink when the plane took off. There were no seat belts on the old twin prop carrier. The only barrier between the pilots and thirty or so passengers was what appeared to be a used shower curtain. Fortunately, the flight was only about a half hour. It was relatively smooth until the final moments.

There was no air traffic control system on the island and no communication link with the ground. All navigation was strictly by line of sight. As we approached the airport, the plane passed the runway, turned and suddenly descended, straight down. Women and children screamed, dogs barked, men fingered their rosary beads. People rolled out of their seats into the aisles. All we could see was ground in front of the cockpit window. Thank God we were all half loaded. Bartles, crawling backed into his seat, turned to the stewardess and asked, "Hey, what the hell's going on here?"

She calmly smiled and said, "Don't worry. Captain Brown, he always lands like this. Don't know why. If you can do better, go up and try."

As the wheels hit the runway, we could see smaller aircraft frantically swerving off onto the shoulder to avoid the big twin prop still traveling close to a hundred miles an hour. When we reached the gate, Captain Brown shut off the engines and slammed on the brakes. Plumes of smoke from the tires enveloped the entire plane. People and cargo flew everywhere. A woman ended up on Hutchinson's lap. Bartles spilled his drink on his shirt and trousers. My brother-in-law summed it up succinctly when he yelled, "Holy shit." Anyway, we were there.

Hutchinson clearly had influence. Gasoline was almost nonexistent on the island, but a young Bahamian police officer in his crisp red uniform was there to greet us, driving a Land Rover. He couldn't have been more than eighteen years old, and he could hardly wait to call his mother and tell her that he was working with the FBI. We traveled about five miles over pothole-pocked roads and encountered no more than two dozen other cars. Most travelers walked. We passed a few nice homes, but most residents lived in handmade shacks with crude doors and no windows. Flies and information seemed to proliferate in the environment. Within minutes, the entire close-knit population knew we were there.

Before we were taken to our hotel, Hutchinson advised us that protocol required us to pay an initial call on the island superintendent of police, a gentleman in his fifties wearing the insignia of a captain. He assured us that his officers would assist us in any way possible, and then politely reiterated that banking or financial information was off limits. To reinforce the point, he said that even soliciting such information was a felony.

The young officer then drove us to the Peace and Plenty Hotel, located on a lagoon leading out into the ocean. We had a huge two-bedroom suite with an additional adjoining room. The view overlooked the adjacent sailing marina. The swimming pool, which faced the lagoon, was about ten paces from our exterior door. The place would do for our two-week stay. We checked in and asked for at least two room keys. This drew a blank stare. There were no keys to the room; no one locked their door. After signing the registration form, we grabbed a cold beer and assembled beside the pool to plan our interview strategy.

For the next seven days, we worked our butts off. I was up by 6:30 a.m. for my daily exercise. We ate breakfast in the room and were on the road by 8:00 a.m. We conducted interviews in teams until about 4:00 p.m., most days walking to our destination. Then we returned to the hotel to dictate memorandums of the interviews we had conducted that day before gathering by the pool for our daily caucus as the sun set. I dutifully kept the ambassador advised, in general terms, of what the agents were doing during the day. But that was only one dimension of our investigation.

In the evening we'd go to the local pub for a beer or two. All the local police officers would congregate there to talk with Jack Bartles and Kirk Hutchinson. Hutchinson, a legendary drug investigator, was just coming off a long-term deep-undercover assignment. The officers were thrilled by his stories and by Bartles's tall tales of busting pimps and bank robbers. Bartles bought beer for the officers and played darts until well past midnight. It would pay dividends later.

*Waiting for the Bahamian Police at the airport in George Town, Exuma.*

After a full week of pounding the pavement, our efforts had uncovered nothing of value. Our mission was to determine if millions of dollars of skimmed bingo profits were being invested on the island. We needed bank records or some type of inside information.

Hutchinson explained that laws in the Bahamas were tough, modeled on the old English common law system. Persons charged with crime were presumed to be guilty until proven innocent. They believed in short periods of intense incarceration, with hard labor sixteen hours a day, six days a week. They also used caning or whipping for any offense involving violence or injury to the victim. The recidivism rate? Less than five percent. Now that's effective justice.

The central focus of our investigation was the Two Turtles Inn, a small boutique motel situated on a spit of land on the lagoon about three miles from where we were staying. It was nicely appointed, but had a lingering musty smell. As we expected, it had a pier-like facility for mooring airplanes equipped for water landing. Supposedly, high-class hookers were being ferried to the island on these planes.

Several days of periodic surveillance revealed little activity. Finally, Bartles approached the front desk and asked for a room. The lady was less than accommodating and claimed they might have something later in the week. What? Every room appeared vacant. Maybe the place was a front for a money-laundering scam.

We eventually learned that we needed to talk to an islander named Johnny Wylie. At one time, Wylie had been the manager of the Two Turtles Inn, and he had been bad mouthing the owners since the day he left. He lived on the other side of the island and drove an old blue pickup truck displaying the Two Turtles Inn logo on its side. Everyone we asked about Wylie's whereabouts said the same thing, "You mean that lying Haitian?" After a few days, Bartles's contacts with local police paid off. They told us where Wylie was staying and loaned us a well-used police Land Rover to travel to the remote location.

We found it with little difficulty. The blue truck was sitting out front. Painted beside the Two Turtles Inn logo was the message, "Who killed my goat should be more careful." It seems that a motorist had struck and killed his goat, but was never identified. To shame the driver, Wylie painted the message on his truck, an island custom. Unfortunately, the "lying Haitian" was not there. He had been tipped off that we were coming and fled the island.

After ten days we were getting a bit desperate. Lydon and his partner decided to confront the desk clerk at the Two Turtles Inn. They walked in, showed their credentials, and displayed photographs of the subjects of our investigation. She curtly denied ever seeing them and politely told the agents she had nothing else to say.

Later that evening, after the rest of our group had retired, Bartles shared his dilemma with a couple of the young Bahamian police officers at the pub. This was a risky move. We knew nothing about the trustworthiness of these two men. Some of our group suspected that they might be trying to set us up by luring us into seeking forbidden banking information. For that reason, Bartles used a different approach. He told them we needed to know who was behind the Two Turtles Inn, who financed the operation, who supplied their equipment, and who was their bookkeeper. This would enable a crude cash-flow analysis without requiring any bank records. It would have provided a starting point. The officers agreed to work on it.

Next day, Lydon, Hutchinson and I walked back to the airport to inspect the customs declarations and see how often our targets visited the island. Although the Bahamian customs agents were cool to me and my brother-in-law, they gladly gave Detective Hutchinson access to the records. They unlocked a large closet door and showed us inside. The five-by-five-foot closet was chock full of thousands of declarations forms tossed into random piles with no semblance of order. Hutchinson called for assistance and directed the customs agents to pile the mounds of documents into the Land Rover. We took the forms to the hotel and spent ten hours combing through them. Not a single declaration was signed by our targets.

We were asleep when Bartles returned from the pub that night, but within minutes we all were clustered around the couch in the sitting area. The Bahamian police officers had arranged for us to interview another former manager of the Two Turtles Inn, who had succeeded Wylie. They were working on the auditor, but that could take several more days.

The next morning I called Bill Cummings and said we needed to extend our stay for several days. After conferring with the heads of the regional IRS and FBI offices, he called back and authorized the extension. I also called home and learned that there were several developments on that front. First, Tara had located a lovely house in Arlington for us to buy. Next, she told me that the local paper had carried an article earlier in the week that the Democrats were planning to file a complaint with the Department of Justice contending that my public statement of proposed candidacy was a violation of the Hatch Act. This antic did not faze me since I would be resigning in two weeks. As slow as the Department of Justice moved, it could take two weeks to open the letter containing the complaint and make up a file.

For almost three solid months my name had been prominently featured several times a week in all local newspapers covering Northern Virginia. Each development in the prostitution and bingo probes merited front page treatment. I also enjoyed an excellent relationship with all the reporters who covered the U.S. attorney's office. Once I confirmed the rumor that I was running, all the papers did extensive profile pieces with photographs. That really ticked the Democrats off. They retaliated with the Hatch Act complaint. My advice to those with ruffled feathers: Buy a jock strap—you'll need it before this campaign is over.

Lastly, Tara told me that Burroughs was going to have primary opposition. John Purdy, a member of the Arlington County Board, was competing for the Democratic nomination. Purdy had minimal legal experience, but he did have a strong political following. Democrats outnumbered Republicans in Arlington

County by better than two to one. I was pulling for Burroughs. Without him, my entire campaign strategy was out the window.

We spent the next few days interviewing the linen supplier, the former manager of the Two Turtles Inn, and the auditor. There was not a shred of evidence that any of the political figures we were investigating had any present interest in the Two Turtles Inn or were smuggling currency onto the island. This didn't mean it wasn't happening—we just couldn't prove it. The return flight was uneventful. Before boarding, we made sure that Captain Brown was not at the throttle.

In the after-action analysis, there were varying assessments of the worth of the trip. On the one hand, everyone was a little disappointed that we had come back empty-handed. But on the other, we could proudly say that we worked as hard to clear our suspects' names as we would have to convict them. After all, that's what justice is all about.

As one of my final acts as assistant U.S. attorney, I recommended that the case be closed without prosecution. My resignation was effective May 4, 1979.

VIII

# THE PEOPLE DECIDE

The transition from the United States Attorney's Office was brief. Monday following my Friday resignation, I moved into a small law office in a building owned by Claude Hilton. Located just around the corner from the Arlington County Courthouse, it would serve as both law office and campaign headquarters. My practice would consist of cases no one else wanted.

I was excited about returning to the courthouse and seeing my old friends. To my dismay, they were not excited about seeing me. I was greeted with the warmth of a winter storm. Those who spoke at all were curt. One former colleague in the clerk's office asked that I not tell anyone that we had spoken. If this was an example of what the campaign was going to be like, it would be rough sledding.

The next week I appeared in Arlington General District Court on two court-appointed criminal cases. Ironically, the assistant commonwealth's attorneys handling the cases, who worked for Burroughs, treated me royally. The judges, whom I knew well, treated me like crap. I was having a terrible time just getting an initial political compass bearing. I had no clients, no money, and few friends.

I sat down with Bill Cummings the following week and told him I'd had enough. I wanted my job back. He summarily cut me off. He said to stop whining and get my ass out and campaign. If I lost, he'd consider taking me back. He also told me, much to my delight, that he had received authority to rehire me immediately as a part time special assistant to prosecute drug cases—my specialty. I walked out with my chin up. The part-time job was a lifeline. It gave me enough income to cover the mortgage.

The next week, at age thirty-one, I publicly announced that I was a candidate for commonwealth's attorney and that I would be seeking the Republican endorsement at the May 15 party canvass. The press coverage was extensive. The

*Washington Post* and the *Washington Star* both characterized the campaign as potentially the bitterest in Northern Virginia history. My campaign slogan was Competence—Not Controversy.

My prior experience managing a campaign had been a disaster. This time, I sought advice from every current and former political office holder in Arlington who would see me—Republican or Democrat. Almost all pledged support, even a few Democrats still holding office. Momentum began to build. Within a month, people were stopping me on the street with words of encouragement.

At the first meeting of my campaign steering committee, campaign manager Dottie Todd calculated from past election results that we would need about twenty thousand votes to beat Burroughs. We spent the next five hours figuring out where to get them. We adopted a back-to-basics intensive grassroots approach with emphasis on favorable voter identification. In other words, identify your supporters and get them to the polls. Don't waste resources on groups or areas who never vote Republican.

Although as an Independent Republican I was swimming against the political tide, I had the advantage of being a life-long Arlingtonian, a rare commodity. I had worked in the courthouse for nine years. Arlington had a transient population of about one hundred thousand in those days, with a population turnover of almost twenty percent each election cycle. This meant that a sizeable block of people who had voted for Burroughs four years earlier probably no longer lived in the county. I had been active in the volunteer fire department, the Masonic Lodge, the Lions Club, my church, and my local civic association. My largest and most faithful base of support however was the Arlington County Police Department.

Tara and I, along with our parents, all of whom lived in Arlington, spent the first few weeks of the campaign making extensive lists of everyone we knew well who lived in the county. I called each of the four hundred or so people on the list, asked for their support, and requested that they walk me around their neighborhood and introduce me to their friends. I was hitting about five neighborhoods a weeknight and close to twenty a day on weekends. My coordinators, David Cayre, Bill Fields, Gerhard Kelm, and Scott McGeary, organized the walks in tight geographic clusters to insure maximum coverage. Unlike random door knocking, which I did a lot of, on my organized walks there was a familiar face to vouch for me. The reception was much warmer than with cold calling. Most had never met my opponent, who knocked on no doors.

Simultaneously, I sent letters to members of every organization I belonged to seeking their personal and financial support. I also mailed letters to everyone who had contributed to the campaigns of the Independent Republicans then in office. Once the pump was primed, return envelopes started pouring in. Coupled with several successful fund raisers, we were flush with cash.

I knew that most small-budget local campaigns founder because of mismanagement of funds. Therefore, I needed to channel my resources, and prepared a budget accordingly. I figured that I knew at least ten thousand Arlington residents who would support me. I needed ten thousand more. Even though I was knocking on hundreds of doors each week, and passing out literature at shopping centers and Metro stops, that was not enough. I decided to rely heavily on mass mailing, particularly to the twenty thousand high-rise apartment dwellers. Mass mailing was the only reliable form of contacting them.

We concluded that it was a waste of time to spend money on those precincts with a solid Democratic base; nothing would change their mind. We therefore sent one letter per month to all registered voters in the swing precincts and those that leaned Republican. I tried to focus my message on crime issues or activities of special interest to those neighborhoods.

I sent a personal letter to every newly registered voter on the assumption that they probably had never heard of Bill Burroughs. Three weeks before the election, I sent a glossy brochure to all registered voters, comparing my background and legal experience with my opponent. One week before election day, we mailed another piece to the same list, focusing exclusively on the Foreman-Shoremaker case.

Thanks to my friend Lou Haskell, I received the endorsement of the Northern Virginia Gasoline Retailers Association. As a result, thirty-five of the county's busiest gas stations put huge picture posters supporting my candidacy in their windows, as did more than fifty other businesses.

I enjoyed the retail side of the campaign, meeting and talking with voters, and encountered a surprisingly small number of hard-core Burroughs supporters. The down side was the public debates. Because our campaign overshadowed all others in the Washington area that year, we were in demand. We debated in front of the Arlington Civic Federation, the Chamber of Commerce, the League of Women Voters, the Bar Association, the Northern Virginia Young Lawyers Association, and the *Northern Virginia Sun* newspaper. In addition, we had daily appearances before regional civic associations—there must have been fifty—and smaller groups and organizations. The joint public appearances were tough. I had to attack Bill's record; there's no other way to beat an incumbent, but I still had a lot of respect and affection for my former boss.

Burroughs used the same canned speech at each of our public appearances. My staff could recite it from memory. He always slipped in the comment that I was a capable lawyer because he had trained me. I learned not to take the bait. I chose a different strategy. Each week, I would focus on a different issue, such as burglary, crime against the elderly, victims' rights, crime in the schools, drugs, or juvenile justice, and how I would handle it better than Burroughs. Cracking down on residential burglary proved to be one of the hottest issues of the campaign.

*Gaining the endorsement of U.S. Senator John W. Warner for Commonwealth's Attorney.*

Each Monday, I would issue an extensive press release unveiling that week's issue. The local papers gave them front page coverage. Then I'd relentlessly hammer away on that issue. To keep my opponent off stride, I never gave the same stump speech twice. I would, however, end each presentation on the same note. "The cardinal issue in this campaign is the quality of legal representation the citizens of Arlington receive. You should select your commonwealth's attorney with the same care you would use to select someone to handle your most important business affairs. If you or a family member are the victim of a serious crime, it could be one of the most important decisions in your life."

*Campaigning for Commonwealth's Attorney of Arlington County at the Cherrydale Safeway in 1979.*

After Labor Day, the pressure and intensity of the campaign increased incrementally with each passing day. Although Burroughs handily defeated his primary opponent, his campaign lacked energy. His response to the issues I raised was tepid at best; I kept waiting for the bomb to drop.

My only respite was the three or four hours I spent each day at the United States Attorney's Office. I was handling clandestine laboratory cases almost exclusively. One of the evolving trends in the drug underworld at the time was the manufacturing of phencyclidine, commonly called PCP. It was a hot item in the drug market. Brewed in crude laboratories, typically in home kitchens, PCP is a veterinary tranquillizer. When ingested into the human body, ordinarily by smoking PCP-treated parsley or marijuana, it causes hallucinations. Most home labs are detected either by neighbors complaining about the noxious odor or by tips to the police from chemical supply houses. When "cookers" order the precise combination of chemicals necessary to formulate the mixture, or actually hand the supplier the recipe, this prompts a call from the supplier to DEA. A dead give away for us was the guy who purchased ten pounds of parsley at the grocery store.

I learned to prosecute lab cases as an assistant commonwealth's attorney. One of the most comical cases I ever handled was a dimethyltryptamine, or DMT, lab.

## What's Cookin'?

On a cool spring morning, the Arlington County Police switch board lit up with more than a dozen calls within a two-block radius. An offensive odor permeated the air, coming from South Wayne Street. The beat officer stepped out of his scout car, took one whiff and called the Special Unit. The source of the odor, which resembled putrefied eggs, was a small duplex. It was overpowering—no one's cooking was that bad.

A forensic chemist from the state lab diagnosed the smell as DMT—a drug rarely encountered in Northern Virginia, and counseled extreme caution. One of the final stages of the brewing process for DMT involves a lithium compound that is highly explosive if handled improperly.

The assigned detective drafted an affidavit outlining the probable cause to search the house, obtained a search warrant from the court, and consulted with me on the method of entry. They were inclined to use no knock—kick the door open and rush inside, providing an element of surprise, but the forensic chemist nixed the idea. If the lithium were spilled, the entire house could go up. They decided to use a more creative ruse-entry technique.

Detective Ruth "Ruby" Emery pulled her undercover vehicle in front of 413 South Wayne Street and walked up to the door. Although bright and well educated, she could play the role of "dizzy broad" masterfully. She knocked on the front door. A young woman answered. Ruby asked if this was 413 North

Wayne Street. The young woman politely said that Ruby had the wrong address; this was South Wayne Street. Ruby said she desperately needed to find 413 North Wayne Street; she had medicine to deliver to an elderly relative. The young woman told Ruby to stay right there while she got her brother. She returned with Winston Monk in tow.

Monk was wearing a face mask, rubber apron, and thick gloves. He removed his face mask to greet Ruby and began explaining directions to North Wayne Street. As Ruby gradually backed toward the door, he followed. When they arrived at the door step, Ruby grabbed Monk's apron and pulled him to the ground, as a horde of detectives swarmed the house and seized the glass of lithium sitting in the dining room window. In the kitchen was a full functioning laboratory. It appeared to be an open-and-shut case.

We indicted Monk for attempting to manufacture a controlled substance. To my amazement, he went to trial, but waived a jury. Generally, this meant the lawyer had something up his sleeve, some type of technical legal defense. Even more disturbing was the fact that I put on two full days of evidence and Monk's lawyer asked only a handful of seemingly trivial questions. We felt like soldiers sitting in a foxhole waiting for a shot to be fired. Where was the loose screw in the case?

At the close of the evidence, Monk's lawyer moved to dismiss the charges on the ground that we had over proven the case. He claimed our evidence showed that Monk had completed the manufacturing process and, hence, his client was not guilty of *attempt.* The attorney argued that the brewing process was in the final stage and had consequently progressed beyond mere preparation, which is the traditional touchstone of attempt crimes. Neither the trial judge nor the Supreme Court of Virginia bought Monk's tortured logic. The court sentenced him to a short prison term.

### Burroughs Self-Destructs

With one month left before the election, I was literally at my wit's end. I was campaigning from sunrise, canvassing at Metro stops, to sunset, knocking on doors. I wore out the soles on three pairs of shoes. Predictably, the campaign became progressively bitter, fueled in part by unprecedented media coverage. In an act of self-destruction, Burroughs filed lawsuits against the *Washington Post* and the *Washington Star* for their libelous coverage of the Foreman-Shoremaker case. He claimed a million dollars in damages. As a result, each paper carried a feature article recounting in detail the alleged shortcomings in his handling of the prosecution. I could not have purchased that type of publicity for fifty thousand dollars.

Furthermore, the poor judgment Burroughs displayed in filing the lawsuits rattled his own political base. Several of his supporters, including a Democratic office holder, called to advise me that I could count on their active support.

Controversy became so intense that Burroughs asked the Arlington County Circuit Court to appoint a special prosecutor to take over the Martin case. In part, this was attributable to Burroughs's announcement that he would be a prosecution witness at the trial. The court set Joseph Martin's trial for the murder of Alan Foreman and Donna Shoemaker for October 25, 1979, the week before the election. Since the trial, the central issue of the campaign, would take at least a week, any blunders by Burroughs in handling the investigation would receive daily press coverage. Again, money couldn't buy this kind of public visibility.

Against the advice of my campaign staff, I decided to take a four-day break in mid-October and go fishing with the Hookers. I hadn't missed a trip in four years. We rented a cottage at Chincoteague, Virginia, on the Eastern Shore. We set up our beach chairs, rod racks, and coolers each day at Fisherman's Point, a narrow strip of land on the southern tip of Assateague Island. To reach the Point, we had to travel twelve miles across desolate sand in four-wheel-drive vehicles. We encountered no one during the day except the park rangers, who loved to stop by and talk with the twelve or so cops in our group. We fished in the surf for blues and sea trout. All of the detectives working the Foreman-Shoremaker case were on the trip, as well as Burroughs's chief deputy, my close friend Ken Melson. We avoided discussing the campaign until the third morning, when the nuclear bomb hit.

## It's Over

Before heading out to the beach, Ken Melson and I stopped at the store to pick up some hot dogs for grilling, and several bags of potato chips. As we got back into my copper-colored Ford Bronco, Ken casually said "Congratulations, you won."

"Won what," I asked?

"The election, what else?" Ken replied, as he showed me the headlines of the *Washington Post.* The October 19, 1979, *Post* reported that Virginia Attorney General J. Marshall Coleman had filed a formal public response to Burroughs's third request for a grand jury investigation of the state police probe of his handling of the Martin prosecution. Coleman's filing, as reported in the *Post,* stated that his office had received corroborated information that Burroughs was suspected of "bribery and a coverup" in the case and that he might have committed other acts that constituted malfeasance of office. According to the *Post,* Coleman's "staff last year turned up allegations that bribery might have been committed by Burroughs in refusing to prosecute a defendant, Joseph Martin, in the murder case," but that the state police investigation did not yield sufficient evidence to warrant criminal charges.

The same *Post* article also reported that Burroughs immediately called a press conference to deny the allegations and denounce Coleman's characterizations. He stated that *his* investigation had uncovered no such allegations, and said he'd have no more to say. In his carefully chosen words, he refused to be lured into "a pissing contest with a skunk." The article noted that Hudson was unavailable for comment.

I had mixed reactions. My first inclination was to go back into the store and pick up another six pack. But I caught myself. One of the basic tenets of campaigning is never to get overconfident and always to run scared. Maybe I'm superstitious, but declaring victory, even to myself, three weeks before the election was risky. It could suppress the adrenaline driving the campaign at the most critical time.

En route to Fisherman's Point, Ken and I reminisced about our experiences with Bill Burroughs. We agreed that the undertone of corruption in the state police report was unfortunate and probably undeserved. Burroughs may have used poor judgment, but he was not dishonest. I refused to accept the notion that the Bill Burroughs I knew would ever consider taking a bribe. No matter how misguided his actions may have seemed to some people, there was no doubt that Bill truly believed he was doing the right thing. I'm glad in retrospect that I was unavailable to comment. The natural tendency would have been to seize the moment, and I am convinced that exploiting the press frenzy by piling on would have been a mistake. Burroughs was hit so hard that I feared it could engender voter sympathy.

We had a delightful day of sunshine and surf fishing. Of course, even when fishing conditions were poor, beer-drinking and cigar-smoking conditions were always excellent. Melson had an exceptional day. He caught two sea trout weighing about ten pounds each in the course of fifteen minutes. He also won the daily jackpots for first fish, most fish, and largest fish—all in two casts. As usual, I caught nothing.

The following day we returned to Northern Virginia. After huddling with the campaign team, I decided, with the political wind at my back, to adopt a "hunker-down strategy" for the final two weeks: Say as little as possible and make no mistakes. The press coverage of the Martin trial and Burroughs's continuing comments kept him on a path of self-destruction. I just stayed out the way.

Even though I had met or communicated by mail with about twenty-five thousand potential voters, I knew that many people showing up at the polls would not recognize my name. I therefore devoted the final two weeks to recruiting poll workers to cover every precinct. Since I hate it when people shove literature in my face, I used a different approach. I called it "whisper in their ear." My poll workers were instructed to approach voters with a smile and say, "Henry Hudson would sure appreciate your vote for commonwealth's attorney. He's running against Bill Burroughs." On election day, we had every polling place covered. More than a hundred police officers, in plain clothes of course, greeted voters on my behalf at the polls, in blatant violation of county policy.

Speaking of county policy, my detractors tried to chill my supporters with claims of forbidden campaigning in the employee parking lot. The county manager, a friend of Burroughs, sent out a memo to all county employees that no cars with political bumper stickers could park in the lot. Literally hundreds of county employees, mostly police officers, had my bumper sticker displayed on their car. The media leaped on the memo like a linebacker chasing a fumbled football. It was retracted the next day.

November 6, finally came. It was cold and snowing lightly on Election Day. My entire family, including my mother- and father-in-law, were working the polls. During the course of the day, I visited about half of the thirty-nine polling places in Arlington. I returned home, along with my campaign team, shortly after 7:00 p.m. when the polls closed. I was drained. Most of the police officers who were members of my fishing club arrived moments later. I mixed manhattans for the group and we waited. My friend Scott McGeary was at the courthouse calling us with the numbers as the precincts reported.

## Victory Blow Out

By 8:30 p.m. the suspense was over. David Green and John Webb, both Arlington detectives, drove Tara and me to the Republican victory blow out. I had won by fifty-nine percent, taking thirty of thirty-nine precincts. We racked up seventeen thousand five hundred thirty-eight votes to Burroughs's twelve thousand one hundred twenty-seven. I received more votes than any Republican candidate in Arlington County history. The Republicans also retained the majority on the Arlington County Board, with both incumbent candidates reelected.

As we pulled up in front of the hotel in Crystal City where Republicans were assembled to celebrate our victory, the obvious struck me. I'd be expected to give a victory speech, something I hadn't even thought about. In an otherwise perfect night, that could cause a problem—I'd already downed a couple manhattans. My father-in-law had drunk at least four. The press was everywhere. The governor and the attorney general were waiting on the phone to congratulate me. With cameras rolling, I gave a two-minute speech, thanking my legion of supporters and pledging to build an effective law enforcement team. Given the risks that Tara and I had taken, the experience was one of the emotional high points of my lifetime. It is no wonder that politics can easily become addicting.

One of the most widely reported comments made that night was by Detective John Webb. Throughout the campaign, Burroughs claimed to have been instrumental in reorganizing the police department. The Arlington County Chief of Police denied the claim, and the rank and file officers resented the comment. Webb, who also had a few manhattans under his belt, told a reporter that, "Last year, Burroughs claimed to have reshuffled the police department. Well tonight, we reshuffled the commonwealth's attorney's office."

Predictably, the chief of police received complaints about his officers working at the polls. After sitting on the complaint for a few days, he responded that there was insufficient evidence to warrant disciplinary action.

Bill Burroughs blamed his defeat on negative press coverage. He continued to maintain that his handling of the Foreman-Shoremaker case was the major accomplishment of his career. He concluded his comments to the press by saying that if he had it all to do over again, he'd do it all the same.

When Tara and I left our house that evening for the victory party, the only people remaining there were my mother-in-law and the chief of police, Smokey Stover. My mother-in-law was preparing a huge pot of chili for some of the key campaign aides. We lived in a modest three-bedroom split-foyer of about twenty-five hundred square feet. When we returned about 10:30 p.m., we had well over two hundred visitors. People were standing on the front lawn. Police cars were everywhere. More than twenty cases of beer and five half-gallons of whisky were consumed that evening. The party broke up around 2:30 a.m. My three-year-old nephew Jake woke me up at 6:30 a.m. to tell me that more people had arrived.

It took me three or four days just to decompress. Tara and I then spent weeks writing more than five hundred thank-you letters. We took a short trip to Myrtle Beach, South Carolina, with the family and I returned home to begin a new phase of my life, still pumped with excitement.

## A Capital Conviction

At trial, Joseph Martin was convicted of capital murder, but the jury declined to give him the death penalty. After eight and a half hours of deliberation, they sentenced him to life in prison. Under Virginia law he would be eligible for parole after serving twenty years. Richard Lee Earman was sentenced to ten years. Earman, the confessed triggerman, later filed a lawsuit against the Department of Corrections complaining about the "intolerable noise emanating from other inmates' radios and televisions." The federal court had little sympathy for the convicted murderer and dismissed his case.

In the aftermath of the campaign, I had hoped to rekindle a peaceful coexistence with Bill Burroughs. It was not to be. Within weeks of my swearing in, Burroughs sued me, Virginia Attorney General Marshall Coleman, and the *Northern Virginia Sun,* alleging that my characterization of his handling of the Earman case in my campaign literature had been libelous. He had earlier unsuccessfully sued the *Washington Post* and the *Washington Star* on similar grounds. His lawsuit against me fared no better, but gaining a dismissal cost me more than four thousand dollars in legal fees.

I was fortunate that the voters returned a Republican majority to the county board, because the Democrats could not resist a final slap. The county manager attempted to reduce my starting salary to that of an entry-level lawyer. The county board quickly intervened and set my salary at the same level as that of the former commonwealth's attorney. Despite his initial antagonism over Burroughs's defeat, the county manager and I soon developed a good working relationship.

The passage of time has dissolved most of the bitterness between me and Bill Burroughs. We now have a cordial relationship. After leaving the Office of the Commonwealth's Attorney, Bill developed a successful private practice and has enjoyed a distinguished career. In each political office I have held over the succeeding years, I have made sure that he has received red-carpet treatment. I owe him no less. In the coolness of retrospect, I must concede that he taught me a lot. I consider him a friend.

Between the election and taking office, I had two cases to finish in the United States Attorney's Office: a bank robbery and a PCP lab. The bank robbery was an effortless conviction. The jury was out ten minutes. The PCP lab was set for a three-day jury trial. However, the weekend before trial, the defendant was killed in a violent explosion. You guessed it: He was mixing another batch of PCP.

## Commonwealth's Attorney

I was sworn in as commonwealth's attorney just after Christmas, and experienced a common political phenomenon. Before the election I met scores of people who claimed to be supporting my opponent, but they must have had a last-minute epiphany, because after the election I could find no one who voted against me.

At 8:00 a.m. on January 1, 1980, two pickup trucks pulled up to the rear entrance of the Arlington County Courthouse. With the assistance of several detectives, Tara and I unloaded my furniture and personal files, and wheeled them into my new office. Sitting in the middle of the desk left by Bill Burroughs was a three-inch stack of documents. On casual glance, I sensed it was my first crisis as "the people's lawyer." Each document bore the name of my friend, Detective David Green. Burroughs had left a note clipped to the top page, "Henry, this one's for you."

# IX
# THE PEOPLE'S LAWYER

The phone rang for almost thirty seconds at the Green residence before Detective David Green answered. Without even identifying myself, I said "David, ninety parking tickets?"

"Yeah," he replied. "I got those doing the Martin case, in my police cruiser no less. Burroughs refused to cancel them. Guess he's still pissed off."

Not wanting to prolong the agony of past history, I whipped out my pen and dealt each one a lethal blow—my first official act as commonwealth's attorney.

The following day I turned to more typical business: residential burglaries and serious juvenile crime. Police Chief Smokey Stover and I spent hours developing a game plan. The issues were closely interrelated. Residential burglaries had reached epidemic proportions. Most were being committed by three categories of offenders—professional silver thieves, certain District of Columbia residents, and juveniles. There was little deterrence. Convicted housebreakers were typically serving about ninety days in jail, a small price for heists that often exceeded ten thousand dollars.

Approximately twenty-five percent of the burglaries were committed by people under eighteen years of age, often during the school day. I immediately suspended all plea bargaining in residential burglary cases. I also began recommending at all sentencing hearings, without exception, that people convicted of breaking into someone's home serve at least six months in jail. And that was for first offenders who returned the property taken and did not trash the house. This was a radical change in policy. Crime victims told me that aside from sexual assault, no offense is more personal or invasive than someone breaking into your house and rummaging though your personal belongings. And it was heartbreaking to see priceless family heirlooms sold at pawnshops for pennies.

Stover and I called a press conference and announced our policy—break into a house, go to jail, no matter who you are. The message resonated with the press, the citizens, and the court.

Although criminal defense lawyers screamed about our hard-nosed approach, the burglary rate plummeted as judges began sending burglars to jail in droves. An unfortunate by-product was the increase in burglaries in surrounding jurisdictions. But that wasn't my problem.

Chief Stover and I also persuaded the county board to adopt an ordinance requiring pawn shops in the county to record the identity of every person pawning property. The law also required that the property had to be held for a specified period before being resold. The ordinance enabled the police to significantly increase the amount of stolen property recovered.

Changing the approach to violent juvenile offenders was not as warmly received. Even in those days, Virginia law allowed prosecutors to petition the juvenile court to certify certain youthful offenders for trial as adults. To satisfy the certification requirements, a defendant had to be over sixteen years of age, have committed a serious felony offense, and be beyond the rehabilitative capabilities of the court. Despite being on the books for decades, the law was rarely used. The historical mind-set had always been that every young person, no matter how lawless and violent, could be saved by the juvenile justice system. Based on my experience as a juvenile court bailiff and prosecutor, I found this notion quixotic. Chief Stover agreed.

The underlying analysis was simple. A significant percentage of serious crime, that is, burglary, rape, and robbery, in Arlington was being committed by juvenile offenders. On close examination, we concluded that a handful of young ruffians was responsible for ninety percent of the serious juvenile crime. Most of these punks had multiple prior felony convictions and previous unsuccessful experiences with probation and counseling. To the horror of the juvenile court staff, Stover and I announced that all juveniles who committed serious felony offenses would be scrutinized for certification to the adult court. In the case of hard-core recidivists, we would seek substantial time in the state pen. No one believed me at first, so I personally prosecuted the first qualifying case.

### Edna Weaver

When the doorbell rang at 11:00 p.m. on a chilly November night, Edna Weaver was suspicious. Her small terrier barked incessantly. She walked to the door as quickly as her eighty-one-year-old frame would permit. Since her husband's death several years earlier, she never opened the door after dark. Who could be calling that late?

She cut the porch light on and asked who was there. A young male voice replied, "Mailman—got a package." Mrs. Weaver wasn't expecting a package, and she knew the postal service didn't deliver mail that late. Then a second young man's voice urged her to open the door. What did these kids want? She began to tremble. Maybe her daughter was right, she shouldn't be living alone.

She ordered the young men to leave the package on the porch and go away. She listened to their foot steps on the wooden stairs leading from the porch. Were they gone? After a few minutes, she extinguished the porch light and headed for the bedroom. Her hands were still shaking, so she decided to call her daughter. With her little dog held tightly in one hand, she picked up the telephone. There was no dial tone. She reclined on the bed with her little terrier by her side. Miraculously, she dozed off to sleep, perhaps to escape the grip of fear, but not for long.

It was shortly after midnight when she was awakened by the sound of breaking glass. Next she heard the splintering sound of wood as her rear door was kicked open. She lunged, but it was too late. Her beloved terrier leaped off the bed and raced into the kitchen barking. Tears filled her eyes as she heard the little dog cry out in pain when the intruders crushed its small skull. She braced as the footsteps came closer, but there was no place to hide.

Mrs. Weaver lived in an upper-middle-class neighborhood on North Edison Street, about two hundred yards from Arlington Hospital. A neighbor might have heard her if she had screamed, but she could not summon the strength. For a moment she thought it must be a dream.

Suddenly the silhouettes of two young men appeared in her room, which was illuminated only by a small lamp on a bedside table. One began to pummel her mercilessly. The other rummaged through her belongings. Within minutes, Mrs. Weaver lost consciousness.

Meanwhile the two thugs foraged through her entire house looking for valuables, but found only a few dollars and a couple pieces of jewelry. Enraged, they took a sledge hammer from the basement, and traveled from room to room, destroying every piece of furniture in the house.

When Mrs. Weaver regained consciousness, she was being dragged into the living room. Her living room furniture had been smashed into pieces and placed in a mound. The two men tossed her on top of the pile and began pouring gasoline all around her. She begged them to kill her, but that would have been too charitable. They removed her nightgown, and one of the young hoodlums defiled her anally.

Officer Roger Estes was the type of cop who knew most of the long-time residents on his beat. When he saw Mrs. Weaver's front door open the next morning, Roger thought he'd better check it out. About ten steps from his scout car he heard moaning and crying. He picked up the pace and called for a back up. Looking inside the door, Roger drew his weapon and proceeded with caution.

At trial, when I showed the jury the photographs taken that morning of Mrs Weaver, several jurors screamed, "Oh my God." They were so distraught that the court gave them a short recess to compose themselves. Mrs. Weaver's face was a deep crimson color from internal bruising. Four bones in her face were broken, as were two in her arm, and one in her leg. She had five broken ribs. After extensive physical therapy, she was mobile only with the aid of a walker. She suffered a stroke during the traumatic event. The jurors placed their heads in their hands as the elderly widow bravely recounted the final indignity visited upon her by her assailants. Forensic testing confirmed the presence of semen in her anal canal.

The pillaging of Mrs. Weaver's residence did not satisfy the appetite of her intruders. They struck again several days later. This time a neighbor called the police, who nabbed the young thugs. Fortunately, the elderly occupant was unharmed. Without the slightest contrition, they boastfully admitted breaking into Mrs. Weaver's house, but had the audacity to claim that the sex was by consent. They told the detectives that they were unconcerned about the consequences. These were juvenile offenders.

Before turning to the epilogue, let me tell you the most disturbing part of the Weaver case. Could there be more?

The day after Mrs. Weaver was discovered by Officer Estes, detectives canvassed her neighborhood to determine if anyone had seen anything suspicious. They interviewed a neighbor with a window facing the rear of Mrs. Weaver's home. Yes, she heard the glass breaking, and watched the two punks kick Mrs. Weaver's rear door open. When questioned, she indignantly dismissed the suggestion that she had any obligation to help protect her elderly neighbor; she said she "was too busy to get involved," and didn't "have time to go to court."

In the months that followed, as I traveled around Arlington County encouraging the formation of Neighborhood Watch programs, this incident, more than any other, captured the essence of our message. Neighbors *should* do unto others as they would have their neighbors do unto them.

## Trying Kids as Adults

Appearing in juvenile court to set a date for a transfer hearing for the two young men accused of breaking into Mrs. Weaver's home turned out to be one of my most memorable moments as a lawyer. The courtroom was packed with juvenile probation officers and court staff. The law did not permit the general public to be present at a juvenile hearing. At first I thought the crowd was gathered to see what type of thugs would committed such a dastardly crime. I was wrong.

The crowd in the gallery was assembled to watch me get my tail chewed by the court for suggesting that these two "kids" be tried as adults. The judge, who I thought was a friend, derided my judgment and scathingly exhorted me that no adult court would send sixteen-year-old "children" to the penitentiary. Emboldened by the encouragement of defense counsel, the judge reprimanded me for a good ten minutes, insinuating that my judgment was flawed. My extremist hard-nosed policies were out of step with these smart folks who, after all, knew what was best for these kids.

I was at a loss for words, but I refused to back down. The judge was reluctant to even hold the young men in the juvenile detention facility pending a transfer hearing—the proceeding at which the court would decide whether they'd be tried as adults.

However, things went a little better at the transfer hearing several weeks later. Although the judge was less than cordial, after hearing the evidence, he was not openly hostile. With minimal argument from the prosecution, he found probable cause that a crime had been committed and that the two young men charged were the perpetrators.

The next legal hurdle was convincing the court that these juveniles were too incorrigible to be rehabilitated by the juvenile court system. To my surprise, the juvenile probation officer who prepared the transfer evaluation recommended that the case be sent to adult court. Without comment, the judge certified the case to circuit court. There, the two would be treated like any other adult offender. Before this case, with few notable exceptions, juveniles convicted of committing serious violent crimes—even those with substantial prior records—were sent to a state facility until their twenty-first birthday.

Once a case reached circuit court, the only procedural difference between a certified juvenile and an adult defendant was sentencing. Virginia has a unique system of sentencing defendants in criminal cases tried before a jury. Ordinarily, the jury both determines the guilt or innocence of the accused and fixes the punishment. The judge then has the discretion to reduce, but not increase, the sentence. Until 1994, the prosecution was not permitted to even mention the defendant's prior record to the jury. Consequently, all defendants with lengthy rap sheets went to trial with a jury to avoid being held accountable for their prior record. When a defendant pled guilty or was tried by a judge after waiving the right to be tried by a jury, the judge could consider the defendant's criminal record. A hybrid procedure was used in the case of juveniles.

In the case of a juvenile certified for trial as an adult, the jury's role was solely to determine guilt or innocence. Because of the multitude of sentencing options available to the court, such juvenile offenders are sentenced by the presiding judge rather than the jury.

In another unfortunate quirk of Virginia law, each defendant in a criminal case is entitled to a separate trial. That meant that poor Mrs. Weaver had to tell the story to twelve strangers twice. It must have been unpleasant, but she never expressed the slightest reluctance. She was a tough lady of firm resolution. The juries returned verdicts of guilty in each case after less than an hour of deliberation. Judge Charles S. Russell, who had a reputation for handing out stiff sentences, ordered a thorough background investigation on each defendant before sentencing. Despite their young age, both defendants had a prior history of significant misbehavior. And of course, the fact that they had been apprehended attempting to break into yet another house didn't help!

The defendants' attorneys presented elaborate plans at sentencing. They suggested to the court that their clients be confined in a juvenile facility for a few years and then placed on an extended period of probation. Judge Russell listened patiently, rejected the lawyer's arguments, and sentenced each defendant to life in prison. Under Virginia law in effect at the time, they would be eligible for parole after serving fifteen years. The sentences sent a strong message to the juvenile court.

On another front, the police chief and I submitted a ten-point plan to the Arlington County School Board to aid in the reduction of juvenile crime. Several elements of the plan were controversial. First, we recommended that all students be required to remain on campus during lunch and study hall. We presented detailed statistics on the number of burglaries and delinquent acts committed by students supposedly "in school." Undercover officers periodically wandered through school parking lots taking note of activity ranging from drug use to sexual intercourse. Not all students, or even a majority, engaged in such behavior, but enough to raise a red flag. About twenty-five percent of all daytime burglaries at that time were being committed by juveniles during school hours.

Local newspapers strongly endorsed the proposal. The school board slowly succumbed to pressure and adopted a diluted version. Surprisingly, many parents complained bitterly. One couple confronted me at a school function. They prefaced their comments by saying that they had voted for me in 1979, but never again. My closed campus policy unreasonably interfered with their daughter's freedom. After all, they explained, she was sixteen years old and could make decisions on her own. I smiled and replied that their daughter was obviously far more mature than I had been at sixteen.

Another aspect of the ten-point plan involved school discipline. Chief Stover and I learned that some school administrators were discouraging teachers from taking students who committed crimes on school property to court, even when the crime included physical assault on a teacher. The administrators did not want the adverse publicity, and the accompanying perception that there was a disciplinary problem at their school. I publicly announced that I would accompany any teacher to a meeting with the school principal if necessary to insure the prosecution of a truly disruptive student. The teachers union, which generally disfavored anything proposed by a Republican, rallied to my support.

To the delight of rank-and-file educators, Stover and I also proposed that students who posed chronic disciplinary problems be expelled from the school system. The school board initially rejected this idea, but over time they were persuaded that a handful of bad actors was causing ninety percent of the problems. Today, Arlington County has no hesitation in expelling students who continually disrupt classes or engage in serious misconduct.

In the early spring of my first year in office, I called a meeting to plan the semiannual Hookers fishing trip to the Outer Banks of North Carolina. During the meeting Steve Kincheloe, a detective, told me he had just been assigned the most bizarre case of his career. We needed to talk as soon as possible.

## An Unsavory Crime

The next morning Kincheloe told me that a young soldier assigned to Fort Myer had supposedly been castrated by three bikers at a local bar. According to the soldier's story, he had gotten into a heated argument with one of bikers. The bar was located on North Pershing Drive, about a half mile from the front gate of the military base. When the soldier left the bar, the bikers jumped him in the parking lot, dragged him to a secluded spot, removed his trousers, and severed his testicles. He was discovered by a military police officer inside the fence of Fort Myer. After he explained what had happened, he was taken directly to the base hospital for surgery.

Based on the physical description of the soldier's assailants, the military officer, accompanied by an Arlington patrolman, went to the bar and arrested three bikers who fit the description. Despite their strident protests of innocence, the magistrate issued warrants for the bikers for malicious wounding. No one had conducted any investigation or asked any tough questions before Kincheloe got the case. They had taken the soldier's story at face value, assuming that no one could have concocted such a horrific tale.

I personally handled the bikers' initial court appearance that morning. Their unsavory, heavily tattooed appearance alone would have been enough to convict them in front of any jury. They looked the part. After hearing the facts, the judge ordered them held without bond and set a date for preliminary hearing.

One of the most difficult tasks facing a detective or prosecutor is confronting the victim of a crime of this type with inconsistencies—things that don't add up—about a story. But it had to be done in this case. The bikers adamantly denied any confrontation with the soldier, much less cutting his testicles off. Such denials, of course, are not uncommon in criminal cases; in this case, however, the bartender confirmed their story. The bikers neither left the bar nor got involved in any altercation that evening. That was just the beginning of the inconsistencies.

Why did the supposed encounter take place in the rear parking lot? The soldier claimed he was on foot. He had no reason to walk to the rear lot, a distance of about fifty feet. The front sidewalk led directly to the military base. How could he possibly have walked back to the base bleeding profusely and in excruciating pain? Why was there no blood on the parking lot pavement, or on the sidewalk leading to the base? Where were the blood stains on the bikers' pocket knives, sheaths, or clothing? The guy had lost at least a pint of blood. No one had heard him scream. Why had he walked a mile to Fort Myer before calling the police? His story didn't wash.

Before reinterviewing the victim, I decided to have each of the defendants polygraphed. Without hesitation, the bikers jumped at the opportunity. The reliability of a polygraph examination depends on the competence of the operator. Detective Clyde Wolfe of the Arlington County Police was one of the best. He ran all three defendants and found no indication of deception. In his opinion, these guys were innocent.

Within an hour of the polygraph exam, Kincheloe and I were sitting in a barracks at Fort Myer listening to the soldier recount his story. Some parts had changed, but nothing important. I asked him how he got back to the base. He said he had walked, as best as he could recall. Why no blood? He said he didn't start bleeding "real bad" until he got back to the base. What?

Why were pieces of tissue from his severed testicles on the ground in a puddle of blood inside the base? No response. I asked if he wanted to change his story. He said he had nothing further to say.

I asked if he wanted to proceed with the case. He said he didn't really care. I told him that we didn't believe his story, and unless I got a satisfactory explanation for the discrepancies, I was dismissing the case. He stood up and walked out without saying another word. We never heard from him again.

That evening, Kincheloe and I took the necessary paperwork to the home of the general district court judge. All three bikers walked free out of the Arlington County Jail at 10:00 p.m. All charges were dismissed. Kincheloe and I were there to offer our apologies. The men were effusively appreciative. But what really happened that night?

Incensed that the soldier had lied, the military police stayed on the case. No one else was ever charged, mainly because the soldier would never come clean. According to military investigators, the soldier had been warned by a senior sergeant to stay away from his young daughter. When the soldier failed to heed the warning, the father took the matter into his own hands, so to speak.

## Stella Mae Harris

From time to time I have been taken to task by the media, liberal members of the public, or some criminal defense lawyers for wasting resources prosecuting prostitution cases. Of course, many of the lawyers fomenting this criticism specialize in representing people connected to this sordid industry. The business is not as tame as some naive commentators suggest. It is highly profitable and represents the quintessence of organized crime. Most women affiliated with massage parlors or outcall services are truly independent contractors who are handsomely compensated. The other, tougher and less glamorous, side of the business is the women who work the street. Many of these women are drug addicts or runaway teenagers enslaved to a pimp. Discipline is strict. Take the case of Stella Mae Harris.

It was shortly after noon when police units responded to the Arna Valley Apartment complex in South Arlington for "gunshots fired." Officers discovered a new pink Cadillac with Alabama license plates with the rear window shot out. A lone witness, who had been too startled to take note of many details, reported that a sharply dressed black woman in a wide-brimmed hat had walked out of an apartment building escorting three white women. As they approached the pink Cadillac, two black males leaped out of a black Cadillac and opened fire with a sawed-off shotgun. The black woman, with the finesse of a western gunslinger, whipped out a long-barreled pistol and returned fire.

Within minutes, the first officer at the scene broadcast a lookout for the black Cadillac. It was easy to spot, with two bullet holes in the hood and a cracked windshield. The occupants were placed under arrest for possession of a sawed-off shotgun. The driver of the car was a well-known pimp from Georgia named "Froggy" Bonneville. Unfortunately, the magistrate set his bond at only a hundred thousand dollars, which he immediately posted. As far as I know, neither Froggy nor his partner has ever been seen again in Virginia.

Officers at the scene of the shooting eventually located the black woman, Stella Mae Harris, and her "girls." Ms. Harris was attractive, about forty years old, with a taste for expensive clothing. She also had a rap sheet five pages long with numerous felony convictions, including murder. She declined to make a statement to the investigating officers and was eventually taken into custody for attempted malicious wounding—shooting at Froggy Bonneville. The officers also interviewed the girls. The two older women told the officers to "pound sand," but the younger one, Lori Lane (that's the name she gave us), was extremely cooperative.

Lori had just turned eighteen and was essentially homeless. Harris had picked her up at a bus station in Georgia where she was "turning tricks" for Froggy. To escape Bonneville's physical abuse, Lori decided to go to work for Harris, who was also a master whore-handler. The crew fled the Atlanta area to avoid Bonneville's enforcers. Obviously a mercenary at heart, Lori maintained telephone contact with Froggy. Apparently that is how he knew their location in Arlington County. When Lori agreed to testify against Harris, the police located a place for her to stay and provided her with a little walking-around money.

We tried to negotiate some type of plea, but it was a hard sell. Harris had almost as much experience with the criminal justice system as the lawyers. Her strategy was obvious on the morning of trial. Our star witness, Lori Lane, was nowhere to be found. I tried the case with the physical evidence recovered at the scene and our only witness, who was conspicuously memory challenged. We were able ballistically to link an expended round of ammunition found on the ground under the pink Cadillac to the revolver seized from Stella Mae Harris. The forgetful witness could not identify Harris, and of course that was the centerpiece of her defense. The jury deliberated almost a full day, but couldn't reach a verdict. Judge Charles H. Duff declared a mistrial and scheduled the case for retrial in three weeks.

The case was not a big deal until Lori Lane mysteriously disappeared. That upped the ante substantially. Since Harris was a previously convicted felon in possession of a firearm, a federal crime, I brought in an agent of the Bureau of Alcohol, Tobacco and Firearms, Darryl Dubose, to assist. The first order of business was to locate Lori Lane. We circulated her photograph to Washington, D.C., vice detectives working the third district (3D), also known as the red light zone. Sure enough, she had been spotted several times over the preceding week, working the streets.

Dubose and I spent two successive evenings combing the Fourteenth Street corridor looking for Lane. There were lots of people on the street, the epicenter of the prostitution market, looking for love, but no Lori Lane. Aside from the two 3D vice detectives, Agent Dubose and I were the only white guys on the street in the roughest area of D.C. Even though we were all armed, the climate was unsettling. The vice detectives were a little rough around the edges. They took us into a gangster bar in search of a pimp who, they felt, might be able to help us. When a patron on a bar stool was less than cooperative, one of the detectives knocked him onto the floor and poured a draft beer in his face. These guys meant business. As they walked through the packed bar, rogues stepped aside and let them pass. Still, we could not find Lori Lane.

*Stella Mae Harris and her gang. At right is Lori Lane.*

The following afternoon I got a call from 3D vice. They had located Lori Lane in the D.C. lockup, busted on prostitution and drug charges. With one week to go before the retrial of Harris. Dubose and I decided to go back out to the scene and "shake the bushes" for additional witnesses. Luckily, we found a man who had some recollection of the incident, and we subpoenaed him for the trial.

On the morning of trial, Stella Mae Harris arrived in her classy clothes and wide-brimmed hat exuding confidence. Lori Lane was not present. She had been arrested the preceding evening in Washington, D.C. for oral sodomy and was back in the D.C. jail. The guys from 3D vice offered to get her out, but it would take an hour or two to process the paperwork. When Harris's case was called, I asked Judge Duff for a two-hour postponement to allow me and Detective Butch Gressley to go to D.C. to take custody of Lane. Despite howls of protest from defense counsel, the judge granted the request, provided that we select the jury before I left.

I returned from D.C. with Lane, and the trial resumed at noon. After brief opening statements, I called the prosecution's first witness, Lori Lane. She took the oath and promptly assumed a seat on the witness stand. The flow of questions proceeded smoothly until I asked her about the shooting incident. Then, with well-rehearsed crispness, Lane declined to testify further on the grounds that it might incriminate her. Harris and her lawyer smiled, knowing that our case was headed drown the drain.

I asked Judge Duff for permission to introduce Lane's earlier statement to the police as evidence, since she was now legally unavailable as a witness. The judge took a brief recess to read the cases I had cited, but returned and denied my request. Her attorney boldly inquired if we were dropping charges at this point. I decided to continue.

I put the crime scene investigators on the stand, along with the eyewitness we had used in the first trial, and the forensic scientist, to connect the shell to Harris's gun. Finally, I called our final witness, the one Dubose and I had located the preceding week, a gentleman in his mid-sixties with neatly trimmed white hair. However, that was not his most distinguishing feature.

What stood out was the white collar. Father Lewis had been visiting a sick member of his parish the day of the shooting. He pulled alongside the pink Cadillac and asked for directions. He was stunned by the sound of gunfire as he spoke to a fancy-dressed black woman. Was that woman in the courtroom, I asked? "Yes," he replied, as he pointed to Stella Mae Harris, who appeared startled.

My next question was, "What happened after that Father?" His answer was that she had whipped out a long-barreled pistol and ordered him to "get your ass out da way." The priest ducked his head as the woman fired three shots at the men in the black Cadillac. He then made a U-turn and headed out of Arna Valley. It was purely fortuitous that he had returned to see his parishioner the day

Dubose and I were canvassing the neighborhood for witnesses. He was preparing to leave her apartment just as we knocked. What a stroke of luck.

Anyway, Harris had a mild coronary and continually mumbled to her lawyer during Father Lewis's testimony. She was visibly upset; her strategy had been foiled. She put on no evidence. Her lawyer, stumbling for verbal traction, said little in final argument except to excoriate me for calling a secret witness. The jury was unimpressed. After an hour and a half of deliberations, the jury returned a verdict of guilty and set Stella Mae Harris's sentence at four years. And what happened to the faithless Lori Lane?

As the jury filed out of the courtroom to begin its deliberations, Lane stood up, stretched her arms, smiled at Detective Gressley seated next to her, and started walking toward the door. Gressley shouted, "Hey, where you going?"

"I'm leaving. You all didn't need me anyway," Lane responded.

As she reached the courtroom door, Gressley was two paces behind her. Waiting in the hallway were the two guys from 3D vice, handcuffs in hand.

"I thought we had a deal," Lane screamed.

"So did I," Gressley replied as the 3D detectives led her to the elevator in cuffs.

## EYEWITNESS IDENTIFICATION

In November, Tara and I purchased a small cottage on the sprawling Piankatank River in Gloucester, Virginia, about three hours from Arlington. The house was small with just two bedrooms, but it had a huge stone fireplace and a large picture window overlooking the river. We began hanging out down there on weekends with friends and family. Fishing was fair, crabbing was incredible. We once caught seventy-five crabs in three crab pots in less than five hours. We had a pier that extended about fifty feet out into the river. I could hunt ducks on a small point about a hundred yards from the house.

One three-day weekend, I brought the Hookers down to catch perch and croakers. The fishing was so good we decided to stay an extra day. About 4:00 p.m., as we were packing up to leave, the phone rang. It was one of my assistants calling to report the results of a highly publicized attempted rape case that had been tried that day.

The attorney prosecuting the case was one of the best. Her voice was charged with emotion. She began by saying that she had three things to tell me. First, the jury found the defendant not guilty. Second, the victim was livid and had blasted her in the press, so I better brace for the fallout. And third, did I remember the pint of Jack Daniel's in the cabinet?—well, she and the paralegal "drank it."

As disappointing as the outcome was, it showed how hard it was to prosecute sexual assault cases before the advent of DNA testing. Actually, DNA testing would not have saved this prosecution, assuming that the defendant was in fact guilty, because there were no bodily fluids for comparison. Many jurors are reluctant to convict someone of a felony and lock him up for decades solely on the strength of a single eyewitness identification. This is particularly true where the encounter was momentary.

In my twenty years as a prosecutor, I convicted at least fifty defendants of assault, rape, or robbery based only on eyewitness identification. The police would develop a suspect based on other similar crimes that the person had been involved in, or perhaps on a tip from an informant. The detective would put the suspect's photo in a group of five or six others, in what is known as a photo spread. The spread would be presented to the victim for identification. If the suspect was selected, the detective would press charges.

Eyewitness identification applies fundamental principles of human psychology and basic logic. When victims focus on the face of someone who has perpetrated a traumatic act of violence against them, it causes them to mentally relive the incident. The image of a perpetrator is indelibly etched in the mind, and is recalled by the one-on-one courtroom confrontation. The victim's initial opportunity to observe the assailant may have been short, but for most, it was the most traumatic few minutes of their life.

The argument played well with a jury. I never had an acquittal in a case turning solely on victim eyewitness identification. In retrospect, do I believe that eyewitness identification is always reliable? I am not sure. In large measure, it depends on the circumstances of the encounter and the victim's opportunity to carefully observe the defendant. The critical element is the perceptiveness of the witness, which the jury has no way to gauge.

Today, as a trial judge, I am increasingly skeptical of uncorroborated eyewitness identification, especially when the defendant and victim are of different racial or ethnic groups. Recent studies by research psychologists confirm that stand-alone eyewitness identification is marginally reliable. DNA testing has proven a good number of uncorroborated eyewitness identifications to be in error. Such evidence should be weighed with care and caution, especially in the absence of other corroborating testimony.

## A Lone Republican

In the years following my election, I continued to be active in Republican politics. As the only Republican commonwealth's attorney north of Richmond, and one of only three in the entire state, I found myself in demand as a public speaker. Party officials began circulating rumors that I was being groomed for statewide office. Since my political base in Arlington County was predominantly Democratic, I was very careful about getting involved in other local political campaigns. I enjoyed an excellent relationship with Democratic officeholders and never spoke critically of them in public. They adopted a similar policy with me, which paid handsome dividends at election time.

While I kept an arm's length from many local campaigns, I took a front-line role in two campaigns of monumental significance: Ronald Reagan's campaign for president of the United States and my good friend Frank Wolf's quest for Congress. Both of them won, but I caught unmerciful flak from my Democratic supporters for aligning myself with Wolf. After three tries, he ousted the incumbent Democratic congressman. Frank and I developed a very close relationship as the years passed.

## 'Escort Services'

During the early months of 1981, my political honeymoon with the media took a downward turn. Although we had successfully rid the county of fixed-based massage parlors, D.C.-based out-call services were proliferating. To clean up their image, they held themselves out as "escort services." The vice section of the police department was receiving weekly complaints from motel managers and security officers that hookers were hanging out on their premises. So the police began using undercover officers to arrange for women to provide services in Virginia. After they agreed to perform sexual acts, they were arrested for prostitution. The owners and operators of the escort services, and their lawyers, raised hell. It ignited a firestorm of adverse publicity, including blistering editorials.

We employed the same strategy as with the fixed-based parlors: Our goal was not to prosecute the masseuses, as the press was implying, but to get the operators. With the help of cooperating masseuses, we convicted several of the big players. Despite a media-generated perception of public outrage, Arlington juries handed down convictions in every case and recommended stiff prison sentences. One case was particularly memorable.

One out-call operator, Dennis Sobin, also published a satirical and sexually oriented weekly newspaper. He dispensed the papers without charge in vending machines at subway stops and large shopping centers. Thanks to him, I had the opportunity to get acquainted with the general counsel and Virginia editor of the *Washington Post.*

In addition to publishing his weekly skin journal, Sobin began distributing a newspaper-like production dubbed the *Washington Pist.* The outward appearance of the publication was almost an exact replica of the *Post.* It was so confusingly similar that regular readers of the *Post* unwittingly grabbed the *Pist* from vending machines. Boy, were they in for a surprise. The *Washington Pist* was a crude and sexually explicit porno publication. My office and the Arlington County Police assisted the *Post* in getting these parodied publications off the street.

Sobin was indicted and tried for his involvment in the out-call business in Arlington County. He was basically a likeable chap, who insisted that his business was strictly an "escort service." Although he was a renowned porno publisher, he adamantly denied any knowledge that his employees were engaging in acts of prostitution. He insisted that he operated an aboveboard dating service and that his people had been warned in writing not to get sexually involved with their dates. Rest assured, each woman who testified against him was confronted with one of these transparent documents.

Sobin testified that the problems with his business were largely attributable to his wife's drug addiction problem. Surprisingly, she took the stand and testified in his defense. She said that her husband was a wonderful father and that he had taken great pride in the birth of their recent child. He had been with her during delivery and was thoughtful enough to take a photograph. On cross-examination, my assistant, Liam O'Grady, asked her if she had ever seen the photo. She admitted that she had not, but defensively insisted that she was there when it was taken.

O'Grady then produced one of Sobin's skin journals and asked her to take a look at the centerfold. She gasped as she gazed at a series of graphic shots of her during childbirth. She audibly muttered, "that son-of-a-bitch." O'Grady had no further questions. Sobin was convicted and fined ten thousand dollars by the jury.

Several years later when I ran for reelection, Sobin, then the publisher of a sexually oriented newspaper called "Free Spirit," ran an advertisement offering a free membership in a sex club to anyone who contributed a hundred dollars or more to my opponent's campaign. Sobin, who was running for the District of Columbia School Board, claimed that I was wasting taxpayers' money in pursuing victimless crimes, particularly those involving homosexuals. Of course, he never mentioned his own legal problems. My challenger had no knowledge of the ad. I publicly expressed sympathy for the adverse publicity he received.

It was true that Chief Stover and I had initiated a program using undercover tactical officers to remove men who hung out for extended periods in men's rest rooms. Only those caught accosting patrons, grabbing their crotch or peeping through cracks in stalls, were actually arrested. In one restroom in a county park, tactical officers discovered men hiding in the ceiling and watching other men relieve themselves. I met with members of the gay community who had expressed concern that homosexuals were being singled out for prosecution. After hearing the facts, they had no sympathy for those arrested and did not condone their behavior. As a result of this meeting, we maintained a constructive line of communication.

One morning in the early spring of 1982, I returned to the office after my daily swing through all the courts. The receptionist had an urgent message. From 8:00 a.m. to 5:00 p.m. each day, the reception area of my office was crowded with lawyers, citizens, and police officers waiting to see me. When Betty Eversberg shouted that I needed to call the White House immediately, lots of heads turned and I could hear the rumor mill grinding. I headed straight to my desk and called the number on the message slip.

X

# Hang 'Um High Henry

"I would be honored."

The opportunity to serve on the National Highway Safety Advisory Committee sounded exciting. But why had President Reagan chosen me, I asked? The lady from White House personnel told me that I had been recommended by Secretary of Transportation, Drew Lewis. They were looking for a state prosecutor with experience enforcing traffic laws. I certainly had that. And because it was a political appointment, solid Republican credentials were crucial.

## Tackling National Issues

The National Highway Safety Advisory Committee is composed of the Secretary of the Department of Transportation, the Federal Highway Administrator, the National Highway Traffic Safety Administrator and thirty-five members, all appointed by the president to a three-year term, with no Senate confirmation required. Its statutory mission is to advise the secretary of transportation and the National Highway Traffic Safety Administration, commonly called NHTSA (pronounced "knit-sa"), on the field of highway safety and related policy issues. Our mandate included making recommendations on projects and programs pertaining to the cause and prevention of traffic accidents.

The committee was an eclectic group. About a third of the members had some connection or background relevant to traffic safety. Several were former members of Congress. The others were wealthy and significant Republican campaign contributors. The members could be roughly divided into two *de facto* classes, workers and observers. Out of the thirty-five members, about eight workers performed the bulk of the work. The others attended the meetings and picked up the tab for lunch and cocktails. As a member of the working class, I had no problem with the division of responsibility.

During my tenure, the committee addressed two major issues: a national program to promote safety-belt use and a campaign to increase drunk-driving enforcement. I assisted in organizing and coordinating the latter project. The focus of our work was to enhance federal funding for state-of-the-art sobriety field-testing techniques and equipment. We also launched a national campaign to encourage judges and prosecutors to get tough on drunk drivers. We literally traveled the country conducting public hearings and promoting demonstration projects. The committee stayed in high-end hotels and ate in the finest restaurants in town. I enjoyed every minute of it. Frills aside, we made a real impact, particularly with respect to roadside field sobriety testing.

My appointment to the committee drew considerable press attention and bolstered my Republican credentials. I made many friends and cultivated a number of contacts that served me well in later years. One was Mike Johnson, the coroner of Ada County, Idaho. He and I would cross paths again with the U.S. Marshals Service at a deadly stand-off with a fugitive named Randy Weaver at Ruby Ridge, Idaho.

My initial appointment was for one year, to fill the unexpired term of a member who had resigned, followed by my reappointment to a full three-year term. My second term would be cut short by another assignment from the president, one less pleasant and far more controversial.

* * *

Apportioning my time between national and local responsibilities involved a delicate balance. Historically in Virginia, a person elected to a constitutional office, like mine, was pretty well assured of life-time tenure. Without a highly publicized scandal or chronic incompetence, knocking off an incumbent commonwealth's attorney was almost unheard of. All you had to do to keep your job was show up for work and not get indicted. Incumbent prosecutors seldom faced opposition. But I knew it would be different in my case.

I was a Republican floating in a sea of Democrats. Sixty-five percent of the Arlington voters were predisposed to support Democratic candidates, regardless of their position on the issues. Why? Because their mothers and dads had always voted for Democrats. Consequently, unlike most of the other constitutional officers, such as the sheriff, clerk of the court or commissioner of the revenue, I knew I had to prove myself everyday. For decades Democrats had occupied the Office of the Commonwealth's Attorney. There was no doubt they wanted it back. I knew they were coming after me in November 1983. But I was ready.

Almost immediately after being sworn in, I began raising a war chest of money to underwrite my reelection campaign. I also kept in touch with the voters by sending out a yearly newsletter entitled, *Your Commonwealth's Attorney*

*Reports* to each registered voter. A four-page puff piece, it highlighted the programs and accomplishments of the office, including an analysis of crime trends and crime resistance tips. I also visited every civic association in the county annually, and met with residents in high crime neighborhoods—something they had not been accustomed to, except maybe in an election year.

Our tough prosecution policy played well with the business community, which was tired of being robbed by D.C. heroin addicts. We tightened the screws on these cases by refusing ever to drop any firearms charges in exchange for pleas to robbery, as had been the practice. This had been an attractive bargaining chip, because each firearm charge carried a harsh mandatory sentence. We also had a policy of informing the jury in these cases that the defendant was a D.C. resident who had traveled into Arlington County to stick up a business. This policy fueled the flames of passion. Criminal defense lawyers screamed foul, but juries would invariably add a few years to the sentence.

## Abduction with Intent to Extort

My stature with the business sector also received a substantial boost from a kidnapping case I personally handled during my first year as commonwealth's attorney. The daughter of one of Arlington County's most prominent businessmen had been abducted at gun point in broad daylight and held for ransom. It took her crafty captor two tries before he succeeded.

John J. O'Grady, age thirty-three, chose his target carefully. Carol Lynn Drewer was the nineteen-year-old eye-catching daughter of Milton S. Drewer, Jr., the wealthy president of the First American Bank of Virginia. O'Grady meticulously studied Ms. Drewer's daily movements and focused on several narrow windows of time when she was most vulnerable. He made his first move on September 18, 1980.

That afternoon, O'Grady grabbed a young nursing student at gunpoint in Alexandria. He sexually assaulted her, blindfolded her, and forced her to drive, in her white nurse's uniform, to the Drewer's elegant home in North Arlington. There, he forced her at gunpoint to serve as a decoy to ensnare his prey. He coerced her to feign illness as he tried to flag down Carol Drewer's car. The ploy was almost successful. Drewer stopped momentarily, but when she noticed a gun in O'Grady's waistband, she became suspicious and took off.

Five days later, O'Grady struck again. At about 8:00 a.m., when Carol Drewer got out of her car in the parking lot of the Tysons Corner branch of her father's bank where she worked, O'Grady was waiting. Ordering her back into the car, he slid into the passenger's seat, gun in hand. He told her that if she followed his instructions she would not be hurt. He instructed her to put on sunglasses and a baseball cap, to drive to five separate branches of First American Bank, and to cash checks at the drive-up windows—twelve hundred dollars in all. O'Grady next directed her to a motel and took her into a room where he bound, gagged, and blindfolded her. As a gesture of kindness, he cut on the TV. Above the sound, Carol Drewer did manage to overhear one telephone conversation in which O'Grady whispered that everything was going fine. He left for about a half hour, presumably to ditch the car.

At about 3:30 p.m., O'Grady placed the first ransom call to Mr. Drewer's office at First American Bank headquarters. O'Grady identified himself as "Franklin," a member of a freedom group, and said that this was their third kidnaping. The demand for Carol's release was fifty thousand dollars in fifty and hundred dollar bills. Mr. Drewer was told that if he contacted the police, he would never see his daughter again. Drewer immediately contacted the bank's chief security officer, a former FBI Agent, who in turn notified the FBI.

Justifiably terrified, the Drewers insisted on following the kidnapper's instructions by leaving the money at the designated drop site without FBI surveillance. The FBI did, however, record the serial numbers of the bills before placing them in a brown bag. As evening approached, O'Grady directed Mr. Drewer through a maze of locations before reaching the ultimate drop site, a trash can in the parking lot of a bank on Leesburg Pike.

Three hours later, at about 10:45 p.m., Milton Drewer received a phone call at his home from his daughter. She had been released and was waiting at an all-night convenience store. She was recovered unharmed, at least physically, after fourteen hours in captivity. O'Grady had already ridden off into the sunset, but a swarm of Arlington police and FBI agents were hot on his trail.

Working around the clock, the FBI and the Arlington police tracked O'Grady to Dulles International Airport in the Northern Virginia suburbs. The most valuable lead was an anonymous tip that a nervous passenger had dropped a huge wad of large bills on the floor at the airport. This resulted in an FBI agent locating a United Airlines employee, who identified O'Grady as having purchased a ticket to San Francisco. He had used eighteen fifty dollar bills matching the recorded serial numbers of the ransom money. Agents also interviewed a baggage screener who had been working a security checkpoint when O'Grady passed through that morning. The screener had noticed one thing interesting about his bag: It contained several metal cylinders stuffed with hundred dollar bills.

The next break came several days later when a passenger identified O'Grady as the person sitting next to him on the San Francisco flight. The passenger's suspicion was aroused when O'Grady pulled out a handful of fifty and hundred dollar bills. The critical link, however, was an off-hand comment O'Grady made to his seatmate about the Fairmont Hotel in San Francisco.

Sure enough, a good looking woman in her early twenties picked O'Grady up and drove him to the upscale Fairmont Hotel. The plot thickened. Was this the real motive for the kidnaping? Was this the person Carol Drewer overheard O'Grady talking to? Later that afternoon, he was arrested in his fashionably appointed hotel room. Agents recovered thirty-three thousand dollars from a safe-deposit box in the hotel. Most of the bills matched the serial numbers of the ransom paid by Milton Drewer.

The FBI attempted to interview the young woman who met O'Grady and drove him to the hotel. She refused to talk, but her roommate confirmed that O'Grady had visited their apartment on at least one occasion.

Agents also discovered a new orange Corvette that O'Grady had rented in the parking lot at Dulles Airport. Inside, they discovered a .22-caliber revolver, similar to the one used in both abductions.

O'Grady was indicted by the grand jury in Arlington County for abduction with intent to extort money and using a firearm in the commission of a felony, and charged with abducting and sexually assaulting the nursing student in Alexandria. In addition, he was indicted by the feds for violating the Hobbs Act, which involves interfering with interstate commerce by extortion, bank robbery, and use of a firearm.

I devoted countless hours to preparing Carol Drewer for her anticipated trial testimony. She was an impressive and courageous young lady with deep emotional scarring. Luckily for her, at the last minute, the defendant pled guilty in Arlington, as he had in Alexandria and in United States District Court. He had no significant prior record, but Judge Winston still sentenced O'Grady to life. In Alexandria, he received life plus fifty-one years. The feds added another fifteen years on top of that. O'Grady expressed no emotion, contrition, or sympathy for his victims at any of the sentencing hearings. His apologies were directed solely to his family.

The Drewer family was most appreciative. Carol even invited me to her wedding. As for the nursing student, after O'Grady was sentenced in Alexandria, she told the *Washington Post,* "I'm just so happy. The ax has fallen and this is it."

## Another Election

A public official sometimes achieves miracles no one ever knows about because word never reaches the street. Therefore, I worked hard to develop a close relationship with the reporters covering the courthouse, giving them almost open door access and a heads up on significant cases and events. It paid dividends in the form of frequent and largely favorable coverage. My staff and the Arlington County Police became an awesome and effective crime fighting team.

When pressed, even hard-core Democrats had to acknowledge that the crime rate had dropped dramatically. One local newspaper carried an interview with a serial burglar convicted in a neighboring jurisdiction. He told the reporter that he stayed "the hell out of Arlington County; they'll put your ass in jail." The comment resonated well with the voters. As liberal as most Arlington voters were on social issues, they had no tolerance for burglars or dope dealers.

Over the years, numerous aspiring Republican politicians have asked me for the secret to my success with the Arlington voters. Several things founded on basic principles of psychology and common sense were central to my strategy.

First, and perhaps most important, I made a concerted effort to disarm the opposition with bipartisanship. Every time Democrats contacted our office for advice or assistance expecting a chilly reception, they received a prompt, friendly, courteous, and thorough response. They were astounded, particularly when I followed up with a personal phone call to ask if they had any further questions. We did the same for civic associations, teachers, and school administrators, all of whom historically supported only Democratic candidates. They loved the sterling service and prompt attention.

As election time approached, even Democrats who opposed me were hard pressed to find fault with our performance. The personal touch really blunted the political cutting edge.

This policy was not limited just to the politically powerful. Each day one of the lawyers on my staff was assigned to serve as the duty assistant. We did not provide general legal advice, but we responded to any question relating to the duties of our office or the enforcement of the law. I also assigned an assistant to serve as our liaison with the school system and with each investigative section of the police department. Helping citizens deal with criminal justice problems was part of being the "people's lawyer." No problem was too trivial.

### There's a Man in My Attic

My office received a call one afternoon from an elderly constituent. My fishing buddy Bruce Bartleson told her to call my office. The lady, who lived alone, called the police department at least once a week to report that there was a man living in her attic. After checking out her attic three times and finding nothing, Officer Bartleson, in desperation, told her to call the Office of the

Commonwealth's Attorney. He told the lady that we could advise her on what legal steps were necessary to "evict" the intruder.

The lady took Bartleson's advice and called our office. One of my assistants, Arthur Karp, a lean athletic bearded lawyer in his early sixties who had the patience of Job, was referred the call. After a few minutes, Karp realized that the lady's problem was more mental than legal. He confided in her that there was only one known solution to her problem—a bug bomb. Karp told her to go down to the grocery store and buy a large can of bug spray. Next, he instructed her to open the attic door and spray the entire can into the attic. He cautioned her not to reopen the attic door for one week.

A week later I was a little hesitant to take the lady's call and did not know what to expect. She was ecstatic. "That Mr. Karp, he's something." Her problem was solved; the man was gone. Only Officer Bruce Bartleson, and perhaps the police dispatcher who took her weekly calls, were happier.

Arlington County was a predominantly upper-middle-class community, with a significant population of retired people, many of whom were seeking an additional challenge and cared little about compensation. In time, I learned to capitalize on this valuable resource. We recruited a cadre of seniors to staff our victim/witness assistance program. Many of these volunteers devoted thirty hours a week to helping other citizens with their court-related questions.

Because seniors are among the most vulnerable to crime, we also developed a crime prevention and educational program geared to their age group. The program was conducted by the Crime Resistance Unit of the police department, with assistance from my staff, and focused on teaching seniors the early warning signs of the most common fraud schemes targeting them. This type of outreach broadly widened our community contacts.

Arlington County, as an immediate suburb of the District of Columbia, was also home to many prominent government leaders, including the chief justice of the United States. Chief Justice Warren Burger and his wife lived in a magnificent home on ten acres of land in North Arlington. Tara and I got to know the chief justice through my selection to assist him with the Anglo-American Exchange Program for judges and prominent lawyers. I had given my card to the chief justice and told him to call me if I could ever be of help. One Monday morning Mrs. Burger, a very graceful and courtly lady, called and told me that there was a "sheath" in her yard and she wanted to speak to a police officer immediately.

Several Arlington police units rolled up to her house moments later expecting to find a knife in her rear yard, which abutted a secluded cul-de-sac. After a brief search, the officers found the "sheath." It was a discarded condom.

As part of my political survival strategy, I also cultivated alliances with other elected officials. I was unquestionably the most controversial and perhaps the highest high-visibility public figure in Arlington. Consequently, I was in demand on the speaking circuit, giving two or three speeches a week. I'd always introduce any other elected officials in the crowd, Republican as well as Democrat, and comment on their fine work. A fraternal bond began to develop with most of my Democratic colleagues, especially with my friends Dave Bell, the clerk of the court, and Sheriff Jim Gondles. It really paid off. None of my fellow constitutional officers ever publicly uttered a derogatory comment about me, even at election time, or even endorsed my opponent. I, of course, extended the same courtesy to them.

The Eighth Congressional District of Virginia includes Arlington County, the City of Alexandria and a sliver of Fairfax County. It has been historically difficult for many aspiring Republican politicians, especially the more ideologically driven, to understand that you must neutralize key elements of the Democratic machine to win there. In other words, you must persuade them to stay on the sidelines or provide only tepid support for your Democratic opponent. It is an incontrovertible fact that no Republican in the Eighth District can survive a full-bore assault from the Democrats, because Republicans are outnumbered and outgunned. However, I confess that ten years later, while contemplating a run for Congress, I learned that this axiom is much easier to preach than practice.

In the run up to my reelection campaign, I was successful in neutralizing a number of Democratic heavy hitters, but a few key Democrats were still irked about my support of Frank Wolf for Congress. Others disliked my aggressive policies, particularly our requirement that all drug dealers and residential burglars serve time in jail. They felt that I lacked compassion for youthful offenders and wasted tax money prosecuting operators of outcall massage parlors and possessors of drugs for personal use, issues that had the political buoyancy of a bowling ball. In fact, I underestimated the depth of my detractors' ire—and how low they would go to get me out of office.

My sources reported that the Democrats were having a difficult time in the summer of 1983 recruiting someone to run against me. However, they were determined not to give me a free ride. Finally, Brendan Feely, an attorney I had worked with during Claude Hilton's era as commonwealth's attorney, was persuaded to run. Although not energetic, Feely was a fine lawyer and a true gentleman. The press characterized him as soft spoken and low keyed. He described me to the media as inappropriately zealous and uncompromising. He told the *Washington Post,* "[The county's top law enforcement job is] a position that requires someone with balanced judgment . . . Henry Hudson sees the world in black and white. He really has no sense of greys."

My campaign mantra was simple—My record speaks for itself. I replied to the *Post* that, "Our conviction rate is ninety percent. Our jail is so overcrowded we had to build a new one . . . [Our crime rate is the lowest it's been in a decade.] We must be doing something right."

Feely, who ran an aboveboard campaign, miscalculated the impact of his kinder, gentler approach to crime fighting on the historically liberal voters of Arlington County. The mainstream voter was liberal, but not naive. I loved to tell undecided voters that the question they had to ask themselves was: How much of a risk are you willing to take with your family's safety? I also enjoyed ending my stump speeches by telling the audience that their popular police chief, Smokey Stover, and I were an effective crime fighting team. If they had any doubt, stop any Arlington County Police Officer and ask them! A group of cops even had large campaign buttons made up that said "I voted for Hang 'Um High Henry."

In the months immediately preceding the election, the *Washington Post,* rarely friendly to Republicans, ran a detailed candidate comparison. They described me as one of the "toughest candidates to beat." People either loved me or hated me. They painted Brendan Feely as a good lawyer with progressive ideas on criminal justice. Absent a bombshell, his chances looked dim.

Feely was a man of integrity. He did not have the stomach for bare knuckles campaigning, so others tried to create an issue for him during the post Labor Day push.

I had just wrapped up the prosecution of a highly publicized manslaughter case. A prominent Arlington dentist, highly intoxicated and driving on the wrong side of a divided highway, struck a young employee of the *Washington Post* head-on. The young man was killed instantly. The trial was hard fought with numerous expert witnesses on both sides. The defendant claimed he was neither drunk nor the cause of the accident, despite being on the wrong side of the road. The jury found his mechanical failure defense unpersuasive. The preelection publicity did not go unnoticed by my Democratic archenemies, who were quietly laying in ambush.

Within days, I began the prosecution of one of the most vicious rapes ever tried in Arlington County. Again, the case dominated the headlines. Out of respect for the victim, whom I came to admire tremendously, I will not use her real name.

### 'JENNIFER WARD'

There was already almost three inches of snow on the ground at 9:00 p.m. when "Jennifer Ward," an attractive thirty-year-old registered nurse, walked from her River House apartment to the parking lot of the complex. The River House is located within sight of the Potomac River, in South Arlington. Although she lived only a few miles from Georgetown University Hospital, where she worked, in Washington D.C., she would take no chances on such an inclement night. As a supervisory nurse, it was her routine to arrive early for her midnight shift. Ms. Ward patiently let her engine warm up before cutting on her defroster to clear the icy windshield.

Moments later someone knocked on her window. She lowered the window of her Subaru station wagon about three inches and confronted Stanley Hunt. Hunt asked for directions to the District of Columbia. Another man, Gregory Church, stood behind him. Seconds into her directions, Hunt whipped out a handgun and said, "Good, you're going to take us there." The two men jumped into her car and, with the gun pointed at her head, instructed her to drive across the Fourteenth Street Bridge into D.C. As they drove, Church rifled through her purse and demanded money. Ward told them to take the fifteen dollars, but just get out and leave her alone. That wasn't all they wanted.

With the revolver still pointed at her head, Hunt directed Jennifer to stop the car on a side street in Northeast Washington. She was terrified and in a complete state of "shock and horror." She was next instructed to pull into the parking lot of an apartment complex. Her heart almost stopped when they pulled her into the back seat. A daunting crowd began to form around the car. Despite her sobbing and begging, they ordered her to undress as men stared into the car, cheering her captors on. She was then forced to have sex with Hunt and Church as the crowd stuck their faces against the window. When the humiliating experience was over, she took a deep breath and sighed, thinking that now they had what they wanted, they'd let her go. It was, tragically, just the beginning.

Pressing a knife against her neck, Hunt and Church ordered Ward to continue driving, but not in the direction of Virginia. Her hands shook so that she could hardly control the car. It took all her strength to hold herself together emotionally. Suddenly, she stalled in traffic and a D.C. police car pulled alongside to assist. She could feel the blade of the knife in her chest. Hunt rolled down the window and told the officers everything was fine. Despite the terrified look on Jennifer's face, the officers sped off.

Hunt and Church next directed her to the Mayfair Apartment complex, a public housing project in the 3800 block of Jay Street, Northeast, one of the roughest neighborhoods in D.C. As a standard practice, no single cop would even get out of the patrol car in that area without backup units.

With a tight grip on her hair and the revolver pressed against her back, the two escorted Ms. Ward through a courtyard into a dark dungeon-like basement with no lights. She was so terrified her legs buckled, and they had to drag her the last few yards.

Jennifer Ward could see matches flickering, and then somebody lit a few candles. They illuminated faces and reflected off teeth. Why were a dozen or so men waiting inside? The air reeked with the smell of alcohol. Again, she pled with her captors, and her body shook from the overpowering terror. Over the next several hours, she was forced to repeatedly engage in oral, anal, and vaginal sex with an incalculable number of men, often with two at a time. Finally three

*The basement in Southeast Washington, DC where "Jennifer Ward" was taken by her captors and viciously raped.*

hours later, they dropped her off at the Deanwood Metro Station. She took the subway back to Arlington and called the Arlington County Police.

While the images of her attackers were still emblazoned in her mind, detectives had a sketch artist prepare a diagram of the kidnappers. A wanted poster was circulated to all Washington area law enforcement agencies within days. Six weeks later, on March 10, an alert Metro transit officer observed Gregory Church, whom he recognized from the wanted poster, walking near a Metro stop. Church was conspicuously intoxicated and the officer placed him under arrest. Several hours later, Church was taken to the D.C. Police Detective Bureau for questioning. Nine hours after his arrest, Church admitted having raped and abducted Jennifer Ward.

Because the initial abduction occurred in Arlington County, the Arlington Police launched an intensive parallel, but well-coordinated, investigation. Although the D.C. Police claimed to have thoroughly processed the crime scene, that was not good enough for Corporal Cindy Wessen, one of Arlington's best crime scene investigators. As a dedicated officer, Wessen was obviously motivated by a desire to crack the case, but as a woman, she was outraged. The morning after the incident, Wessen scoured every inch of the basement and found assorted items, such as match books and torn paper, not seized by D.C. officers.

With Wessen's assistance, fingerprint examiner Deborah Davis lifted several latent prints, and eventually connected some to the known fingerprints of Hunt. Another forensic scientist identified one of Hunt's hairs in the victim's socks. In addition to Church and Hunt, a number of other thugs were eventually identified and taken into custody. Church and Hunt were indicted in Arlington County for abduction, robbery, conspiracy to commit rape, and use of a firearm in the commission of a felony. Church tried to convince the court to throw out his confession, claiming that he was too high on PCP and vodka to understand his rights. The court was not persuaded.

Despite the confession, both Church and Hunt insisted on going to trial. The other assailants were indicted and tried in D.C. The only issue in Church's trial was his contention that he and Hunt had not conspired, or formed any type of agreement, to rob or rape Ms. Ward in Virginia. He claimed that they made that decision in the District of Columbia, divesting the Virginia courts of jurisdiction over the most serious offense. Why was that important? The D.C. courts are notoriously lenient, and Church's chance of beating the charges in front of a D.C. jury was significantly higher than in Virginia.

Unlike most other jurisdictions, under Virginia law, each criminal defendant has a right to a separate trial. I set them two weeks apart, in late September.

Detective Robin Jones and I spent countless hours preparing Jennifer Ward to testify, and developed a close working relationship with her. She was a petite lady, charming and dignified, with at times a reserved and formal demeanor. She was articulate and well-educated, with a master's degree in nursing. But she was tough and fearless, perhaps the most resolute witness I ever called to the stand.

We tried and convicted Church, age twenty-seven, first. He was on both probation and parole at the time the crime was committed. The jury sentenced him to seventy-one years. The most powerful and emotionally laden moment occurred during the codefendant's trial. The defense lawyer was cross-examining Ward on her ability to identify her assailants in the poorly lit basement. Patience thinning, Ms. Ward interrupted and cut his question short. She explained that it might be something he could not comprehend, but at the time, she was determined to look him (pointing to his client) straight in eye—because she wanted to see what type of person would subject a woman to the unforgettable humiliation of ejaculating in her face—while holding a knife to her throat. Not much more needed to be said. The jury convicted Hunt of all counts and sentenced him to fifty-five years in prison.

Even though Jennifer Ward was a courageous lady of impressive constitution, the prospect of telling her story multiple times was unnerving. She confided this frustration to a friend. Somehow, perhaps misconstrued, it was conveyed to a Democratic member of the Arlington County board of supervisors, one who held me in low regard. In the middle of the second trial, the board member contacted the chief of police and demanded a meeting with Ms. Ward. The board member told the chief that she had been notified by a concerned citizen that a rape victim was being mistreated by the commonwealth's attorney and that a delegation, composed of course of all Democrats, needed to meet with her immediately. Detective Jones, as instructed, set up the meeting. We learned later that the press corps had been alerted that a public statement could follow that afternoon.

I was in a state of total shock and was noticeably distracted in court. Although I suspected that the meeting was politically motivated, I decided to avoid any contact with Ms. Ward that morning, to avoid even the appearance of tampering. If she had any complaints, she had never voiced them to me or to Detective Jones.

The meeting with the "delegation" lasted about five minutes. Jennifer Ward, who knew me well enough to know that I was in the midst of a reelection campaign, instantly smelled a rat. She advised them that she was fine, and then politely told them to go screw-off. The delegation quietly retreated without further comment.

The balance of the campaign was uneventful. I was reelected by fifty-five percent of the vote. Despite weak opposition and a lackluster campaign, the margin was closer than four years previously, by several thousand votes. It occurred to me that maybe my luck was running out.

* * *

Ever had an irrepressible urge for a cold beer? I did during the early morning hours of August 20, 1984. I'd been hanging around the hospital for almost twenty-four hours. The temperature outside was hovering at a hundred degrees. Just before 3:00 a.m., I seriously entertained the vagrant thought of slipping out for a burger and a cold one. Then reality hit me: my mother-in-law, seated next to me, would never let me live it down. If I had gone out, I would have missed one of the most exciting moments of my life, the birth of my son, Kevin.

## Using Science to Solve Cases

In 1984, the extensive use of forensic, or scientific, evidence to solve criminal cases was the new legal frontier. Although fingerprint comparisons and blood typing had been around for decades, the use of soil sample comparisons, glass fragment analyses, tool mark impressions, footprint examinations, and ballistics evidence was uncommon. It was expensive and labor intensive. Evidence of this type was reserved for the most extraordinary cases, such as bombings or serial killings.

My second in command in the Office of the Commonwealth's Attorney, Ken Melson, was an adjunct professor of forensic science at George Washington University and a well-known expert in the field. As deputy commonwealth's attorney, Ken reviewed each case to insure that the charges were provable before presenting an indictment to a grand jury. He was constantly on the lookout for new opportunities to use scientific evidence to enhance the quality of our courtroom presentations. It was about this time that the State of Virginia began to expand the depth of talent at the Bureau of Forensic Laboratories, which provided forensic examinations in criminal cases. The lab was able to recruit a number of former FBI agents who were nationally recognized in their fields.

In addition, the Arlington County Police sent a number of officers to specialized schools to learn how to gather evidence and preserve it properly for scientific analysis. These officers, called police agents, were paid at a higher level than those assigned to ordinary patrol functions and carried an array of crime scene processing gear in their vehicles.

In the initial stage, aside from fingerprint evidence, which was virtually unimpeachable, we primarily employed scientific evidence to corroborate other forms of proof, such as eyewitness identification or a composite of circumstances. As our skill in forensics progressed, we began to test its outer limits.

For example, I used blood type comparison evidence to link a sexual predator to an assault on a six year-old girl, which occurred in a large supermarket. The little girl wandered away from her mother, apparently in search of a restroom. She was seen by store employees talking to the defendant, who later claimed that he was merely showing her the way to the bathroom. He was later observed walking briskly from the restroom area minutes before the little girl bolted out of the door crying. She pointed to the defendant and told her mother that he had "pee-peed in my mouth."

The child was terrified, and embarrassed talking to a stranger. I spent hours with her, even attempting to recreate the incident with dolls. She wouldn't talk about it and her parents insisted that I not press further. It would have been a tough, even impossible, case to prosecute until I got the report from the forensic laboratory.

Right after the defendant's arrest, I obtained a court order requiring the defendant to furnish a sample of his blood for serological comparison. A serologist with the state lab compared his blood type, AB positive, to the traces of semen found on a piece of chewing gum that had been in the victim's mouth at the time of the assault. The result was a match. It was not smoking gun evidence. But in concert with the other circumstances, it was enough to persuade the defendant to plead guilty to sexual assault, rather than face an outraged jury that would also set his sentence. More important, it spared the little girl, who was then receiving psychological therapy, from the trauma and embarrassment of testifying. Her parents were thrilled with the result.

Admittedly, most forensic evidence in the pre-DNA era had limited utility. The results are either consistent or inconsistent with a known fact, such as a pry mark on a door that microscopically matches the characteristics of a screwdriver found in the defendant's pocket. In isolation, a shard of glass or a drop of blood is merely another piece of circumstantial evidence. However, logically, the more layers of consistent forensic evidence the prosecution can offer, the stronger the case. Juries tend to accept scientific evidence as reliable and trustworthy, untainted by bias. It provides a level of comfort to lay jurors, who may be hesitant to convict someone of murder or rape based solely on circumstantial evidence. Joseph Francis O'Brien learned this the hard way.

# XI
# THE PATCHWORK QUILT

The phone just continued to ring when Murray Jacobson called his good friend and coworker Betty J. Konopka's house on the morning of June 6, 1984. He was concerned but not disturbed. Maybe she was still in the shower. They had the same routine each day. He'd call at 5:30 a.m. to wake her up. She'd unlock the front door. While she was dressing, Jacobson would let himself in and make a pot of coffee. They'd sit around drinking coffee for a while before heading into the office. But not that day.

When Jacobson arrived that morning at her small home on North Woodrow Street, to his surprise the front door was still locked. That had never happened before; maybe she had forgotten. He reached under the porch light and pulled out the hidden door key. Inside, the house was dark, so he turned on a lamp. Maybe she wasn't home. But why hadn't she called? He decided to take a quick look around.

He panicked when he found a window in the rear door broken and the door ajar. He repeatedly called her name. No answer. He paused to resolve a dilemma—call the police or walk through the house? His heart pounded. After several seconds of disoriented thought, he bounded up the stairs two at a time and found Betty Konopka in her bedroom.

Detective Chuck Shelton of the Arlington Coundy Police Department's Robbery/Homicide Unit arrived at Mrs. Konopka's house within minutes of the initial call. Other officers were in the process of securing the scene. Shelton was taken directly to the upstairs bedroom where he found the nude body of a middle-aged lady lying across the bed. The cause of Mrs. Konopka's death was obvious: nineteen stab wounds. Shelton's job was to determine who did it and why.

The latter question was answered fairly quickly. A citizen found a variety of credit cards and assorted identification bearing Betty Konopka's name strewn under a bush several blocks from her house. The documents appeared to have been tossed on the ground. No purse or wallet could be found anywhere in her house. At Shelton's request, the U.S. Army combed the neighborhood using search dogs in an attempt to locate Konopka's purse and keys. The results were disappointing.

On the surface, robbery appeared to be the motive, but Shelton remained skeptical. To a seasoned cop, this did not appear to be "a burglary gone bad." The crime scene had none of the characteristics of a typical burglary. The house had not been ransacked, no other valuables had been taken. It also had been Shelton's experience, as a former burglary investigator, that housebreakers usually hauled ass when confronted, to avoid physical contact with the occupants. The obvious exception was cases where the burglar intended to assault the occupant. But the question still hung in the air, why Betty Konopka?

Crime scene investigators, headed by Police Agent Ray Spivey, meticulously scoured Konopka's house for any particles or traces of evidence, such as hairs, fibers, or glass, that might provide a scientific clue. Several items recovered appeared to be of particular value. A hair was recovered from the blanket on Mrs. Konopka's bed. A piece of blue velcro fiber was found in the carpet in the victim's bedroom. Neither she, Jacobson, nor any member of her family owned shoes with blue velcro fasteners. All these items were sent to the state laboratory for examination by a forensic scientist.

*The rear door of Betty Konopka's home. Forensic analysis of glass fragments from a windowpane in the door sent her killer away for 50 years.*

In examining the shards of glass around the rear door, Agent Spivey identified a near pristine shoe print left on a large piece of broken glass. The impression was first captured on high resolution film and then submitted, along with all the other glass particles, for forensic testing.

Also significant to the investigators was the jagged edge of a piece of glass remaining in the broken pane. There was a high probability that the perpetrator had cut or scraped his arm or wrist when reaching inside to unlock the door, and that the wound had left traces of blood on the glass. It was also possible that clothing was torn in the process. As this case demonstrated, when it doubt, seize it as evidence.

The first break in the case came the following day. A man called the Arlington County Police to report that his son had just stolen the family car, with several firearms in the trunk. The man was concerned because his son had just been released from jail two days before—for burglary. And where did this man live? About one hundred sixty yards from Mrs Konopka. Shelton and his partner scrambled.

Within the hour, Shelton was sitting in the residence of Joseph Francis O'Brien talking to his parents. O'Brien's father was a former criminal investigator with the IRS and was fairly cooperative at first. He explained that their son had taken the family car on the morning of June 6, the day of Konopka's murder. Mr. O'Brien confided to Shelton that his son could be a suspect in their neighbor's murder. He explained that when his son arrived home at about 1:30 a.m. that morning, roughly a half hour after Mrs. Konopka had been killed, he was "covered with blood." Even more startling was their son's request to use the washing machine to wash his clothes—at 1:30 in the morning. They were surprised to learn that he even knew how to operate a washing machine!

Shelton sensed that he was on the right track, but to arrest Joe O'Brien for murder at that point would have been premature. There was lots of suspicion, but little hard evidence. So Shelton decided to obtain an arrest warrant for Joseph Francis O'Brien for auto theft only. This was a strategic move designed to enable him to arrest O'Brien and perhaps get an incriminating statement or comment. Even a false alibi would help animate an otherwise circumstantial case. But Shelton knew from a quick glance at O'Brien's rap sheet that he was dealing with a hardened criminal.

The next step was to locate O'Brien. Again, they sought help from his parents. Using the information they supplied, Shelton and his partner, Bob Carrig, called a few of Joe O'Brien's friends who lived in the area. One friend revealed that he had spoken to Joe O'Brien earlier that day, and expected him at his house later that afternoon. Shelton and Carrig staked the place out. In time, O'Brien showed up and was arrested. Under the front seat of the stolen family car, an officer found a loaded revolver. The parents, at that point, were relieved and appreciative. This attitude proved to be evanescent.

O'Brien was taken directly to the Arlington County Jail for booking. It was there that Shelton discovered one of the most incriminating pieces of evidence. When O'Brien was being fingerprinted, the detectives noticed deep incisions in his right arm, consistent with cuts from jagged glass. After the booking process, Shelton told O'Brien that they were going to take a few photographs of his arm. O'Brien had other ideas.

It took six police officers to restrain O'Brien while the photographs were being taken. One officer sustained a broken wrist in the process. It was worth it. The photos would form the basis of scintillating expert testimony at trial.

O'Brien told the detectives that he had cut his arm in a fight at Misty's Bar, located just across the Arlington line in Fairfax County. Later, he explained to a physician's assistant at the jail that he had either been stabbed with a bottle in a fight at Misty's or cut on a "pane of glass" in the parking lot. He couldn't recall which. However, Fairfax County Police who responded to the altercation at Misty's interviewed a number of witnesses. None saw O'Brien injured in the scuffle.

Before O'Brien was lodged into the jail, Shelton decided to seize his new Stadia athletic shoes. The detective knew a shoe print had been lifted near the rear door of the victim's house. O'Brien had purchased the shoes within hours of his release from jail—about eighteen hours before Konopka was killed. The shoes were sent to the state forensic laboratory for comparison with the print.

The next day, Shelton received a call from Officer Harry Foxwell of the Fairfax County Police Department, one of the officers who had responded to the fight at Misty's Bar. He vividly recalled having contact with O'Brien on the night of the homicide. Foxwell arrived at the bar, located in the Culmore area of Fairfax County, around midnight on June 5. Foxwell added that he immediately recognized O'Brien from a prior case. During an interview in the parking lot, O'Brien complained of being dizzy and told the officer that he had been struck in the head with a bottle.

Foxwell gave O'Brien a ride to a point just inside the Arlington County line. O'Brien was in his presence for about twenty minutes. Foxwell looked O'Brien over carefully before allowing him in his scout car. He saw no cuts or bruises on his arms. The officer last saw O'Brien at 12:38 a.m., walking in the direction of his home, located just down the street from Mrs. Konopka's. From the point where Foxwell dropped O'Brien off, Konopka's house was less than a half mile away.

O'Brien was eventually indicted for capital murder, robbery, and burglary with the intent to commit robbery. He pled not guilty and steadfastly maintained his innocence. I served him with formal notice of our intent to seek the death penalty. The trial was a slugfest. His very capable lawyer, John C. Youngs, did a magnificent job of tossing mounds of sand into the government's gears at every turn of the case.

As even the Virginia Court of Appeals later noted, the prosecution of Joseph Francis O'Brien was built solely on circumstantial evidence. Chuck Shelton and I were a little apprehensive that we might not be able to sell this multi-layered confection of scientific opinion and conflicting statements to a liberal leaning Arlington jury. Rather than roll the dice, with the concurrence of the Konopka family, I offered O'Brien the chance to plead to first degree murder and avoid the death penalty. Sensing the potential weakness of our case, he rejected the offer. Up to then, no one had ever been convicted of capital murder in Northern Virginia on the strength of scientific evidence alone.

As the trial date approached, we discovered a dynamite witness that we thought might tip the scales in favor of the death penalty. There are two stages in a capital murder trial. In the first, the jury hears the evidence pertaining to guilt or innocence. If the jury finds the defendant guilty of capital murder, the case progresses to the second, sentencing, stage where the jury decides whether to impose the death penalty. During the sentencing stage, the prosecution puts on evidence to prove the aggravated nature of the crime or the future dangerousness of the defendant. The defendant, on the other hand, has the opportunity to put on evidence in mitigation. The jury then sorts it out and determines the fate of the accused.

The witness we stumbled on was a correctional officer at a Virginia prison work camp where O'Brien had previously served time. The witness told us that one Friday afternoon while he was on vacation, he stopped at the prison camp to pick up his paycheck. Because he was running errands that day, his severely retarded eight-year-old son was with him. As he walked through the entry gate with his son, O'Brien, who was working in the yard, threw a soda bottle and struck the son in the head. O'Brien thought it was hilarious. The little boy was rushed to the hospital, where several stitches were required to close the wound. We hoped this would help sway the Arlington jury. After all, the case was about a guy who stabbed a defenseless lady nineteen times on the very day he was released from jail after serving a year on a burglary charge.

The option of imposing the death penalty always adds a complicating layer, known as "death qualification," to the jury selection process. As a prerequisite to sitting in judgment on a capital case, a prospective juror must provide assurance under oath that he or she can consider all sentencing options, including the death penalty if warranted.

In Virginia, the decision to seek the death penalty resides solely with the elected commonwealth's attorney. It is an awesome responsibility, but in this case I had no reservations. The effectiveness of the death penalty as a deterrent is topical in academic circles. The logic supporting their doubt is usually based on surveys of convicted murderers who profess that they never considered the lethal consequences of their acts before killing the victim. In my view, this argument is counterintuitive. How do you determine how many assailants choose not to kill the victim because of fear of the death penalty? This is critical information that is conspicuously absent in the argument advanced by death penalty opponents.

I must have been right to seek the death penalty in O'Brien's case. He made it clear that one of *his* priorities after being released from prison would be to kill me and Chuck Shelton.

Even including the death qualification process, jury selection in Virginia is relatively quick. It took about three hours in the O'Brien case. We began opening statements right after lunch. Predictably, they represented polar opposite views of the case, built entirely on circumstantial evidence. I described the evidence as an "interlocking patchwork quilt." John Youngs, O'Brien's lead counsel, depicted it as a bunch of random circumstances woven together by fantasy.

It took me almost a week to present the commonwealth's case. The first few days set the scene for the high impact scientific stuff. Mr. Jacobson described the discovery of Mrs. Konopka and the condition of the rear door. Agent Spivey explained in painstaking detail how he processed the crime scene and identified the items he collected, including the rear door. Spivey actually reconstructed the jagged edges of glass in the rear window for the jury.

Officer Foxwell recounted his encounter with O'Brien on the night of the homicide and the absence of any cuts on his arms, and, perhaps most importantly, placed O'Brien within a short distance of the crime scene minutes before the murder. Shelton testified about O'Brien's arrest and the scuffle when they photographed his arms. He told the jury that O'Brien lived a hundred and sixty yards from Mrs. Konopka. He also described O'Brien's conflicting explanations for the cuts on his arm, as did the jail physician's assistant. Another officer told about the recovery of Konopka's credit cards and identification a few blocks from O'Brien's house.

The tempo picked up the third day. Dr. James Beyer, the deputy chief state medical examiner, outlined the results of his autopsy of Konopka's body. He established the time of death as approximately 1:00 a.m. on June 6, about twenty-two minutes after Officer Foxwell dropped O'Brien off. The next line of questioning was explosive.

Over the high-decibel objection of defense counsel, I qualified Dr. Beyer, who was board certified in both anatomical and forensic pathology, as an expert in wound patterns. The jury was impressed when he explained that he had examined more than two hundred fifty thousand wounds in his thirty years of practice, including hundreds of glass incisions. While serving in the military as a combat pathologist, he had examined scores of such wounds daily. Because Dr. Beyer had not prepared a formal report, I had no obligation to warn the defense in advance of what was coming.

I next showed Dr. Beyer the photograph of the incision taken during the booking process. Aside from showing the wounds, the photo also depicted a large tattooed death skull on O'Brien's arm. That went over big with the jury. Dr. Beyer was then asked to come down off the witness stand and examine the rear door with the glass pane earlier reconstructed by Spivey. I then asked Beyer to compare the wound track on the photograph to the jagged pane of glass in the door. Almost simultaneously, all twelve jurors leaned forward in their seats.

In his ever confident resonant voice, Dr. Beyer explained in professorial detail how O'Brien's wounds were consistent with the jagged glass pattern of the door. In his opinion, the cuts were caused by the rotation of his arm as he turned the interior door knob. Beyer demonstrated with his own arm. There was little the defense could do on cross-examination. There were too many potential land mines. Defense counsel knew that cross-examining "Doc" Beyer was like wrestling a wounded rhinoceros. After thirty years of testifying in homicide cases, Dr. Beyer took great pride in twisting the knife deeper on cross.

The next forensic scientist compared the piece of blue velcro fastener found on the rug in Konopka's bedroom to the blue velcro fasteners on O'Brien's Stadia shoes. He testified that the two had identical chemical and optical properties. Another match.

A scientist had also examined a strand of hair found on the bedding where the victim's body was discovered. Her tests revealed that the strand was consistent in physical properties with those of the defendant and inconsistent with the hair of the victim. Ordinarily such evidence would have minimal impact, but in concert with the web of circumstances being spun before their eyes, the jury's attention was riveted. Just in time for the coup de grace.

We called a forensic geologist as our last scientific witness. He had microscopically examined O'Brien's newly purchased Stadia athletic shoes. The soles were almost unblemished; they bore few if any pock marks or scrapes from wear. This was something the geologist had rarely encountered. Moreover, he further explained that the ridges on the soles of Stadia shoes were truly unique. He had seen only one other pair in his seven years with the Virginia Bureau of Forensic Laboratories, where he examined about a thousand pairs a year. The witness did a microscopic comparison of the ridge pattern on O'Brien's shoes with the characteristics of the shoe print on the fragment of broken glass found next to the rear door. The print was definitely made with a Stadia shoe. Moreover, the print matched the unique ridge pattern of O'Brien's shoes. The cuts and scrapes in the ridges were identical in all respects on both surfaces. But that's not all.

The forensic geologist discovered forty particles of glass embedded in the soles of O'Brien's shoes—which had been purchased only fourteen hours before Shelton seized them. The tiny shards of glass from O'Brien's shoes matched the chemical and optical properties of the glass from the window in Konopka's rear door, indicating that they were most likely produced by the same manufacturer. Not one sliver was inconsistent. Now that's a hell of a coincidence.

My final witness was the defendant's father, but his attitude had done a one-eighty. He claimed no recollection of his comments to Detective Shelton and denied that his son's clothes had been blood soaked on the morning of the murder. Given the strength of our case, I was unconcerned.

After two days of deliberation, we began to wonder if the jury agreed with our assessment. The defense put on no significant evidence and tried to create the illusion of innocence by arguing to the jury that there was reasonable doubt of O'Brien's guilt. What was the hang up?

Finally, the jury knocked on the door and filed into the jury box. The clerk of court read the verdict, one charge at a time: robbery—not guilty; burglary—not guilty. I looked over at Chuck Shelton and braced for the worst. On the last charge, the vicious stabbing of Betty Konopka, the jury found O'Brien guilty of first degree murder, and fixed his sentence at fifty years. It was a respectable verdict and, because of his record, O'Brien would not be eligible for parole for twenty-five years. (Parole was not abolished in Virginia until 1994 and it would not have affected his sentence.) However, we found the results disappointing. O'Brien would probably have agreed to plead guilty if I had agreed to recommend a sentence of fifty years. So what happened?

Several months later, Detective Shelton ran into the foreman of the jury at the grocery store. The guy was somewhat apologetic and provided some insight into the jury's deliberations. He explained that the jury first concluded that Mrs. Konopka was most likely dead when her purse was taken. Therefore, technically the theft could not have been a robbery. Okay, the underlying logic was basically correct, if they found that she was actually dead when the taking occurred. They were evidently not convinced, as we were, that she had been killed during the course of forcibly taking her property.

Next, since they acquitted on the robbery, they deduced that they could not convict him of burglary with the intent to commit robbery. Why else would he have killed the victim rather than simply fleeing? For that reason, Shelton and I flatly rejected the notion that theft alone was O'Brien's motive.

The jury foreman then turned to the murder charge. Within minutes of retiring to the jury room to begin their deliberations, one of the jurors stood up and said he was intractably opposed to the death penalty, contrary to his earlier representations under oath. The verdict was the best compromise they could agree on. However, technically, proof of the robbery was critical to the capital murder charge. That's why I decided to indict for robbery as opposed to larceny. It was the only option that enabled us to pursue the death penalty, which this guy deserved.

## Turning the Tables

Experienced officers learn to compartmentalize their emotions and suppress their opinions. Few become attached to routine cases. Most learn to respect and accept, sometimes begrudgingly, the court's decision. But inevitably, in the course of every officer's career there is a case or two where seemingly extraordinary acts are the subject of senseless judicial criticism or inexplicable public scorn. Unquestionably, one of the primary responsibilities of the judicial branch is to check lawless police behavior, but too often, cases distill down to second guessing the split-second judgment of an officer in a perilous situation. An officer confronted with a life-threatening crisis on the street does not have time to call a lawyer or do legal research.

In many precedent-setting cases, it takes years, dozens of judges and multiple levels of review, scores of law clerks and paralegals, a modern law library with computerized legal research, and hundreds of pages of memoranda to pass judgment on a decision made by a single police officer in less than one minute. As a commentator once noted, courts review by the coolness of the evening what cops do in the heat of the day. That's the way our system of justice works. And on balance, it works well. But the public perception that a well-meaning officer has blundered because of a subtle misapplication of law can be demoralizing. The best illustration was a case I prosecuted involving my friend Officer Mike Kyle of the Arlington County Police.

Detective Ed Gabrielson, a robbery-homicide investigator, reached for his radio mike as he attempted to penetrate late morning traffic en route to a bank robbery call in the Buckingham area of Arlington County. This time it was the Washington-Lee Savings and Loan. Gabrielson was aware that another bank in the same area had been robbed the previous day by two black males driving a green Dodge Dart or Plymouth Duster with District of Columbia license plates.

On a hunch, Gabrielson broadcast a county-wide lookout for the vehicle. Unfortunately, Gabrielson could not get an immediate confirmation or a description of the robbers from the scene. The first detective to arrive at the bank was a female juvenile investigator. They refused to admit her into the bank because she had forgotten to bring her badge and credentials. Fortunately, the perpetrators had already fled, because she had also forgotten her gun. She also proved to be of little value later in interviewing witnesses because she didn't have a pen or paper.

Meanwhile, Officer Mike Kyle was patrolling Route 50, also known as Arlington Boulevard, which divides the county into north and south. He was driving a marked police unit. After hearing Gabrielson's broadcast, Kyle accelerated to the Virginia end of Memorial Bridge, which linked Arlington, Virginia, with the District of Columbia. He pulled to the shoulder. This was the logical escape route for someone fleeing the Buckingham area heading into the District of Columbia. Nine minutes later, a green Plymouth Duster with D.C. plates occupied by what appeared to be two black males breezed by. The driver resembled pictures Kyle had seen earlier that day of the suspects in the previous day's bank robbery. Kyle pulled out into traffic and casually followed the vehicle while trying to get a detailed description of the suspects from officers at the scene of the bank robbery. Both vehicles were traveling within the speed limit.

Kyle remained behind the green car as it proceeded onto the Theodore Roosevelt Bridge, which also connects Virginia with the District of Columbia. Eventually, Kyle decided that he had to pull the vehicle over before it got lost in dense D.C. traffic, so he activated his overhead lights and siren, and alerted the Arlington County Police dispatcher that he was stopping the suspect vehicle. He was getting a little annoyed since he still had not received a definitive description of the holdup men. The green car proceeded down the E Street ramp off the bridge and pulled to the shoulder of the road. They were now in the District of Columbia. As Kyle placed his scout car in park, he was advised by the dispatcher that the D.C. Police and United States Park Police were being advised of his situation, and would presumably be arriving soon to assist. However, as a veteran officer, he knew you couldn't always count on D.C. in a pinch.

Before Kyle could get out of his car, the driver of the green Duster, Lyntellus Brooks, got out with his hands up and walked toward Kyle, heightening Kyle's suspicion. Brooks left his car door open. Kyle stepped out with his service revolver drawn. He turned Brooks around and escorted him back to the light green Plymouth, and directed him to place his hands on the trunk of the car and remain there. Kyle, however, did not close Brooks's car door, seize the keys, handcuff or frisk Brooks, or order him to lie on the ground. Kyle walked around the car and looked into the passenger side to gain a clearer picture of what he was up against. At the same time, he again asked the dispatcher for a description of the robbery suspects.

The suspect took advantage of the momentary diversion of Kyle's attention. In a split second, Brooks leaped back into his car and accelerated, spraying dust in his path. Kyle gave chase with his emergency lights flashing and siren blaring. He pursued the Plymouth Duster down the E Street Expressway and through the E Street Tunnel. Kyle stayed well behind Brooks's car, which was traveling at speeds approaching eighty miles an hour. As they exited the tunnel, a man leaned out of the rear side window and began firing shots at Kyle. Kyle slowed down at that point and discontinued use of his siren. He proceeded on E Street in the general direction of travel of Brooks's vehicle, hoping the D.C. Police would soon appear.

Brooks continued to accelerate and ran the red light at Twentieth Street, still traveling at least seventy in a thirty-mile-an-hour zone. Brooks arrived at the next intersection, Nineteenth Street, just as another vehicle entered it. The Duster driven by Brooks struck the other vehicle in the intersection and careened off onto the sidewalk, pinning a pedestrian against a light pole. Tragically, the pedestrian was severely injured and eventually lost both of his legs. Brooks attempted to flee, but was restrained by an angry mob of kicking and flailing pedestrians. Kyle arrived just in time to save Brooks from some well-deserved "street justice." Two handguns and several rounds of ammunition were recovered from the demolished Duster, along with proceeds from the robbery.

I had no problem convicting Lyntellus Brooks and his sidekick, Orlando Dorantes, of several bank robberies and related firearms charges. The jury found little of a redeeming nature about either of them and handed down sentences approaching seventy years. The case then took an ironic turn.

As anticipated, the injured pedestrian filed a lawsuit, not against Brooks and his band of desperadoes, but against Mike Kyle and Arlington County. The pedestrian claimed that Kyle had been negligent in conducting the initial traffic stop. He contended that Kyle should have seized Brooks's keys and secured all occupants of the vehicle on the ground in handcuffs. However, at that point the car had been stopped based on a description of a vehicle used in a bank robbery the day before. Kyle had no description of the perpetrators or the getaway vehicle from the robbery of the day he stopped them. It was what lawyers would call articulable suspicion.

The injured pedestrian also alleged that Officer Kyle was negligent in conducting a high speed chase in the District of Columbia, in technical violation of Arlington County Police regulations. To add brine to the wound, he also claimed that Kyle had been poorly trained and supervised. The worst insult was that the liberal-leaning D.C. federal court agreed.

In a bizarre twist, reminiscent of a man-bites-dog story, the pedestrian's star witnesses against Kyle were the two stick-up men, Brooks and Dorantes. Imagine Kyle's reaction as he sat there in the courtroom—in the defendant's chair—as Dorantes calmly explained how he blasted away at Kyle's pursuing scout car. Under prevailing U.S. Supreme Court precedent, in order to return a verdict against Kyle, the jury had to find that his actions were "so egregious, so outrageous, that it may fairly be said to shock the contemporary conscience." The standard implies near purposeful and deliberate endangerment on the officer's part, a high evidentiary hurdle to satisfy.

Considering that he was being tried by a D.C. jury, Kyle was prepared for the worst. When the jury awarded the pedestrian five million dollars Kyle was shocked but not shaken. It was only when the court ordered Mike Kyle, whose salary was probably under fifty thousand dollars a year, to pay one million dollars *personally* that he became apoplectic. How do you think his wife reacted? Is there any wonder that the D.C. Police had a morale problem, and that the city had such a high crime rate?

Fortunately, several large corporations in northern Virginia were so outraged that they chipped in and paid off the financially crippling judgment against Officer Kyle. Although initially stunned and a bit demoralized, Mike remained with the police department and advanced in rank. His commitment never wavered, but his perception of the mission was unavoidably affected. Stories like this cause officers to hesitate when confronted with risky situations. That moment of hesitation—and inaction—can place both the officer and those he or she is sworn to protect in danger. And unfortunately, the feeling is contagious. Most police officers are willing to put their lives on the line to protect the public, but unless they intentionally act lawlessly, or maliciously cause serious injury, putting their families in financial jeopardy is beyond the call of duty. The conundrum can be paralyzing. Just ask Mike Kyle.

## Duty Calls Again

Ordinarily, I'd rush right to the phone to return Congressman Frank Wolf's call. But I couldn't resist pausing to tell my staff, and anyone else in the reception area, the hilarious experience I had just had in court.

I was trying three men from D.C. charged with armed robbery. I took a personal interest in the case, because the victim was the vice president of Jack Daniel Distillery, maker of my favorite whiskey. He was staying at a high-end motel in Crystal City, a cluster of commercial high rises and apartments located in South Arlington within sight of the D.C. line. He casually strolled down the hall to his room after attending a conference at the D.C. Convention Center. As he stuck his key in the door, two thugs stepped out of a stairwell, pointed a revolver at his face and relieved him of his wallet.

They were apprehended later that evening, along with the driver of the getaway car, by a tattered-clothed police tactical unit, as they attempted to enter another hotel in the immediate area. They matched the general description provided by the liquor executive. One was carrying a revolver and the other had several of the victim's credit cards. The plain clothes officer returned the two suspects to the scene of the robbery, where they were identified without hesitation by the victim. All three were placed in handcuffs and charged with robbery.

Because the defendants had substantial prior records they pled not guilty and insisted on a jury trial. As I've mentioned before, in those days the prosecution was prohibited from introducing evidence of the defendant's record, even though the jury was responsible for setting the sentence. All three were tried together. Two had retained prominent criminal defense lawyers. The third had a relatively inexperienced court-appointed lawyer. The trial was a hoot. I put on two witnesses, the victim and the arresting officer. My direct examination took about thirty minutes. Cross-examination took more than two hours.

Each time the court-appointed lawyer asked a question on cross-examination, the other two defense lawyers would object. They would then argue among themselves about the objections in front of the jury, which found it humorous. The tension between counsel escalated as the objections became increasingly personal and derogatory. The court-appointed lawyer, in turn, objected to almost every question asked by the other two. The jury laughed incessantly for almost two hours. The judge kept his face covered with a handkerchief to conceal his amusement. I hardly said a word. What could I say?

Sensing self-destruction in the making, I kept my final argument brief. It was the proverbial open-and-shut case. Defense counsel continued to bicker during their arguments to the jury, provoking periodic giggles. The jury deliberated for more than three hours before convicting two of the defendants. They were unable to reach a verdict on the third guy—the one represented by the court-appointed lawyer. I always wondered if it was the result of confusion or sympathy.

Two weeks later, the victim sent me a half gallon of Jack Daniel's Sour Mash whiskey as a token of his gratitude. The Kentucky gentleman also sent a note politely declining to come back to Virginia for a retrial of the third guy.

He'd seen enough of Arlington County. That left no option except to dismiss the remaining charges. As for the other two defendants, the ones with the high-dollar lawyers, they're probably still in prison.

Once the laughter subsided in the reception area, I walked back to my office, message in hand, to return the congressman's call. As Northern Virginia Republicans, Frank Wolf and I were an endangered political species. In the early 1980s, there were damn few Republican office holders in the Commonwealth of Virginia. Our minority status, and relentless efforts to survive politically, created a strong and lasting bond between me and Congressman Wolf. I was prepared to do almost anything he requested, within reason.

However, I'd have to think about this one.

XIII

# The Commission on Pornography

Several months before I received the phone call from Congressman Wolf, I'd been invited to the White House for a meeting with the president. The invitation was extended by Morton Blackwell, then serving as a special assistant to the president. Morton had played a significant role in my election as county prosecutor. President Ronald Reagan had scheduled a meeting with a number of political, community, and religious leaders to discuss the proliferation of pornography in America. To my astonishment, Morton told me that President Reagan wanted me in attendance. I later learned that Morton had extolled our track record of vigorous enforcement of obscenity laws in Arlington County, and how we had closed all the adult book stores and massage parlors. The president was left with the clear, but mistaken, impression that I was an expert on obscenity.

About a dozen people were present at the meeting, which was held in the ornate cabinet room. I could become accustomed to this lifestyle. After everyone was assembled, President Reagan quietly entered the room without pomp or ceremony. His introductory comments were simple but eloquent and articulated with the precision of the broadcaster he had been in the past.

He began by going around the room and allowing everyone, except me, to speak. Each voiced a common theme. They demanded stricter enforcement of the nation's obscenity laws. The president then turned and introduced me to the other people present. It was a heady moment for a thirty-four-year-old.

President Reagan briefly explained how I had successfully used Virginia's obscenity laws to shut down all the adult bookstores in Arlington. Everyone nodded and smiled with apparent approval. He closed by commending me for my extraordinary work, agreeing that a significant problem existed, and promising the attendees that his staff would develop an action plan. I added one profound comment, "Thank you, sir."

As I walked toward the door, Morton motioned for me to follow him to the Oval Office. There, President Reagan greeted me with a handshake. We then posed for a photograph, which he later signed and sent to my office. He concluded by reiterating his appreciation for my fine work. The president's kind remarks were later part of a national press release.

Meeting with the president of the United States had provided an unparalleled emotional rush. I stepped out of the White House that day with my self-confidence at an all time high.

When Congressman Wolf explained what he wanted during our phone call, all the pieces fell into place. In response to political pressure, and at Wolf's urging, the president planned to establish a national commission on pornography, and he wanted me to serve as chairman. It would be an uncompensated, part-time position on top of my duties as commonwealth's attorney.

My visceral reaction was to jump at the opportunity. It would undoubtedly be a high visibility post, giving me national exposure. The down side was the constituency I represented in Arlington County, a jurisdiction at least twenty degrees left of center. As a Republican in a Democratically dominated town, I could expect fierce opposition for reelection. As the press frequently reminded me, voters either loved me or hated me.

I needed time to reflect and consult with my political advisors. Most people thought it was a dangerous move. Even my wife Tara had serious reservations. My deputy, Helen Fahey, called it an act of political suicide. I was on the fence.

Pressure intensified the day following Congressman Wolf's call. Paul Trible, then the junior United States senator from Virginia, called and added his personal encouragement. I valued the senator's judgment. It had served him well. He was a former commonwealth's attorney who had been elected to Congress three times and to the Senate before his fortieth birthday. He strongly supported the commission and concluded our conversation by telling me that President Reagan was counting on me. Within minutes, I called Wolf and agreed to serve.

My formal appointment was preceded by an extensive vetting process. I spent more than two hours meeting with various people in the White House Personnel Office. Their mission was to examine the purity of my Republican pedigree. Next, I devoted an entire day meeting with officials from the Department of Justice, including a half hour with Attorney General William French Smith.

## Chairman of the Attorney General's Commission on Pornography

In about two months, President Reagan formally announced the formation of the Attorney General's Commission on Pornography, and my appointment as chairman. The announcement commanded the front page of every newspaper in the nation. Before the print was even dry, the media went on the attack. The press characterized the Commission on Pornography as a full-scale assault by the right wing on American First Amendment rights. They persisted in portraying the commission as a government censorship board, poised to ban fine literature from local libraries. It became clear that few journalists understood our mandate or found it commercially advantageous to describe it accurately. The frenzy of hysteria sells far more newspapers than reasoned analysis.

Contrary to media portrayal, the Pornography Commission's mandate specifically excluded literature or similar printed material. Its focus was on visual imagery or photographs. We were asked to place special emphasis on materials depicting children or women being abused, degraded, or sexually exploited. The president, in publicly unveiling the commission, announced that our charter was, "to determine the nature, extent and impact on society of pornography in the United States—and what we can do about it."

Newly confirmed Attorney General Edwin Meese and his staff further expanded our charge. We were to determine the extent of the national problem, the adequacy of governing laws, the sufficiency of law enforcement efforts, any connections with organized crime, and any identifiable correlation with criminal activity or deviant sexual behavior. He also requested specific law enforcement policy recommendations for the Department of Justice.

The attorney general also directed us to devote special attention to child pornography: to report on its prevalence in the United States, the nature of the industry, and the methods used for its distribution, and we were to assess the correlation between child pornography and child abuse. Despite this clear, precise, and highly publicized definition of our role, literary organizations throughout the nation seemed to band together to form a joint defense coalition founded on a near-hysterical fear of censorship. Our integrity was at issue from the moment of conception.

This misunderstanding, fostered in large part by the media, was exemplified by an incident during a public hearing in Chicago. It was late in the day, and only four other commissioners were still in attendance. One was a renowned forensic psychiatrist; another, a nationally known clinical psychologist. One of the last witnesses was a distinguished and scholarly lady about sixty years old, a professor of library science at a major university with a doctorate in her field.

Her disdain for the commission was palpable from the moment she walked to the podium. She began with a discussion, in classic pedagogical timbre, of the cultural value of literature in our society and a reminder of the cherished role of freedom of expression in our history. Next, she challenged our lack of qualifications—both personal and intellectual—to judge the quality and propriety of literary works. She ended her presentation by curtly conveying the idea that every book has a message—if you're just smart enough to understand it. We remained patient and said nothing.

As the librarian assembled her papers in a folder, she asked if we had any questions. I handed three publications to a staff investigator to present to her. The cover of the first, *Lesbian Lovers,* portrayed two women engaged in oral sex. That of the second book, *Animal Lovers,* depicted a man performing fellatio on a horse. The third publication showed a man on the cover with his arm stuck up to the elbow into the anus of another man.

The librarian grimaced in disgust as she glanced at the covers of the magazines. She then gave us a bewildered look. I posed a simple question.

"Doctor, can you explain to us the message in these three books?"

I'm sure she considered my question a cheap shot, but after collecting her thoughts, she muttered, "This is not what I'm talking about."

One of my colleagues responded, "But Ma'am, that's what this Commission is all about." She retreated from the hearing room gracefully.

The weeks following President Reagan's announcement of the Pornography Commission were hectic. I had twenty requests for press interviews every day. Reporters were waiting for me outside the courtroom each morning and in the parking lot each night. Paparazzi everywhere, each hoping I'd say something stupid. The Department of Justice had to assign a full time staffer from the Public Affairs Office to answer inquiries and serve as my handler.

Press coverage intensified as our initial meeting in Washington approached. On the weekend preceding that first hearing, I was a guest on all the Sunday television talk shows, and the commission was the subject of editorials in most of the national newspapers, none complimentary. Most focused their pens on the composition of the commission, which they characterized as a right wing group with a preordained mission. There certainly was an expectation that the commission would recommend stronger enforcement of the nation's pornography laws, particularly with respect to materials depicting children and violence. However, philosophically, the members represented widely divergent interests and opinions. No one could possibly have forecast the robust debate or deep divisions that emerged.

Besides me, the commission was composed of ten other members, apparently selected by Attorney General Meese.

• Dr. Judith V. Becker, an associate professor of clinical psychology at Columbia University and director of the Sexual Behavior Clinic at the New York Psychiatric Institute. Dr. Becker had published extensively on sexual aggression, rape, victimization, human sexuality, and behavior theory.

• Diane D. Cusack, vice mayor of Scottsdale, Arizona.

• Dr. Park Elliott Dietz, a prominent forensic psychiatrist and professor of law, behavioral medicine, and psychiatry at the University of Virginia. Dr. Dietz had served as an expert witness in numerous high-profile cases with insanity defenses, and as a consultant to the FBI Behavioral Science Unit. He had also authored scores of publications on visual imagery and deviant sexual behavior.

• Judge Edward J. Garcia, a United States district court judge for the Eastern District of California. He had previously served as the deputy district attorney for Sacramento County, California.

• Ellen Levine, who resided in New Jersey, was editor-in chief of *Woman's Day* and vice president of CBS magazines.

*United States Attorney General Ed Meese introduces me to the press as Chairman of the Attorney General's Commission on Pornography in 1985. (Courtesy of the U.S. Department of Justice.)*

• Tex Lezar, a practicing attorney in Dallas, Texas, had formerly been chief of staff to Attorney General William French Smith, and assistant attorney general of the United States for legal policy. He was undoubtedly one of the original architects of the commission.

• Reverend Bruce Ritter, an ordained Catholic priest, was the founder and president of Covenant House, an international child crisis center.

• Dr. James C. Dobson was a syndicated radio broadcaster and president of Focus on the Family. He had practiced clinical psychology for seventeen years and was a former associate clinical professor of pediatrics at the University of Southern California School of Medicine.

• Frederick Schauer was a professor of law at the University of Michigan. He had authored several books on the First Amendment and obscenity.

• Deanne Tilton was president of the California Consortium of Child Abuse Councils. Her organization concentrated on broad-based child abuse prevention and treatment programs.

The executive director was Alan E. Sears, an assistant United States attorney from the Western District of Kentucky. Alan was detailed to the commission by the Department of Justice, as were most other members of our staff. To oversee our review of social science research, we hired Dr. Edna Einsiedel. We also had a cadre of investigators from numerous federal and state law enforcement agencies, including FBI, U.S. Customs, Postal Inspection Service, Arlington County Police, and Metropolitan Police Department.

These were bright, well-educated, independent-thinking people. Each had at least a graduate level degree. None was easily influenced. As a result of the onslaught of critical media chatter, most commissioners were determined to publicly demonstrate their freethinking autonomy. This was readily evident at our first meeting.

The meeting was held in Washington, D.C., at the Department of Justice. Its stated purpose was to define the national problem of pornography. It allowed an array of public officials to express their sentiments, including the attorney general, the director of the FBI, the commissioner of Customs, the chief U.S. postal inspector, members of Congress including Senators William Roth of Delaware and Mitch McConnell of Kentucky, and numerous police officials from around the country. At the accompanying organizational meeting, an undercurrent of dissension began to form that would reach critical mass in the tense moments of internal debate over our final report a year later. Its resolution was beyond my control.

The well-spring of continuing controversy was the duration, funding, and research limitations on the commission. Our charter had a one-year sunset provision and a total budget of five hundred thousand dollars. We were prohibited from undertaking or contracting for any independent research, except to ask Surgeon General C. Everett Koop for assistance. My request for additional time and money was rejected out of hand by the Department of Justice.

Inevitably, the scope and depth of the inquiry was compared to that of its predecessor, the 1970 Commission on Obscenity and Pornography. That commission, which essentially found no identifiable social harm and no connections with organized crime from pornography, operated for two years with a two million dollar budget. That commission also hired prominent social and behavioral scientists to conduct specific research. Factoring inflation into the equation, in actual 1985 dollars, the 1970 commission had sixteen times our funding. This disparity was publicized by our detractors and proved to be a liability from the inception.

Several members of the commission with scientific backgrounds found our limitations unsettling. They questioned whether purely "anecdotal" and "impressionist" evidence could form a defensible basis for respectable findings. I candidly acknowledged that the limitations were a handicap. However, I reminded them that this was a practical, commonsense exercise that would rely heavily on logic and human experience. I drew the analogy of a jury deciding a case based on the facts presented. There are hundreds of people on death row based solely on circumstantial evidence. This was a fact-finding project. It was never intended to have the rigor of a scientific study. This view gave limited solace.

Since we couldn't do independent research, we drew our data base from five general sources: existing research, submissions from the public, interviews conducted by staff investigators, information from law enforcement sources, and public hearings. Scores of vice investigators from throughout the nation sent us endless boxes of seized materials and copies of interviews with sex offenders. Usually, the offender had admitted using pornographic material to ignite sexual arousal before preying on the victim.

Many members of the commission detected a correlation between the visual images found in the possession of sex offenders at the time of their arrest and the type of sexual transgression committed, especially with bondage and other forms of violent visual imagery. The behavioral linkage was interesting. The psychiatrists and other behavioral scientists on the commission explained that arousal to sexually coercive themes is a product of classic human conditioning. A number of other organic, psychological, and cultural elements must be factored into the analysis.

In simple terms, someone who reads materials containing violent sexual imagery and who derives sexual pleasure through fantasy or masturbation, in time learns to become aroused by these materials. This is the same way a fetish to leather, shoes, feet, silk, purses, or even cigars is acquired. I worked on a case involving a pedophile with a strange cigar fetish during my final few months as U.S. attorney.

An informant told the FBI in Richmond, Virginia, that a certain real estate agent was plotting to kidnap and molest a child. The investigation shifted into high gear when agents observed the man on three successive afternoons watching the same young blond-haired boy riding his bike, at the same location, and at about the same time. After corroborating some additional information, my office applied for and obtained authority to tap the man's phone. At first, we thought the conversations we intercepted were merely fantasy, but after several days of listening and watching, the horrifying plot began to unfold before our eyes. This guy was dead serious.

Our "subject," as cops called such suspects before the advent of the term "person of interest," was planning to kidnap the child. For days, he and his coconspirator from Alexandria, Virginia, discussed the details. On a designated day and time, these guys intended to grab the kid off his bicycle, toss him in the back of a windowless van, knock him out with chloroform, place him in a heavy canvas bag, take him to a secluded cabin, and sexually molest him. And after that, they planned to kill the boy and bury his body at a specific location in a remote area of North Carolina. The subject had already rented the windowless van. The burial site described in the intercepted conversations, on the bank of a stream in dense woods, actually existed. Now for the fetish connection.

These two perverts intended to fulfill their masturbation fantasy. Their plan was to bind the youngster's hands, blindfold him, and make him smoke a cigar—while they jerked off. After arresting these guys and searching their homes, we learned they were part of a national group with a common source of sexual stimulation: watching kids in bondage smoking cigars. The group even publishes a periodic newsletter. In each defendant's house, FBI agents seized mounds of child pornography. The guy from Alexandria also had an elaborate torture chamber in the bedroom of his suburban high-rise apartment. Both defendants were convicted of assorted federal crimes and received sentences of forty years.

Some forms of paraphilia, as clinicians prefer to call fetishes, are common and acceptable in society today, as demonstrated in many popular over-the-counter men's magazines. Most people with such tendencies have the willpower to control their behavior. If it is bizarre, they keep it a dark secret. This partly explains why there are otherwise respectable, family-oriented men, and occasionally women, who patronize prostitutes. It's the only available vehicle to fulfill their sexual obsessions without the humiliation of revealing their secret. Sometimes these trysts have tragic consequences, such as blackmail and extortion. People with weird sexual foibles often pay large sums to avoid having their secrets told. It's a facet of the prostitution industry that rarely surfaces in discussions among those who oppose governmental regulation of the trade.

There are people who cannot control the temptation to act out their fantasies. Those who "get off" on violence have the potential to be dangerous. For example, Ted Bundy, the notorious serial killer, told investigators that he routinely looked at magazines with violent sexual imagery before torturing or killing his victims. That's the dangerous side. On the other side, there are people who do not engage in deviant behavior and simply claim to derive pleasure from these materials.

The commission's finding with respect to violent imagery may not satisfy the scientific gold standard. However, where a significant number of criminal investigators report finding such material routinely in the possession of sexual predators, the association seems intuitive, if not self-evident. Here is another practical illustration.

Would you as a parent feel comfortable allowing your minor child to hang out at a neighbor's house if you knew that person's pleasure reading included magazines depicting youngsters in bondage being forcibly sexually violated? Would you let your teenage daughter date a guy who read that kind of stuff? The answer is a simple *hell no!* And I'll bet you wouldn't need a psychology professor's opinion or scientific study to reach that conclusion. Too often in the sterile laboratory environment, logic and common sense are dismissed as unacceptably inexact.

In addition to input from law enforcement officials, behavioral scientists and outpatient sex offenders, the commission invited comment from the general public and the publication industry, as well as the academic and legal communities. We held six public hearings, each with a different emphasis. Beyond the initial meeting in Washington, D.C., we held three days of hearings each in Chicago, Houston, Los Angeles, Miami, and New York.

The Chicago hearing focused on the law. A bevy of First Amendment scholars gave us their take on what constitutes pornography and how it is legally distinguishable from obscenity. The boundaries are difficult to stake out. We concluded that we could devote our entire existence to the task of formulating a definition of pornography. The inherent difficulty was the commissioners' inability to compartmentalize their personal value judgment of the activity depicted and to agree on an objective definition. Therefore, we decided to place the material in working categories and make an assessment of its social harm.

The public hearing in Houston drew national attention, including a three-page spread in *Time* magazine. The meeting was devoted to behavioral science and a discussion of the state of the existing research. A number of prominent psychiatrists and psychologists presented their theories and experiences. With the consent of their patients, some also shared interviews with outpatient sex offenders. These were quite revealing. Some patients of the presenters admitted molesting dozens of children.

No consensus emerged but most presenters, despite a lack of strict scientific validation, acknowledged some association between violent sexual imagery and the potential to act out the depicted conduct. All encouraged additional research. The commission concurred.

Several behavioral scientists in Houston presented research findings demonstrating a correlation between the frequent viewing of materials depicting women as docile, subordinate sexual partners who crave being sexually exploited, and the acceptance by the viewer of the notion that woman derive pleasure from such humiliation and abuse. The more the subjects saw of such imagery, the more inclined they were to accept it as appropriate behavior. The presenters referred to this process as "desensitization," and added that few of the research subjects were conscious of the effect until they reviewed the results. Since the research was conducted over a short period of time in an academic context, it is difficult to gauge whether the effect is long term. However, these findings were useful in crafting our final report. They also proved valuable in enlisting many women's groups as supporters of the commission's work.

However, it was not the behavioral research that drew the attention of the national media. It was the televised unannounced visit to three seedy adult bookstores in downtown Houston by eleven commissioners and staff, a half-dozen Houston cops, and about twenty-five reporters. As we walked in, some patrons rushed toward the door, while others leaped out of peep show booths and scrambled to the exit. When a vice detective opened the door to one video booth, the commissioners observed two men engaged in a sex act. Several booths had

*The initial meeting of the Pornography Commission in Washington, DC on June 19, 1985. (Courtesy of the U.S. Department of Justice.)*

crudely bored holes allowing a man to stick his penis into the adjacent booth to facilitate fellatio.

The materials on display were pretty much what we had expected, and were tame compared to some of the stuff we had seen. Most of the hard-core magazines were stored in the back or under the counter. However, after perusing more than a thousand "dirty books," our thresholds of sensitivity had reached new heights.

My colleagues found the peep show booths the most revolting. Dr. Judith Becker told a reporter from the *Washington Post* that she needed a steamy shower after the tour. "The hygiene in these places is upsetting, and the viewing rooms and booths just smelled bad back there."

Deanne Tilton told the same reporter, "It was a restroom ambiance. The floors were sticky, the air was musty. I was astonished at the ability of some people to be sexually aroused in a place like that."

Quite an understatement!

Our next hearing was devoted to the production of pornography. Naturally, it was held in Los Angeles. Most domestically created porn films were made in California. Most hard-core films are home-produced using amateur actors. A lengthy parade of actors and producers appeared before the commission. Some saw smut production as a respectable commercial enterprise. Others found varying degrees of job satisfaction. Later in the hearing at New York City, we heard testimony from Linda Lovelace Marchiano, star of *Deep Throat,* a film destined for the Pornography Hall of Fame. Ms. Marchiano claimed that she was forced at gunpoint to participate in some pornographic productions.

Other actors reported being abused during filming, but most participated willingly. Some had been lured into the business with the expectation of launching a film career. This aspiration was never achieved. The reputation of a porn star is hard to live down. The average career spanned less than six months. Many had drug habits and needed the income. Others were exhibitionists and enjoyed flaunting their stuff. Only a select, easily identifiable, few were well paid. Most earned less than a thousand dollars per film. The producers, on the other hand, made big bucks. *Deep Throat,* an adult theater box office hit, cost twenty-five thousand dollars to make and as of 2005, had yielded more than six hundred million dollars in profits.

It was at our Los Angeles meeting that we viewed the most gruesome film of all, and we'd seen some raunchy flicks. It was a video in which a man paid a long-legged, huge-busted woman in a thong bathing suit fifteen hundred dollars to cut off his testicles with a knife, on camera. Blood splattered everywhere. My friend Park Dietz, a physician who was sitting next to me, remarked in revulsion that it was no simulation. Several commissioners chose not to watch the film. Others gasped in horror. Compounding our amazement was the frustration of getting no answers to the obvious follow up questions—Why? Was it money or sexual gratification? Was he on drugs? Did he survive? If so, wouldn't you love to get his reaction the next day? The movie had apparently been seized from an adult book store.

Just another day in the life of a porn commissioner.

A few months later in Miami, we turned our attention to child pornography. This was undoubtedly the most emotional and stirring of all our public hearings. In 1985, many states did not outlaw the possession of child pornography. The materials we viewed ranged from seemingly innocent poses of youngsters in underwear to an adult male sexually violating a six-month-old infant. We learned that large amounts of child porn were produced overseas in gritty sweat shops using forced child labor, and smuggled into the United States. Customs seized tons of it each year during shipment across the U.S. border. The rest was either home produced or created by small cottage-type industries. The demand was limited, so very little was produced for profit in the U.S. However internationally, the production and distribution of child porn was a four billion dollar industry.

The most informative presentation at the Miami meeting was a detailed explanation of how child pornography is used by pedophiles to seduce their prey. A pedophile will show a child magazines with pictures of adults and children engaged in sexual activity, initially to excite their interest. Then they will use the magazine as a confidence builder. In other words, they will try to persuade the child that there is nothing wrong or to be afraid of. If the sex act portrayed were not okay, these people wouldn't be doing it, and they wouldn't be shown in a magazine. The experts described this as an effective and frequently encountered form of chicanery.

The commission was readily convinced that child pornography was harmful. We all concurred that the social damage was self-evident, and recommended that its mere possession be declared unlawful. We also recommended that interdicting illicit trafficking in such material should receive increased law enforcement attention. The United States Congress agreed on both fronts.

Our final public hearing was held in New York City. There we heard several days of presentations from state and federal criminal investigators concerning the involvement of traditional organized crime families in the pornography industry. A collateral issue was the definition of organized crime. Our charter did not specify La Cosa Nostra (LCN), or what is known as "traditional" organized crime families. The evidence clearly revealed that materials that would satisfy the legal definition of obscenity were being produced by structured organizations formed to do something the law forbids. So technically they met the definition of "organized crime,"

However, we found that La Cosa Nostra's role in the production of obscene materials, while sporadically present nationally, was geographically limited to the Los Angeles and New York areas. The director of the FBI reported that a survey of all field offices disclosed "some involvement of [La Cosa Nostra in the obscenity industry], but no verifiable information." Our investigation revealed that several LCN families from New York and Los Angeles controlled the east and west coast production and distribution of obscenity—the Galante family in Los Angeles and the DeCavalcante family in New York.

Contradicting the report of the FBI director, former Capo (mob boss) Jimmy Fratianno of the L.A. family told our investigators that "ninety-five percent of the families are involved in the porn industry." A number of "gangland style shootings" were reportedly connected to competition among LCN families for control of the New York and L.A. markets. Our presentations disclosed some involvement of traditional organized crime families (La Cosa Nostra) at the retail level, but not enough at the production end to conclude that any significant linkage existed on a national scale.

The festering divisions within our numbers began to percolate to the surface at our next two working sessions, at Scottsdale, Arizona, and Washington, D.C. In Scottsdale, we categorized the various genres of materials and debated their harmful effects. After days of robust discussion, we voted on each category, specifically, how it would be described, and our assessment of the perceived harm.

We divided the universe of materials into four working classes. Class I encompassed sexual activity, actual or simulated, in a violent context. Class II featured sexual activity, actual or simulated, with degradation, humiliation, or domination, but without violence. Class III consisted of sexual activity without violence, domination, humiliation, or degradation. Lastly, Class IV involved pure nudity, without sexual activity, violence, or degradation. Aside from child pornography, we agreed on very little.

Our debate was plagued from the outset by our inability to define critical terms or agree on our analytical framework. We could not reach a consensus on the standard of proof we would use to measure the evidence. We concluded that legal terms of art, such as *beyond a reasonable doubt* or *preponderance of the evidence,* were not transferable to a non-judicial context. The Commission therefore elected to employ "ordinary words," such as *convinced, satisfied* and *concluded.*

Our deliberations were also mired down in high-decibel dialogue over what constituted harm in each of the designated classes of materials. This discussion consumed a full day. The passions of several commissioners were stoked by comments yelled from the audience by our ever-present detractors. The crowd was packed with representatives from groups hoping to dilute our findings. I sensed that our traction was slipping. But, after a recess, things got back on track.

We decided that harm would be assessed from three perspectives: social science evidence, totality of the evidence, and moral, ethical, and cultural evidence. Next, we ground the gradations of harm even finer. We identified five categories: acceptance of rape myth, degradation of women, association with replication or acting out, effects on the family, and social harm. I took a separate vote on each class in each individual category of harm from each perspective.

Members were willing to compromise in some areas, but remained intractable in others. In many categories, only one vote controlled the result. A growing chorus of commissioners complained of inadequate time, research, and information. It was a grueling experience. Many of our tough decisions were purely judgment calls reflecting personal values. Several books have been written over the years on the deliberations of the commission. Almost uniformly, the commentators—both pro and con—have faulted me for pushing too hard for consensus. Despite our shortcomings, it was my duty to deliver a report to the attorney general, and I intended to do so.

After four headache-provoking days, we walked out of the hearing room with the understanding that we had reached sufficient consensus on every issue to enable the drafting of a final report. There were hard feelings and emotional scars, but we left with our friendships intact. I directed the staff to prepare a draft for our Washington meeting, to be circulated to all commissioners in advance of the final vote.

I breathed a sigh of relief as I headed to the Scottsdale airport. It was a relaxing return flight. I looked forward to reporting to Attorney General Meese that our mission was accomplished—on time and within budget. In addition, I hoped I'd earned some points with the president. As it happened, things did not turn out quite that way.

Under the supervision of Executive Director Alan Sears, a hard-hitting federal prosecutor, the staff diligently prepared a working draft of the final report. It exhaustively surveyed the material we had reviewed and captured in detail the presentations at our hearings. The draft also contained proposed findings and recommendations. The findings generally tracked commissioner discussions, but presented the staff's understanding of our conclusions, in certain, forceful, and strident terms. Many of the aggressive recommendations in the draft were devised by the staff based on the suggestions of the presenters, without input from the commissioners. The recommendations were admittedly hard hitting including, for example, mandatory minimum sentences for repeat offenders, forfeiture of assets of purveyors of illegal pornography, lifetime probation for chronic child porn traffickers, and increased penalties in the states for the possession of child pornography.

Within minutes of my calling our final Washington meeting to order, and without any prior notice, Professor Fred Schauer announced that he could not sign the proposed report, and pulled from his briefcase his own draft. Several other commissioners were in league with him. Schauer indicated that his stature as a law professor could be jeopardized by the quality and tone of the proposed report. In his opinion, many of the proposed findings were not sufficiently supported by the evidence to survive peer review.

Striving to regain balance, I reminded Professor Schauer that the staff-created draft was not intended to be the final report, but a starting point for discussion. However, the message was subtle, but clear—adopt Schauer's version or at least four commissioners would refuse to sign.

As we started discussing the Schauer draft, the group began to divide along a philosophical fault line. The more conservative members insisted on the certainty of findings and damnatory language of the staff report. The debate became intense and, at times, personal. Our findings of harm for each category of material, especially those without violence or gender subordination, provoked continuing controversy. We decided to take a break and return in several hours. As the clock began to tick toward our sunset, I had all but concluded that our impasse was unresolvable.

During the break, I huddled with several commissioners and placed a call to the attorney general's chief of staff. The response from the Department of Justice was simple. Do the best you can, but bring it to closure. After about an hour of private discussion, our small caucus came up with a proposed compromise.

When the commission reassembled late in the evening, I proposed that we adopt Schauer's draft with some modifications as the commission's report, and that the staff version, also modified, be attached as an appendix. At that juncture, most commissioners were exhausted and frustrated. No one wanted to walk away and live with the stigma of failure, memorialized in the headlines of every national newspaper. For me, it would be politically ruinous. We all had too much invested. One by one the commissioners' heads began nodding affirmatively. We had the makings of a report, but it couldn't be completed before our commissions expired. We voted to request a short extension. With some trepidation, I agreed to call Attorney General Ed Meese.

The attorney general's reaction was unexpected. With my pledge to produce a quality report in thirty days, he granted the extension. My fellow commissioners were elated. A wave of conviviality engulfed the group and we all headed out for dinner together. No words could describe my personal relief.

There was a sea of reporters in the Great Hall of the Justice Department on the July morning that Attorney General Meese and I publicly unveiled the report. I could feel the dampness of sweat on my collar as he and I waited to step up on the podium. I felt the anxiety of a defendant waiting to walk into the courtroom to hear what would surely be a guilty verdict. General Meese made a few introductory comments, received the report, praised our work, and turned the press conference over to me for questions. I remember the lonely feeling as I watched Ed Meese step off the podium. With sweaty palms, I responded to press questions, and after being pelted with verbal rocks for about an hour, I fully expected a lashing in the press the next day. I wasn't disappointed. Editorials in national newspapers ran about twenty-five to one negative.

*The Final Report of the Attorney General's Commission on Pornography* resembled a Manhattan phone directory. It was two thousand pages long and a Government Printing Office best seller at fifty-three dollars per two-volume copy. I suspect the government recouped a substantial portion of the commission's budget on the profits. *People* magazine called the report "Uncle Sam's Dirty Book" and "one of the most provocative documents in recent years."

Three commissioners, Ellen Levine, Judith Becker, and Deanne Tilton, dissented. In their collective view, our information base and analytical depth were too shallow to support conclusions that would guide public policy. Individual commissioners muttered comments of discontent on all sides of the issue.

Although the report contained an exhaustive explanation of the evidence we heard and the materials reviewed by the staff, most readers, particularly reporters, went straight to the findings on harm. Surprisingly, the next most popular and often-quoted section was the list of more than twenty-three hundred steamy magazines reviewed by the staff. Almost every editorial had to cite examples, such as *Tri-Sexual Lust; Teeny Tits, Big Boobs to Chew and Suck On; Lisa and Her Dog; Pregnant Lesbians; Asian Slut; Anal Girls That Like Black Cock; Ass Masters; Big Busted Ball Buster,* and *Fire My Rear.*

The centerpiece, and ultimately the hallmark of our report, was the findings on harm that we methodically hammered out. In essence, we drew the following conclusions, based on our four classes of materials:

• Class I consisted of sexually violent materials, either actual or simulated. This group was represented by bondage and sadomasochistic publications. In our near unanimous opinion, the clinical and experiential evidence supported the finding that substantial exposure to sexually violent materials bears a causal relationship to antisocial acts of sexual violence. In other words, there appears to be a correlation between the frequent reading of magazines in this category and sexually aggressive behavior—not in every reader—but enough to raise a red flag. We also determined by majority vote that, for some people, substantial exposure to sexually violent materials can cause an attitudinal change with respect to women. Men can become desensitized and more accepting of the notion that women enjoy being coerced into sexual activity (sometimes known as the rape myth) or that women enjoy feeling pain in the sexual context.

• Class II was composed of materials depicting sexual activity, actual or simulated, nonviolent, but characterized by degradation, domination, subordination, or humiliation. Our conclusions in this category, by majority vote, paralleled those in Class I. However, our opinion was offered with less confidence in the supporting evidence. Formally expressed, we determined that substantial exposure to materials of this type bears some causal relationship to the level of sexual violence, sexual coercion, or unwanted sexual aggression in the population so exposed. We were not comfortable quantifying the causal relation. We also noted that regular reading of this genre of material appeared to effect the reader's sensibility toward women in society.

• Class III materials were characterized as those portraying sexual activity without violence or degradation. The *Final Report* captures this group as being composed of materials with "fully willing participants occupying substantially equal roles in a setting devoid of actual or apparent violence or pain."

It was difficult at this stage of the deliberations to yield a clear majority on any of the subsets of harm. The Commissioners had widely divergent views on the morality and social acceptance of the depicted activities. This subjectivity began to infect the process. What some perceived as harm was in actuality an expression of judgment on the underlying behavior. Under any standard of measure, Class III did not pose the type of public danger identified in Classes I and II. Some commissioners were even convinced that this genre of imagery had some arguable educational and therapeutic value that might enrich the sex lives of consenting partners. They therefore voted to classify this group as having "mixed effects" on the family, some arguably positive, some arguably negative.

A majority, however, was convinced that materials in Class III have the potential to erode "the moral fiber," in that they could conceivably project social condonation of promiscuity, adultery, and oral sex. A minority was concerned that even simple depictions of sexual activity could promote the notion that women are mere sex objects. In the final analysis, most of us agreed that as a matter of public policy, the social acceptability of such behavior distills to personal choice between those who engage in such activity.

Unlike the materials in Classes I and II, which fall into a grey area, publications in Class III indisputedly enjoy First Amendment protection and probably would not be considered obscene. We found no evidence of any correlation with violent or aggressive behavior for them. The only unanimously accepted potential harm dealt more with use than with content. Everyone concurred that Class III materials could be harmful when used by pedophiles to lure youngsters into believing that the portrayed sexual activity is appropriate for people their age.

• Class IV publications depicted mere nudity without other sexual activity. The commission was nearly unanimous that these materials stir the reader's passion, a natural and socially acceptable reaction, but have no harmful effects.

The *Final Report* also featured an array of remedies that communities can take to combat the distribution of inappropriate materials—ninety-three recommendations in all. I parted company with some of the other commissioners in recommending what type of materials should be regulated. Community standards differ drastically from state to state and from city to city. Each locality should decide for itself, without direction from a federal agency.

Our report strongly encouraged the Department of Justice to step up the enforcement of the nation's obscenity laws, especially as to child pornography and material in Classes I and II. William Webster, director of the FBI probably struck the right balance. He told the commission that enforcement of federal obscenity laws should not be the highest priority of the FBI, but it should not be the lowest either.

The *Final Report of the Commission* is less relevant today than it was then. Times have changed drastically in the last twenty years. Our culture is coarser and far more sexually oriented, as evidenced by the language and subject matter of television programming. Do you recall seeing erectile dysfunction ads on TV every fifteen minutes in 1986?

In an era of intense media coverage of crime-related news, it is interesting to note the number of child molesters and sexual predators who are arrested with large stashes of Class I and II publications in their possession—a coincidence?

Congress adopted many of the recommendations in the *Final Report* pertaining to the regulation of child pornography. Ironically, the legislation was sponsored by Democrats, who were originally critical of the commission's mandate. I was proud to stand at President Reagan's side as he signed the Child Protection and Obscenity Enforcement Act of 1988, enacting our child pornography regulations into law. Before we entered the room for the signing ceremony, Jim Dobson and I had a few personal moments with the president. He commended us on the work of the commission and added that hundreds of people from around the nation had expressed their appreciation for our work. Characteristically, President Reagan said he believed that ninety-five percent of the people in America agreed with the findings of the Commission, but unfortunately, the other five percent are newspaper editors.

Talking about newspaper editors and the *Final Report,* a personal experience illustrates the president's point. About a week after the *Report* was released, a friend of mine, Herman "Obie" Obermayer, called me with unsettling news. Obie was the owner and managing editor of the *Northern Virginia Sun,* a small but widely read local publication. The *Sun* had endorsed me for election in 1979 and usually treated me quite favorably. I was bewildered when Obie politely informed me that he was finishing up an editorial—and I wouldn't like it. He said it was about "that darned Pornography Commission. Henry, I just don't agree with it."

I asked Obie to explain what he took issue with and to "show me" in the Report.

He reluctantly confessed that he didn't have a copy of the *Report.* He'd never seen it, only a summary prepared by the American Civil Liberties Union. I reminded him that the ACLU had been one of the most vociferous critics of the commission's work. I then added jokingly, "How would you like to be indicted by someone who never bothered to read the material you were being charged with publishing?"

Obie, who was intellectually honest to a fault, paused and then admitted that maybe he should do a little more research. The editorial was never published. I've often wondered how many other authors of acerbic editorials never bothered to read the report.

The only truly negative fallout from the commission in the ensuing months was the lawsuits. Several associations of magazine publishers and distributors, as well as *Playboy, Penthouse,* and *Hustler* magazines, filed civil rights suits against the commissioners and the attorney general. The litigation was sparked by a letter that had been sent by the commission staff to Southland Corporation, owner of forty-five hundred 7-Eleven stores and an additional thirty-six hundred franchises nationally.

The letter was intended to elicit a response from Southland to highly publicized testimony that 7-Eleven stores were major retailers of porn magazines. The commission did not necessarily agree with that position, and wanted Southland to have the opportunity to respond. The resulting letter, prepared by the staff, regrettably was perceived as having an intimidating tone. Consequently, Southland and other similar chains chose to discontinue selling *Playboy* and *Penthouse.* Both publishing companies lost considerable revenue and filed suit.

In an attempt to settle the lawsuit, I had a telephone conversation with Christie Hefner, president of Playboy Enterprises. I assured her that the commission never intended to insinuate that *Playboy* was obscene, or anything other than a quality publication. Ms. Hefner was very bright, self-confident, and pleasant to deal with. She left me with the distinct impression that all her company really wanted was a public statement that *Playboy* was a cut above pornography. If it had been within my power, I would gladly have issued the statement.

The United States District Court for the District of Columbia kept our motion to dismiss under advisement for five years before finally throwing the cases out. The decision was affirmed by the court of appeals.

The pending lawsuits gave me particular heartburn. In early 1986, on the recommendation of my friend U.S. Senator Paul Trible of Virginia, the president had nominated me to serve as the United States attorney for the Eastern District of Virginia. As I completed the mound of required paperwork and impatiently awaited Senate confirmation, several nagging questions heightened my anxiety level. Would critics of our report launch a full-scale attack? What about all those newspaper editors? Would the Democrats on the Senate Judiciary Committee cave under pressure and block my nomination?

I was able to divert my attention, and maintain my sanity, by total immersion in the most bizarre homicide case of my career. I vividly recall, at the preliminary hearing, asking the first officer on the scene, Bob McFarlane, to describe his impressions. His response, reported in every local newspaper was, "I got the feeling I was in a Steven Spielberg movie."

# XIII

# A Deadly Exorcism

It was approximately 4:50 a.m. on a Monday morning when the call was received at the Arlington County Emergency Communications Center. Dialing from a public telephone at an all night gas station in North Arlington, the caller, in a calm steady voice, told the dispatcher that he wanted to report a possible death. He declined to give details, but when pressed, said the guy "had a problem with demons" and that he'd prefer to explain the rest when the police arrived.

Officer Robert A. McFarlane rolled up to the house several minutes later, under the impression that it was a routine "DOA call," denoting a natural or non-suspicious death. McFarlane found Robert C. Bloom, twenty-seven years old, lying face down on a coarse carpet, with bruises on his throat, mouth, and chin, and what appeared to be a bite mark on his forearm. Drama turned to mystery when the officer asked Bloom's roommate, Daniel R. Kfoury, age thirty, to explain what had happened.

Kfoury began by saying that he and Bloom had been wrestling. Glancing at Bloom's pummeled body, Officer McFarlane noted that it must have been a hell of a wrestling match. Sensing that the officer was not buying the story, Kfoury coyly added that he was trying to get the demons out of Bloom. A bit bewildered, McFarlane said he'd need a better explanation.

Kfoury finally began to elaborate. He said that he had clamped Bloom's head between his legs and pounded Bloom's spinal area to purge the demons. It made Bloom "vomit and spit up quite a bit." McFarlane instinctively pulled his police radio from his belt and asked the dispatcher to send a homicide unit.

Detective Chuck Shelton arrived about 6:00 a.m. After a short conversation with Kfoury, he learned that Kfoury and Bloom had been living in the basement of Bloom's parents' home. They had separate bedrooms and shared a common kitchen, living room, and dining room area. Shelton observed religious books scattered around the floor and several religious posters on the wall, citing biblical phrases. He also saw what appeared to be blood stains around Bloom's body. Shelton directed a uniformed officer to transport Kfoury to the station for further questioning. The detective then patiently awaited the arrival of the medical examiner. She arrived ten minutes later, officially pronounced Bloom dead, and determined that the cause of death was most likely asphyxiation.

Once the crime scene was secured to Shelton's satisfaction, he went upstairs to interview Bloom's parents. The father, William R. Bloom, said he and his wife had been home all evening and heard nothing suspicious. He had been awakened by the flashing lights of police cars in front of his house. The Blooms were startled to learn that their son had been killed.

Mr. Bloom described his son as the eighth of eleven children. He had been an excellent student and had been on the dean's list at Northern Virginia Community College. Unfortunately, following his freshman year, Robert had sustained severe brain injuries in a bicycle accident while traveling to see his brother in Oregon. On the return trip, he had been hit by a truck in Memphis, Tennessee. The resulting litigation culminated in a civil settlement in excess of one million dollars.

In an interview with the *Washington Post,* Mr. Bloom said that after the accident, his son became "very disoriented, his speech pattern was interrupted, and he was not able to concentrate." According to Mr. Bloom, "He lost his judgment, his discrimination." Bloom also told the *Post* that his son had been reared a Catholic, but in the months preceding his death, he had begun searching for a new religion. Five weeks before his death, he discovered the Five Fold Ministry, which met several times a week in the basement of a twelve-story apartment building in the vicinity of Seven Corners in Falls Church, Virginia. It was there that he met Daniel Kfoury.

In speaking with the *Post,* Mr. Bloom doubted that it was religion that drew his son to the Five Fold Ministry, which had about a hundred members. In his opinion, his son was attracted by the opportunity to meet people. Robert was a lonely young man seeking fellowship. Before the accident, he had had an active social life and dated frequently. After the accident, his old friends seemed to have abandoned him.

During the conversation with Detective Shelton on the morning of his son's death, Mr. Bloom recalled one item among his son's possessions that he thought might be of interest. It was a brochure, apparently produced by the Five Fold Ministry, describing a videotape on demonology. Shelton made a note to check it out.

After concluding the first of several interviews with Mr. Bloom, Shelton headed straight to the station to talk to Kfoury. After being advised of his Miranda rights and signing a waiver-of-rights form, Kfoury began by saying that he had met Robert Bloom one week earlier at the Five Fold Ministry, a "charismatic Christian group." Unemployed, he moved in with Bloom four days before the murder.

Kfoury described the events of earlier the previous evening as an exorcism. Although he denied a sexual relationship, he said that he was very fond of Robert. "It hurt my heart to see a man so bound by demons. They were hurting me; they were hurting Robert. They wanted to destroy us."

In a detailed two-hour videotaped statement to Shelton, Kfoury recounted his attempts to purge the demons. He pinned Bloom between his legs for nearly seven hours and pounded on his back to "cast out the demons"—two thousand demons by Kfoury's count. Kfoury struck Bloom between one and two hundred times, causing vomiting, first of mucous, then of blood. This was his fourth attempt to perform an exorcism on his roommate.

Kfoury explained that exorcism involved purging the demons in progression, or rank, order—from the "privates to the generals." According to Kfoury, the lesser-ranked demons were expelled rather easily, at a rapid pace. When he reached the higher ranks, like the colonel area, the task became considerably more difficult. At that point, Kfoury said that he had been forced to bite Bloom as well as pound the spinal area with his fist and elbows, because the demons "would only leave two at a time." Finally he came face to face with the highest-ranking demon, "Orion."

Kfoury told Shelton that he had a great deal of trouble with this recalcitrant spirit. "Sometimes I had to strike him hard . . . a good healthy blow. I wanted to get this animal, this beast out of him."

At some point, he noticed some discoloration through Bloom's shirt; it appeared that his skin was turning yellow. After hours of pounding, Kfoury said that he was able to expel Orion, "but when Orion left Robert's body, he also took Robert's life with him."

Kfoury then had what he described as "an encounter with the Lord." He prayed for a while, thought about calling the pastor, but decided to call for an ambulance. The delay in calling the police had been necessary to collect his thoughts, to decide how he would describe what happened.

At the conclusion of the interview, Shelton headed straight to my office. The question was, What do we do with this guy? Was this a homicide, an act of negligence, or just an accident? More important, was Kfoury mentally sound? Could this have been drug induced? We needed answers.

There was little doubt in Shelton's mind that Kfoury, who presented himself as a deeply religious person, truly believed that he was acting as a disciple of God. Unless he was putting on one heck of an act, Kfoury sincerely believed that by exorcizing the demonic spirits, he could relieve Bloom of his physical and mental impairments.

From a purely legal perspective, there was no evidence of any ignoble motive or malice. Of course, our investigation was still in its infancy. On the other hand, as a practical matter, Kfoury beat this guy to death—he was even spitting up blood. Kfoury was clearly mentally disturbed. Could he be a homicidal maniac? We didn't know, nor did we know where he would go if released. He appeared to be a drifter.

There were too many unanswered questions to take any chances. I told Shelton to charge him with murder and to ask the magistrate to hold him without bond. We needed to sort this out, piece by piece.

Shelton's next step was to learn what he could about Daniel Kfoury, who described himself as a maintenance worker. What made this strange guy tick? He punched Kfoury's name into the Arlington Police information network. Within seconds the screen lit up.

According to police records, shortly before 1:00 a.m. on October 23, five days before Bloom's death, an Arlington Police officer encountered Kfoury and Bloom slumped down in the front seat of a small blue car. The approaching officer could hear someone yelling for help. Kfoury appeared to be bent over choking Bloom. The officer directed both occupants to sit up in their seats and demanded an explanation from Kfoury. Kfoury calmly explained that there was nothing to be alarmed about. He said that Bloom was possessed by demons and that he was choking them out of him.

Kfoury assured the officer that he knew what he was doing. He was skilled in performing exorcisms. When Bloom said that he had no interest in pressing charges, the officer left thinking it was some kind of joke—until the next night.

Shortly before midnight the following day, the same officer, Mike Fortune, was dispatched to a fight in progress in the 3500 block of Columbia Pike, about five miles from the location of the prior night's incident. Fortune was astounded to again discover Kfoury in the front seat of the car with both hands around Bloom's neck. Kfoury stated that they had just come from church and that he was still trying to purge some of the more stubborn demons from the docile, marginally conscious Bloom. Fortune's first reaction was to arrest Kfoury, but Bloom insisted that everything was being done with his consent. Fortune walked away confused and frustrated after warning them that he'd lock them both up next time.

Shelton's next task was to gather information on Kfoury's background. Kfoury had been discharged from the Army that past August, after a tour of duty in Germany. Prior to moving in with Bloom, Kfoury had been living with his mother in Arlington. Mrs. Kfoury admitted to Shelton that she had been concerned about her son, because he wouldn't find a job. He just sat around her house all day reading books about demons.

Kfoury's father painted a similar picture. He denied that his son was a drug user, a factor Shelton and I had not ruled out. Mr. Kfoury revealed that his son had been acting strangely since leaving the Army. He was obsessed with demons. Mr. Kfoury said that his son had studied theology for two years after graduating from high school, one year at Valley Forge College in Pennsylvania and one year at Gordon College in Massachusetts.

The day following Kfoury's arrest, he made his initial appearance in the Arlington County General District Court. After hearing the strange circumstances of Bloom's death, the judge set bond at one hundred fifty thousand dollars, and scheduled a date for the preliminary hearing. The defense then had one request of the court, and I had two. Kfoury's attorney, John C. Youngs, who had previously represented Joseph Francis O'Brien in the Betty Konopka murder case, asked the court to order a mental examination to determine if Kfoury was competent to stand trial. I joined in the request. We needed to get that resolved up front. That motion was granted.

I next requested that the court direct Kfoury to supply a sample of his blood for analysis and a dental impression or bite sample. I argued that the blood analysis would show whether Kfoury was acting under the influence of any mind-altering drugs, as we suspected. The dental impressions would be used by a forensic dentist for comparison with the various bite marks identified on Bloom's body. Even though we had what amounted to a full confession, I was taking no chances. Given the mystery enshrouding this case, we were preparing for all eventualities.

Although the law was clearly in our favor, Kfoury's lawyer opposed both motions. His reasoning was thin and unpersuasive. Both motions were granted.

As absurd as it may seem, we could foresee the possibility of the religious legitimacy of Kfoury's crude demon deliverance becoming an issue at trial. Kfoury never wavered in his insistence that he was acting at the direction of the Lord. Was there any arguable basis for his belief? Do any recognized religious sects accept such demon purging as part of their founding doctrine, in practice or in theory? These were questions we needed to answer. These were issues we'd inevitably confront at trial, along with a probable intertwined insanity defense. Prior to this case, the only thing I knew about exorcism came from watching the movie, *The Exorcist.* What I eventually learned was eye-opening.

To tackle these issues, I decided to bring in reinforcements, so I asked the best trial lawyer on my staff, Liam O'Grady to join the prosecution team. His Catholic background proved to be an asset.

Our first task was to learn more about the occult Five Fold Ministry, so Shelton casually showed up uninvited at one of their meetings. Even after identifying himself as a homicide detective, several young disciples volunteered that they had assisted Kfoury in attempting an exorcism on Bloom—several days before his death—right there on the church floor. Shelton was amazed by their ease and self-confidence in talking about it—no sign of reluctance or discomfort—in telling it all, to a cop no less. There was something very unsettling about this so-called "church."

Shelton tracked down the pastor, the Reverend Nathan Robinson. Before the detective had completed his introduction, Robinson adamantly denied that his church taught or practiced exorcism. He admitted that Bloom and Kfoury were part of his congregation, but he professed no knowledge of the attempted exorcism at his church. According to the pastor, when Kfoury began talking about demons, he was warned by other church members "to get out of that area." (the *Washington Post,* December 26, 1985). He described his church to Shelton as religiously independent and as subscribing to the "full gospel of the Lord," and disclosed that the church's services were often delivered in tongues. Meaning what? Robinson declined to elaborate.

When asked about the demonology video mentioned by Bloom's father, the reverend fumbled momentarily for words. He agreed that he was familiar with that tape, and that he had plans to show it to the congregation. He denied, however, that it related to any of the church's precepts. The video had been produced by the pastor of another church. When asked if that church was affiliated with the Five Fold Ministry, "Well, not directly," the pastor replied.

"Then why are you showing the film? And what about the pamphlet describing the film, isn't it available at your church?" Shelton asked the minister.

Robinson again paused and cautiously responded that he "just thought it might be something of interest."

Nothing Robinson said allayed Shelton's suspicion that something lurked under the surface of the Five Fold Ministry.

The physician conducting the initial competency examination found Kfoury competent to stand trial. We were not surprised, but we sensed that this cursory examination would not put the issue to rest. We were convinced that his mental state was destined to be *the* central issue.

As was the custom, the preliminary hearing was an abbreviated proceeding—to determine if there was probable cause to believe that a crime had been committed and that the accused committed it. The general district court judge made the requisite findings and forwarded the case to the grand jury. The following week, Kfoury was indicted in circuit court for first degree murder, although we had no illusions that he would be convicted of that.

I asked Circuit Court Judge Paul Sheridan to send the defendant to Central State Hospital for a comprehensive mental examination to determine, not only his competence to stand trial, but also his mental soundness at the time the crime was committed. The defense offered no objection, and inferred that an insanity defense was being contemplated.

While Kfoury was being examined, we wasted little time. Liam O'Grady and I continued to seek out sources of information on exorcism. A close friend of mine, a pathologist at Arlington Hospital, was well connected academically with the staff at Georgetown University, a Catholic school with a distinguished school of theology. The school initially resisted disclosing any information pertaining to exorcism. It was their unwritten policy to refuse even to acknowledge the religious use of the ancient practice. Finally, the university arranged for O'Grady and me to meet a member of the theology faculty with expertise in this area. Our meeting had an added element of intrigue. It was held within yards of where *The Exorcist* was filmed.

Our meeting with the priest was enlightening. He was reticent about discussing any church policies or doctrine relating to the cleansing of evil spirits. He explained that without an appropriate background in the tenets of Catholicism the concept of exorcism would be meaningless. By inference, he did concede that exorcism was an available spiritual tool, but used sparingly. He refused to divulge the type of physical or mental condition that would warrant its use. The priest also declined to discuss how an exorcism was performed, "let's just say—that it's something we don't talk about."

O'Grady and I gave the priest the facts of our case. He smiled momentarily, then stated categorically that what Kfoury had performed on Bloom bore no resemblance to an exorcism.

We next asked if any organized religious sect would employ such a brutal ceremony. He responded that his answer would depend on how I defined "organized religious sect." Yes, he supposed that it was possible that a group organized around some unorthodox religious teaching could endorse a different form of demon deliverance than other recognized religions. But, again he stressed that such pommeling was alien to the theological principles underlying exorcism. He added that those who believe to the contrary have been deluded by *The Exorcist,* which in his view was not moored in reality.

We ended our tutorial by asking if the priest was willing to testify as an expert witness that what Kfoury did to Bloom was not an exorcism. This obviously touched an academic nerve. "But perhaps to him it was an exorcism," the priest noted.

"Okay Father," O'Grady replied, "what about testifying that no recognized religion would condone this type of act."

"And where would that get you?" the intellectually agile priest shot back. "Even if totally grounded in spiritual fantasy, the fact remains that you'll never prove that he had the intent to kill."

Liam and I took a deep breath. Thank goodness this guy wasn't representing Kfoury. In conclusion, I posed the question again, "can we count on your testimony, if necessary?"

A smile came across his face as he answered, "I will gladly do as the bishop instructs." Fat chance we'd ever see him again.

In time, we received the report from Central State Hospital. A diagnostic team consisting of a clinical psychologist and a forensic psychiatrist concluded that Kfoury suffered from a schizophrenic disorder. Kfoury reported hearing the voice of God, which commanded him to do certain things. Whether he was psychotic and delusional was a closer call. However, in the final analysis, the team determined that he understood the judicial process and was competent to stand trial. They further believed that although his thought process was impaired, he was able to appreciate the criminality of his acts at the time the crime was committed. Hence, they found that he was not insane at the time he killed Bloom.

Realizing that the success of the prosecution's case turned entirely on the statements Kfoury had made to the police, Kfoury's lawyers turned their attention to having them thrown out. Their strategy was creative. At first glance, Kfoury's statements satisfied every constitutional standard of voluntariness. He was advised of the Miranda warnings and waived his rights in writing. There was nothing coercive about his discussion with Officer McFarlane or his interview with Detective Shelton. Employing the traditional objective standard, there was also nothing threatening or overreaching about the conduct of the police—at least that a reasonable person could logically draw.

But the lawyers added a new twist. They argued that because of his mental condition, Kfoury was unable to make a conscious choice as to whether it was in his best legal interest to talk to the investigating officers. It was their contention that, because of his mental illness and deeply ingrained religious notions, he was unable to comprehend the potential illegality of his acts. The effect was to obstruct his judgment and compel him, against his volition, to explain his actions. He was simply following God's direction.

Furthermore, despite the well-reasoned conclusions of the psychiatric evaluation team at Central State Hospital, Kfoury's lawyers continued to maintain that their client was incompetent to stand trial, on an equally novel theory. They argued that his mental condition, coupled with his religiosity, precluded him from rationally selecting a theory of defense. The lawyers asked Judge Sheridan to appoint another psychiatrist to examine Kfoury and, they hoped, to serve as the defense expert.

Knowing that a colossal battle of the experts was brewing, I countered by seeking the appointment of a rebuttal expert for the Commonwealth. I didn't ask for just any expert; I asked for the renowned Dr. Park Elliott Dietz, probably the best known forensic psychiatrist in the nation. Park had served with me on the Pornography Commission, and I knew he'd salivate over a case like this one. Judge Sheridan granted both the defense and prosecution motions, and set the case for a hearing on May 21, 1986, on the admissibility of the statements to the police.

## United States Attorney for the Eastern District of Virginia

There was one complicating wrinkle. Following my formal nomination by President Reagan, I had finally on, May 17, been confirmed by the United States Senate as United States Attorney for the Eastern District of Virginia, and had submitted my resignation as commonwealth's attorney effective at the close of business, May 21. However, I figured there was no way the hearing could go more than one day. I was cutting it close, maybe too close, but I wanted to take some time off between jobs.

* * *

O'Grady and I felt confident we'd be able to fend off the defendant's motion to suppress the confession. The motion really had two separate theaters of debate. From a factual perspective, was the defendant mentally capable of knowing and intelligently waiving his constitutional right to remain silent? If we prevailed on this front, it was over. The court would deny the motion and the statement would come into evidence.

On the other hand, if the court ruled that, because of mental illness, Kfoury was incapable of rationally deciding to waive his rights, the legal issues became far murkier and more complex. It was our position that the statement should not be excluded as evidence, since the police did nothing wrong or improper to induce the confession. Excluding that statement would be an improper and absurdly sweeping application of the so-called exclusionary rule, which was judicially created to deter police misconduct and preserve the integrity of the fact-finding process. Although few courts had favorably entertained the defendant's theory, the issue was far from well settled.

O'Grady and I remained convinced we'd never reach the novel legal issues. Both the clinical psychologist and the forensic psychiatrist from Central State Hospital were prepared to testify that Kfoury was mentally capable of making a conscious choice to speak to the police. We thought the evidence was overwhelming, at least until we received the report of my good friend Dr. Dietz, the prosecution's expert.

As predicted, the two doctors from Central State Hospital testified that Kfoury had not been laboring under any delusions when he was interviewed by Detective Shelton. However, in a shocking role reversal, Dr. Dietz ended up testifying as a defense witness. Dietz disagreed with the doctors from the state mental hospital. He described Kfoury as "obsessed with demonology" and as having exhibited chronic symptoms of mental illness. In his opinion, Kfoury did not fully comprehend the consequences of his decision to talk to the police. Kfoury believed that if the police had understood the religious implications of his actions, he would never have been arrested. Dietz said that in Kfoury's view, the police did not understand that he was performing a "valorous act" in the service of God. Dr. Dietz characterized the defendant's statements as pressured, rather than compelled, speech.

Kfoury's court-appointed expert, Dr. Erich Rhinehardt, was a bit more equivocal. He believed that Kfoury was competent to stand trial, but that his ability to understand the legal significance of making a potentially incriminating statement to the police was "borderline." Rhinehardt also concluded that Kfoury was psychotic and delusional at the time of the homicide. If asked, Dr. Rhinehardt would probably have opined that Kfoury was insane when he killed Bloom.

Neither the substance nor the length of the hearing proceeded as anticipated. Dietz's findings were unexpected and required protracted cross-examination to blunt the cutting edge of his opinion. At 5:00 p.m., I had to ask Judge Sheridan to recess for the day. My resignation as commonwealth's attorney had taken effect. I scrambled to locate Judge Winston, the chief judge, who then appointed me for twenty-four hours to fill the vacancy created by my own resignation.

The next morning the court heard legal arguments from both sides. The issues were close, but in the final analysis, we concluded that Judge Sheridan, a conservative former Marine infantry officer, would never put this guy back on the street.

The following day, Judge Sheridan issued an extensive and well-reasoned opinion. The judge concluded:

> Despite some expert testimony suggesting that Daniel Kfoury indeed was suffering from a schizoaffective disorder at the pertinent times, and despite the disturbing nature of the contents of Kfoury's statements, the Court concludes that the Commonwealth has carried its burden of proving that, considering all the circumstances, Daniel Kfoury had sufficient capacity to comprehend his rights, the nature of the acts he described, and the factual and legal framework in which he was talking to the police, and that [his] motion to suppress statements . . . should be denied. (Letter opinion, May 23, 1986)

The hearing served as a reality check. O'Grady, who assumed responsibility for the case after I left, was reminded that a first degree murder conviction was not in the cards. As bizarre as Kfoury's actions may have been, he had no intention to kill—or perhaps even harm—Robert Bloom, whom he professed to love. At best, the facts supported involuntary manslaughter, which is defined in Virginia as "the killing of someone accidentally contrary to the intention of the parties, in the prosecution of some unlawful, but not felonious act, or in the improper performance of a lawful act." Kfoury's attorneys agreed and recommended to their client that he plead guilty to involuntary manslaughter, which carried a maximum penalty of ten years. Kfoury was steadfast that he he had done nothing wrong, and refused the offer. As the trial date approached, Kfoury's lawyers offered a counterproposal.

Kfoury agreed to plead guilty to involuntary manslaughter if he did not have to concede his guilt. Known as an Alford plea, named after the U.S. Supreme Court decision in *North Carolina v. Alford,* this allows defendants in a criminal case to plead guilty because they feel that, based on the strength of the prosecution's case, it is in their best interest to do so rather than go to trial. This was acceptable to O'Grady, who was personally amenable to Kfoury serving any sentence imposed in a mental facility, but refused to join in a specific recommendation to that effect.

In entering his plea of guilty, Kfoury told the court that he feared a jury might not understand his religious beliefs, especially since the case involved an exorcism. Judge Sheridan accepted Kfoury's plea of guilty, but stunned the lawyers by rejecting out of hand his attorney's recommendation that his client receive probation or that any sentence be served in a mental institution. In imposing the maximum sentence, the judge remarked that it "would trivialize that death with anything less than a ten year sentence . . . I have to consider the man who isn't here today . . . Robert Bloom. He was helpless and unable to fight back."

Several months later, my star witness Dr. Dietz and I had a chance to revisit the Kfoury case before a room full of lawyers, psychologists, and psychiatrists at a Forensic Symposium at the University of Virginia Institute of Law, Psychiatry & Public Policy. There were about fifty participants with fifty separate opinions as to how the Kfoury case should have been handled. I still wonder what a jury would have done.

After leaving the Office of the Commonwealth's Attorney, I had little time to worry about Daniel Kfoury. Just one month after I was sworn in as United States attorney for the Eastern District of Virginia, my transition period screeched to an abrupt halt.

Black smoke bellowed for days from riots at one of the most notorious prisons in America, located right in the suburbs of Northern Virginia. Although it was operated by the District of Columbia, it was a federal enclave and, hence, my responsibility. A long-festering point of community controversy erupted into boiling outrage. My orders from the attorney general of the United States were clear: Clean that place up—now.

# XIV

# The Notorious 'Prison Farm'

For the former "porn czar," the path to the attorney general's fifth-floor office at the Department of Justice was a familiar one. I was still a little apprehensive and didn't quite know what to expect in my new capacity. The smiling faces of Ed Meese's staff put me at ease. Then I looked into the waiting area and saw about ten other people, including Norman Carlson, director of the Federal Bureau of Prisons, and James Palmer, head of the D.C. Department of Corrections. It sunk in. This was going to be a heavy meeting.

The Lorton Correctional Complex was located about twenty miles from Washington, D.C., just off I-95 in the southern portion of Fairfax County, near the intersection with Chain Bridge Road. In 1986, it consisted of eight interrelated facilities: Maximum Security, Central Facility (medium security), Occoquan I and II (minimum security), a women's detention facility, two for juveniles, and an industrial plant. The complex was situated on three thousand acres of prime real estate surrounded by family-oriented residential neighborhoods.

The component facilities collectively housed about forty-five hundred inmates who had been convicted of offenses ranging from passing bad checks to multiple homicides. The overcrowded complex had been designed to accommodate only thirty-five hundred. Numerous federal lawsuits had been filed over the years to control its burgeoning population. In order to comply with the court-ordered population caps, the D.C. Department of Corrections (DCDC) would bus prisoners between facilities just before the official head count. They had even parked buses of inmates along the road to avoid exceeding the ceiling. Ninety-eight percent of the prison population was black. Escapes were frequent. There were six escapes from one youth center alone during a six-month period. Two escapees required more than a year to recapture. A loud siren would scream into the night to alert the panic-stricken neighborhood—often several hours after the inmate had made it over the wall and a citizen was calling the police to report an inmate running through the back yard.

The Lorton Reformatory, as it is commonly called, was once a good neighbor. Supposedly, in the early 1900s there was insufficient space within the District of Columbia itself to construct a prison. So the federal government and the District of Columbia entered into a long-term lease for several thousand acres of desolate, undesirable farm land, located too far out in the boonies to bother anyone. At the time of the lease, the land had a probable value of less than a million dollars. By 1986, its value approached one hundred million dollars, and its current value has increased at least another fifty percent.

The original concept was to develop a prison farm that would raise crops and cattle to feed the inmate population, then consisting of only a few hundred. No one ever contemplated that the facility would proliferate into the sprawling complex it eventually became, or that high-end residential communities would abut it. After a couple of incidents where escapees broke into houses to steal a change of clothes, or where housewives were taken hostage and sexually abused, the community was up in arms.

Even more disturbing were the riots and prisoner uprisings. To avoid bad publicity, DCDC would call for assistance from neighboring jurisdictions only when the situation was out of control. More than once, Fairfax authorities first learned of massive disturbances from terrified residents near the institution.

The prison was literally a powder keg. In December 1983, two hundred inmates staged a night-long riot at Youth Center I over the alleged mistreatment of a female visitor. Thirteen correctional officers were injured. At the same facility on April 28, 1986, three hundred fifty inmates incited wholesale disorder during a power outage. The crazed crowd set fourteen separate fires in the maintenance, academic, and administration buildings. Five fires were apparently ignited by firebombs. One correctional officer was severely beaten. Fires burned out of control for almost three hours. It required one hundred twenty-five correctional officers in riot gear and ninety-eight tear-gas canisters to suppress the uprising. The resulting search of the rioters yielded a horrifying mound of baseball bats, hand-crafted knives or shanks, blackjacks, and metal pipes. This followed an incident ten years earlier at Maximum Security where one hundred armed inmates held ten guards hostage for almost twenty-four hours.

By July 1986, the Lorton Reformatory was a white-hot political issue. As firefighters doused flaming buildings during the April riot, members of the Fairfax County Board of Supervisors had held press conferences along the fence line.

Board Chairman Jack Herrity passed out marshmallows suitable for roasting as he grinned for the press cameras. The prevailing mantra was, "Lorton must go." Aside from consternation in the community, Fairfax citizens were forking out millions of un-reimbursed tax dollars each year to provide police and fire protection for a D.C. government facility. This was the political climate when the two minimum security facilities, Occoquan I and II, burst into flames in the early morning of July 10.

It was obvious that the July 10 riot was well-organized and carefully executed. At precisely 12:30 a.m., fires were kindled in fourteen buildings using blankets, mattresses, and assorted rubbish. Within hours, flames were shooting forty feet into the air. The Fairfax County Fire Department was delayed in entering the facility for more than an hour because the guard staff could not bring the inmate population under control. More than twelve hundred inmates, many armed with crude weapons, roamed the grounds. To restore order, twenty-nine prisoners were either shot, or injured by tear gas. Nine correctional officers and six firefighters also sustained injuries. At least two female guards were sexually assaulted. Thousands of inmates were relocated temporarily to other institutions.

Except for the smoldering, the conflagration was pretty much extinguished by daylight. Six buildings had burned to the ground. Several others were uninhabitable. The fire trucks had left, but the fire was far from out. It continued to burn in the craw of every resident of South Fairfax living within five miles of the Lorton Reformatory. The smell of smoke lingered for days. And that's what instigated the meeting at the office of the nation's chief law enforcement officer.

I had hardly had a chance to greet the other people in the attorney general's waiting area when his chief of staff opened the door and summoned me into the boss's office. It was obvious that Attorney General Ed Meese was not happy. As expected, the General had received an earful from the Northern Virginia congressional delegation.

The congressmen made clear that unless prompt corrective action was taken, they intended to introduce legislation requiring the Federal Bureau of Prisons to absorb all forty-seven hundred-plus Lorton inmates into the federal system. Just discussing the idea gave Director Norm Carlson heartburn. D.C. inmates were notoriously lawless, and were accustomed to unprecedented control over the institution. They were generally unwelcome at every other prison in the nation.

In 1978, U.S. Attorney Bill Cummings assigned me and an FBI agent the task of conducting a security survey at Lorton and making recommendations on how to shore up the place. The survey was inspired by the increasing number of stabbings and homicides there. Most of the weekly woundings at the medium security facility were done with crudely crafted knives, commonly called shanks. These weapons of choice were made from strips of metal smuggled out of the prison work shop. Inmates ground one end into a jagged point, and used electrical tape to form a handle at the other end. Some were a foot long, and left an ugly and often lethal wound. People in their path often bled to death before arriving at the hospital.

In our report, we recommended that magnetometers be installed at the exit points of the metal shop and that a closed-circuit TV camera be installed along the perimeter to prevent inmates from tossing pieces of metal out of windows. The U.S. attorney and the director of the DCDC agreed with our common sense recommendation. There would be a cost associated, but only a fraction of the expense for the medical treatment of the half dozen or so inmates shanked each month. We were impressed by the DCDC's response. The recommended security equipment was installed sixty days later. The stabbing incidents declined precipitously. Several months later, they again increased dramatically. Why? Because the magnetometers and cameras were no longer functioning. Why? Because the inmates complained, and the guards didn't want to risk a disturbance by ticking them off. That was the theory of management at Lorton. Keep the inmates happy and they won't riot. My shift ends in seven hours, thirty-five minutes and forty-two seconds. Norm Carlson, a burly well-educated man with close cropped hair, would never put up with that kind of crap. And that was the rub.

Ed Meese was action oriented and bottom-line focused. No way was the Federal Bureau of Prisons taking responsibility for Lorton. He wanted my thoughts before the meeting began. I told Meese that I intended to recommend the formation of a Lorton Task Force, composed of prosecutors from my office, the D.C. U.S. Attorney's Office, the Office of the D.C. Corporation Counsel, and the FBI. It would be a high-visibility full court press. Our initial focus would be those responsible for the July 10 fire. Every significant crime would be vigorously prosecuted—prisoners, guards, administrators—let the chips fall as they may. There was a momentary deliberative twitch of the jaw, and the attorney general nodded his head, "Okay." He stood up and I followed him into the conference room. We had a plan.

The meeting began on a cordial note. Meese welcomed everyone with a smile. Then with ascending seriousness, he launched into an abbreviated summary of the two riots occurring at Lorton during the preceding three months. Director of the DCDC James F. Palmer began to squirm and stare at his deputy seated by his side. As the attorney general began to transition from the April riot at the youth center to the July inferno at Occoquan I and II, Palmer politely interrupted. Palmer, a former U.S. Marshal, defensively noted that too much had been made in the press of the April 28 dustup. He explained that, in essence, it was just a handful of rowdy teenagers who got a little disorderly when the power went out. Palmer added that the correctional staff never lost control, saying, "I wouldn't call it a riot."

Frustration soon overcame Norm Carlson's forbearance. "Wait a minute Jim, didn't they shoot eleven inmates during that disturbance?"

Palmer conceded that they had opened fire with shotguns when a stampeding crowd of inmates charged a group of guards.

"Sure sounds like a riot to me," Carlson noted, smiling to defuse the escalating tension.

Discussion turned to the July melee. Palmer confided that major personnel and structural changes would be forthcoming shortly. It would require at least six to nine months to rebuild the destroyed dormitories. He then made a pitch for federal money to build an additional facility to ease the overcrowding. Meese abruptly responded that it would only be considered if the structure were located somewhere in the District of Columbia. Apparently coached by the mayor, Palmer shook his head and claimed that the mayor wanted to build an eight hundred bed prison in D.C., but the voters were opposed to it. He reiterated his need for federal assistance to upgrade Lorton. Meese just stared straight ahead.

As a conciliatory gesture, the attorney general, over Carlson's objection, agreed to house some of the twelve hundred displaced DCDC prisoners within the Federal Bureau of Prisons until parts of Occoquan I and II were rebuilt. However, Carlson was successful in his demand that a predetermined deadline for their return to DCDC be established. Meese then indicated that he was willing to offer some federal help in the form of a task force of federal agents and prosecutors to tighten down on Lorton. I interjected that I would personally handle the investigation and prosecution of the group that torched the facility on July 10.

Palmer, with a conspicuous lack of enthusiasm, thanked the attorney general, adding that he was not sure *that* was the type of help they needed. The problem, in his view, was overcrowding. On that note, the meeting broke up.

## The Lorton Task Force

Later that morning Joseph DiGenova, United States attorney for the District of Columbia, and I held a press conference at my Alexandria office to publicly unveil the task force. It would consist of five full-time prosecutors drawn from our respective offices, a team of FBI agents, and several Deputy U.S. Marshals. I opened my remarks by stating that our primary mission was to "wrest control from the prisoners at Lorton and place it back into the hands of law enforcement officials." DiGenova used his time at the podium to blast the mayor's handling of the DCDC in general, and his mismanagement of Lorton in particular. He observed that Lorton had never been "viewed as a penal institution" by the prisoners or guards, but as a "home away from home."

A reporter asked if D.C Police or corrections officials would be included in the investigatory group. I replied, "No." We had no problem with the D.C Police, but we had "lost confidence in [the Department of Corrections] and they were being excluded."

Joe DiGenova added that they could well be potential targets of the investigation. In response to other questions, I revealed that we expected early indictments of those responsible for the July riot. We already had prisoners coming forward to cooperate in the investigation. Inmates were angered over the loss of their possessions in the fire and their temporary relocation to more restrictive federal prisons thousands of miles from home.

Our comments did not go unrebutted. D.C. Mayor Marion Barry called a counterpress conference to defend the city's Department of Corrections. He adamantly denied that the prior Thursday's riot showed a lack of control. Instead, he blamed it on the ingenuity of the inmate population, which he described as "rebellious and smart as hell." He said the prisoners had "outmaneuvered the authorities." In the same breath, the mayor praised the DCDC for its excellent management of the facility.

Our press conference and the mayor's response was the lead story on every evening news broadcast in the Washington area. For the new U.S. attorney for Eastern Virginia, the pressure was on. The media would follow this story and keep my feet to the fire. My district and the District of Columbia were unique from all the other federal prosecutors' offices in the country because the president of the United States, the attorney general and almost every member of Congress reads the *Washington Post* every day.

The *Post* had reporters assigned to our offices on almost a full-time basis. Many politicians in Washington complain about biased coverage in the *Post.* My experience was to the contrary. In my five years as U.S. attorney, the coverage of my office was fair, thorough, and well balanced. I had no hesitation in discussing sensitive but appropriate issues off the record or in confidence with fine Post reporters like Rob Howe or Caryle Murphy.

Given the high visibility of this project, failure was not an option. I therefore put one of my best—and toughest—prosecutors, Karen P. Tandy, in charge of the task force. Tandy, who was later appointed head of the Drug Enforcement Administration, had an unparalleled reputation for conducting thorough and meticulous investigations. I also assigned David Cayre, now a circuit court judge in Charlotte, North Carolina, and Roscoe C. Howard, Jr., who was subsequently appointed United States attorney for the District of Columbia, to the prosecution team. Stripped of the varnish, their mission was to kick ass and take names.

The Lorton Task Force wasted no time in letting its presence be known. FBI interviews with disgruntled inmates had confirmed that much of the contraband in circulation at Lorton had been smuggled in by correctional officers. Not all, or even most, of the guards at Lorton were corrupt. On the contrary, most were upstanding people working in a virtual hell hole. But there were rogues, and the honest officers really resented it.

As the sun rose on a Monday morning several weeks later, hundreds of correctional officers clad in dark blue uniforms funneled into the entrance of the medium security Central Facility. A surprise confronted them as they stepped inside for the usual cursory pat down. Rather than the smiling faces of their cohorts, they encountered FBI agents and drug-sniffing dogs. The news traveled through the line at the speed of light. Dozens of correctional officers turned and ran for the parking lot. A couple of officers were ensnared before they could retreat. Others passing through the screening process praised the FBI and expressed their appreciation.

Why hadn't the DCDC done something like this earlier, as most prisons do periodically? Because the agreement between the DCDC and the correctional officers union required union notification in advance of any such screening procedure. The union expressed outrage that my office and the FBI would ignore the agreement, but they eventually got used to it. There was a new sheriff in town.

Prior to the inception of the task force, the prosecution of crime at Lorton was one of lowest priorities in the U.S. Attorney's Office. There were several reasons. First, there was no pressure. Neither the inmates nor the correctional staff were cooperative. An inmate could be stabbed twenty times in front of a dozen other inmates and three guards, and invariably no one saw anything. It was a part of the Lorton culture that inmates settled their differences among themselves. And second, it was hard to convince a jury to convict an inmate for injuring another prisoner unless the circumstances were unusually brutal, like decapitation by a broken ashtray.

But the task force was prepared to play hard ball, including prosecuting uncooperative guards and transferring recalcitrant inmates to rough federal prisons far away from home. Tandy had her team review every pending case, and within a month indictments began to flow—a half dozen at a time—charging inmates as well as guards.

The only people who abhorred Lorton cases more than our office were the U.S. district judges. Our policy of strict prosecution did not go over well with the bench. To reduce the prevalence of shanks, I instituted a policy that every inmate caught with a shank would be prosecuted, rather than merely getting restricted privileges, as before.

We also decided to recommend six-month consecutive sentences in every shank case. Justin Williams was covering court when the first shank case came up for sentencing. Judge Bryan ordinarily displayed great deference for sentencing recommendations made by Williams. On this occasion, the judge abruptly cut him off and asked rhetorically, "Six months? For carrying a shank at Lorton? Heck, I couldn't imagine anyone in their right mind walking around Lorton without a shank as dangerous as that place is." The message was clear.

Judge Bryan was a strong believer that D.C. should clean up its own problems. The fact that D.C. courts were notoriously lenient did not justify the large number of Lorton cases in his court. He strongly reinforced this point one morning several months later. At about eight o'clock, I received a phone call from one of Judge Bryan's law clerks. The judge wanted to see me. It was a routine request. I had an excellent relationship with the judge, who was tough but quite pleasant, at least most of the time. The judge was seated at his desk with a thin smile on his face. He motioned for me to enter his cavernous office.

"Henry, what's this I hear about indicting [a certain unnamed D.C. official] in Alexandria?"

Surprised that the judge was even aware that the idea had been privately discussed, I replied that no decision had been made.

"We don't need that kind of publicity over here," Bryan remarked in his slow southern drawl. "And remember," he added, "you may decide who gets indicted, but I decide who gets a parking space at this courthouse."

The judge punctuated his admonition with a smile. I got the message.

## Keeping a Courtroom Presence

When the first batch of indictments was handed down, I startled the staff by volunteering to try a routine stabbing case myself. The U.S. attorney for the Eastern District of Virginia had historically been an administrator, rarely making a court appearance. With four staffed offices, in Alexandria, Richmond, Norfolk, and Newport News, forty assistants and fifty other support staff, management was a full-time job. Although based in Alexandria, I spent several days each month in Norfolk and Richmond. Most Newport News cases were covered by the Norfolk office.

My decision to maintain an active but small caseload was driven by several factors. I wanted to maintain my reputation as a trial lawyer, someone capable of slugging it out in the courtroom if necessary. A good trial lawyer's ability to settle contentious cases is directly dependant on the adversaries' perception of the threat of having to duke it out in the courtroom. But mainly, it was an issue of leadership.

The U.S. Attorney's Office for the Eastern District of Virginia had a national reputation for handling some of the toughest cases in America. It is the venue preferred by the Department of Justice for the trial of espionage and terrorists cases, as well as massive fraud and drug conspiracies. A tour as an assistant U.S. attorney in Eastern Virginia is a passport to success as a high-dollar trial lawyer or a stepping-stone to high-level government service. We received well over a hundred applications for each vacancy. To provide direction and counsel worthy of the staff's respect, I believed it was critical to demonstrate that I could block and tackle as well as they could.

The case I selected was fairly typical—two inmates shanked another prisoner in the shower. One grabbed, one stabbed. You'd think it would be a slam dunk since a correctional officer had been standing about five feet away. Not at Lorton. When first interviewed, the victim refused to cooperate, and the guard claimed he could not identify the men involved. (My earlier recommendation that all inmates be required to wear their name prominently displayed on their clothing was not well received by the DCDC.)

Under more aggressive questioning by task force agents, the correctional officer finally admitted that he knew the identity of the stabber. The agents were also able to track down another guard who had seen the other participant toss a bloody tee shirt into a trash dumpster minutes after the stabbing occurred. I spent two hours with the victim, including feeding him a couple of cheeseburgers, fries, and a shake. After I agreed to write a letter to the D.C. Parole Board on his behalf, and convinced him we had two other eyewitnesses testifying, he began to limber up, and eventually identified the perpetrators.

My maiden court appearance as the chief federal prosecutor was memorable. The courtroom was packed with staff members who wanted to see the boss in action. No one was more surprised to see me than Judge Bryan. My opening statement went well, but it was down hill from there. The victim, who still had five more years to serve, vaguely recalled being shanked with a nine-inch piece of metal. "Could you be more specific, man, 'bout what you talking 'bout?" was his initial answer. His memory had faded, or perhaps been overcome by more exciting events. He couldn't remember who else was involved. It was "no big deal." Heck, he only spent nine days in the hospital, and had a six-inch scar.

The correctional officer who had witnessed the assault began on a positive note. He hedged a bit, but identified one defendant, the grabber. In response to my questioning, "looks like him." However when confronted on cross-examination with his earlier inconsistent statement to the FBI denying that he could identify anybody, the witness self-destructed and went up in smoke. He did an immediate one-eighty. He really couldn't be sure. He only knew what the FBI told him to say.

Fortunately, the second correctional officer nailed the grabber. He'd seen the guy running from the dorm where the stabbing occurred within minutes of the shanking, bare chested and carrying a bloody tee shirt. Predictably, the jury acquitted the stabber and convicted the grabber. Judge Bryan gave him ten years.

After the trial, Bryan called me into chambers. He began by telling me that in his twenty-five years as a United States district judge, he had never before had the U.S. attorney personally try a case before him. And why this crappy case? The logic was simple. If I didn't immediately take a case and dive into court, I would spend the next four years or so immersed in the bureaucracy of management, constantly making excuses about why I was too busy to try cases. I assured the judge he would see me regularly in court, and I kept that promise.

## What Do You Do If a Fight Breaks Out?

During the year that followed, Karen Tandy and our team of FBI agents spent hundreds of hours interviewing Lorton inmates and guards, trying to build a case against the band of thugs that torched Occoquan I and II. I personally devoted more than a hundred hours questioning reluctant witnesses and talking to prisoners at Lorton. I will never forget a statement made by one of our witnesses. She was a plump, friendly, well-spoken female correctional officer about thirty-five years old, and a single mother of three.

She worked the midnight shift at Occoquan II. Her assignment? Guard the top floor of an un-air-conditioned dormitory where ninety inmates slept on crowded bunk beds. Most beds were eighteen inches apart. She sat inside the door on a folding chair. The door was locked with a padlock, to which she had a key.

"Do you walk around, check the area during the night?" I asked.

"You're kiddin'," was her response. One other guard was responsible for the first floor, which housed a similar number of residents, also packed in like sardines. A supervisor sat in a booth downstairs and, if awake, supposedly checked on her every hour.

As I began my transition to the night of the fire, Karen Tandy quizzically remarked, "I'm curious. What do you do if a fight breaks out, or something? I mean, you're by yourself with all those men?"

The correctional officer stared at Karen for about thirty seconds.

Then she said, "Tell ya the truth. I run like hell."

Many of the correctional officers at Lorton were women, single mothers desperate for a well-paying job. Most were terrified of the inmates. Of course, the male guards were too. Woman officers were known to go to extreme lengths to keep the prisoners under control, often ingratiating themselves with the meanest or most influential guy in the cell block. Several female guards had been raped multiple times on the night of the July riot.

There were approximately twelve hundred inmates in Occoquan I and II on the night of July 10, 1986. Only two were Caucasian. Both had been released on parole at the time of our investigation and were therefore easy for the FBI to track down. They proved to be our best sources of information. They told a story of absolute hell. Every day was the same—fight or submit to abuse. One of the two was a college graduate who served six months at Lorton for passing bad checks. The other was a street-tough drug pusher. Between the two of them, they were able to finger all the major players who planned the riotous rampage. Their stories were corroborated by several extremely cooperative correctional officers, some of whom described July 10 as more frightening than an enemy ambush in Vietnam.

The FBI interviewed more than six hundred inmates. Most were indignant and totally uncooperative. Several, however, were initially willing to testify. They were transferred to safe and relatively comfortable facilities. As the trial date approached, however, many became increasingly hostile. The most probative inmate testimony came from a young man named Earl Latham. Latham and a group of former Lorton prisoners had been shipped to the Federal Correctional Center at Petersburg, Virginia, for temporary housing.

According to Latham, two former residents of Occoquan II, Rodney Jenkins and Carl Henderson, had boastfully admitted torching the dormitory. Their motive was to destroy the facility to force the D.C. government to release them on early parole, in order to avoid sanctions for exceeding the court-ordered prison cap. Crazy?

Not really. The D.C. government has done it before. Maybe Mayor Barry was right. These guys may have been smarter than we gave them credit for.

## An Indictment

Finally, on July 13, 1987, one year and three days after the riot, we indicted the nine people principally responsible. They were charged with arson, inciting a riot, damaging government property, witness tampering, and obstruction of justice. Three pled guilty before trial and agreed to testify. Barry Tapp, an assistant U.S. attorney from D.C., Karen Tandy, and I tried the other six before a jury for three days. It was a rocky road.

Most of the prisoner witnesses spun us by changing their testimony. One of the Caucasian former inmates, the check buster, was excellent; the other was unimpressive. He had recently been rearrested and was going through drug withdrawal. One correctional officer tried to wiggle out of his original story and had to be declared a hostile witness. We were forced to "impeach" his testimony by confronting him with his prior statement implicating the defendants. The other correctional officers pulled it out. They were powerful and unshakable witnesses. The jury deliberated for two days. It was a split decision: Three were convicted and three were acquitted. We were satisfied with the result.

The Lorton Task Force continued its work until the prison was eventually closed and all inmates were transferred to federal custody. Now, thousands of homes and townhouses are being built on the land where the correctional complex once stood, bringing gridlock to already overcrowded roads, and forcing schools to instruct children in trailers. On reflection, some community activists are now saying that maybe that old prison wasn't that bad after all.

## Alleviating Overcrowded Conditions

When I entered the U.S. Attorney's Office as United States Attorney for the Eastern District, it had changed considerably since I left in 1979. It was still located in a three-story storefront building in the heart of Old Town Alexandria, just across from the Federal Courthouse. (Today, that structure houses Pier I Imports.) The assistant U.S. attorneys had increased from nineteen to twenty-nine, and there was a perception that the office had been poorly managed under my immediate predecessor. Virginia Senators John Warner and Paul Trible directed me to "clean house" and get the office in shape. However, it was apparent to me that the office did not need a wholesale change in personnel—the existing staff needed leadership and direction. To accomplish that, I enlisted two of my most trusted confidants in the office—my long-time friends Ken Melson and

Justin Williams. I made Melson the first assistant, or second in command. Williams, who turned down the first assistant's job, took over as chief of the Criminal Division. I also created a new position of chief of the Special Prosecutions Unit, which turned out to be the hottest spot in the office. Joe Aronica was tapped for that extremely demanding job. Within six months, the office had regained its national stature, but for us that was not good enough.

As our track record improved, our case load swelled. Because the U.S. District Court in Alexandria moved cases faster than any other court in the nation, and the judges were renowned for handing down tough sentences, the Department of Justice resumed steering many nationally significant cases there. As a result, we had at least a dozen lawyers on temporary assignment from the DOJ, designated as special assistant U.S. attorneys, continuously camped out throughout the office, along with endless boxes of documents.

It looked more like a warehouse than a law office. In time, our staff doubled in size, to one hundred fifty-nine employees—fifty-four of them assistant U.S. attorneys. Finally, the Alexandria Fire Marshal, who was working closely with us on several investigations, served me with a fire-code violation notice for gross overcrowding, which was forwarded to the DOJ. As a result, we were forced to relocate to plush offices with balconies and views of the Potomac River. The fire marshal was instantly elevated to "most favored client status." Thereafter, he always received red-carpet treatment from my staff.

In hiring our assistants, Melson and I looked for young attorneys with experience and a demonstrated ability to try cases. We could care less where they went to law school, what their grades were like, or whether they had been selected for law review. We were looking for critical skills, such as the ability to cross-examine a witness, properly organize a case, and give a compelling final argument. With a huge field of applicants, we could be choosey. Like the well-remembered George Allen, legendary head coach of the Washington Redskins, we only wanted veterans with a track record of performance.

Each applicant was subjected to several rounds of interviews, culminating in a one-hour meeting with Melson and me. The final interview was anything but routine. It included a series of practical legal problems designed to test the applicant's ability to approach and solve everyday legal problems. About seventy-five percent of the applicants washed out after the oral exercise. There was one other important criterion. Although we wanted aggressive people, they had to understand that we were lawyers first—and prosecutors second—always courteous, ethical, and aboveboard.

## Finding a Focus

To attempt to achieve everything as U.S. attorney would inevitably result in achieving nothing, so I focused attention on white-collar crime, developing a closer working relationship with state and local law enforcement to combat drug trafficking, and devising a more effective scheme to stem the flow of illegal firearms. I also shifted the historical prosecution perspective from a purely reactive caseload to a proactive response to crime problems. Through an active line of communications with federal law enforcement agencies and our state and local counterparts, we would identify criminal activity and get aggressively involved in the initial investigative stages.

The only downside was the results. The office was awash in high visibility, labor intensive cases by mid-1987. I deserved minimal credit. Our dedicated prosecution teams became relentless engines, cranking out one indictment after the next. At one point, we had fifteen wiretaps running simultaneously, and scores of federal agents assigned to our office. Grand juries were hearing evidence almost every day. At times, the stress became hard to handle. Without the capable leadership of Ken Melson, Justin Williams, and Joe Aronica, I would have been swept under.

## The Pizza Connection

Several of our cases were national in scope. One that I particularly enjoyed was a team effort with Rudy Giuliani's office in New York. Guiliani had just stepped down as associate attorney general of the United States, the number three post at the Department of Justice, to serve as the United States attorney for the Southern District of New York. The investigation began in New York City in 1984, when the FBI learned that organized crime families were using pizza parlors as fronts for laundering drug money. Brutal interfamily rivalry and ruthless competition eventually flushed out enough informants to launch an investigation that grew to span the entire east coast, including Virginia.

The target of the investigation was a rapidly expanding joint venture between members of the Sicilian Mafia and the Medellin cartel, controlled by Jorge Ochoa Vasquez, one of the world's largest cocaine distributors. The press dubbed the case "the Pizza Connection." Only a small part of the case was based in Virginia and D.C., but the cells we identified were the seeds of major organized crime in the Washington area. At a press conference later, Joe DiGenova, the U.S. attorney for D.C., characterized it as "highly sophisticated criminal elements" of traditional organized crime families infiltrating the D.C. area to take advantage of the "booming drug market."

The cocaine syndicate was operated from unobtrusive pizza outlets in the Washington area. It was a perfect marriage. The parlors enabled the Mafia to launder money by investing in low-visibility cash businesses financed with drug money. For the cartel, the pizzerias became factory outlets for Colombian cocaine, shipped to the shops dissolved in canned tomato paste. Upon arrival from New York in secret compartments in trucks, the drugged paste was decanted and chemically dried into powder. Nine cans yielded approximately one pound of cocaine. The organization was moving about one hundred pounds of cocaine a month. Up to that point, it was the biggest drug operation uncovered in the D.C. area, and it was developed through the ingenuity of Special Agent James L. Glass, Jr., of the FBI. Justin Williams and I could not resist the temptation to jump on board.

Glass had an eye for the mobsters, having spent years with the FBI investigating organized crime. He also knew from the New York investigation that the Washington-area market appealed to the Sicilian Mafia bosses. Glass began hanging out in some of the Sicilian pizza shops. He struck gold at the Alfredo and Miriam Pizzeria on Vermont Avenue, about five blocks from the White House. After several weeks of surveillance, Glass identified an array of suspected organized crime figures. The owner of Alfredo and Miriam Pizzeria was Alfredo Toriello, known as "the Butcher," whom Glass knew by reputation was connected to the Genovese family. Toriello earned his nickname as a ruthless debt collector for the New York family.

Three other frequent patrons drew Glass's attention: Benjamino Centurino, Giuseppe Luciano Cottone, and his brother, Sal Cottone. All three were known to be "made members" of the Sicilian Mafia. Centurino owned the K Street Eatery, a pizza carry-out in the heart of the Washington business district. The Cottone brothers operated Pizza Delight franchises in the Springfield Mall and in a small shopping center in Winchester, Virginia. A review of informant data on file at the FBI revealed that Sal Cottone was believed to be a high-level Sicilian mob boss.

In addition to carry-out, the K Street Eatery featured delivery of high-grade cocaine concealed in pizzas to select customers. Undercover FBI agents were able to place several orders for home delivery using an elaborate system of code words gleaned from a court-authorized wiretap. The pizza was delivered in piping hot boxes. A later search warrant resulted in the seizure of more than a dozen cans containing cocaine suspended in tomato paste.

The Virginia connection proved tougher to penetrate. Outwardly, Pizza Delight appeared to be a typical over-the-counter food franchise inconspicuously occupying a corner space in the food court of a suburban Virginia shopping mall. The Springfield Mall was a sprawling structure of three floors accommodating well over a hundred stores. The food court was situated on the third floor. Fast food vendors encircled sections of wooden tables where shoppers dined. Even on a weekday, hundreds of shoppers roamed the corridors of the immense enclosed shopping complex. On weekends, it was a mob scene, in more ways than one.

FBI agents knew from wire intercepts coupled with limited informant data that Pizza Delight was actually a wholesale outlet for massive quantities of nearly pure cocaine. Based on the conversations intercepted, and surveillance of Joe Cottone's movements, the FBI expanded the wiretaps to include the home phones of two members of the Medellin cartel, Diego and Elieser Hoyos. Further intelligence analysis suggested that the Hoyos brothers were the Washington connection. Now, Glass had to connect the dots.

During his investigation, Glass had developed an insider as an informant, a wiseguy who suspected that his days might be numbered. The informant introduced an undercover FBI agent, John Brown III, to Joe Cottone. Brown deftly played the role of a high-rolling cocaine wholesaler. Cottone fell for it and, within days, sold Brown several ounces of cocaine in the Springfield Mall parking lot and, later, in front of Pizza Delight in Winchester. Brown continued to make purchases to elevate the confidence level. This set the stage for the final act—a scene with all the players.

Brown ordered up six pounds of cocaine. To lubricate the deal, he was willing to pay top dollar, but he needed it quick. This sent the syndicate into overdrive, casting security to the wind. The phone taps gave the FBI total control. Cottone called his immediate supplier, Alexandria Del Sordi, who in turn called the Colombian pipeline, Elieser Hoyos. Two hours after Brown's call to Cottone, FBI agents watched Hoyos hand Del Sordi a plastic bag in the parking lot of a Denny's restaurant. It appeared to contain cans of dog food and kitty litter. Del Sordi proceeded directly to the parking lot of Commonwealth Doctors' Hospital in Fairfax County, where he delivered the bag to Joe Cottone.

Later that evening, agent Brown linked up with Joe Cottone at the Crystal City Holiday Inn in South Arlington. Brown took the bag of canned goods, containing three kilograms of uncut cocaine, and handed Cottone one hundred five thousand dollars cash. The loop was completed when Cottone met up with Del Sordi in front of the First American Bank at the Burke Center Plaza in Fairfax County to deliver the cash. And it was all caught on tape.

Eventually, the decision was made to take down the operation in a nationally coordinated roundup. By this time, Special Agent Brown had purchased more than twenty-four pounds of cocaine with four hundred twenty thousand dollars in FBI funds. In all, twenty-two people were arrested in Virginia and D.C., including a receptionist with the Colombian Embassy who had direct ties to drug kingpin Ochoa-Vasquez. All defendants pled guilty to cocaine trafficking charges and agreed to cooperate, despite the traditional consequences for breaching the code of silence.

The results on the New York end were legendary, and helped propel the assistant U.S. attorney heading the investigation, Louis Freeh, to the position of director of the FBI. But for our office, the investigation wasn't over.

Despite the blizzard of commendations, Glass was not satisfied. The investigation had failed to touch the man overseeing the mob's interests in the pizza parlors, Sal Cottone. After the Washington bust, Cottone relocated to Norfolk, Virginia, where he opened Michelangelo's Restaurant and a beverage wholesale business. Glass eventually learned that another FBI agent had cultivated an informant within the Sicilian Mafia. Through the mob network, the informant arranged a meeting with Cottone at his restaurant in Norfolk. Circumspect by nature, Cottone refused to exchange more than casual greetings with the informant until a recognized Mafia member vouched that he was "a friend of ours."

Once the informant was appropriately introduced, he spent several weeks nurturing the confidence of Cottone. A recurring topic of conversation was Cottone's abhorrence of Frank Casali, the guy who had introduced Special Agent Brown to his brother Joe, who was now serving time in the federal pen. Cottone desperately wanted the guy taken out, but knew that he was still too hot to arrange a hit. The informant was quick to accommodate a member of the family. He'd get back to Cottone.

# XV

# IMPEACHMENT?

A week later, the informant returned in company with an associate of the New York mob known to be a brutal enforcer. The hit man confided to Cottone that he knew where the witness protection program had stashed Casali. The cagey Cottone was not convinced. He wanted proof—current photos, particularly one of Casali wearing his ostentatious signature diamond-studded medallion. Two days later, Cottone's eyes lit up when the mobster returned with the photos. Cottone was convinced that this guy was for real. He had two special requests. He wanted Casali blown away with a sawed-off shotgun, and he wanted the medallion as a souvenir. Neither was a problem. Unknown to Cottone, the hit man was an FBI agent who had penetrated a New York family and remained in deep cover for years.

Cottone insisted on knowing the precise date and time of the hit. He wanted to have an air-tight alibi. They chose October 11, 1988.

Several days later, the hit man returned to Michelangelo's Restaurant. Cottone danced with delight when the undercover agent produced a staged photograph of Casali's blood-spattered body, covered in dirt like a piece of breaded fish, lying in a roadside ditch. The picture had required five bottles of catsup to create. As added proof that the deed was done, the agent tossed the medallion on the table, along with an added bonus—Casali's gold watch. Cottone yelled, "God bless America."

On that note, Special Agent Jim Glass stamped the case file closed. Cottone was convicted of a host of racketeering-related charges and now resides permanently in a federal prison.

## CAROLYN HAMM

I hadn't given the Carolyn Hamm murder case much thought after leaving the Office of the Commonwealth's Attorney, until I received a call to attend a meeting at the Arlington County Police Department. When I entered the conference room, I was a little surprised by the number of people in attendance. It was a full house—Chief Stover, Helen Fahey (who succeeded me as commonwealth's attorney), Detectives Shelton and Carrig, and a host of others. After some light conversation, I took a seat, still somewhat tense. Detective Joe Horgas placed a few charts on an easel and began his presentation. Horgas, a well-respected veteran homicide investigator with whom I'd worked many times when I was a state prosecutor, laid out in elaborate detail his theory of who killed Carolyn Hamm.

Horgas meticulously analyzed the characteristics of several similar burglary cases in the Arlington area in which the victim had been brutally sexually assaulted, carefully identifying the common elements. He next compared those characteristics with the modus operandi of Timothy Spencer, the notorious "Southside Strangler," who had recently been convicted of capital murder in Arlington County and sentenced to death in a case whose facts closely resembled the Hamm case. These included entry through a basement window, trashing the contents of the house, and dumping the victim's purse near the front door. Each involved strangulation of the victim with a ligature or rope. In most of the sexual assault cases discussed by Horgas, Spencer had been linked by DNA evidence to the crime scene. The bottom line was that in Horgas's opinion, Spencer had also killed Hamm. Stover and Fahey agreed.

Horgas's presentation was impressive. He had a lot of experience; his conclusions carried weight. I figured that if he, Stover, and Fahey believed that Vasquez was innocent, I had no reason to second guess them. Carrig and Shelton were a little miffed that their judgment was being second-guessed, but in time they'd get over it.

Fahey told me that they were going to ask Governor Gerald Baliles for a full pardon for David Vasquez. I expressed no opposition. If he was truly innocent, he should be set free as soon as possible.

Governor Baliles, a personal friend for whom I have immense respect, granted Vasquez's petition and gave him an unconditional pardon. The Virginia General Assembly awarded him a structured one hundred seventeen thousand dollar compensation package, with a payout of about nine hundred fifty dollars a month. I certainly wish him the best, and regret what happened. However, I offer no apologies.

Every author who has written a book about Vasquez or the Hamm murder, and a number of reporters doing follow-up articles, have asked me how I would have handled the case differently. I would have done nothing different.

Based on the eyewitness identifications, people who knew David Vasquez, and his statements to police, I believed there was probable cause that he was

somehow involved in the Hamm murder. Obviously, Detectives Shelton and Carrig, as well as their supervisor, agreed. A neutral magistrate reviewed the evidence and concurred by issuing a warrant for Vasquez's arrest. A general district court judge heard most of the witnesses and examined Vasquez's statements at the preliminary hearing. The court found that there was probable cause to believe that Vasquez was involved. When the case was presented to a grand jury, those seven citizens heard a summary of the prosecution's case and concluded that there was sufficient probable cause to indict Vasquez for capital murder. My duty at that point was to present the case to twelve jurors. It was their job to decide—that's the way the system works in America. Vasquez chose to fold his cards.

Was there enough evidence to convict David Vasquez? Reasonable minds could differ, but apparently David Vasquez thought so. He pled guilty and accepted an agreed sentence of thirty years.

Was this a flimsy case?

### Fraud in the Defense Industry

It began with a late afternoon briefing—one that would belie its eventual significance. Joe Aronica, chief of the Special Prosecutions Unit, had mentioned in passing that the FBI and the Naval Criminal Investigative Service (NCIS) wanted to bring me up to speed on a developing fraud case. A small group of agents casually walked into the office and sat down on the leather couch. They had suspected for some time that there was an undercurrent of corruption within the Department of Defense (DoD) procurement system. A network, perhaps involving faithless government officials, that enabled sensitive inside information to be leaked to contractors, was undermining the integrity of the procurement process. For years, the FBI and NCIS had detected symptoms, such as four hundred dollar toilet seats and hundred twenty-five dollar hammers, and heard rumors from disgruntled bidders, but never had the opportunity to penetrate the network—until now.

An unusual alignment of the stars created a unique window of opportunity. On the morning of September 5, 1986, a former civilian employee of the Navy Department called the regional fraud unit of the NCIS at the Washington Navy Yard. The caller, who was then employed by a small defense contracting firm, revealed that a procurement consultant had offered to sell him his competitor's bidding information on a pending U.S. Navy contract. This would have enabled the contractor to file a "best and final offer" developed with inside information, a total perversion of the DoD contracting system. The contractor agreed to cooperate with the investigators. The agents ran a quick background check on the con-

sultant attempting to peddle the numbers and learned that he was awaiting trial on felony charges in state court. This gave the agents maximum leverage.

Much of what the cooperating contractor said appeared to check out. If the agents could corroborate the rest, they might apply for authority to "go up" on a wiretap. I pledged whatever resources were necessary to make it happen. They agreed to keep me posted.

Like a submerged submarine, they filed quietly out of the office. In time they would resurface. But, no one ever imagined what lurked below the surface—one of the largest fraud schemes in American history.

## Lyndon LaRouche

There were many memorable moments during the three-year investigation of perennial presidential candidate Lyndon H. LaRouche, Jr., and his band of groupies. His comments before being sentenced in U.S. District Court in Alexandria for masterminding a massive fraud scheme stand out. As part of a rambling statement, LaRouche told Judge Bryan that he had irrefutable evidence that Queen Elizabeth II of England was an international drug dealer, that the Department of Justice was part of a conspiracy to cover it up, and that former Secretary of State Henry Kissinger was a Soviet agent. It was entertaining but without effect.

I vividly remember the day LaRouche was sentenced. Hundreds of people were on the streets of Old Town Alexandria, some to support their political hero, others wondering how to recoup money fleeced by his organizations. And there were dozens of cops—federal, state, and local—who had relentlessly pursued the inscrutable crook, patiently awaiting the moment of reckoning.

That afternoon, just before the sentencing proceedings began, Liam O'Grady, whom I'd recently brought over to the U.S. Attorney's Office from Arlington, and I were walking down King Street to the bank. It was a cool sunny day and protestors, for and against LaRouche, were standing along the street wearing large signs. On the return trip, one caught my eye. The sign proclaimed in huge letters, "Impeach Henry Hudson." The young man holding the sign had a neatly trimmed goatee and was wearing a tee shirt proclaiming that LaRouche had been "framed." We just walked on by. Suddenly, unable to resist, I turned and, with a disarming smile, approached the youth.

"Hey," I inquired, "who is this Henry Hudson?"

"I don't know," he candidly replied, "but I can tell you one thing, he's a real asshole."

Liam and I laughed and walked away. Guess it goes with the territory.

When the LaRouche organization relocated from New York City to Loudoun County, Virginia, in 1984, it was not warmly received. Located in the heart of Virginia horse country, Loudoun County is one of the fastest-growing communities in Virginia. Per capita income ranks in the top bracket, nationwide. Traditionally populated by self-proclaimed Virginia aristocracy, polo and fox hunting are popular pastimes. Just thirty-five miles west of Washington,D.C., the county is home to many capital city rich and famous who enjoy country living. Lyndon LaRouche did not exactly fit in, although he promised the local newspaper that he would be a quiet neighbor. And he kept his word, at least for the first six months. Things began to deteriorate when he publicly accused the local garden club of being a bunch of drug dealing, homosexual, communist sympathizers.

By early 1985, John R. Isom, sheriff of Loudoun County, had reached his wit's end. Within a span of less than six months, the sheriff's office had received more than a hundred complaints of unscrupulous fund-raising activities. Their "phones rang everyday" with reports of heavy-handed solicitation.

An elderly person would report being inveigled into loaning money at an exorbitant interest rate, ten to fifteen percent, to one of the LaRouche organizations for what appeared to be a noble purpose, such as combating teen drug use. In all, his group solicited about thirty-four million dollars in loans. Few were ever repaid, unless the lender hired a lawyer and threatened to file suit. We were able to establish from documents later seized by federal agents that the group had a corporate policy of stonewalling creditors.

Other complaints to the sheriff were from people who had been accosted by a "LaRouchite," as his followers were called, at an airport, shopping center, or post office and persuaded to purchase a subscription to a magazine published by LaRouche, using a credit card. Frequently the amount actually charged on the credit card slip was inflated; for example, from twenty-five to two hundred fifty dollars. In addition, his band of solicitors prepared "contact cards" on everyone who contributed or subscribed to one of the magazines: *Fusion, New Solidarity,* or *Executive Intelligence Review,* among others.

The contact cards were used by a cadre of LaRouche telephone solicitors to hound people for additional loans or contributions. Some people received as many as thirty calls in one week—four or five calls a day from the boiler-room operation. The scheme targeted elderly people with conservative viewpoints, many of whom embraced some of the political positions of Lyndon LaRouche.

Because LaRouche and his National Democratic Policy Committee were based in Loudoun County, law enforcement agencies around the nation directed victims to contact Sheriff Isom. It soon became more than he and his deputies could handle. Isom enlisted the assistance of the FBI and the Virginia State Police, but little action ensued. Isom next proceeded to Richmond and met with Attorney General Mary Sue Terry, who promptly energized the State Police.

By the time I was sworn in as U.S. attorney in June of 1986, the LaRouche investigation had been gaining momentum for almost eight months. Because the Boston office of the FBI had been actively working the LaRouche organization, our office had been playing a subordinate role. That changed in August. Within the course of a week, I received calls from Attorney General Terry, Sheriff Isom, and the superintendent of the Virginia State Police, all requesting our assistance in leading a concentrated effort to curb LaRouche's fraudulent activities. By the end of the week, I'd also received a call from William Weld, U.S. attorney for Massachusetts, who wanted to join our collaborative investigative team.

The following week I was off to Boston with two of my assistants to discuss the case with Weld and his staff, who had been hot on LaRouche's tail for almost a year. The quick response was necessitated by Weld's imminent departure from his Boston post to the Department of Justice in Washington. He had just been confirmed by the Senate to be the assistant attorney general of the United States in charge of the Criminal Division. Fortunately, that placed almost unlimited DOJ resources at his disposal.

Weld's staff had already made considerable progress. Scores of victims had been interviewed by the FBI, many of whom had testified before a federal grand jury. Bill Weld, who would later be elected governor of Massachusetts, was impressively organized and had formulated a game plan in advance. He suggested that his office focus on the credit-card fraud and that Virginia take the lead on the mail-and-wire fraud. Boston would also indict members of the LaRouche organization for obstruction of justice and destroying evidence subpoenaed by a federal grand jury.

LaRouche associates were suspected of sending potential witnesses to Europe to avoid testifying before a federal grand jury, and burning and shredding subpoenaed documents. The FBI office in Boston had obtained internal documents written by LaRouche security personnel to staff advising them that "paper burns at 451 degrees Fahrenheit." A federal judge in Boston had already fined the LaRouche organization twenty-one million dollars—forty-five thousand dollars a day—for failing to turn the documents over to the grand jury.

Weld envisioned the centerpiece of our investigation to be the simultaneous execution of search warrants on the offices of the various business entities controlled by LaRouche, most of which were located in Loudoun County. Always results oriented, Weld wanted to serve the warrants in three or four weeks, an aggressive time frame for such a sensitive case.

The raids would require extensive planning, particularly since LaRouche had told his supporters that any attempt to arrest him would be tantamount to attempting to kill him. Consequently, LaRouche claimed that he would not submit "passively" to arrest, but would defend himself. LaRouche later reiterated the message in a personal telegram to President Reagan. LaRouche lived in a rented mansion converted into an armed fortress patrolled by guards. He justified the security by claiming to be targeted for assassination by the Soviet KGB.

An FBI agent in Boston testified that a high-level LaRouche associate had said on several occasions that Bill Weld "deserved a bullet between the eyes." The raids on the base of operations would clearly require extraordinary security precautions.

Lyndon LaRouche was no stranger to Alexandria federal court. In 1984, he filed suit against NBC for broadcasting a story that accused him of being anti-Semitic. NBC filed a counterclaim for interfering with network operations. According to the complaint, a LaRouche follower, identifying himself as an NBC employee, canceled an interview the network had set up with U.S. Senator Daniel P. Moynihan of New York.

LaRouche employed his usual litigation strategy of tossing a monkey wrench in the works. Even before the trial began, he was fined by the judge for walking out during a deposition. At trial, LaRouche continually attempted to delay the proceedings with his outrageous demands for additional personal security. He believed that he had been targeted for assassination because of his strident opposition to drugs and his conservative viewpoint. The judge's patience thinned quickly.

LaRouche's evasive trial tactics failed to ingratiate him with the jury. In response to NBC's questions on cross-examination, he would launch into lengthy diatribes about communism or worldwide drug-smuggling conspiracies. The judge repeatedly admonished him to answer the question asked. Maintaining control of the circus-like atmosphere took full time. At one point during cross-examination, LaRouche turned the chair on the witness stand toward the wall as a gesture of disrespect. His antics scored no points with the court.

The jury rejected his claim against NBC and socked him on the counterclaim. The jury awarded NBC two thousand dollars in compensatory damages, and a whopping three million dollars in punitive damages. The numbers were so disproportionate that the judge, in a consummate act of dispassionate judgment, reduced the punitive damages to the more reasonable sum of two hundred fifty thousand dollars. The stonewalling really began at that point.

Despite living on a rented two hundred acre estate in Loudoun County, valued in excess of $1.5 million (1986 dollars), with horses and a huge swimming pool, LaRouche professed to have neither money nor any source of income. His affiliated organizations owned approximately $4.2 million in real estate in Loudoun County. All of his expenses were paid by generous benefactors. He claimed he didn't even know who owned the clothes he was wearing. After devoting almost two years to collecting their judgment, to no avail, NBC asked the court to compel LaRouche to truthfully answer questions concerning his assets. Rather than divulge the details of his financial underworld, LaRouche paid up.

Preparation for serving search warrants on the offices of the LaRouche enterprises was greatly aided by the advance work of the Boston prosecutor's office. It had already prepared a rough draft of the affidavit needed to secure the warrant from a judge. The Virginia attorney general, the State Police and the Loudoun County sheriff were ecstatic about the accelerated time frame. While we burnished the final version of the affidavit, the FBI—now joined by the IRS—and the State Police made final plans for the raid. The completed game plan was as detailed as any crafted by a military strategist, complete with armored vehicles and aircraft.

During the last stages of preparation, an undercover state trooper purchased a subscription to two LaRouche publications at Washington National Airport. The subscriptions to *Fusion: Science, Technology, Economics and Politics* and *Executive Intelligence Review* cost $75. The trooper also provided the information necessary for the LaRouchite to prepare the contact card, including a specifically dedicated undercover phone line. Over the next seven days, LaRouche representatives made twenty-two calls to the undercover phone, haranguing the trooper to loan money to LaRouche's campaign.

The week preceding our raid, ten LaRouche associates had been indicted on credit-card fraud and related charges in Boston. Also charged in that indictment were a number of LaRouche organizations, including the LaRouche Campaign, Independent Democrats for LaRouche, Campaigner Publications Inc., Caucus Distributors, and the National Caucus of Labor Committees. In all, the indictment alleged that more than a thousand people had lost in excess of one million dollars. The one hundred seventeen count indictment was placed under seal, and arrest warrants were issued for the ten indictees. Coincidentally, the day of the Boston indictment was the same day the U.S. Supreme Court refused to hear LaRouche's appeal of the NBC decision.

Monday, October 6, 1986, was the appointed day. Not since the Confederate Army of the Potomac paraded through the town of Leesburg on September 5, 1862, led by General Robert E. Lee en route to the Battle of Sharpsburg, had the citizens of Loudoun County witnessed such an impressive showing of governmental might. The predawn procession extended almost two miles, with one hundred fifty federal agents, one hundred forty-five Virginia State Troopers—some in armored vehicles, others with canines—and about fifty sheriff's deputies. The brigade was covered by air support. A tank was brought in on the back of a tractor trailer. The designated staging area was the 4-H Fairgrounds. Citizens crowded the street. "what the hell's going on?" was the frequently heard question. Word spread quickly. Finally, something was being done. Loudoun County Supervisor Frank Raffo danced in the street, yelling that we had "made his day."

The targets of the search warrants were two of the business offices of the LaRouche organization located in the heart of Leesburg, the historic county seat of Loudoun County, 20 South King Street and 722 East Market Street. Two large trucks rented by the FBI transported more than three hundred boxes of materials from these locations. Federal agents described it as "a gold mine." LaRouche's employees were totally cooperative.

Among the records seized were documents that had been withheld from the Boston grand jury, and extensive files on Bill Weld, his family, neighbors, and in-laws, along with a number of semiautomatic weapons. FBI agents also searched a branch office of Caucus Distributors, Inc., located in Quincy, Massachusetts, in the outskirts of Boston. Six indicted members of the LaRouche organization there were also taken into custody.

In his public response to the searches, which he described as a "panty raid," LaRouche reiterated his intention to seek the presidency a fourth time in 1988. In his opinion, three people were responsible for the raids: White House Chief of Staff Donald Regan, U.S. Attorney William Weld, and Soviet leader Mikhail Gorbachev. Mikhail Gorbachev? Yes, supposedly Gorbachev had demanded "his head" as a price for the Iceland summit with President Ronald Reagan.

LaRouche characterized the transactions in the Boston indictment as purely campaign contributions. He could not repay the millions of dollars in outstanding loans because the government had shut his businesses down. The organization was the subject of lawsuits in fifteen other states around the nation, extending from Alaska to Delaware to Texas to California.

Simultaneously, I asked our financial litigation expert, David Schiller, to devise a legal means by which we could assist the victims in recouping their losses. This would necessarily entail seizing the assets of the various operating

*Discussing final plans for serving search warrants on the executive offices of Lyndon LaRouche in Leesburg, Virginia in 1986.*

LaRouche entities before they were depleted. Schiller suggested a rarely used procedure called an involuntary bankruptcy petition. It is the converse of the typical bankruptcy action. The creditors, rather than the debtor, petition the court for bankruptcy relief. In the LaRouche case, there were thousands of potential creditors in amounts varying from a hundred to a hundred thousand dollars. All were clamoring for their money back, but few were willing to come forward to serve as specifically named petitioning creditors.

Schiller developed a novel approach. The United States, on behalf of all the unnamed creditors, would petition the U.S. Bankruptcy Court for involuntary relief against the LaRouche organization. Theoretically, this would place all LaRouche assets under the control of that court and afford the creditors an opportunity to file claims for repayment. The procedure was admittedly unorthodox, but Schiller was an exceptionally bright lawyer. I authorized him to file the petition. The bankruptcy judge had no hesitation in issuing an order placing all of LaRouche's corporate and political assets under the jurisdiction of the bankruptcy court. This enabled federal agents to quickly identify and freeze almost everything.

As expected, Lyndon LaRouche went on the offensive. First, he called a press conference to denounce the seizure as "a political dirty trick," an attempt by the Reagan administration to derail his contemplated 1988 campaign for President. In his unsuccessful 1984 bid, LaRouche had received 78,773 votes, or nine hundredths of one percent of the total votes cast. The chairman of the National Democratic Policy Committee, an arm of the LaRouche political network, told the Associated Press that LaRouche was running "the cleanest political organization in the country." The chairman also added that if LaRouche was indicted, the Reagan administration "will be condemned by history."

Next, LaRouche unleashed his bevy of hard-hitting lawyers, who filed a motion with the Bankruptcy Court to dismiss the involuntary petition. His legal team told the *National Law Journal* that litigating against the government was the "equivalent of guerilla warfare." I was prepared to personally argue the motion before the court, believing that the importance of the matter deserved the full dignity of my office. However, as a diversionary tactic, LaRouche's lawyers subpoenaed me as a witness and subjected me to more than an hour of cross-examination on my rationale for filing the petition. They would pull the same stunt later, during the criminal trial in district court.

Ultimately, the court was sympathetic but unpersuaded that the petition was properly filed. Only bona fide creditors have standing to file such an action. Our case on behalf of the bilked creditors was dismissed. I accepted a mild scolding from the court and moved on. Besides, our secondary objective had been achieved. We confirmed that the LaRouche empire had no assets; it floated on a platform of defaulted promissory notes.

The aftershock of the Boston indictment tested the fealty of many LaRouche followers, variously estimated to be between a thousand and fourteen hundred. When confronted by federal agents, numerous "defectors" folded and agreed to cooperate fully. Although we were ready to proceed with the Virginia portion of the case, we allowed it to ferment slowly, to enable Boston to complete the credit-card facet.

In time, our patience dissipated. A federal grand jury in Alexandria returned a thirteen count indictment on October 14, 1988, charging LaRouche and six key associates with conspiracy to commit mail fraud, various specific acts of mail fraud, and income tax violations. LaRouche tersely described the indictment as "a piece of garbage."

Over the objection of many of the federal agents participating in the LaRouche Task Force, I decided to honor the request of his attorney and allow LaRouche to turn himself in rather than subject him to a photo-op arrest. Several considerations drove this decision. First, we had already sent a message to the LaRouche organization. Second, it was the typical practice in the Eastern District of Virginia to honor such a request. To do otherwise would invite the public appearance of overkill and grandstanding. Lastly, we could not contend in good faith that he posed a risk of flight. LaRouche relished the opportunity to be publicly viewed as a victim of government persecution. A former Marxist who had taken a sharp political right turn after a sudden doctrinal epiphany, he looked forward to the inevitable political drama.

LaRouche's lawyers soon realized that they were operating on tougher legal terrain in Virginia than they had encountered in Massachusetts. The wheels of justice turn very slowly in Boston, where the original indictment was returned on October 6, 1986. The United States obtained a superseding indictment in July 1987, which added LaRouche himself as a defendant. Jury selection for the Boston trial began in September 1987. It took the Boston judge two months to select the jury. The trial began on December 17.

The LaRouche legal team took control of the Boston trial from the kickoff. They contested every point and requested hearings outside the presence of the jury at every twist and turn, sometimes lasting for days. The United States district judge, a scholarly former Harvard University law professor, was totally flummoxed. The trial moved one step forward and three backward every day. After four months, the jury was on the brink of mutiny. Concern turned to panic when the judge casually commented that the trial could take another year to complete. In response to increasingly clamorous protests from members of the jury, the judge finally declared a mistrial on May 4, 1988, based on "severe hardship" to the jury. The trial was reset for January 3, 1989.

LaRouche and his inner circle got their first taste of the "rocket docket" on October 17, 1988, when they were arraigned before Judge Bryan in Alexandria—three days following their indictment. The docket in the Eastern District of Virginia moves at the fastest pace in the nation. First, LaRouche's lawyers wanted to transfer the case to Boston. That request was promptly denied. They next asked for an autumn 1989 trial date, so there would be no overlap with the January 3, 1989, date set for the Boston trial. Judge Bryan assured them that the Boston date would pose no problem.

They gasped for oxygen when the judge scheduled the trial to begin four weeks later, on November 21, 1988. When Judge Bryan denied their motion to postpone the trial, LaRouche appealed. The court of appeals summarily upheld the decision. The attorneys immediately notified my office that I was a prospective witness, thereby precluding me from serving as trial counsel. Frankly, I would have added little to the prosecution team.

LaRouche's defense was consistent with his public statements. A self-perceived economics scholar, LaRouche contended that his concentration on world affairs was unencumbered by the day-to-day operation of his various enterprises and political entities. Although LaRouche did not testify, his lawyers continually argued that their client was totally ignorant of the business side of the campaign. Memoranda unearthed in the searches and the testimony of former associates belied this contention. On December 16, 1988, LaRouche and his band of associates were convicted on all counts. LaRouche was sentenced to serve fifteen years. His associates received sentences ranging from three to five years.

The Boston case took a strange twist. The U.S. Attorney's Office asked the court to dismiss the pending indictment set for retrial on January 3, 1989. The Boston prosecutor was apparently convinced that enough resources had been spent on the LaRouche clan. The court granted the request over the strenuous objection of LaRouche. In a shocking act of defiance, LaRouche opposed the dismissal. He claimed that a Boston trial would present an opportunity for him to prove that his Virginia conviction was the product of a government conspiracy, or as his lawyer called it, "systemic government misconduct." An assistant U.S. attorney characterized LaRouche's argument to the court as "a journey to the twilight zone." LaRouche even took the unimaginable step of appealing the dismissal of the charges against him.

Confinement in a federal prison did little to hinder the political crusade of Lyndon LaRouche. Operating from a prison cell, he continued his quest for the presidency of the United States. His platform included quarantining AIDS patients and establishing a permanent colony on Mars. Don't laugh—the American taxpayers were forced to foot the bill. When the Federal Election Commission tried to cut off his public funding while he was serving his sentence, the decision was reversed by a federal appellate court in 1993. In all, LaRouche has received almost six million dollars in federal matching campaign funds.

After serving five years, LaRouche wasted no time before returning to the campaign trail. He returned to Loudoun County, Virginia, to a smaller, more secluded residence. His campaign rhetoric now focuses on the wars in Afghanistan and Iraq, which, he contends, only he is capable of bringing to closure. LaRouche sees these wars from a "deeper perspective" than other U.S. policymakers.

No matter how intellectually scattered or disoriented LaRouche's logic may seem, there is always a common thread underlying his conclusions—conspiracy.

In his widely espoused view, the September 11, 2001, attacks on the Twin Towers were not the handy work of Osama bin Laden and the al Qaeda network. They were an attempted coup orchestrated by the United States military. His views may be farfetched, but they're being disseminated at taxpayer's expense.

## Extortion or Murder?

"Melissa, if you can hear Mommy and get to a phone, please dial our number like I've taught you to. Please call home. I miss you and love you very much. Please come back. Mommy's waiting."

The tearful words of Tammy Brannen resonated with every parent in the Washington, D.C., area as she faced scores of television cameras on a cold winter night in December 1989. The impact was seismic. Thousands of people who had never met Tammy or her daughter Melissa cried each evening as the nightly news displayed the heart-wrenching photos of the blue-eyed, five-year-old dressed in her Big Bird sweater and plaid skirt. Where was Melissa?

Every year the Woodbine Apartments in South Fairfax held a community Christmas party, popularly referred to as the Annual Yuletide Fest. Tammy Brannen was reluctant to attend on December 3, 1989. A single mother working two jobs, as an accountant during the week and jewelry store clerk on weekends, she really just wanted to relax. But the love of her life, her daughter Melissa, dressed in her Big Bird sweater and plaid skirt, insisted. Although a little on the shy side, Melissa loved parties. So her mother couldn't resist.

Melissa sat on her mother's lap through most of the festivities, but as they prepared to leave, the little three-foot-tall girl wanted to grab a few potato chips to take home. Meanwhile, her mother walked over to get their coats and wish a few friends, "Merry Christmas." When she turned around, Melissa was gone. In a panic, she frantically searched the community clubhouse, then the surrounding neighborhood. Within hours she was joined in the search by police and firefighters from every jurisdiction in the D.C. area, along with more than three hundred soldiers and marines and hundreds of civilian volunteers. Every area-based television station ran periodic public service announcements.

Not a clue turned up.

Tammy Brannen waited, seemingly endless lonely nights and days, sitting in her apartment praying her daughter would call. She knew Melissa had memorized the number, so she refused to disconnect the phone or change the number. As a result, she had to endure almost daily crank calls, even from young girls claiming to be Melissa. It was an ugly and painful symptom of escalating social sickness. But not as sickening as the call she received at 8:00 a.m. on February 14.

"It's time to take care of business, Mrs. Brannen. Follow my instructions. I hope you don't think this is a joke, because your daughter's safety is riding on this." The caller then explained that they had been holding her daughter and would release her for seventy-five thousand dollars. He warned her not to contact authorities, and closed by saying that she'd receive further instructions the following day.

Tammy Brannen immediately notified the FBI who responded quickly, but doubted the call was genuine. Kidnappers don't hold a screaming five-year-old child ten weeks before placing a ransom call. Agents installed a recording device on Tammy's phone and a mechanism to decode the telephone number of incoming calls.

The next call came the following afternoon at 4:15 p.m. Tammy was to take the seventy-thousand dollars in cash to 111 Massachusetts Avenue, in northwest Washington, at 7:00 p.m. and deliver it to a waiting courier. The caller added that, "As long as the money is delivered safely, without any outside involvement, your daughter will be set free at the nearest police department as soon as we are assured of our safety."

One Eleven Massachusetts Avenue was an eight-story office building then occupied primarily by the Union Labor Life Insurance Company. At 7:00 p.m., FBI agents observed a commercial courier pacing restlessly in front of the building. They patiently waited. About 7:15 p.m., the courier was seen placing a call from a pay phone. Moments later, Tammy Brannen's phone rang but, as instructed by the FBI agent at her side, she didn't pick it up. The call was traced to a dormitory room at Howard University located about two miles from the drop site. Before the caller could recradle the phone, a team of agents was burning rubber to that location to set up surveillance.

Once the agents were in place at Howard University, a female FBI agent posing as Tammy Brannen turned the corner and approached the courier with an envelope containing the money in marked bills. The courier advanced in her direction, took the package, jumped in his car and hauled tail to Howard University. Two young men waiting in a dorm room were all smiles when the courier, who knew nothing of the ransom plot, handed them the plump envelope. The next thing they knew all three were being handcuffed at gun point by FBI agents. The party was over. Both extortionists, later identified as Anthony G. McCray, twenty-four, and Emmett M. Grier, twenty, admitted their involvement in the ransom plot, but adamantly denied any knowledge of the whereabouts of Melissa Brannen. They just wanted to make a few bucks at Tammy Brannen's expense.

The courier was questioned and released. He told the agents he thought it was a drug deal. As for McCray and Grier, after spending the night in the notoriously rough D.C. jail, both men appeared the next morning before United States Magistrate Jean F. Dwyer, who characterized the crime as one of the cruelest she'd seen in thirty years. Usually calm and soft spoken, Magistrate Dwyer severely tongue lashed the two young thugs for the outrageous distress they caused the emotionally scarred mother of Melissa Brannen. Outraged, she ordered them both held without bond and directed that they be transferred to Virginia for trial.

Hitting the rocket docket, the two men were indicted and arraigned seven days after their arrest.

I told the media that, "We want this aspect of the case concluded as quickly as possible, to hopefully relieve the tension suffered by the Brannen family."

To underscore the significance of the case, I decided to personally handle the trial.

Over the years, I had tried many cases with psychologically fragile victims, but I was a little nervous the afternoon that FBI Agent Charles K. Dorsey and I met with Tammy Brannen. Victims of tragic experiences at the hands of callous criminals show various reactions. Some suffer pangs of guilt. Others are hostile, and still others seek to suppress the experience. I didn't know what to expect.

Agent Dorsey, the principle investigator on the case, had met with Tammy previously and found her to be a woman of truly amazing strength. But Dorsey and I wondered how she would hold up emotionally on the witness stand. Could she relive the horrifying nightmare? Was she still experiencing terrifying flashbacks of the evening her daughter was kidnaped? How could anyone keep it together? Maybe her doctor would intervene and tell us she couldn't testify.

Five minutes with Tammy Brannen proved she was a lady of invincible spirit. Charming and intelligent with remarkable resilience, Tammy was deeply wounded but steadfastly committed to finding her daughter. This case was one more skirmish in her never-ending battle for her daughter's return.

One of the extortionists, Emmett Grier, elected to plead guilty and testify for the prosecution. He had no prior record and had been contrite and cooperative from the moment of his arrest. On the other hand, the mastermind, Anthony McCray, who was already on probation, demanded a trial by jury. His defense? The money used to pay the ransom had not traveled in interstate commerce because it had been borrowed from a D.C. bank. Consequently, McCray argued, there was no federal jurisdiction. In order to prove a violation of the federal extortion law, the prosecution must prove that the act affected interstate commerce.

Obviously it was a defense of desperation, probably designed to pressure Tammy Brannen into agreeing to some type of plea bargain to lesser charges. Man did they miscalculate this lady.

At trial, an FBI agent testified that the drop money was loaned by Riggs National Bank in D.C. as a public service. An officer of that bank explained to the jury that Riggs was one of the largest banks in the Washington area and did business with people, corporations, and corresponding banks in all fifty states. It was logical for me to maintain that any transaction with Riggs, given the geographic reach of its operations, affected interstate commerce. The court agreed and found our evidence sufficient to show the necessary link to interstate commerce. The jury convicted McCray of conspiracy, extortion, possession of ransom money, and use of a telephone in furtherance of criminal activity. Despite my request for a twelve-year sentence, McCray was later ordered to serve only seven years in federal prison. His accomplice, Grier, who testified as a prosecution witness, was sentenced to forty-six months.

Tammy Brannen was a powerful and articulate witness. McCray's lawyer wisely offered her his heartfelt sympathy and waived cross-examination. Women on the jury closed their eyes as Tammy bravely recounted the events of December 3, 1989. In the end, she was a little disappointed, but said she could live with the sentences handed down. Tammy was destined to have another day in court—this time with the kidnaper.

As our case progressed in federal court, Fairfax County Commonwealth's Attorney Robert F. Horan, Jr., was preparing an indictment against the prime suspect, Caleb Hughes, a newly hired groundskeeper at the apartment complex where Melissa had been abducted. Attention focused on Hughes moments after the little girl disappeared. Tammy had found the attention Hughes devoted to her daughter at the neighborhood Christmas party strange. Minutes before Melissa disappeared, she was seen sitting on Hughes's lap. Earlier in the evening, he had offered to escort Melissa to the restroom.

When questioned by detectives, Hughes could not account for his whereabouts for the two and a half hours after leaving the party. He claimed that he just drove around from 10:00 p.m. until after 12:30 a.m. On a sub-freezing December night?

Police next discovered a witness who saw Hughes shave—not just scrape—the sides of his shoes several hours after leaving the party. Detectives theorized that Hughes was attempting to rid the soles of his shoes of the little girl's blood.

Fairfax Police soon hit a dead end, concluding that other investigative leads were exhausted. Even though their grounds were a bit thin, they decided to get a search warrant for Hughes's wife's car, the one he was driving on the night of the Christmas party. Their hunch paid off big time. Using an evidence recovery vacuum, they lifted more than fifty blue acrylic fibers, twelve reddish cotton fibers, five dyed rabbit hairs, and one human hair follicle from the seats of the car.

The FBI obtained a Sesame Street outfit from J.C. Penney, identical to the one worn by Melissa Brannen on the night of her disappearance. An FBI forensic scientist compared the physical and chemical properties of the fibers recovered from the car with the fabric of the supplied Sesame Street sweater and skirt. The results exceeded the typical match. The expert concluded the physical and chemical properties of the fibers used to construct the sweater and skirt were microscopically unique. Powerful, damning evidence.

The proverbial noose was drawn tighter when the FBI Forensic Science Laboratory also found that the physical properties of the rabbit hairs from the Hughes vehicle matched those of Tammy Brannen's fur coat. Trace hairs are routinely transferred when someone brushes against a fur coat of this type. Standing alone, such evidence has minimal value. But in concert with the fiber comparison, it was dynamite. Especially when you add the human hair follicle, which matched the general physical properties of little Melissa's hair.

Fairfax prosecutor Bob Horan, a trial lawyer of legendary skills, crafted the indictment against Hughes to achieve the most severe sentence possible. Rather than simply charge him with abduction, which he could easily prove with the forensic evidence, he elected to indict for the aggravated offense of abduction with the intent to defile. It upped the ante from a penalty range of one to ten years to that of twenty years to life. But it also created monumental proof problems. What evidence, other than strong suspicion, was there that Hughes intended to sexually molest the little girl?

Horan employed masterful psychological strategy. He had an amazing compass for navigating the mind and emotions of jurors. Horan knew it would not take much to convince the jury to formally conclude what they already probably suspected—that Hughes was a sexual predator. What other logical motive was there for kidnaping Melissa? But Horan needed something concrete he could point to that would support his theory.

Two women attending the December third Christmas party testified that Hughes had tried to pick them up that night. "He was obviously looking for love." Neither of them was that desperate. Horan also highlighted the fact that in order to leave fibers from her skirt and sweater on the seat, Melissa's coat must have been removed. The temperature that night was below freezing. How else could the large number of fibers be explained? Again, Horan persuasively deployed logic and common sense.

Horan's smoothly presented symphony of circumstantial evidence, reinforced by the near irrefutable testimony of the forensic scientists, guided the jury to a swift verdict. In the process, the jury rejected the alibi testimony of Hughes's wife whose recollection was riddled with uncertainty. Following the return of the verdict, several jurors conceded some discomfort in returning a verdict of guilty without knowing what had happened to little Melissa. But not enough discomfort to prevent them from sentencing him to fifty years in prison. The verdict provided Tammy Brannen with some palliative, short-term relief.

Just as the waves of her life began to calm, the Virginia Court of Appeals reversed Hughes's conviction, finding that the evidence of his intent to sexually molest the child was insufficient. A panel of three judges concluded that the verdict had been based on speculation and conjecture on the jury's part. Horan was privately outraged and asked the full court—all nine judges—to hear the case, which they agreed to do. By a vote of five to four, the full court reversed the three-judge panel and reinstated Hughes's conviction. Tammy Brannen told the media she was overjoyed, but it was not a victory in her mind. She could "never win" until Melissa came home.

Horan was relieved by the court's change of course. A retrial would have been traumatic for the Brannen family. One judge on the original three-judge panel that earlier reversed Hughes's conviction even changed his position on further reflection and voted to uphold the conviction. Historically, issues pertaining to intent in criminal cases are decided by the jury and are overturned on appeal only if there is no evidence to support their findings. Whether the Virginia Court of Appeals would have ruled the same way if they had been on the jury is irrelevant. The determinative question is whether there was specific evidence in the record supporting the jury's factual conclusions. Yes, the evidence was thin, but the law requires a prosecutor's case to provide proof beyond a *reasonable doubt*—not all possible or conceivable doubt.

The decision of the initial three-judge panel of the Virginia Court of Appeals exemplifies a disturbing trend in the law. Logic and common sense are often dethroned in the analytical process in favor of a rigid construction of facts and a strict black letter legal interpretation of legal principles. In considering the evidence, juries should be encouraged to draw upon their collective human experience and to view the evidence in that context. Common sense is a critical element of the fact-finding process. Otherwise, trials could be conducted by computers. Why was a five-year-old girl in Hughes's car that night with her outer garment removed? Why did she never return?

To this day, the Melissa Brannen case remains a source of festering frustration. Horan firmly believes that Hughes killed Melissa Brannen and that Hughes should be prosecuted for murder, but the evidence isn't there. Tammy Brannen, more than a decade after the loss of her daughter, still prays for that miraculous phone call. She still hangs a Christmas stocking, and bakes an annual birthday cake for Melissa. Caleb Hughes remains in prison until 2013. Tammy Brannen has communicated with him on several occasions, begging for information about her daughter. He remains mum. His account of what happened on December 3, 1989, would bring some closure to Tammy's agonizing ordeal. But, for Caleb Hughes, it could be a ticket to death row.

## Espionage

The Soviet Embassy gets lots of strange calls, and perhaps this was one of them. A recently retired U.S. Navy senior NCO, with more than twenty years of experience in the highly classified field of antisubmarine warfare, called the publicly listed phone number at the embassy one morning. As reported by Peter Jennings on ABC's "World News Tonight," the caller told the receptionist that he needed to talk to the KGB—the Soviet intelligence agency. The lady answering the phone carefully chose the words of her response. Is there a message I can give someone? Yes, he replied. He succinctly explained his military background and then asked if they had any KGB agents monitoring the movement of submarines at the Norfolk Naval Shipyard. If not, he'd like to volunteer, because his home was an excellent observation point. Besides, he had lots of information. The lady coldly agreed to pass the message on.

Undoubtedly, the embassy cast it aside as another crank call. Someone else, however, took it seriously—damn seriously.

# XVI
# Spy Trap

One of the most enjoyable things about my monthly visit to the Norfolk Office was the view of the shipyard. From my desk I could see naval vessels, cruisers, battleships, and aircraft carriers either moored in Hampton Roads or in transit in the bay. At times, the thundering roar of jets overhead would disrupt meetings. To us it was not an annoyance. It was the sound of freedom.

Several months before I took office in June of 1986, my staff, working in league with the Internal Security Section of the DOJ, had wrapped up the espionage prosecution of John A. Walker, Jr., along with his son, brother, and close friend. One of the most insidious spies in U.S. history, Walker, an officer in the U.S. Navy, casually entered the Soviet Embassy in Washington, D.C., in the autumn of 1967. He was not a tourist. He asked to speak to a KGB agent, and was promptly accommodated. Moments into the meeting, he brushed aside the small talk and got right down to business. The young naval officer wanted to sell secret information to the Soviets. And sell he did. Over a seventeen-year period, Walker sold more than a million classified documents and related information to Russian agents. Of course, he was well compensated with cash and lovely ladies. His lifestyle became so conspicuously lavish and immoral that his own wife became an FBI informant. Was he worth the money?

The KGB described him later as one of their most valuable intelligence assets. Thanks to Commander Walker, the Navy lost an entire generation of top secret communications codes and war fighting tactics. The rebuilding process was estimated to take a decade.

That's why the FBI was so disturbed by that strange call to the Soviet Embassy. Craig Dee Kunkle, a thirty-nine-year-old resident of Virginia Beach, wanted revenge. But he also wanted money. He'd been booted out of the Navy after twelve years as an acoustics instrument operator. He was skilled in operating the highly classified and sophisticated systems used to analyze the sounds of the sea to detect the presence and movement of submarines. Once recognized as the Atlantic Fleet Sailor of the Year, Kunkle's life had deteriorated. He left the Navy as a Chief Petty Officer with a less than honorable discharge and found employment as a security guard at Portsmouth Hospital. Inspired by John Walker, Kunkle thought he was sitting on a treasure trove of information—and he was determined to cash in.

The day following his call to the Soviet Embassy, Kunkle received a return call from "Mikhail," who represented himself as a Soviet intelligence operative. "Mikhail" expressed cautious interest, but wanted proof of Kunkle's bona fides. Drawing on the exploits of Walker, Kunkle expressed an interest in traveling around the world to exotic places to meet and exchange secret information. In an effort to seal the deal, Kunkle told "Mikhail" that he was smarter and much more professional than John Walker. Kunkle confided that he was surprised Walker had not been arrested earlier, he was such an amateur.

"Mikhail" instructed Kunkle to send a sample of his information to a post office box in Alexandria which would serve as their "drop box." Two days later, on December 9, 1989, Kunkle mailed a package of handmade documents and diagrams, along with a few photographs, to the drop box. The materials contained enough classified data to excite "Mikhail's" interest.

After several follow-up conversations, "Mikhail" told Kunkle that the Soviets were ready to do business. They arranged a meeting at a motel in Williamsburg, Virginia, about thirty miles from Norfolk. To add a dimension of intrigue, Kunkle was instructed to wear a gray raincoat and carry a folded magazine in his left hand. They also agreed on a secret password.

On January 10, Kunkle met with the Soviet spy master and his associate. After a satisfactory exchange of introductions, the group retired to a room to negotiate. Kunkle produced a forty-page self-created document containing a detailed description of the Navy's acoustic intelligence techniques. It also contained an explanation of the operation of highly classified acoustical instrumentation on which Kunkle had received extensive training while assigned to a P-3 Orion antisubmarine patrol squadron. The P-3 Orion aircraft has a distinctive dome radar and drops buoys to sound out enemy submarines in the ocean.

Kunkle emphasized to the Soviet agent that he wanted to supply secret information on a continuing basis. He reiterated that he was far too clever to get caught. His price for providing the classified information up to that point was a paltry five thousand dollars. "Mikhail" counted out five thousand in U.S. currency and handed the cash to Kunkle, who smiled as he pocketed the money. His Soviet handlers then presented him with a receipt for the money, which Kunkle signed without hesitation. "Mikhail" then dropped the bomb, whipping out his FBI credentials. Kunkle was escorted to a waiting car in handcuffs. He had been ensnared in an operation known as "False Flag."

I had been anxious for some time to personally prosecute a spy case, particularly in the Norfolk division. This was the perfect combination. I teamed up with Rob Seidel, the assistant U.S. attorney supervising the criminal section in Norfolk. Trial preparation was exciting. In order to better understand the submarine warfare acoustics systems, we finagled a visit to the U.S.S. *Flying Fish,* a nuclear attack submarine, and a tour of a P-3 Orion aircraft.

Initially, Seidel and I were excited about the prospect of trying a high-visibility espionage case. Classified information has several gradations, ranging from confidential to top secret. Some supersensitive data, such as that pertaining to the Star Wars System, is even more highly classified. Military experts assigned to assist us described the materials supplied by Kunkle as containing some secret and top secret information. When Seidel and I finally had the opportunity to review the material ourselves, we were disappointed. We expected something—well—a little juicier.

Our first reaction was, How could this stuff possibly be classified? Even the military experts conceded that most of the information was in the public domain, for example, in *Jane's Fighting Ships.* However, their steadfast position was that it had never been publicly confirmed by the U.S. Navy. Moreover, our expert was prepared to testify that its disclosure would damage the national defense. This we also found perplexing. Even the FBI agent assigned to our case harbored some candid doubt.

Obviously, Seidel and I were prepared to follow the instructions of the Department of Justice zealously. Unlike most other types of cases, prosecution decisions in national security cases are driven by the Justice Department, and not by the U.S. attorney in the field. Our directions in this case were full speed ahead. However, unlike the folks at the DOJ, who deal with cases from a distance, Seidel and I knew how a jury in Norfolk, home to one of the world's largest navel bases, would react to these facts. They would undoubtedly be outraged by Kunkle's disloyalty, but we were sure they would be unimpressed with the information

Kunkle sold, particularly when defense counsel pointed it out in publications available to anyone in major bookstores. Wouldn't a reasonable jury conclude that the Soviets already had this information?

Fortunately, Rob Seidel was personally acquainted with the chief of Naval Intelligence, who had served as an expert witness in the John Walker spy case. We met with the admiral at the Pentagon to discuss the information Kunkle had passed to the FBI. We explained our concerns. He was sympathetic, but confirmed that the information was indeed classified. His assessment of the resulting damage was, in our view, a little more realistic. In his opinion, there was damage but it was probably minimal.

An important trait of an effective prosecutor is the ability "to know when to hold 'em" and "know when to fold 'em." Rob and I decided it was time to talk settlement, if an agreement could be reached that required Kunkle to serve a significant period of time. Surprisingly, the Navy did not disagree. The Department of Defense is always a little nervous in cases where classified information could potentially be exposed. We received authority from the Internal Security Division of the DOJ to offer a plea agreement with a specific sentencing recommendation of not less than ten years. We began negotiations at fifteen years. After a short volley of counter proposals, we settled on an agreement that Kunkle would serve twelve years in a federal prison. The United States District Court accepted the agreement. On my public representation that the documents were "harmful, but not highly damaging" and that "there would be no significant damage to national defense," the judge followed our recommendation and sentenced Kunkle to twelve years.

For me, the lesson learned in Kunkle was to always make a personal assessment of the practical, as opposed to the legal, significance of purported classified information before setting the tone of the prosecution. Many people in Norfolk must have wondered why we sold out so cheap after all the press conferences and hype attending Kunkle's arrest. Then again, they never saw the so-called secret documents.

## A Generation at Risk

Early in my tenure as U.S. attorney, the national focus of drug enforcement began to shift to one of the most devastating drugs to hit the streets—cocaine base, commonly referred to as "crack." The street name is derived from the crackling sound made when the substance is lit for smoking in handmade pipes, tubes, or even beer cans. Cocaine base is a chemically denuded version of cocaine hydrochloride, the form of cocaine that results from the initial postharvesting process.

As with many new and exotic drugs, the crack epidemic began on the west coast. An amateur chemist stumbled on the conversion process in his basement in Los Angeles in the mid-1970s. Street gangs began pushing it and really made the big bucks. Through the gang network, its popularity spread to New York and, in the mid-1980s, to Northern Virginia. The trend was alarming.

Detective Jerry McHugh, a narcotics investigator with the Alexandria City Police, captured the essence of the problem:

> Any kid with a few hundred bucks, a pan, a stove and a box of baking soda can become a little drug lord. Crack is easy to make, easy to sell and easy to become addicted to. You can't use the stuff without wanting more.

Crack is kind of a poor man's cocaine. Unlike the traditional powder form, which sold in 1987 for between a hundred and a hundred twenty-five dollars a gram, crack is sold in lumps or rocks—fractions of a gram—for five to twenty-five dollars a chunk. You could purchase a hundred-dollar gram of powder-form cocaine (cocaine hydrochloride), convert it into crack, and sell it in rocks on the street for about two hundred fifty dollars.

Any idiot can make crack cocaine, although few do it safely. Boil a pan of water, dissolve the cocaine hydrochloride, add baking soda, and stir until the cocaine base is crystalized into lumps of crack. The finished product is then dried on paper towels. The residue of the baking soda (sodium bicarbonate) makes the crackling sound, sort of like Rice Krispies cereal in milk.

Crack cocaine has a much lower melting point than powder cocaine. The rock is heated in a smoking pipe with a long-flamed butane lighter. The lower melting point preserves the psycho-active properties of the drug. Powdered cocaine has to get so hot to dissolve that it loses a lot of its mind-altering properties. The operative element of crack is the potent vapor. Because of the incredible profits from pushing the stuff, some call it the "vapors of gold." Detective McHugh was fond of saying, "You pay twenty bucks for a few minutes in outer space." The resulting high is intense, euphoric, some describe it as "orgasmic." The vapor is fat and soluble and is absorbed into the brain in a matter of seconds. Once it dissipates, the user crashes fast and craves more. Consequently, addiction is near instantaneous. Consumers of the drug develop a habit or dependence almost immediately, creating a quick high-demand market. Some users go on binges and stay high for days at a time, totally neglecting their job, kids, and personal hygiene.

As the flow of crack cocaine spread south from New York, so did the unprecedented level of accompanying violence. Drug distribution has always been a ruthless business, but never like this. There are a number of contributing factors. Unlike the tamer drugs, or even heroin, the price of crack is cheap, and predisposed people have the opportunity to develop a hard-core addiction. And it is a hard-core addiction. People will kill for a ten dollar rock of crack. The demand is intense.

The potential profit is unfathomable. As Detective McHugh pointed out, young men living in an economically depressed public housing area—with little to lose in life—can become unimaginably wealthy in a matter of weeks. Their flashy jewelry, expensive cars, and fast women are coveted in communities where many residents are looking for money for their next meal. The resulting market is therefore lucrative and keenly competitive.

By virtue of sheer strength and intimidation, much of the crack cocaine market in 1987 was dominated by street gangs for whom violence was a tool of the trade. Encroachment by one gang on another's territory usually ended in bloodshed. Moreover, the pharmacology of the drug itself promotes violence. Once the high begins to ebb, the user fades into a depressive stage, where tempers flare quickly and behavior becomes unpredictable.

As addiction to crack cocaine reached epidemic proportions in Northern Virginia, the law enforcement community rapidly exhausted every available means of control. Attempts to educate the public proved unavailing. Too many people dismissed it as just more antidrug hype. Meanwhile, many loosely associated groups of neighborhood kids were motivated to link up with ruthless street gangs to share the bounty reaped from the "vapors of gold." To insulate themselves from the risk of street pushers "flipping" and cooperating with the police, many gangsters relied on juveniles to do the retail work.

In those days, most juveniles busted on drug charges faced little more than a period of probation. Consequently, the police had little legal leverage. Unlike with adults, there was no legal incentive to "work off" a charge. They couldn't bargain away a prison sentence in exchange for active investigative assistance, such as introducing an undercover officer or providing testimony against retailers or managers.

Regrettably, many parents, most of whom were single mothers living in public housing, turned a blind eye to their kids' activities. For them, it was a source of vitally needed income—food, clothes, and in many cases, a new car. Sadly, it was an immense economic boost to an otherwise impoverished subculture. Besides, as the addiction epidemic spread, more and more mothers themselves became hooked, often from their own children. This enabled dealers to literally convert the house into a retail outlet, because the parents were doped to a point of unconsciousness. As a consequence, the exchange of gunfire became common in many public housing projects. Stray bullets penetrated windows. Innocent neighbors were mortally wounded. The projects became social powder kegs.

Today, as a federal district judge, I often chastize convicted crack cocaine dealers before sentencing by telling them that "crack cocaine has literally destroyed a generation of young Americans." These are not my words. They were crafted by an eloquent African American pastor in the city of Alexandria, surrounded by a dozen community leaders and elderly residents of the projects, begging me for federal assistance with the crack problem. I also heard, "Please stop all this killing." Several days before this meeting, my old friend Smokey Stover, chief of the Arlington County Police, called with the same message, and suggested that we assemble a regional crack task force. If I had had any doubt about his wisdom, it was dispelled by the community meeting. I was convinced that our response to the crack problem had to be the moral equivalent of war.

## The Crack Task Force

Public policy has two components: a bright idea and the money to make it happen. Therefore, our first step was a meeting with Congressman Frank Wolf. Wolf's father had been a career police officer in Philadelphia, Pennsylvania, and the congressman was an enthusiastic supporter of law enforcement. He required little convincing. If Smokey and I needed it, he'd find the money to underwrite the task force.

And find the money he did—almost one million dollars in federal grant money to fuel the effort. The following week, we assembled the police chiefs and commonwealth's attorneys from every jurisdiction in the Washington, D.C., area along with the regional commander of the Virginia State Police and the agent in charge of the DEA, at the United States Attorney's Office.

The response was enthusiastic. Almost every department was willing to commit at least one investigator to the regional task force. Even those police departments historically reluctant to "work with the feds" were willing to bury the hatchet and join forces. As an added incentive, and to assure our state counterparts of full partnership in the venture, I announced that the DOJ had authorized me to cross-designate assistant commonwealth's attorneys from participating jurisdictions as special assistant United States attorneys. This was something rarely permitted on a large scale, and enabled the state prosecutors to serve as cocounsel on cases developed by investigators from their jurisdictions. This significantly raised their comfort level and reduced their fear of losing control of the cases directly effecting their geographic area. DEA would manage and administer the group because it was funded by a federal grant. The operation was christened the Northern Virginia Regional Crack Task Force.

Our game plan was simple and based on a number of commonly accepted assumptions. Our best source of raw intelligence was the local police departments. They came into contact with street-corner crack dealers every day. The stakes were low in state court. Some suspects agreed to assist the task force in exchange for a break on their charges. Others chose to hang tough. Most pled guilty in the end and were sentenced to a couple of months in jail followed by a few years of probation. And that, unfortunately, was a major part of the problem. From a risk versus benefits perspective, selling crack won out—hands down.

But when the small-time dealers walked out of jail, they were being greeted by a task force agent armed with a subpoena ordering them to testify before a federal grand jury. Some failed to show up and were awakened the next morning at daybreak by federal agents who whisked them off to jail in handcuffs. Those who appeared were politely advised of the rules of engagement. They had two options: Identify their source; or be held in contempt and jailed until they did, or for the life of the grand jury, typically eighteen months. Those who lied bout their supplier were charged with perjury.

In most cases, the investigators had a reasonably good idea who the street dealers were working for. To test their veracity and further pin down the identification, witnesses were asked to pick out photos of the people they had described from a group of pictures. The next step, using the testimony of the street pushers, locked in by their grand jury testimony, was to indict the middle men, managers, and wholesalers.

For larger-level crack traffickers, federal prosecution is their worst nightmare. Federal law provides a combination of stiff mandatory minimum sentences and harsh sentencing guidelines that escalate with the quantity sold. To up the ante even further, the sentencing guidelines hold a person convicted of conspiracy responsible for the drugs sold by his coconspirators. A low-level supplier linked to a small local crack syndicate could easily be held accountable for a quarter to a half pound of crack cocaine—less than a standard coffee cup would hold—and end up facing about fifteen years in prison without parole. Prior felony convictions jacked up the guidelines even further.

The mandatory minimum sentences for distributing crack cocaine or possession with the intent to distribute are equally tough. Some argue that the penalties are draconian. For cases involving five grams, which is enough to cover the average fingernail, the mandatory punishment is five years without parole. And for fifty grams, or about a teaspoonful, ten years without parole. Federal law also presumes that drug traffickers are a flight risk, so few are released before trial.

Imagine the reaction of the petty crack pusher—cocky, defiant, and decked out in gold jewelry—busted by the feds. He's accustomed to being released on bond and back on the street in an hour, so he tells the cops to screw themselves. Doing a few months in jail is nothing. It's a badge of manhood and the girls love it. But the bravado evaporates when they're held without bond and their lawyer explains that they are looking at ten years without parole. Some cool guys actually passed out on the spot. At that point, we were ready to do business.

Federal law provided only one escape route from mandatory minimums for convicted merchants of misery—cooperation with the prosecution. If the United States attorney told the court that a defendant had rendered substantial assistance to the prosecution, the judge then had the authority to impose any sentence he or she wished. This law, which went into effect in November 1987, changed the entire dynamics of federal drug prosecutions. No longer did assistant U.S. attorneys have to cajole drug pushers to cooperate. It became a race to the prosecutor's door and a bidding war between defense attorneys claiming their client had the most to offer. There was no scarcity of fallen pushers who wanted to finger the big guy and, ultimately, of big guys begging to give up the kingpin.

Statistically, the Regional Task Force was a remarkable success. We shipped off almost a hundred crack dealers to federal prison, some for life, during my tenure as U.S. attorney. The media was complimentary. Public officials were convinced that the scourge of crack cocaine was under control. We knew better.

Undoubtedly, the task force put a significant dent in the Northern Virginia crack market. But on analysis, we knew that our relentless efforts were only stimulating a continuous process of upward mobility. The big guy goes down and the void is filled by someone further down the chain. The process continually repeats itself. It is hard to accurately assess how many people were actually deterred from crack trafficking by the tough sentences reported weekly in the press. As unfathomable as it may seem, harsh mandatory sentences seemed to be no deterrent to many people entangled in the street gang culture. Sure, the dealers we nabbed regretted getting caught and dreaded doing time. But even factoring the potential for long sentences into the equation, the benefits seemed to outweigh the risks in their minds. For those who had developed a habit themselves, it was probably the only means of garnering the cash necessary to keep the crack flowing. In addition, from their perspective, it was safer and more lucrative then sticking up stores or banks.

Intense enforcement rid many neighborhoods of the crack trafficking bands of thugs who had controlled their streets. I am convinced that hundreds of lives were saved by the Northern Virginia Regional Crack Task Force, but thousands remained at risk. However, a disturbing fact hampers the control of the crack problem. Crack addicts rarely respond well to treatment. The addiction is difficult to overcome, because the craving is so intense, and few crack addicts have a sincere desire to conquer their habit. Consequently, consumer demand never subsides.

A rarely recognized victim of the crack epidemic is middle-aged and elderly African Americans. A disproportionately high percentage of crack addiction affects the young black segment of our population, particularly in the inner city. Chronic use of the drug distorts the user's judgment and values. Women, in particular, will engage in indiscriminate sexual activity in exchange for a rock or two of crack. This results in a significant increase in illegitimate children, many of whom suffer from birth defects as a consequence of their mother's crack addiction. Many crack mothers have only a vague notion of the father's identity, and many are too irresponsible to care for their children. For these women, life is narrowly focused on their obsession with the tantalizing vapors of cocaine base.

By default, a large percentage of children born to crack addict mothers are raised by grandparents who were fortunate enough to mature before the crack epidemic. Many of these fine people are living on fixed income with thinly spread resources, sometimes forcing them to return to work to support their grandchildren. Most of these grandparents provide youngsters with an appropriate value structure, but many find it difficult to compete with peer pressure drawing kids to the street scene as the teen years approach. This tragic cycle is exacerbated by the lack of a true father figure in the life of too many of these young men. The evolving phenomenon is explosive. There are no simple answers. And another drug epidemic is just around the corner—crystal methamphetamine. Experts contend that if the spread of "crystal meth" is left unchecked, it could have the same effect on Caucasian users that crack has had on African Americans.

In my current position as a United States district judge, fifteen years after having left the United States Attorney's Office, over fifty percent of my criminal docket is composed of cases involving crack cocaine, and the attendant violence hasn't slacked off one bit. There are suggestions that we should simply surrender, and abolish the mandatory minimum sentences and tough sentencing guidelines for crack pushers. The argument is predicated on the assumption that the laws discriminate against African Americans, since crack is most prevalent in the black community. Further, it is contended that the law should punish traffickers in powder cocaine and crack cocaine the same. The punishment for crack is about ten times as tough as for powder cocaine, because pharmacologically, the drugs are not the same. One is highly addictive and the other is not.

It gives me pain that many of my distinguished judicial colleagues and other purported legal scholars don't grasp the devastation caused by crack cocaine. They should sit down over a cup of coffee with a group of senior and middle-aged citizens from an economically depressed area ravaged by widespread crack addiction and hear their side of it. It's the story of the destruction of an entire generation of Americans. For their sake, and for generations to follow, the war must go on.

# XVII
# Rogues in the Pentagon

The agents investigating corruption in the Department of Defense procurement system resurfaced sooner than I expected. Joe Aronica, chief of the Special Prosecutions Unit, had been keeping me briefed on the procurement probe, but things had been moving at a faster pace than our regular briefing schedule. The FBI and the Naval Criminal Investigative Service needed my authority to take the case to unprecedented heights—a place where surreptitious listening capability had never been before.

The cooperating defense contractor had truly gone beyond the call of duty. Wearing a concealed transmitter, he met with the crooked consultant who had offered to sell inside information on a pending military contract. Sure enough, for a hefty price the consultant could provide him with the bid numbers for all the competitors on the multimillion dollar contract. Under the direction of federal agents, the contractor took the next step and purchased the confidential information. The numbers squared with the closely held information at the Navy Department Acquisitions Office.

Obviously, no competing contractor would give up bid information. It would be like a pro football team publicizing its game plan. Many contracts were worth hundreds of millions of dollars. In 1986, the DOD budget for weapons and related war-fighting materials was a staggering 2.2 trillion dollars a year. The Pentagon spends about three hundred thousand dollars a minute on acquisition. It has fifty thousand employees who do nothing all day but buy things. The lives of our men and women in combat depend on the integrity of the system to provide them with the best weapons available.

Armed with the recorded conversation, agents paid a visit to the defense contract consultant who had sold away a competing contractor's secrets. Of course, he knew nothing about any inside information and flatly denied selling the bid numbers. One of the agents then pulled the tape out of a briefcase and played the conversation for the startled consultant. Before he could regain his mental balance, they told him he had just committed a federal crime—intentionally lying to a federal agent. He had two options: cooperate or be prosecuted. He choose the former—and cooperate he did.

On the strength of the information gathered, we had already received authority to tap the phones of several rogue consultants. These also proved to be virtual gold mines. Each tap sprouted additional shoots. Application for electronic surveillance authority is an elaborate process. Federal law requires that all wiretaps in federal cases be approved by the attorney general of the United States or his designee, usually the assistant attorney general in charge of the Criminal Division at the Department of Justice. The FBI files the formal application with the concurrence of the U.S. attorney in the jurisdiction where the underlying case is pending. The supporting affidavit, which tends to be extensive in scope and detail, must present sufficient facts to demonstrate probable cause that a federal crime is being committed, that the targeted individuals are implicated, that the phone to be tapped is being used to further the crime, and that all other normal investigative techniques have been exhausted.

If these standards are met, the assistant attorney general signs the formal application, which is then presented to a U.S. district judge. If the judge also finds that all statutory elements have been fulfilled, he or she signs the wiretap authorization order. At that point, the FBI plugs in the recording equipment.

The agents wanted my approval to apply for authorization to tap the phones of the Office of the Assistant Secretary of the Navy in charge of acquisition. The investigation was now beyond my pay grade. Based on the information they provided, I concurred in the request. It was obvious that closely held information was being leaked from that office, perhaps at the highest levels. Before it hit the fan, I thought it was time to give Attorney General Ed Meese a full briefing. Regardless of the outcome, this one was destined for the president's desk.

For me, this was a career-defining case. As a career prosecutor and political aspirant, these were the moments I'd be measured by. Tension escalated daily. It was comforting to know that I had direct access to my friend, Ed Meese. Unfortunately, I soon hit a bump in the road.

## Turf Battles

Most people believe that the expression "war on crime" refers to locking up bad guys. At the United States Attorney's Office we knew better. To us the popular saying referred to the interminable bureaucratic turf battles within the

Department of Justice. Many divisions at the DOJ were staffed with politically appointed budding legal scholars salivating to engage in intellectual combat. They may have had stellar academic credentials, but few had ever seen the inside of a courtroom. The product of this crucible of cerebral firepower was often cleverly crafted solutions relentlessly in search of a problem.

For our defense procurement investigation, the sound of heavy ordinance could be heard in the halls of the DOJ within minutes of the attorney general's announcement that he was disqualifying himself from any involvement in the defense probe. It was jump ball; every division with a claim to jurisdiction wanted a piece of the case.

For the preceding year, Attorney General Meese had been at the vortex of an acrimonious investigation by a judicially appointed independent counsel. The underlying allegation of conflict of interest, dubbed the "Wedtech" scandal by the media, arose from actions Meese had taken while serving at the White House as counsel to President Reagan. An independent counsel was appointed because of the inherent conflict created if the DOJ were obligated to investigate its own Department head.

When Meese learned that the attorney representing him also represented several potential targets of the procurement investigation, he wisely elected to recuse himself. The resulting disorder cast the seeds of mass confusion.

Within days of learning that our office had launched a nationwide probe of the defense procurement industry, sharks within the Criminal Division at the DOJ were on the prowl. They pressed the deputy attorney general, the number-two guy who ordinarily functions as the chief operating officer of the DOJ, to require our office to turn control of the case over to main justice. For years, the DOJ had maintained a well-funded Defense Procurement Fraud Unit with a poor track record for developing significant cases. The unit had recently been dinged by the General Accounting Office and several key U.S. senators for "lackadaisical, careless, hands-off management . . . the government is losing the war against defense fraud." In its defense, the feisty deputy assistant attorney general overseeing the program responded by telling Congress "to put its money where its mouth is." In her view, the unit was grossly underfunded.

Heading this probe would justify the Defense Procurement Fraud Unit's existence and rehabilitate its lackluster reputation. The lawyers in the Unit were certainly competent, but once cases are sucked into the bowels of main Justice, you can expect endless delay. The process of making a decision at DOJ has the grace and speed of an aircraft carrier executing a U-turn.

Therefore, the FBI and NCIS were adamantly opposed to divesting me of operational control of the case. The agents felt comfortable with Joe Aronica's leadership. Besides, having the local federal prosecutor handle the case provides a home-field advantage DOJ lawyers will never enjoy. Fortunately, I had a strong ally on my side, Assistant Attorney General Bill Weld, who occasionally joined me on bird hunting trips.

After the attorney general recused himself from the case, he designated Weld to act in his stead. This included the signing of wiretap authorizations on his behalf and rendering all decisions at the department level. Weld was familiar with the quality of my staff having worked with us on the LaRouche case, and as a former U.S. Attorney favored field-directed investigations.

As a compromise, the case was left under my supervision. However, I agreed to send advance copies of all proposed indictments and plea agreements to the Defense Procurement Fraud Unit for "comments" and to Weld's office for approval. That seemed reasonable, as long as the process did not unduly delay the case. In retrospect, I probably should not have been so gracious.

I dutifully kept the brass at DOJ generally abreast of developments in the case over the next twenty months. It spread wider with each passing hour, because we were simultaneously operating twenty-six wiretaps, and intercepting thousands of conversations each day. Of that number, about fifty a day were incriminating. It evolved into the most labor-intensive fraud investigation ever conducted by the FBI. Scores of clerks under the supervision of dozens of agents reviewed and methodically stored the conversations for use as evidence. By the time we shut down the wiretaps in early June 1988, we had a solid case on a number of major defense contractors and consultants and a few Pentagon officials—and the investigation was just gaining momentum. In time, its dimensions compelled the attorney general to reassume personal command.

## Search Warrants

The next step was to gather documents to support or confirm the intercepted transactions. We had two options, subpoenas or search warrants. Given the high stakes in this case, the decision was easy and unanimous. With the personal approval of the attorney general, we decided to raid the offices of all companies and contractors implicated through the wiretaps and seize any incriminating documents. We also obtained search warrants for the homes of several key targets and five offices in the Pentagon, including the office of an assistant secretary of the Navy; forty-two search warrants in all, involving locations in twelve states and more than four hundred federal agents. Most importantly, we also agreed to operate in total secrecy. But of course this was Washington, D.C., where leaking confidential information to the press is a way of life.

Serving the search warrants was only part of our game plan. A member of each search team was assigned to interview designated people at every location searched. This required extensive preparation, because the targeted individuals were generally people whose incriminating conversations had been intercepted on the wire. The technique capitalized on the anxiety naturally experienced by anyone whose home or business is being searched, an approach particularly effective on less-hardened, white-collar criminals whose will to resist is overborne by an almost irrational combination of fear and guilt. Our targets sensed that their world was crashing around them. Most came clean quickly.

For those who chose to play hardball, the agents were ready. Each team was equipped with recorded snippets of incriminating intercepted conversations, which they would play to "prime the pump." People who feigned total ignorance were confronted with their own conspiratorial words and were asked if that refreshed their recollection. This backed most of them into a corner with only two paths of retreat—confess or take the Fifth.

As June 14, 1988, the day appointed for the simultaneous raids, approached the lid of confidentiality remained tightly fastened. That soon changed. About a week before unveiling "Operation Ill Wind," I was directed by the attorney general to brief the secretary of defense and his staff on the investigation, and to be in the attorney general's Office at 10:00 a.m. on the morning of the searches to provide a final update.

## Briefing the Secretary of Defense

Resplendent with captured war relics and military souvenirs, the cavernous Office of the Secretary of Defense was memorably impressive. Visitors sitting before his huge desk, richly appointed in leather and brass, enjoyed an expansive view of the Capitol and assorted memorials. On the far end of the office, there was a secluded sitting room with a bed and kitchen area.

My conversation with Secretary of Defense Casper Weinberger and his staff of generals was pleasant, but at times tense. People at that level of the military tend to be impatient with any resistence to their authority. Knowing that the walls of the Pentagon are notoriously porous, I was not about to reveal too much. Even an unintentional leak could tip off our targets and result in lost evidence.

Weinberger, who was in his final days as secretary of defense, appeared outwardly appreciative, but seemed annoyed with the level of the briefing. He had clearly expected to learn specific names of the officials and contractors under investigation, and was frustrated when I declined.

The military officers in the room, mostly two- and three-star generals, dealt daily with the nation's most closely held secrets, and were understandably restive.

The overview that I provided was generic, but sufficient to engender heartburn and panic. I explained that more than eighty defense contracts were under review. A staff member asked if they should halt work on those contracts. A yes would have absolved DoD of any further responsibility if the contract later turned out to have been fraudulently obtained. On the other hand, if the contract was clean, DoD would publicly castigate me for holding up production of the weapons system. Moreover, to stop work, I would have to reveal the contracts under investigation. Perhaps that was what they wanted. I may have read too much into the question, but the dialogue appeared to be carefully calculated to create a moral, if not legal, obligation to disclose more.

Given the prevailing hysteria, which would reach hurricane force in the days to follow, any mention of a specific contract would have resulted in an immediate suspension of work. Because most contracts were worth between ten and a hundred million dollars and affected hundreds of employees, an affected contractor would inevitably file a federal lawsuit against the DoD to enjoin the suspension. This in turn could cause the court-ordered discovery of confidential information critical to the ongoing investigation—a risk I was not prepared to take. I told the secretary that it was premature to draw any conclusions, and moved on.

I said that our investigation had revealed a scheme similar to insider trading, but that in this instance it involved bid rigging of defense contracts. We suspected (actually, we knew) that the scheme had been facilitated by bribing Pentagon officials, sometimes with cash, sometimes with promises of future employment. Almost five thousand employees left the DoD annually to take jobs with defense contractors, often those they had interacted with in their official capacity.

About fifteen defense consultants, mostly former DoD employees, were procuring confidential bid information for all competitors on multimillion dollar contracts from Pentagon procurement officials, and then selling it to a competing company for a big fee. You have to understand that the defense procurement process has two stages: the initial bid, and the best and final offer. The initial bid is the contractor's first response to the request for proposal issued by the DoD. The initial bid is evaluated by the DoD and returned to the contractor with comments, ordinarily addressing technical requirements. Then, each contractor wishing to progress to the final stage submits a best and final offer, a BAFO. If a company is privy to the initial bid of its competitors, the strategic advantage in formulating its BAFO is obvious. That was just one facet of the contract manipulation scheme.

If the numbers wouldn't fit, other options were available. Rogue consultants could persuade procurement officials to tailor contract specifications to make them more favorable to their client. Sometimes this occurred between the initial bid and the BAFO stage, and might entail tweeking a few words in the technical specifications to require a certain type of equipment. Occasionally the revised technical requirements eliminated all close competitors. Didn't the companies that got screwed complain? You bet, but never formally. Bid rigging was a way of life among many of the nation's largest defense contractors. Each had something on the other. Anyone filing a formal protest ran the risk of being likewise exposed. Most such disputes were easily resolvable. To accommodate competitors, consultants would often negotiate collusive alliances. One client company would be the designated prime contractor and the other, in exchange for not underbidding the prime, would receive a lucrative undisclosed subcontract. This arrangement also had the advantage of precluding one company from driving the bidding process down to an unprofitable level. The result was the total perversion of the procurement process, something akin to price fixing.

There was another explosive aspect of Operation Ill Wind which I chose to hold back in my briefing of the secretary. Why were multimillion-dollar defense systems being funded by Congress over the objection of the DoD? Some had no conceivable role in any present war-fighting strategy. One funded torpedo could not be used by any submarine then in the U.S. naval fleet.

I concluded the briefing by promising to update Secretary Weinberger—or his designated successor, Frank C. Carlucci—as the investigation unfolded. As a mild tonic, I also agreed to alert his staff before we publicly divulged the identity of any implicated contractors, consultants, or public officials. As I departed, Weinberger reiterated his frustration.

As Weinberger cleaned out his desk in preparation for departure from office, I'm certain he pondered his legacy. It happened on his watch. Would military historians forever associate his name with the scandal, rather than his impressive progress in building a six-hundred-ship navy? He wanted the record to reflect that he had taken immediate corrective action to contain the damage. I'm sure he viewed me as an upstart stonewaller. Unfortunately, we couldn't take the risk of a leak.

In retrospect, I have no doubt about the bona fides of the secretary and his staff. Their proposed actions were spawned by mixed motives—protect the integrity of the procurement process and provide political cover. As the investigation progressed, however, a dramatic institutional transmutation of perspective took place, also arguably inspired by the national interest.

Ironically, as the investigation began to expose improprieties by the nation's foremost weapons producers, those that produced the bulk of our nation's war-fighting technology, the DoD circled the wagons. When we recommended suspension and debarment of companies convicted of illegal procurement practices, the military brass went berserk. How unpatriotic on our part to derail the production of weapons critical to the national defense! Although a bit hyperbolic, there was a thread of truth. No one else could produce these weapons systems with such extraordinary ramp-up periods. This also demonstrated the awesome power of the military industrial complex.

## The Raid Is On

The afternoon prior to the actual raids, at the direction of the DOJ I returned to the Pentagon for a meeting with the newly appointed Secretary of Defense, Frank C. Carlucci III.

At that meeting, I revealed for the first time that we would be serving search warrants on several offices at the Pentagon the following day. I then dropped the bomb and told the secretary that a number of phones at the DoD had been tapped, including those of high-level officials. It was a tough way for Carlucci to begin his second week as secretary of defense. As before, I declined to provide further details. The following day I was glad I hadn't.

The U.S. Attorney's Office was abuzz early on the morning of June 14, 1988, as federal agents across the country headed out to serve forty-two search warrants. By 8:00 a.m., every phone line in the office was lit up with a call from the media: about one every three minutes. Even Howard Stern called for an interview. Literally every major news network in America called for a comment. As directed by the attorney general, I made no comments for the record and took only calls from reporters I knew. By 9:00 a.m., we were besieged with phone calls from members of Congress demanding to speak with me personally. Again as directed, I declined to accept them, with the exception of Senator John W. Warner of Virginia, with whom I enjoyed a close relationship. In violation of my instructions from the DOJ, I gave the senator a succinct briefing and promised to touch base with him later in the day. A member of the Senate Armed Services

Committee, Warner wanted to be out front on the issue. Since my job depended on his political patronage, I intended to cooperate fully.

The most disturbing phone calls that morning came around 7:30 a.m. from the Pentagon correspondents for two national television networks. I took one, because my previous contacts with the caller had been positive. She brashly explained that her schedule was tight and she needed to know exactly where within the Pentagon—a big place—the search warrants were going to be served. She wanted to have a camera in place when the agents arrived. She promised to hold the story until after the search began if I would provide the information she wanted. I declined to be sucked into the deal. Damn, I was glad I hadn't given the Secretary of Defense's staff any more details on the investigation.

I was a little winded at 9:55 a.m. when I arrived at the Office of the Attorney General for a prearranged briefing, before a national press conference later that morning. The following week, I would be spending a day on Capitol Hill briefing members of Congress. Associate Attorney General Frank Keating, the number three person at the DOJ, would accompany me to the Hill, since several members of Congress could be implicated. Although Keating was going as a "handler," he would actually deflect some of the heat. When members pressed me for information beyond our boundaries, I could defer to Keating and let him be the heavy. He was one of the brightest minds at the DOJ and a delightful guy to be around. The leadership he exhibited years later as governor of Oklahoma during the tragic bombing of the Oklahoma federal courthouse will always be remembered.

As I began explaining a few late breaking events, the attorney general abruptly cut me off. He had been ordered to the White House in thirty minutes to bring the president up to date on the investigation. Meese smiled and said that he'd prefer for me to give the briefing.

The attorney general's limousine, following closely in the tail wind of an FBI vehicle with his security detail, whisked through the White House gate without pausing a second. When Meese and I emerged, we were escorted directly into the West Wing. In less than a minute, we were standing at the front door of the Oval Office chatting with President Reagan's personal secretary. Moments later a cavalcade of dignitaries paced down the hallway, including Vice President George H. W. Bush, General Colin Powell, the national security director, presidential Chief of Staff Howard Baker; Counsel to the President A.V. Culvahouse, the director and the deputy director of the FBI, and other assorted high-level White House staff. After a brief exchange of greetings, we proceeded into the Oval Office and awaited the arrival of the president.

President Reagan slipped into the room with characteristic grace and dignity. Sharply tailored and immaculately groomed, the president smiled, shook everyone's hand, and motioned for us to take a seat before the fireplace. Reagan and Bush sat in winged chairs directly in front of the fireplace. Everyone else took seats on couches and chairs around them. A White House photographer captured it on film. The picture is proudly displayed in my office.

I was nervous, but the briefing was uneventful, and pretty much paralleled my presentation to the Secretary of Defense. I did add that we strongly suspected that members of Congress might have received significant campaign contributions from defense contractors, generally through third parties, in exchange for supporting funding for unneeded weapons systems.

Vice President Bush was palpably shaken, and aggressive with his questions. He wanted to know who was responsible and how it had happened. The president was cool, calm, and collected. He asked only one question: How long will the investigation take?

I responded by saying that we already had a number of people cooperating, some of whom would probably be pleading guilty in the next ninety days. The president then gently shook his head and made a comment I'll never forget:

"Henry, be careful. Remember when it hits the fan at the Pentagon, everyone runs for cover."

His insight proved to be correct as the investigation progressed.

When the meeting broke up, I spent about ten minutes discussing mutual political friends with the Vice President and talking about bird hunting, one of his favorite pastimes. Several years later, my personal contacts with Vice President Bush would pay dividends. Initially, the genesis of his passion during our meeting eluded me. I subsequently realized that the Vice President had a personal stake in the Pentagon investigation. Bush was in the midst of a hard-fought campaign for President against Governor Michael Dukakis. Prior to the Reagan administration, most military procurement contracts had been let on a sole-source basis, without competitive bidding. To control spiraling costs, President Reagan directed the DoD to implement a system of awarding contracts on the basis of competitive bids. The competitive process achieved its intended purpose, but the tidal shift in policy was not well received in the industry—and spawned a black market for insider information.

Political analysts and newspaper editors began speculating that the Pentagon scandal could become Bush's nemesis. Guilt by association is a classic indictment in the hardball Washington world, where politics is a contact sport. Some theorized that, rather than wield it as a sword, Dukakis would use the issue as a

*Briefing President Reagan, Vice President Bush and key White House aides on Operation Ill-Wind. The investigation uncovered massive fraud within the defense procurement industry. (Courtesy of the White House.)*

shield to deflect criticism for his soft record on the military. In the end, Dukakis did neither.

As we exited the West Wing, Meese and I were greeted by a throng of reporters and dozens of news cameras. The story was white hot. Although we'd hold a formal news conference later that morning, the attorney general decided to take a few questions. One of his answers haunted me for the next year.

A reporter asked when indictments were expected to be handed down. Meese, misconstruing my comments to the president, responded that I had promised the president there would be indictments within ninety days. What I had told the president was that some cooperating individuals would be pleading guilty in about ninety days: not the same thing. Meese's comment put the investigation on an unattainable time track and put me in a perpetual defensive posture with the press. The problem was compounded by my remark to several reporters as we walked toward the car that, over time, I expected "a blizzard of indictments." It was a nice sound bite, but the allusion created a standard by which the media would later measure the success of our work. How many indictments constitute a blizzard? Damned if I knew!

After an extended press conference with Meese at Main Justice, I headed over to Capitol Hill. I began with a private meeting with the two U.S. senators from Virginia, John Warner and Paul Trible. As a former secretary of the Navy and member of the Senate Armed Services Committee, Warner wanted to take the lead in recommending immediate and swift corrective action. Within hours, he would be on national television recommending structural changes to the military procurement regime.

Warner also asked me to accompany him to the office of Armed Services Committee Chairman Sam Nunn for a brief overview of the scope of our investigation. Senator Nunn, of Georgia, with whom I would have extensive subsequent contact, was undoubtedly one of the finest gentlemen serving in the United States Senate. In the ensuing months, Warner and Nunn would frequently seek my counsel on whether presidential appointees appearing before the Senate Armed Services Committee were implicated in the scandal.

On one memorable occasion, the Office of the Secretary of Defense called my wife, Tara, who was then a civilian employee with the U.S. Marine Corps, early one Friday morning to locate me. Apparently, the nomination of a candidate for Deputy Secretary of Defense was pending confirmation before the Senate Armed Services Committee. Senators Nunn and Warner insisted that the committee vote be postponed until they got my assurance that the nominee was not a subject of the Ill Wind investigation.

Tara informed the secretary's aide that I was playing golf in Myrtle Beach, South Carolina, and would return on Monday. Not good enough. The secretary wanted the vote to take place that day. Tara, being a DoD employee, was effusively cooperative, but informed them that she had no idea what course we were playing that morning. The secretary's directions were simple. Find me, quick. The Secretary had just dispatched a Navy helicopter to the general area to pick me up.

Tara contacted the wives of all the other guys in our group and learned that we were playing Myrtle Beach National. The golf course was notified to find me and direct me to call Senators Nunn and Warner. The copter was standing by. My best friend, Bob Holmes, and I could hear the giant rotors pounding as the assistant golf pro located me on the fifth hole. The pro, a retired New York City police detective, shuttled me to the clubhouse. A quick call to Washington dislodged the nomination, my golf buddies gave me generous bogeys on the four holes I missed, and the pro bought me a beer.

I returned to Capitol Hill to complete my briefings on June 23, again accompanied by Associate Attorney General Frank Keating. After meeting with about a dozen Senate leaders individually, I concluded with a joint presentation

*The Ill-Wind prosecution team meeting with FBI Director William Sessions, center. (Courtesy of the U.S. Department of Justice.)*

to about twenty members of the House, including Speaker Jim Wright of Texas. Man, was I glad to have Keating along.

At the close of our meeting, the Speaker asked if any member of Congress was under investigation. As instructed by Keating, I carefully replied that no member of Congress had been served with a subpoena or been the subject of a search warrant or a wiretap. Apparently, the Speaker misunderstood my response. Later that afternoon, at a hastily called press conference, Speaker Wright proudly announced that I had assured lawmakers that no member of Congress was a target of the investigation. The comment was promptly countered by Keating, who stated emphatically that I had made no such comment, and that it was too early to tell who might be implicated.

Over the two years that followed, the results of the Ill Wind investigation were gradually unfurled as a succession of indictments were handed down. In time, the investigative team consisted of eight full-time prosecutors, seventy-eight FBI agents and fifteen Navy investigators. Much of my attention, however, was diverted by a routine drug investigation in Virginia Beach, one so politically explosive that it would eventually cost me my job.

# XVIII
# Political Powder Keg

To properly set the stage for a discussion of the Virginia Beach investigation, two things must be kept in mind. First, although to the casual observer Virginia Beach is a family-oriented city with one of the most conservative voter bases in the state, there is also a fast-lane undercurrent below the surface. Second, it is an indisputable fact that a busted drug trafficker will attempt to finger anybody imaginable to save his hide.

So when a DEA agent brought an informant hoping to "work off" drug charges to the U.S. Attorney's Office in Norfolk for a debriefing, assistant U.S. attorney Bob Wiechering was skeptical. But when the informant told Wiechering that he had seen the former Democratic governor of Virginia hanging out at parties where cocaine was being used openly, Bob almost fell out of his chair. Never. Not Chuck Robb, former Marine officer, married to President Johnson's daughter. Bob and I both dismissed the notion as ridiculous.

As DEA and the Virginia Beach Police continued to investigate drug trafficking at the oceanfront resort, the governor's name surfaced several more times. Sources alleged that between 1982 and 1986, while Robb was serving as governor, he would occasionally show up at parties where cocaine was reportedly being used. According to these informants, Robb enjoyed hanging out with the young ladies in attendance. The information became increasingly difficult to push aside, but Wiechering and I were still convinced that Robb was too clean-cut to hang with that crowd.

DEA and the Virginia Beach Police began to give the information a closer look when two of the former governor's friends from the beach, a dentist and a restaurant owner, pled guilty to federal drug charges. Both were well known for throwing parties at their oceanfront estates. And yes, Chuck Robb occasionally showed up. At that point, the investigators had to begin asking why. According to press reports, the Virginia attorney general and the State Police had advised the governor to be cautious about the company he was keeping.

The local newspaper had been closely following the investigation of drug trafficking in Virginia Beach. Sixteen people were eventually convicted. Ten were social acquaintances of the former governor. DEA held a press conference to publicize the results of the investigation. The following day, the press picked up on the Robb connection, sparking a feeding frenzy. The reporter following the story contacted everyone who had either pled guilty or testified before the federal grand jury in connection with the case. Smelling the scent of political blood, he also scoured the beachfront for information. Slowly the story unraveled in the press.

The coverage culminated in an editorial in the Norfolk newspaper in which the author contended that a highly placed federal source had confirmed that Governor Robb was under investigation. Governor Robb and his political supporters concluded that I was the anonymous source, and went on the offensive. They accused my office of leaking information to the local press. Both were figments of their imagination. What sparked the hasty conclusion?

In the spring of 1988, Robb had floated an interest in pursuing the U.S. Senate seat then occupied by my friend, Paul Trible. Robb and his supporters believed that the limited inquiry concerning Robb's presence at the parties was part of a sinister plot hatched by me to dissuade Robb from running. Robb's ego inhibited his ability to come to grips with the fact that his popularity was miles wide, but only centimeters deep. As a diversionary tactic, the Robb camp alleged that our inquiry was part of a political vendetta by me and the entire Tidewater law enforcement community, to smear the former governor. Horse manure! Perhaps paranoia?

I scrupulously avoided any discussion of the Robb matter with Senator Trible. He never even asked about it!

Robb's almost daily counterattacks, while annoying, were nothing new. At that stage of my career, I was used to having my integrity impugned by people under investigation. I had nothing to gain personally or politically from asking questions about Robb, except heartburn and his constant hints of retaliation. Several aspects of the investigation deserve illumination.

First, Chuck Robb was *never* the target of any federal investigation, and we could have cared less about his social life. This was a highly publicized angle cultivated entirely by the media on its own, and man, did the daily verbal jousting sell newspapers!

Our investigation focused solely on drug trafficking, not mere personal use. Even if the investigation had revealed that Robb was present when drugs were used, it would not have been a matter of interest to the feds.

Robb adamantly denied ever using cocaine or witnessing it being used. His steadfast position was that, viewed in its worst light, he was simply in the wrong place at the wrong time. That may well have been the case. Robb also contended that he wouldn't recognize cocaine if he saw it. That also is possible, but if you saw someone snorting white powder at a party, even the most naive person would be suspicious.

Even today, I'm inclined to believe that Chuck Robb never used cocaine. I also doubt that it was cocaine that drew him to the beach parties. He was too straight laced. Beyond that, in my opinion, the evidence is less clear.

Second, the U.S. Attorney's Office neither initiated nor suggested any inquiry concerning Robb. His name was first mentioned by DEA agents, and appropriately so. The last thing a U.S. attorney wants is to be involved in the investigation of a person as popular and politically powerful as Governor Robb. However, once the issue of Robb's appearance at parties frequented by drug dealers was raised by the investigators, we had a duty to follow through. The seriousness of the inquiry was greatly magnified by the intensity of the media coverage. Because Robb presented himself as an heir apparent to the throne, anything he did was news.

Despite my skepticism, I believe it would have been patently improper to direct the investigators to simply disregard information that came from multiple sources. No person, regardless of position or pedigree, is above the law or beyond public scrutiny. In time, it would become increasingly apparent that Chuck Robb disagreed.

Third, the U.S. Attorney's Office never leaked any information from the grand jury. Most of it remains to this day clothed in a veil of secrecy. When witnesses walked out of the grand jury room in Norfolk during the Virginia Beach investigation, they were greeted by a gaggle of reporters. Almost all of them freely discussed what they had told the grand jury, as the law allows them to do. Although prosecutors and jurors can be jailed for violating the secrecy of grand jury proceeding, witnesses have no such restriction.

As for the highly placed source that confirmed that investigators were asking questions about Robb, I have my suspicions, but it sure as hell was not me. As I'm certain the reporter would confirm, I've never spoken to him in my life. I had no desire to fan the flames of this controversy.

The most perplexing aspect of our inquiry was its aftermath. I was never convinced that there was any credible evidence that Chuck Robb did anything illegal. Some of the investigators disagreed. Whether he exercised good judgment is best left for the court of public opinion. Anyway, during the Virginia

Beach investigation, Paul Trible made the startling announcement that he would not seek reelection to the U.S. Senate, having opted to pursue the governorship. Robb announced his candidacy for the Senate. However, even as the campaign headed into the fall stretch, he still couldn't dodge the continuing press questions about the investigation. One day, I received a phone call from a gentlemen who, as I recall, identified himself as Robb's director of communications.

Given the public pounding I'd received from Robb and his followers, I reluctantly agreed to meet with George Stoddart. Maybe I was a fool, and perhaps he simply performed his lines well, but he and I hit it off from the first minute. I explained to Stoddart the genesis of our inquiry and my conclusion that there was no believable evidence that former Governor Robb had done anything illegal. He was relieved, but said that Robb would be deeply appreciative if I could make a public statement to that effect. I explained that such public statements were contrary to the policy and tradition of the Department of Justice. It had never been done before in Virginia as far as I knew. But would I consider it? Yes, I agreed to think on it.

Several factors weighed heavily on my final decision. First, while I had no desire to abandon my media-fostered image as an aggressive prosecutor, I did want a balanced reputation for fairness in judgment. Second, our limited inquiry concerning the former governor had spiraled beyond anyone's expectations, in large measure because of the media frenzy over his alleged consorting with young ladies at beach parties. Our routine questioning concerning drugs frankly did not deserve the attention it received. Third, I did not need to make a lifetime enemy of Chuck Robb, someone for whom I had a great deal of respect, at that time.

On the other side of the ledger, I knew my Republican friends and evolving base of political supporters would be furious if I made the statement, and the investigators frowned on the idea. But the decisive consideration was prosecution ethics. A politician's stock in trade is his or her reputation. An uncontrolled canard, no matter how vagrant in origin, can be politically fatal if left unchecked. In the final analysis, I concluded that our duty-bound inquiry probably had stoked the scandal, even though the local press had been hot on the story first. Therefore, it seemed only right that I put it to rest—or at least try to.

During my tenure as U.S. attorney, I followed the same policy with respect to every investigation of an elected official. If they were cleared by an investigation that received press coverage, I said so publicly. The policy conflicted with the prevailing DOJ practice, but I was the one who had to live with my record in office.

I spent several hours with Stoddart hammering out the language of the press release. On the one hand, I wanted to do the right thing. On the other, the message had to square with our findings. In the end, we agreed to a statement about there being no credible evidence of any wrong doing on former Governor Robb's part. It was my understanding that Robb himself, or a high-ranking person on his campaign staff, concurred with the agreed upon language.

The press release went out. I repeated the agreed-upon statement at least a half dozen times during televised interviews. To my surprise, the statement was well received in both Republican and Democratic circles. I thought it put the matter to rest. The cloud was virtually removed as a campaign issue. Chuck Robb was elected to the U.S. Senate that November by a wide margin, with only token opposition. However, the storm clouds soon returned—this time accompanied by thunder.

Within weeks of Robb's swearing in, the media began to speculate that his ultimate goal was the White House. This, coupled with his princely image as someone with all the trappings of aristocracy, fueled even more intense interest in his personal life. *Regardie's Magazine* did a feature article entitled, "Beach Blanket Bimbo, Chuck Robb's Never-Ending Party Problem." The cover featured a cartoon depiction of the senator with his rear end showing.

Meanwhile, a private investigator named Billy Franklin, from Virginia Beach, conducted his own investigation of Robb's presence at beach parties where cocaine was reportedly used. The investigation was bankrolled by an anonymous source, later identified as a Richmond physician and Republican activist. There were also published reports that the project was financed in part by Republican contributors. Perhaps working in league with at least one reporter, Franklin interviewed anyone and everyone involved in the case who would talk with him. The results of his probe were eventually published in the book *Tough Enough.* The subtitle was *The Cocaine Investigation of United States Senator Chuck Robb.* Robb was understandably furious. However, I can say unequivocally that neither I nor Wieckering ever spoke to Franklin or anyone working with him. The last thing we wanted was to resuscitate the controversy. To our dismay, things soon got worse.

In anticipation of the book's publication, Senator Robb's Chief of Staff David K. McCloud went on the offensive. He filed a complaint with the Federal Election Commission (FEC). In essence it alleged that Franklin's book had been financed with illegal Republican campaign contributions. McCloud also contended that my office had abused its prosecutorial function and was in active complicity with Franklin. The complaint offered no factual support for the claim. There was none to offer.

Backed into a corner, I asked the DOJ Office of Professional Responsibility (OPR) to conduct an immediate investigation of McCloud's complaint. OPR investigates all ethical complaints against DOJ employees. Within a week, Assistant Counsel David P. Bobzien was assigned to review the complaint. Bobzien spent several hours interviewing my staff in Norfolk. After examining the transcript of the grand jury proceedings, he found McCloud's complaint concerning the U.S. Attorney's Office and the federal agents working the case to be baseless. The FEC soon agreed. Through third parties, I made repeated overtures to meet with Senator Robb or his staff to set the record straight. He adamantly refused. He preferred to lob verbal missiles.

Meanwhile, one afternoon I received a telephone call on my private office line from David McCloud. He was cordial and almost pleasant. He wanted to stop by my office to talk. I welcomed the opportunity. When McCloud arrived, he was all business. He never even cracked a smile. His proposal was simple. If I wanted Robb's help (the clear inference being in keeping my job as U.S. attorney), I needed to help him. Okay, with what?

Senator Robb wanted to know who hired Billy Franklin to investigate his personal life and write the scandalous book. I told McCloud I had no idea and that I'd never met Billy Franklin. McCloud, leaning forward for emphasis, looked me in the eye and said, "Well then, find out." He then stood up and walked out.

Several days later, I called McCloud and told him that I was unable to determine who had hired Billy Franklin. In a cold voice, McCloud said "okay" and hung up. That was our last contact. To my dismay, I later learned that McCloud might have cultivated an attorney in my office as an informant. The attorney had no involvement in the Virginia Beach investigation, but he apparently pipelined his impressions—a tortured confection of extrapolation, speculation, and spin—to Robb's chief of staff. The attorney apparently had some expectation of political reward. As far as I know, the only thing he received was the ostracism of his peers.

As for McCloud, his zeal and appetite for intrigue eventually ended his political career. The following year, he pled guilty in federal court to unlawfully disseminating the contents of an illicitly taped telephone conversation of Governor L. Douglas Wilder. Two other Robb aides were also implicated. Wilder, who was then lt. governor of Virginia, speculated during the conversation that Robb's career was "finished" as a result of hanging out at wild parties at Virginia Beach while serving as governor.

McCloud, who was extremely contrite and agreed to fully cooperate with federal investigators, was fined ten thousand dollars. It was a sad ending for a man with a bright political future. McCloud told the United States district judge at his sentencing that he had "lost perspective of what was important."

With only a few months left on my four-year appointment as U.S. attorney, I called Senator Warner's chief of staff, with whom I had an excellent relationship, and asked if I should start looking for another job. She advised me to come in and meet with the senator as soon as possible.

My relationship with John Warner had become quite close as a result of the Ill Wind investigation. We could discuss matters with unvarnished candor. He explained that Robb intended to block my reappointment, which he could do with Democrats holding a majority of the seats in the U.S. Senate. However, at Warner's urging, Robb had agreed that I could remain in office until the Pentagon probe was completed. "How much time do you need?" Warner asked.

"One year," I replied.

The senator promised to do what he could. It was understood that I would publicly indicate my intention to step down at that point, and not seek reappointment. Warner's chief of staff called me a day or two later. The deal was struck. I would later learn, however, that Robb's appetite for revenge was still not satisfied.

## Ill Wind Blows Favorably

By the end of June 1991, my designated time of departure, most of the Pentagon procurement investigation had been completed, although a number of defendants were still in the midst of protracted plea negotiations. The final corporate defendant to plead, Litton Systems, Inc., held out until January 1994, and pled guilty to conspiracy to defraud the government, wire fraud, and misappropriating confidential procurement information. Litton admitted paying a consultant ninety-six thousand dollars to obtain secret bid information on its competitors for three Navy contracts. The corporation agreed to pay $3.9 million in fines, penalties, and civil damages.

In all, fifty-four individuals and ten corporations were convicted. The office also collected more than three hundred sixty thousand dollars in fines and penalties. The investigation revealed that a number of members of the House of Representatives had received illegal campaign contributions. Two congressmen were believed to have lost their seats as a result of the probe. More than fifty corporate executives, defense consultants, and military procurement officials were convicted. The most prominent government official convicted was former Assistant

Secretary of the Navy Melvyn Paisley, who received the longest sentence of any defendant, forty-eight months in prison. Also pleading guilty to fraud-related charges were Stuart Berlin, a former high-level Navy Department supervising engineer, and Victor Cohn, a former deputy assistant secretary of the Air Force.

A number of the nation's most prominent weapons and support systems manufacturers pled guilty and collectively paid hundreds of thousands of dollars in fines, including United Technologies Corporation, Loral Corporation, Unisys Corporation, Hazeltine Corporation, LTV Aerospace and Defense Corporation, Litton Systems, and Teledyne Corporation. Unisys paid fines and penalties of one hudred ninety thousand dollars for illegal activities occurring when the company was known as Sperry. Teledyne paid twenty thousand dollars. Executives of both companies were convicted of bid rigging.

In commending Joe Aronica for his extraordinary leadership in supervising Operation Ill Wind, Attorney General Janet Reno described the case as "one of the most successful investigations and prosecutions ever undertaken by the Department of Justice against white-collar crime." Reno further noted that "Ill Wind fundamentally changed how white-collar crimes are investigated and prosecuted."

The Ill Wind investigation leveled the playing field, allowing more small contractors to compete for military contracts, and it cleansed the procurement process of the most flagrant corruption. But are our nation's weapon systems better off?

## Robb Again

As I completed my final plans for departure from the U.S. Attorney's Office, like a smoldering forest fire, the Robb scandal was rekindled—this time by national television. In a scathing one-hour prime time exposé, narrated by NBC news anchor Tom Brokaw and entitled "The Senator's Secrets," the network recounted previous news reports of Robb's presence at beach parties where cocaine was reported used. It included interviews of people with first-hand information. Even more explosive was an interview with a former Miss Virginia with whom the senator had an encounter at a New York hotel in 1984. She claimed they had sex. Robb contended that they simply shared a bottle of wine and she gave him a massage. The story hit *Playboy* magazine the following month.

As is his style, Robb with his band of brothers went on the offensive. Rather than cross swords with Brokaw or NBC, they again came after me—the most convenient target. In a personal letter to Brokaw, Robb claimed that he had been unfairly singled out by me. However, as the NBC feature clearly demonstrated, Robb's name was not randomly selected from a phone directory by federal agents.

Robb also told Brokaw that I had exploited the federal grand jury for partisan purposes. My public reply was that I wished I could release the grand jury proceedings for public review. However, the law does not allow for the release of transcripts of grand jury testimony without a court order. Court authorization is usually given only in extraordinary circumstances, such as if its contents are the subject of criminal or civil litigation. When the shark came back for a second bite, I was prepared to seek such an order.

## A Miracle

Leaving the United States Attorney's Office was one of the most difficult experiences of my life. Fortunately, I had a number of career options available, thanks to Congressman Wolf and my friends at the White House Office of Personnel. I made a concerted effort to be appointed the United States Customs commissioner—one of the true plum jobs in the administration. Despite strong backing from White House personnel, the secretary of the Treasury selected Ambassador Carol Boyd Hallett—a sharp lady and a superb choice.

As a consolation, the White House offered me the position of assistant secretary of Labor, with responsibility for overseeing enforcement of the nation's labor laws. I spent a day with the incumbent in that job and decided it was not for me. Perhaps it was ego, but I enjoyed being in the public eye—sound bites and press conferences. The Labor Department job was too confining.

Much to my wife's chagrin, I decided to run for Congress in the Eighth Congressional District of Virginia. The incumbent congressman, Jim Moran, was an unabashed liberal Democrat and a personal friend of mine, but my name identification and popularity made the race competitive. I joined the law firm of Reed, Smith, Shaw and McClay as counsel. The folks at Reed, Smith were wonderful, and willing to accommodate my campaign schedule.

Although campaigning was nothing new for me or my family, running for Congress was grueling. Even in the early stages, I had dozens of phone calls and three or four meetings or speeches every day, seven days a week. Almost every group I met with wanted my solemn pledge, sometimes in writing, to support a certain position on their issue of interest—guns, schools, taxes, abortion. I stumbled in the door each night about 10:00 p.m. with a headache, and the campaign was still in the preliminary stages.

After about six weeks of campaigning, I realized the obvious. The Eighth Congressional District was gerrymandered for a moderate-to-liberal constituency. History has shown that a conservative Republican cannot win. My campaign strategy combined high name identification with philosophical acceptability. I envisioned the latter element as being an amalgam of conservative views on national defense and law enforcement with a more tempered position on social issues. My Republican base would have no part of it. Many Republican activists would rather cede the election to a Democrat than have a Republican candidate with a tempered message. Increasingly dispirited by the resulting conundrum, I finally concluded that my worst nightmare was being elected and having to serve. I quietly began fumbling for the parachute cord and waiting for my miracle.

One morning it happened. I was sitting in my Tysons Corner law office bemoaning the endless succession of speaking engagements and public appearances on my calendar when my friend Monie Ryder from the Office of White House Personnel called to ask how I was doing.

Since she asked, I candidly responded "Miserable."

She then asked if I would be interested in serving on the U.S. Parole Commission. "Tempting, but no thanks," I replied. Congress had recently abolished parole for federal inmates and the commission was on a gradual path to oblivion. She said she'd keep her eye out for something I might be interested in.

I then asked Monie if the president had selected a new director of the U.S. Marshals Service, the nation's oldest federal law enforcement agency. I'd heard from friends on Capitol Hill that none of the names submitted thus far had excited much interest. Monie said it was her impression that a decision was imminent, but she was not exactly sure where things stood. She'd check on it and call me back.

Not even an hour had passed when Chase Untermeyer, director of the Office of Presidential Personnel called. Chase had been very supportive of my unsuccessful quest for the Customs commissioner job.

"Hear you're interested in the U.S. Marshals job."

"Absolutely," I responded, looking down at my calendar hopelessly in search of a free evening that month.

"Okay." Chase casually intoned. "I think this one's going to be easy. Hopefully we can start the paper work right away."

"Don't you need the president's blessing?" I asked.

"Already got it. He thinks it's a perfect fit. And Bill Sessions (director of the FBI) agrees." Chase added.

"How long will the process take?" I asked.

"Hard to predict, we've got to get the current guy confirmed first. It could take a while." Chase replied.

The incumbent director was awaiting confirmation as a United States district judge for the Southern District of Florida. I breathed a sigh of relief, felt the emotion drain, and savored the priceless feeling of freedom. The campaign was over. Time was now my own.

Throughout most of my adult life, I had bounded out of bed at the crack of dawn, excited about the challenging work day ahead, but I dreaded every day of private practice. The structured bill-for-every-breathing-moment environment was not my style. And unlike most of our friends in the legal field, my wife and I had modest material ambitions. I wanted adventure, and few things could compare to the excitement of heading a federal law enforcement agency.

After pinching myself several times to be sure it was not a dream, I called Tara to share the good news. Then I walked out of the office to perform a less pleasant task—explaining all this to the managing partner of the law firm, and then to my political supporters. Thankfully, they understood and accepted my decision. But not all days ahead would be halcyon. There would be tense moments as my nomination ran its course. As it happened, an ambush awaited me just around the bend.

On November 20, 1991, the president formally announced his intention to nominate me to serve as director of the U.S. Marshals Service, a strategic step in the candidate vetting process. Announcement follows the preliminary background check and serves as a trial balloon designed to smoke out any serious opposition. None emerged in my case, at least not publicly. But in Washington, the real threat is rarely the surface ships. It's the lurking submarines.

The FBI completed my background check in two weeks. Most of the participating agents had known me for years, and I'd been through two prior "full field" background investigations. The only obstacle at that point was the incumbent director. His confirmation was unexpectedly held up for four months. Meanwhile, my law firm was kind enough to allow me to remain in place, drawing full salary and, frankly, able to take on little significant work. I used the interregnum to prepare for the new challenge by meeting with the directors of all federal agencies and components of the DOJ that regularly interacted with the Marshals Service. It was my intention to have a defined game plan in place the minute I took command.

In mid-February 1992, my predecessor was finally confirmed as a federal judge and I was formally nominated. The legal landscape had changed a bit in the preceding four months. We were eight months away from a presidential election. That didn't really worry me, because President George H. W. Bush, who was twenty-three points ahead, had only token opposition from a little-known governor named Bill Clinton, from Arkansas. But as the election cycle progressed, it became increasingly difficult to get confirmed by the Democratically controlled Senate. It was apparent that confirmation could take a few months.

The day following my predecessor's departure, the deputy attorney general called to ask if I would accept an appointment as acting director. He also cautioned me that the DOJ did not necessarily recommend the move, because any blunders that might occur on my watch could be an obstacle to confirmation. Nominees serving in an acting capacity are constrained to keep a low profile—something that historically had not been my style. On the other hand, I had been waiting for almost six months, and was beginning to trespass on my law firm's charity. With the enthusiasm of a child on Christmas morning, I couldn't wait, so I accepted. I was so excited that I spent the Friday afternoon before the Monday effective date of my appointment at the Marshals Service headquarters. With the deputy directors in tow, I walked through the entire building in shirt sleeves shaking hands with all eight hundred employees assigned to headquarters. It set a personal tone for the days to come. Many had never met the head of the service.

The adrenaline rush of my introductory tour was only exceeded by the thrill of entering the front door the following Monday morning. I will never forget walking up to the security checkpoint, displaying my leather-bound credentials with gold badge, reaching out my hand, and introducing myself as the new director. It was an unparalleled honeymoon moment, uncontaminated by the avalanche of problems and pressure sitting on the desk upstairs.

One of the best kept secrets in Washington was the breathtaking view from the director's office in Arlington County, Virginia. Situated on the twelfth floor of a glass-enclosed high rise on Army-Navy Drive overlooking the Pentagon, virtually every monument in Washington, including the White House and the Capitol, was visible from the director's desk. On a clear night, you could lounge in the sitting area on the front side of the office and see for more than ten miles. The director's office suite included a conference room, a personal bath with shower, and a private dining room and kitchen. And of course, I had a new Lincoln Town Car at my disposal, with an assigned driver. A ten-passenger business jet was also available, but I generally opted to fly commercially. It required far less paperwork.

At 7:30 a.m. on Monday, February 24, 1992, I officially took command of more than five thousand employees, including more than twenty-five hundred deputy U.S. marshals located in all fifty states and U.S. territories. More than any other law enforcement badge or emblem, the silver star carried by each deputy U.S. marshal symbolizes the history of law and order in America. From rounding up outlaws in the wild west to enforcing controversial school desegregation laws, the history of America's judicial system is the history of the U.S. Marshals. The price of freedom on our home soil has been costly. More than two hundred U.S. marshals or their deputies have died defending our Constitution—more than every other federal law enforcement agency combined. Four were killed during my service as director.

## History of the U.S. Marshals Service

Among the initial pieces of legislation passed by the First Session of the United States Congress was Senate Bill No. 1, which created the federal judiciary. It provided for one U.S. district judge for each of the thirteen states. To carry out the judges' orders, the Judiciary Act of 1789 also established the Office of U.S. Marshals, one for each judicial district, just as today. Marshals were appointed to serve a four-year term, "at the pleasure of the president," and were required to post a twenty thousand dollar bond. They were also required to carry out all orders of the president and Congress.

The Judiciary Act also allowed for the appointment of such deputy marshals as may be needed to perform the duties assigned. For almost a hundred years, U.S. Marshals were the law of the land. The U.S. Customs Service, which admittedly predates the U.S. Marshals, frequently touts the honor of being the nation's oldest law enforcement agency. This is technically untrue. The original Customs agents could collect duties and tariffs, but they did not have general law enforcement powers. It was many years after the establishment of the U.S. Marshals that Customs agents were vested with the type of police powers they exercise today. Originally, U.S. Marshals served under the direction of the State Department. Currently, they are a branch of the Department of Justice.

Although the original thirteen U.S. Marshals appointed by President George Washington were the chief federal law enforcement officers in their respective districts, their jurisdiction was quite limited. In the early years of the Constitution, Congress was loath to cede much power to the federal government. There were only three federal crimes in 1789—counterfeiting, treason, and piracy. Eventually, as the national banking system was spawned under the direction of Secretary of the Treasury Alexander Hamilton, U.S. Marshals became responsible for tracking down bank robbers. Today, there are more than five thousand federal crimes, and fifty federal agencies with some type of law enforcement powers. The steady growth of the federal law enforcement community has progressively overshadowed the legacy of the roots of federal police powers.

## Statutory Duties

Modern day marshals have a broad portfolio of responsibilities. Most federal agencies with law enforcement powers were created to perform a narrowly defined mission, such as the IRS, the Bureau of Alcohol, Tobacco, Firearms and Explosives, and the Environmental Protection Agency. The U.S. Marshals Service, on the other hand, has general federal police powers and can technically enforce all federal laws, if assigned to do so. For that reason, many federal agencies, including the FBI, occasionally request that their investigators be sworn as special deputy U.S. marshals to expand the statutory scope of their enforcement powers. An example of mass deputization occurred in 1992 when federal agents were dispatched to Los Angeles to restore order.

In the wake of the adverse publicity surrounding the arrest of Rodney King, riots broke out in several Los Angeles neighborhoods, resulting in massive destruction and personal injury. At the request of the governor of California, the attorney general of the United States ordered U.S. Marshals to L.A. to restore order. Never wishing to be upstaged by another federal agency, the FBI also prevailed upon the attorney general to allow it to go as well. The federal law that empowered marshals to enforce state law to restore civil order did not extend to the FBI. I, therefore, gladly deputized all the FBI agents, who despite occasional rivalry, worked quite well with our people.

Today, the principal statutory duty of U.S. Marshals remains the same as it was in 1789, protection of the judicial process. However, their mission has evolved extensively. In addition to serving court orders, protecting the judiciary, and maintaining order in the courtroom, marshals are responsible for all federal prisoners from the time of arrest until their formal surrender to the United States Bureau of Prisons to serve their sentences. In February 1992, the Marshals Service (USMS) had more than twenty thousand federal detainees in its custody, most of whom were spread out across America in rented jail space.

As a perceived cost-cutting measure, in 1992 Congress had appropriated money to house only eighteen thousand prisoners. However, the USMS has no control over the inmate population. It is driven entirely by the federal courts, which have the exclusive power to order defendants into custody. Maintaining a burgeoning inmate population during an escalating war on crime on a shoestring budget was my biggest daily source of heartburn as director. By mid-1993, the inmate population had grown to twenty-two thousand, costing almost a half billion dollars a year to house. Today that number is pushing sixty thousand.

Closely allied with inmate detention was prisoner transportation. Employing an elaborate system of aircraft and buses, the USMS in 1993 moved about fifty-six thousand prisoners. Some moved across a state, others across the nation. Because of a scarcity of bed space in Hawaii, we were forced to transport dozens of inmates back and forth from California to Hawaii several times each week. Hawaii was grateful for federal assistance with its drug trafficking problems, but refused to yield any detention space for the resulting arrests.

To accommodate prisoner movement, the USMS operated a fleet of commercial and business-size aircraft affectionately dubbed "Con Air." To support air operations, scores of USMS personnel meticulously plotted each prisoner's movement from our hub at Oklahoma City.

Another component of our responsibility to protect the judicial process was the Witness Protection Program, referred to within the agency as WITSEC. Serving as a WITSEC inspector is one of the most prestigious, and challenging, assignments for a deputy marshal. Time has changed the mission somewhat, from protecting Mafia members desperately seeking a safe sanctuary to young and restless gangsters champing at the bit to complete their cooperation and get back on the street. The former appreciated marshal protection. The latter resented it. In 1993, WITSEC had almost ten thousand protectees, including their families. Despite the more resistant attitude of its current protectees, WITSEC continues to maintain a perfect record. No program participant who has followed instructions has been killed while still under active protection.

The most exciting task assigned to the USMS is pursuing federal fugitives, foreign and domestic. With a list of exceptions too long and technical to recite, the USMS is responsible for apprehending anyone who fails to appear after being charged with a federal offense. In 1993, U.S. Marshals collared more than seventeen thousand fugitives—more than every other federal law enforcement agency combined. Here, more than any other area, the USMS finds itself engaged in jurisdictional turf battles with the FBI.

All assets seized by federal agencies for forfeiture are the responsibility of the USMS. In the 1800s, this duty was limited to pirate ships on the high seas. Today it includes aircraft, cars, houseboats, jewelry, art work, houses and active businesses. Hundreds of millions of dollars in assets, from new Porsches to decades old Hondas, from ocean side mansions to tenement row houses, from snakes to race horses, from hamburger huts to gambling casinos—the Seized Assets Division has seen it all. The San Diego office alone took more than one hundred cars per week into custody on the Mexican border. USMS was responsible not only for maintaining the property, but also for liquidating it at or close to fair-market value.

Every threat against a member of the federal judiciary or their family is investigated by specially trained court security inspectors. Threats are analyzed at the USMS headquarters for validity and seriousness, where a thorough background investigation is conducted on the suspected source of the threat, often including a personal interview of the person. Then a response decision is made. This could vary from periodic checks on the judge's residence to around-the-clock protective detail.

Perhaps the least known duty assigned to the USMS is the protection of all nuclear missiles in transit between silos in the United States. From the moment a nuclear missile leaves a military reservation in transit to the next silo in its rotation, it is escorted by heavily armed deputy marshals. This fills a void beyond the boundaries of any other agency's jurisdiction.

## The Fate of My Nomination

My first few months as director of the Marshals Service were spent immersed in budget and personnel issues, with which I was familiar, but never on such a grand scale. As time passed, I became progressively concerned that my nomination appeared to be dormant and that, with the election approaching, the gate would close on the confirmation process. My nomination had been placed on the Senate Judiciary Committee calendar several times, but had been passed over for hearing, an ominous sign. I learned from two sources on the committee that the chairman was still waiting for one of my home state senators to return his "blue slip." I felt a bit helpless since the fate of my nomination lay in Democratic hands. The majority party controlled the committee calendar.

Under Senate rules, the home state senators for each nominee are sent a blue form on which they indicate whether they support or oppose a nominee. In some cases, such as a nominee for U.S. attorney, U.S. marshal or U.S. district judge, a negative blue slip is fatal because the geographic jurisdictional boundaries of the office are limited to the senator's state. In such a case, the nominee will never receive a confirmation hearing and the nomination will die in committee. Whether or not a negative blue slip would have a lethal effect on a nominee for a Justice Department position, one with national responsibility like director of the Marshals Service, largely depends on the chairman of the committee with jurisdiction over the nomination. No one was sure how Senator Joe Biden of Delaware would react.

My case was slightly different from the norm, and in some respects unprecedented. Senator Chuck Robb had not returned his blue slip. John Warner, the other Virginia senator, a strong ally, returned his within forty-eight hours, noting his support. Robb sat on his for almost four months. Senator Warner's chief of staff, Susan Magill, repeatedly urged Robb to return the slip, but to no avail. Finally, I asked my friend Duke Short, chief of staff for Senator Strom Thurman of South Carolina, the ranking minority member of the Judiciary Committee, if he would intervene.

A former IRS Special Agent, Short was perhaps the most powerful and respected staffer on Capitol Hill. Always courteous, respectful, and eager to help any friend of Senator Thurman, Short had the confidence of most senators on both sides of the aisle. As Senator Thurman approached a hundred years of age, his health began to fail, and Duke Short was afforded many privileges on Thurman's behalf rarely extended to a staff member.

In an attempt to resolve the impasse, Short spoke to Senator Robb on the Senate floor one afternoon. With his distinctive South Carolina accent, he asked Robb if he would kindly return my blue slip as soon as possible, and added that the Judiciary Committee was anxious to conduct a hearing on my nomination. As a compromise, Duke even suggested that the senator might want to just sign the slip without indicating his position on the nomination. Robb politely responded that he intended to do so after conferring privately with Senator Biden. Days passed, but no blue slip. The following week, Short called to tell me that Robb had met with Biden and, not surprisingly, urged the chairman to tube my nomination. Robb, however, refused to put his opposition in writing and never filed the blue slip.

Absent a filibuster by Robb, there was no question that I would be confirmed if I could ever get a hearing. All of the Republican members of the Senate Judiciary Committee supported my nomination. My special assistant, Sterling Epps, who had previously served as a lobbyist for many federal law enforcement organizations, maintained daily contact with members of the staffs of Senators Biden, Simon, Kohl, and DeConcini. Two Democrats on the committee had even sent letters on my behalf to Chairman Biden, as had Senator John Breaux, a Democrat of Louisiana. Still, the committee was reluctant to move on my nomination without Senator Robb's blue slip, which he steadfastly refused to return.

By failing to return the blue slip, Robb avoided taking a public position, thereby averting another media frenzy rehashing accounts of his Virginia Beach frolics. He also dodged the embarrassment of exposing his petty and boorish vindictiveness to his dwindling constituency.

As I awaited a break in the deepening impasse, my Democratic supporters on Senate Judiciary tried to allay my worry. They described Robb as a likeable guy with minimal influence among his colleagues. They also assured me that Biden was reasonable and open minded.

To intensify pressure on the committee, I called a number of politically influential U.S. marshals and solicited their help. Every U.S. marshal needs a United States senator or powerful political figure's blessing to be appointed. Collectively, they packed a hell of a political wallop. Thanks to their persistent agitation, more than twenty United States senators contacted Biden's office and asked that a hearing be scheduled on my nomination.

The National Fraternal Order of Police and the National Sheriff's Association, which together represented hundreds of thousands of law enforcement officers, also petitioned Biden to move my nomination. Thanks to incessant pressure from Don Cahill, national vice president of the Fraternal Order of Police and a personal friend of Senator Biden, my nomination was tentatively scheduled for the last date on which hearings would be held before the presidential election, July 22, 1992, if Biden's investigator could resolve a few questions concerning my background.

According to unimpeachable sources, Biden informed Robb that if he had opposition to my confirmation, the committee would hear him out. It was an unprecedentedly bold move by Senator Biden, for which I am eternally grateful.

Senator Biden had Harriet Green of his staff call me that afternoon. As I had expected, her inquiry focused on the Virginia Beach investigation. I carefully traced the genesis of the investigation and reiterated that Robb had never been a target and that there was no investigative interest in his social life. I gave her as much information as the law would allow. Ms. Green spent considerable time dwelling on allegations that federal prosecutors had leaked information to the press concerning the grand jury investigation.

I categorically denied that any leaks had occurred and explained that witnesses exiting the grand jury room would immediately (and legally) submit to detailed press interviews. Ms. Green was skeptical of my answer, but I was prepared to go further. I offered her the telephone number of a Norfolk reporter who had covered the story and would verify my account. At that point, she seemed satisfied. My hearing was placed on the Senate calendar for July 22.

Of course, no one thought that Robb would show up for the hearing, but I'd come too far to take any chances. I called U.S. District Judge J. Calvitt Clarke, Jr., in Norfolk, who had overseen the grand jury, and asked if he would authorize the Senate Judiciary Committee to review select portions of the grand jury proceedings, under an appropriate confidentiality order. Nothing would better demonstrate the good-faith basis of our inquiry if it became an issue. Judge

Clarke agreed to "seriously consider" my request if the integrity of our inquiry was called into question. Fortunately, the issue never resurfaced.

My family and I arrived early on the long-awaited day with about fifty friends and colleagues from the Marshals Service in tow. Mine was the second hearing scheduled for that day, behind my former DOJ colleague Frank Keating, who had served as associate attorney general during the Ill-Wind case. In 1992, Keating was serving as general counsel of the Department of Housing and Urban Development. He had been nominated for a judgeship on the United States Court of Appeals for the Eighth Circuit.

Senator Biden began the proceedings on an unexpected note. He asked everyone in attendance to join him in singing "Happy Birthday" to Senator Ted Kennedy's mother, Rose. He then gaveled the committee to order and began Keating's hearing. Unexpectedly, Keating was subjected to more than six hours of agonizing character assassination orchestrated by Senators Kennedy, Biden, and Metzenbaum, all Democrats, concerning legal opinions issued by his office at HUD. As the dust cleared, it was apparent that Keating's nomination would never clear the committee. As disappointed as he may have been at the moment, it proved to be a blessing. Keating later served two terms as governor of Oklahoma and rose to hero status for his leadership in the wake of the Oklahoma City bombing. He was far too energetic a personality to fade into oblivion as an appellate judge.

In the aftermath of Keating's pelting, I was a little apprehensive as I walked forward to be sworn, but felt better when I saw some friendly faces join Biden on the dais: Senators Paul Simon (D., Ill.), Orrin Hatch (R., Ut.) and Chuck Grassley (R., Ia.). Senators Hatch and Grassley gave warm and supportive opening statements on my behalf. Senator Simon, with whom I had an excellent relationship, began on a positive note, but soon took a disturbing turn. Simon wanted to know what had gone wrong in Chicago the prior week, and what I intended to do about it.

## A Tragic Night in Chicago

Jeffrey E. Erickson patiently waited for the right moment. The thirty-four-year-old former police trainee and Marine Corps marksman took careful note of the daily routine of the deputy U.S. marshals at the Dirksen Federal Courthouse in Chicago, looking for a window of vulnerability.

Court recessed at 5:00 p.m. on the afternoon of July 20, 1992. It was the end of the sixth day of Erickson's trial for bank robbery and wounding a police officer during his escape attempt. Erickson's wife, Jill, described by friends as "drop-dead gorgeous," had died during the shootout.

After committing seven bank heists and walking away with more than one hundred eighty thousand dollars in cash, Erickson had finally come clean and disclosed his secret side job to his wife. Bracing for a blast of fury, he was caught off balance when she thought it all sounded exciting—so "cool" that she wanted in on the action. Erickson told a friend that the intrigue whetted his wife's sexual appetite to an insatiable level.

Jill Erickson's good looks and effervescent personality masked her dark side. Over the years, she had been diagnosed with a host of psychological disorders. No question, she was serious in her intent. During the final robbery attempt, she wore a dark wig and held customers at gunpoint. The directions she barked were spiced with just enough profanity to convince her victims that she was for real.

After bolting through the front door of the bank after their last stickup, Jeffrey Erickson surrendered to heavily armed FBI agents who had the parking lot staked out. Not Jill. The agitated driver peeled out of the bank parking lot in her Ford Econoline and accelerated to speeds in excess of 110 miles per hour. During the dramatic eleven-mile chase, she emptied three handguns at the procession of police pursuers. The van eventually went out of control and struck a cement wall. She apparently used the last round in her .45-caliber to take her own life. It left her husband seething in anger.

Fast forward to the evening of July 20, 1992. After court recessed, Erickson was patted down as usual by deputy U.S. marshals before being transported to the Metropolitan Correctional Center for the night. Erickson was relieved when the deputies stuck to their normal routine—so far so good. He grew excited when the young marshals handcuffed him in front and walked him onto the prisoner elevator with a half dozen other detainees.

Two deputy U.S. marshals were assigned to move prisoners that day, Terry Pinta and Roy Frakes. Both had nine month's experience on the job. Frakes was a regular deputy and had just completed twenty-three weeks of training at the Federal Law Enforcement Training Center in Georgia. Pinta was a part-time deputy who had received no formal training, only on-the-job instruction. Dedicated and enthusiastic, she had been an intern with the Illinois State Police before joining the Marshals Service, had qualified with her firearm, and had received some additional training in self-defense.

Frakes went down to the parking garage to pull the van into position near the elevator door to load the prisoners, while Pinta accompanied them on the elevator. No regular deputy was overseeing the prisoner movement. As the elevator descended, Erickson spit a concealed handcuff key into his hand and unlocked his cuffs. Large in stature and muscular, Erickson shoved the prisoners in front of him aside. In the blink of an eye, he punched Pinta in the stomach, put a choke hold on her, pushed her against a wall, and knocked her to the ground.

When he ripped her revolver out of its holster and pointed it at her chest, she yelled to Frakes that Erickson had her gun.

Perhaps not understanding what Pinta had said, Frakes walked around the van to an exposed position. As he emerged, Erickson was sprinting down the walkway leading from the elevator to the waiting van. Using his police training, Erickson crouched to steady the revolver with both hands and fired, killing Frakes.

On the other side of the garage, Judge James H. Alesia, who was presiding over Erickson's case, was pulling out of the underground parking lot. Just seconds behind him, Erickson headed for the exit ramp. En route, he passed the court security officer's post. Harry Belluomini, who had recently retired from the Chicago Police Department after thirty-three years, was the officer responsible for the parking garage that day. When Belluomini pulled his revolver and stepped out of his glass-enclosed booth to confront Erickson, he was instantly gunned down.

Despite his fatal wounds, Belluomini returned fire with four shots, one of which struck Erickson in the back. Erickson stumbled, but kept running up the exit ramp, about thirty yards from Judge Alesia's car. He was yelling that he was going to die anyway, "So I'm taking everybody with me." Erickson staggered halfway up the ramp, pointed the pistol at his chin and fired. Seconds later, a group of pursuing deputy marshals, and eventually Judge Alesia, found Erickson's lifeless body on the ramp. The emotional judge remarked that he "owed his life to Harry." If Belluomini had not shot Erickson, the judge believed that the ruthless bank robber would have killed him.

Coincidentally, I was in Chicago that evening to speak to a law enforcement group only a couple of blocks from the federal courthouse when the tragic events occurred. Arriving just after the bodies had been removed, I headed straight to the emergency room where I encountered Frakes's near-hysterical wife and young son. Doing what I could, I spent the next hour comforting them that evening. Roy Frakes had died a hero and his sacrifices were appreciated. I promised Mrs. Frakes that we could undertake a complete investigation of Erickson's escape, with disciplinary action as appropriate.

Wendy Frakes is a fine lady who was extremely devoted to her husband. Despite my continuing efforts to persuade her to the contrary, she will eternally hold me personally responsible for her husband's death. I spent the next few hours sitting on a bench in a public park, trying to sort out the evening's events with my special assistant, Kathy Deoudes.

The following day, I visited the Belluomini family at their home in the Chicago suburbs. The atmosphere was somber but Mrs. Belluomini was calm as we discussed the tragic consequences of her husband's act of extraordinary valor. As a court security officer, Belluomini served under the direction of the Marshals Service, but was technically employed by the General Services Administration. Nonetheless, his death in the line of duty was mourned by every man and woman who proudly wore the silver star. Harry Belluomini's name was added to the list at Marshals Service headquarters, of heros who have made the ultimate sacrifice to insure the security of the judicial process. [3]

## The Hearing Continues

Senator Simon seemed satisfied by my response and asked that I give him an update when our investigation was completed. He thought the Courthouse needed security improvements, with respect to both structure and policy. However, the central ingredient necessary for any security upgrade is money, and the Marshals Service did not have it. We were the smallest agency at the federal feeding trough, and were routinely pushed aside by the FBI, DEA, and the INS at budget time. That was partly because we were rarely involved in headline-grabbing cases and received minimal publicity. But I intended to change all that.

The questions that followed were softballs. I sailed smoothly to confirmation by the full Senate on the evening of August 13, 1992, with no negative votes.

As promised, I assigned Deputy Director John Twomey to conduct a thorough investigation of what occurred in Chicago on the evening of July 20. Twomey, a former U.S. marshal in charge of the Chicago office, left no stone unturned and identified a number of errors in the handling of prisoners in that office. The most obvious blunder was carrying an exposed firearm in a confined elevator while moving prisoners. It would have been easy to terminate Terry Pinta, but I did not. She had minimal training and inadequate supervision. Our disciplinary action focused on those responsible for supervising her.

[3] Four weeks later, Mrs. Belluomini sued the Marshals Service for seven million dollars.

In a subsequent investigation by the FBI, the inmate who supplied the handcuff key to Erickson was convicted of aiding his escape and sentenced to twenty years in federal prison.

As wounds healed and memories faded, the saga of Jeff and Jill Erickson lived on. The exploits of the bank-robbing couple were portrayed in a 1996 Hollywood film called *Normal Life,* starring Luke Perry and Ashley Judd and in a 1997 made-for-television movie, *In the Line of Duty: Blaze of Glory,* starring Lori Loughlin and Bruce Campbell.

## Plenty of Headlines

Freed of the strain of pending confirmation, I was started work in earnest. One of my first acts was to authorize preparation of final plans for the arrest of an Idaho fugitive, Randy Weaver, who had been eluding capture. The Idaho Marshals office had taken considerable heat from the local federal judge for the delay. But we knew the guy was dangerous, and had vowed to kill any federal agent that came on his property. The best minds in the Marshals Service had carefully reviewed the meticulously crafted arrest strategy, but I wanted to be sure that we employed the safest approach possible. The chief of our Enforcement Division directed the arrest team to conduct another reconnaissance mission before submitting a final tactical plan to me for approval.

*My formal swearing in as Director of the U.S. Marshals Service by Attorney General William P. Barr. My wife Tara and son Kevin are with me. (Courtesy of the U.S. Department of Justice.)*

As the team headed back to Boundary County, Idaho, to walk through the proposed arrest plan one more time, my family and I took off on Friday, August 21, 1992, for a one-week vacation in the Smokey Mountains of western North Carolina. At 2:00 p.m., about fifteen miles into our holiday, my cell phone rang. I would spend the next two years explaining to the media, Congress, a federal court, and a federal grand jury what happened during the forty-eight hours that followed.

# XIX
# Ruby Ridge

The rugged, thinly populated territory occupying the panhandle of Idaho is a paradise for those who love the outdoors. The air is crisp. Trout fill the mountain streams. Wildlife abounds in the endless pristine timberland. Snow graces the mountain peaks most months of the year. Life in this region lacks rigidity and structure. Time is measured in terms of productive daylight hours. The inhabitants like it that way. That's why they live there. The panhandle area has a reputation for harboring those seeking freedom from urban frenzy, oppressive government, unwanted family ties, and often, the law.

Naples, Idaho, is situated within Boundary County about forty miles from the Canadian border. Mountainous and in places desolate, Boundary County offers residents comparatively simple life, built on a bedrock system of time-tested values and traditions. Staunchly conservative, folks from Boundary County resist government in their lives, and distrust its representatives, particularly those who threaten their way of life. The outdoors plays a central role in their bucolic lifestyle. It is said that people from Northern Idaho learn to shoot before they learn to walk. Whether that is true or not, one thing's for certain. People in Boundary County believe the Second Amendment to the U.S. Constitution gives them an inalienable right to own and use firearms—of all types. No right is more fundamental, no notion is more commonly held.

You won't find any industrial plants, military bases, or business parks in Boundary County. Its nine thousand or so residents live off the land—farming, hunting, fishing, or trapping. There's a special sanctity to their land. Poaching or trespassing can be hazardous. Folks prefer self-help legal remedies to anything the law could provide. But it would be unfair to call these people lawless. Law to them is a social contract to live and let live; not governmentally pronounced and enforced rules of conduct.

Boundary citizens are proud of their independence. They neither request nor expect any form of assistance from the federal government. They live by a simple creed—a government that governs least, governs best.

Why would the Bureau of Alcohol, Tobacco and Firearms (ATF) be interested in a man who lived in virtual isolation with his family on a mountainside called Ruby Ridge? That was a question Randy Weaver and his family continually asked, as did his neighbors in Boundary County, Idaho. In time, the same question would be asked by U.S. Marshals.

In December 1990, Randall Weaver was indicted by a federal grand jury in Idaho for allegedly selling two sawed-off shotguns to a confidential informant, working under the direction of an ATF agent. According to the indictment and related documents, Weaver sold the undercover operative a Harrington and Richardson .12-gauge single-shot shotgun with a barrel cut to thirteen inches. The gun measured a total of 19.25 inches. In addition, Weaver provided the agent a Remington .12-gauge pump action shotgun with a barrel cut to 12.75 inches. This weapon had an overall length of 24.5 inches. The purchase price was a hundred fifty dollars each.

Federal law prohibits the sale or possession of a shotgun with a barrel length under eighteen inches, or with an overall length of under twenty-six inches. Although not every sportsman agrees, Congress and every state legislature in America have concluded that sawed-off shotguns have no legally recognized purpose. United States Attorney for Idaho Maurice Ellsworth told the press that the types of shotguns sold by Weaver were ". . . weapons of drug dealers and terrorists." Such shotguns are easily concealed and "shoot ammunition at a wide angle, inflicting deadly injuries," according to the ATF.

Following Weaver's indictment, a warrant for his arrest was issued by a federal judge. To avoid a confrontation, ATF agents, assisted by state officers, had employed a ruse to effect Weaver's arrest on January 18, 1991. That afternoon, Weaver and his wife, Vicki, had driven their snowmobile three miles down the ridge from their cabin to a clearing where they kept an old pickup truck for driving into town for supplies. As the Weavers drove the truck along a narrow U.S. Forest Service road that day, they encountered a bridge blocked by a disabled truck with attached camper. The hood of the truck was up and a distraught man and woman were standing next to it.

When Weaver alighted from his truck to ask if the couple needed help, heavily armed ATF agents emerged from the adjacent woods, and Boundary County Sheriff Bruce Whittaker bounded from the rear of the camper. Weaver was cuffed and transported to jail in Coeur d'Alene, but was released the following morning after posting a ten thousand dollar bond. Weaver jumped bond and never appeared for trial. United States District Judge Harold Ryan issued a bench warrant for his arrest, and informed the U.S. Marshals that he wanted Weaver arrested as soon as possible.

Weaver had no intention of surrendering to agents of a government he deeply distrusted. He and his family sought refuge in his remote cabin on Ruby Creek Ridge. Weaver's cabin was east of Priest Lake, not far from Roman Nose, in an area that is accessible only certain times of the year, and then only by four-wheel-drive vehicles. The secluded hideaway was described by Idaho U.S. Marshal Michael Johnson as "the most remote place that's possible to find in the state of Idaho . . . the closest thing to having a castle with a moat."

Aside from Randy and his wife Vicki, the Weaver family consisted of a twelve-year-old son and two daughters, one ten and one fourteen years old. Another child was born in the cabin during the early months of 1992. Kevin Harris, a twenty-four-year-old family friend and loyal follower, also resided in the cramped cabin.

Randy Weaver was an angry man. An avowed racist and white supremacist, Weaver purported to worship "Yahweh," a transliterated name for the God of the Old Testament. Despite evidence to the contrary, he denied any affiliation with the Aryan Nation, a white supremacist group headquartered in nearby Hayden Lake.

During an interview with Mike Weland of the Northern Idaho News Network, Weaver reportedly called his life a "religious crusade" and vowed never to be taken alive by what he considered to be the forces of evil. In his rantings to Weland, Weaver added, "We don't have freedom of religion or politics in this country . . . our situation is not about shotguns. It's about beliefs. They want to shut our mouths." Weaver, who once commented that he would surrender his life before his freedom, told Weland, "Even if we die, we win . . . . We'll die believing in Yahweh."

In trying to understand the events that occurred at Ruby Ridge, you have to keep in mind that the actions of the Weaver family were guided by their fervent religious beliefs. The Weavers were ardent followers of the racist-based Christian Identity religion. Based on a strained revisionist interpretation of the Old Testament, the religious schism embraced the notion that white Anglo-Saxons are direct descendants of the ten lost tribes of Israel. Followers of Christian Identity believe a racial war will mark a climactic event, pitting whites against a non-white minority. They view the federal government as a destructive force in the racial and religious destiny of the white people.

To prepare for the "inevitable" racial holy war, adherents to this religious doctrine stockpile food, clothing, and weapons. This was the lifestyle of the Weavers, who sought refuge in a remote mountaintop redoubt to fend off the evil government or, as they called it, the "new world order." What drew Weaver to this unorthodox view of life?

Randy Weaver was born and raised in Iowa. After graduating from high school, he enlisted in the U.S. Army and was assigned to a special forces unit. Following his discharge, he married Vicki and enrolled in a community college in Fort Dodge, Iowa. He soon concluded that additional education was a waste of time, so he secured a job at the John Deere Tractor Plant in Waterloo. After eight years at John Deere, in 1981 Weaver moved his family to Idaho. They purchased a remote twenty-acre tract of land for seventy-five hundred dollars. Weaver paid half the purchase price in cash and the balance by conveying an old pick-up truck.

The Weaver's neighbor and family friend, Mary Lou Curnick, told a reporter for the *Spokane Review* that the Weaver family "were able to live pretty primitively, growing their own food and stuff like that." Mrs. Curnick described Vicki Weaver as "a real good seamstress who knitted all the time." Vicki's religious and political views were reported to be much more hard-core than those of Randy, and she was instrumental in providing the children with a home-based education.

Aside from working a few odd jobs, Randy devoted the bulk of his time to constructing the family cabin out of plywood and two by fours. He took a job at Paradise Dairy in Bonner's Ferry, Idaho, but left after the first year. In the days that followed, the Weavers adopted a totally self-sustaining lifestyle, living off the land. Weaver's agitation reached a flashpoint in 1985 when he filed an affidavit with the clerk of the court of Naples, Idaho, placing them officially on notice of the potential for an armed confrontation with the United States government.

Weaver declared under oath, "I make legal and official notice that I believe I may have to defend myself and my family from a physical attack on my life." He continued, "We are the victims of a smear campaign of our characters and false accusations made against us to the Federal Bureau of Investigation and the United States Secret Service by some local residents who have a motive for my decease."

In the final paragraph of the affidavit, Weaver concluded, somewhat presciently, that, "My accusers hoped that the FBI would rush my home with armed agents hoping I would feel the need to defend myself and thus be killed or arrested for assault on a Federal official."

In 1988, Randy Weaver sought the Republican nomination for Boundary County sheriff. He vowed during his campaign to enforce only those laws that people liked. His opponent, Joe Allen, branded Weaver a "right-wing extremist." Weaver was soundly, defeated garnering only one hundred two votes.

Deputy U.S. Marshal David Hunt knew these basic facts when Judge Ryan's bench warrant was placed on his desk for service. Hunt, a seasoned deputy, was assigned to the Boise, Idaho office, several hundred miles from desolate Boundary County. Through law enforcement contacts in the area and conversations with ATF agents familiar with the case, Hunt learned that any confrontation with Weaver was potentially volatile.

After gathering as much background information as possible and waiting for the ground to thaw, Hunt surveyed the terrain of Ruby Ridge. It was going to be a challenge; conventional surveillance techniques would never work in that location. From the position of Weaver's cabin, the family could observe any vehicle traveling up Ruby Ridge Road. Road was a misnomer. Actually, it was a crudely cleared path up the mountainside. The topography, as viewed by Hunt from a distance using high-powered binoculars, was an endless succession of rocks, hills, and thick foliage. The only possible advantage was the cover afforded by the dense foliage—perfect for hunting, but perilous for the hunted, as marshals would later learn.

Hunt learned from discreet contacts with Weaver's neighbors that the entire family honed their shooting skills on a regular basis. Vicki, the son, and two daughters routinely carried sidearms, as did Kevin Harris. The neighbors recounted seeing Harris, Randy, and his son, Sam, toting rifles while walking the perimeter. The message was clear—keep your distance.

The United States marshal for Idaho was a politically savvy friend of mine. Mike Johnson and I had served together on the National Highway Safety Advisory Committee. A former Boise County coroner, Mike perceived the danger posed by Randy Weaver and his family, and wisely chose to avoid armed confrontation if possible.

The Weavers had no telephone. Aside from mail delivery, the only contacts the family had with the outside world were through a generator-powered radio and occasional friends and neighbors who dropped by to visit. Over the ensuing months, Marshal Johnson sent Randy Weaver two letters requesting that he contact the Marshals' Office to discuss turning himself in. Johnson received no reply. The marshal then told Deputy Hunt to brief Judge Ryan on the significant risks presented by attempting to forcibly arrest Weaver. Hunt suggested that they

*An aerial photograph of Randy Weaver's compound at Ruby Ridge, Idaho. This was the site of a tense standoff between federal agents and fugitive Randy Weaver. (Courtesy of U.S. Department of Justice.)*

might want to let things cool off a while. Judge Ryan would have no part of it. He wanted Weaver arrested as soon as possible. Tension began to ratchet up.

Because of the difficulty devising an effective arrest plan for Weaver, Johnson and Hunt turned for assistance to the Enforcement Division at the Marshals Service headquarters. Members of this unit specialized in apprehending fugitives. Inspector Arthur Roderick, a nine-year veteran of the USMS and a member of the Special Operations Group that is trained to carry out the most dangerous, high-risk missions, was assigned to oversee the development of an arrest strategy. William "Huff" Hufnagel, an expert in electronic surveillance, was assigned to assist.

Hufnagel engineered a series of unobtrusive systems that enabled the arrest team to remotely monitor the movements of the Weaver family on the grounds surrounding their cabin. Two cameras were situated at points one half mile and three quarters of a mile from the cabin, and operated continuously for almost two months. The videos revealed that Randy Weaver was armed seventy-two percent of the time he left the house, Kevin Harris sixty-six percent, fourteen-year-old son Samuel eighty-four percent, Vicki Weaver fifty-two percent, sixteen-year-old daughter Sara thirty-eight percent, and ten-year-old daughter Rachel thirty-one percent. Extreme caution was in order.

For months, small groups of deputy U.S. marshals, led by Roderick, Hufnagel, and Hunt, conducted periodic covert surveillance missions from property adjacent to the Weavers. Fortunately, most of the adjoining property was either unoccupied or owned by the U.S. Forest Service. In all, they preformed six surveillance missions spanning several days each, watching patiently and taking notes.

A number of factors complicated Roderick's task. First, many citizens of Boundary County, including law enforcement officials, were Weaver sympathizers. The deputies were therefore forced to operate in a constant near-undercover capacity, revealing their identity only to a select few.

Second, the layout of the Weaver property and his militant response to even the slightest unidentified noise necessitated that most reconnaissance activity be conducted under cover of darkness. Any suspicious sound or movement on Ruby Ridge would result in all members of the Weaver family except the infant rushing from the house fully armed, and assuming a predetermined combat position behind a boulder or rock cluster strategically located in the yard. Often, it was the bark of Weaver's yellow Labrador retriever that would call his family to battle stations. The dog, Striker, was not people friendly.

Third, many of their neighbors found Randy Weaver and his son Sam's obsession with firearms intimidating. They were not anxious to cooperate with the USMS or to allow their property to be used for surveillance. From a tactical perspective, the results of the initial surveillance were disappointing. The Weaver family was totally self-sustaining and never left the compound. Randy Weaver rarely strayed beyond the immediate perimeter of his cabin. Food and other provisions were delivered by friends and sympathizers. Neighbors reported that the house was well stocked with food and ammunition, including six rifles, two shotguns, six pistols, and about forty-five hundred rounds of ammunition. Family members seldom stepped out of the cabin without a firearm. This was going to be a perilous gambit. The tactical plan would require surgical precision and expert timing.

I was still in my first month as director of the Marshals Service when the chief of the Enforcement Division, Tony Perez, stopped me in the hallway and asked if he and Art Roderick could brief me on the Weaver case. Because the mission was potentially hazardous, Perez wanted my approval before agreeing to any proposed arrest strategy.

That afternoon when I walked into my conference room, it was a full house. In addition to Perez, Roderick, Hufnagel, and Marshal Johnson of Idaho, both deputy directors, the associate director of Enforcement, the commander of the Special Operations Group and my general counsel were present. Hufnagel began the presentation with a videotape of the Weaver residence and surrounding terrain. Roderick outlined those strategic options he had eliminated because of the high potential for an armed confrontation with family members. He candidly acknowledged that an exchange of gunfire with a child was a realistic possibility, unless Weaver could be drawn away from the cabin and the rest of the family.

We discussed using a ruse to divert the Weavers' attention or lower their guard, but this technique had been used to ensnare Weaver the first time around. We concluded that this guy, a former Green Beret, was too street smart to fall for same trick twice.

I told them to hold that point and suggested that we consider having the bench warrant withdrawn and the indictment sealed from the public. Once Weaver got word the coast was clear, that he was no longer wanted by U.S. Marshals, in all likelihood he would resume circulating freely in the community. Everyone present liked the idea. I told them to wait right there while I called United States Attorney for Idaho Maurie Ellsworth, to see what he thought.

I had known Ellsworth since my days as U.S. attorney. He was familiar with the Weaver case and recognized that any attempt to apprehend him was fraught with danger. He patiently listened to my proposal that the arrest warrant be withdrawn and the indictment be quietly placed under seal. The U.S. Marshal and U.S. Attorney's Offices would then let it be known in Boundary County—where news travels fast—that Randy Weaver was no longer wanted by federal authorities. If Weaver called the court to confirm, the clerk's office could truthfully respond that there was no outstanding warrant for his arrest. After Weaver resumed moving about freely in the community, a second bench warrant for his arrest would be issued, but its existence would be closely held within law enforcement circles. Marshal Johnson, who participated in the telephone conversation, strongly endorsed the plan.

Although the strategy was a bit out of the ordinary, so were the hazards of this case. Our proposal provided a critical element of control unobtainable in a high-risk confrontational approach. It would enable marshals to arrest Weaver away from his fortified compound and heavily armed children. We believed it would also reduce the possibility that Weaver would be armed at the time of his arrest.

After hearing us out, Ellsworth said that he had already considered and rejected a similar approach. However, he agreed to reconsider and call me back as soon as possible.

Mike Johnson and I returned to the meeting and reported that, in our view, Ellsworth would go along with the proposal. Meanwhile, Roderick was told to continue developing a tactical plan to forcibly arrest Weaver on the Ruby Ridge compound if all other options failed.

The next day, Maurie Ellsworth called. He said that he personally supported our proposal, but that the assistant United States attorney assigned to prosecute Weaver was opposed to it. The assistant then joined the conversation and explained that the U.S. district judge would not participate in any arrest scheme that involved the public withdrawal and surreptitious reissuance of the bench warrant. Period.

Despite my frustration, I thanked Maurie for his time and summoned Tony Perez to my office. I told Perez, one of my most trusted aides, to tell Roderick to move forward with the arrest plan. I also suggested that he contact the elite FBI Hostage Rescue Team and seek any advice and counsel they could provide. Lastly, I asked that either Marshal Johnson or Deputy Hunt contact the Idaho ATF office to inquire if this case was really worth putting federal agents in harm's way. That had been done. ATF had told us to move forward.

Over the next few months, Inspector Roderick and his colleagues painstakingly gathered as much information as possible about the daily routine and personal habits of the Weaver family. Quietly concealed in foliage on neighboring property and using high-powered binoculars, the team of investigators watched

Weaver's every movement for hours on end, looking for a strategic point of vulnerability. It finally came unexpectedly.

One morning, Roderick heard a vehicle approaching along the rock-strewn path leading to Weaver's cabin. As customary, Weaver darted from his house, but this time he actually walked off the twenty-acre compound alone, to confront the occupants of the truck. To Roderick's surprise, Weaver lowered his weapon and appeared to be hospitable, engaging them in friendly conversation. He then got in the truck and accompanied the visitors as they drove around the Ruby Ridge area. Roderick was able to learn that the people in the truck were interested in purchasing property near the Weaver cabin. Even though Randy Weaver knew in advance that they were coming, he still greeted them with a rifle in hand. But to Roderick, this seemed to be the break he was looking for, and maybe the key element of an arrest strategy.

The arrest plan that Roderick proposed would entail undercover deputy U.S. marshals contacting persons in the vicinity of Weaver's home who were known to be interested in selling portions of their property. The marshal would arrange to look over the property. Roderick envisioned that the seller would notify Weaver that a prospective purchaser would be visiting Ruby Ridge to view the property.

We hoped that, with this preclearance, Weaver would again greet the vehicle occupied by deputy marshals and, if invited, would join them in surveying the property. Roderick thought that, once Weaver was in the car, they could easily overpower him, seize his weapon, cuff him, and get him out of there before the other members of his family could respond.

To me, the most appealing feature of this approach was avoiding an armed confrontation with Weaver's children. Subject to some refinement, I approved the plan in concept and asked Inspector Roderick to complete the details. I candidly admit that I was stalling.

It was now approaching July. If I was ever going to get a confirmation hearing, it had to be soon. We were in the last few months of President George H. W. Bush's first term. The election campaign was surprisingly close. The spread between the president and his challenger, Governor Clinton, had shrunk to about ten points. Knowing that any dustup would send my nomination into the darkness of oblivion, I was running on a caution flag. Given the political volatility of the times and the extreme danger inherent in any attempt to apprehend Randy Weaver, it was the unanimous view of upper-level management at the Marshals Service that Weaver's arrest should be delayed until after my confirmation. Despite some criticism from the Idaho press, it was the appropriate decision.

Immediately following my confirmation on August 13, 1992, and formal appointment by the president several days later, I gave Tony Perez the nod to finalize the Weaver arrest plan. At my direction, he instructed Art Roderick to go back to Ruby Ridge for a final look—a last reconnaissance mission just to make sure the plan had no screws left unturned.

Roderick and his hand-picked arrest team swung into action. The following day, they assembled at Sand Point, Idaho. It was far enough away from Boundary County to avoid arousing suspicion and still be within a reasonable commute to Ruby Ridge. In addition to Roderick, the team consisted of Deputy U.S. Marshals Larry T. Cooper of Jefferson City, Missouri; David Hunt of Boise, Idaho; Joseph Thomas of Cleveland, Ohio; and Frank Norris, an emergency medical technician assigned to headquarters. Also joining the reconnaissance team was William F. Degan, Jr., of Boston, Massachusetts, a highly decorated, well-seasoned deputy marshal with a remarkable record. A Lieutenant Colonel in the U.S. Marine Corps Reserve, Bill Degan had just received the Attorney General's Distinguished Service Award, conferred by Attorney General Dick Thornburgh, for commanding a unit of the Special Operations Group that restored order on St. Croix, United States, Virgin Islands, in the lawless aftermath of Hurricane Hugo. Degan's presence reflected the importance of the mission.

The surveillance team focused its attention on four areas: First, to determine how the arrest team could move about the periphery of the compound without exposure; second, to identify locations where countersnipers could be placed; third, to identify areas where Weaver could be arrested without engaging the rest of the family; and fourth, to devise a plan of action in case the worst happened, a siege situation, including a safe path of retreat.

The team was also considering an alternative strategy, one that might have lessened even more the likelihood of an armed confrontation with the children. As before, it entailed having an undercover deputy marshal drive up Ruby Ridge Road, after prior notification of Weaver by the realtor, to view property listed for sale. The deputy would meet and talk to Weaver as other interested purchasers had done, but instead of arresting Weaver at that point, the deputy would actually purchase the property for several thousand dollars and begin construction of a cabin with the help of, perhaps, another member of the arrest team. Over time, the undercover marshal would, at least theoretically, develop enough rapport with Weaver to lower his guard. If Weaver wandered over to chat or check the progress of construction, he would be arrested and removed from the property before his family could mount an armed response. In the end, the team favored the original plan.

On August 20, 1992, after two days of analyzing all newly acquired information, conducting an inventory of all necessary equipment, and ensuring that it was in sound working order, the team headed to Lincoln County, Washington, just west of Spokane, for a day of concentrated weapons practice. In addition to a sidearm, each team member had an M-16 rifle, except Larry Cooper, who carried a fully automatic SMG equipped with a silencer. The next morning, the scouting party would covertly infiltrate Ruby Ridge for one last look before carrying out one of the most perilous missions ever conducted by U.S. Marshals.

At 3:30 a.m. on August 21, the team, equipped with night-vision devices, left Sand Point, Idaho, in two vehicles. Their first destination was the home of Sheriff Bruce Whittaker in Bonners Ferry. From there they proceeded in a Jeep Cherokee to the residence of Wayne and Ruth Rau, who lived on property adjoining the Weavers. Once friends with the Weavers, the Raus eventually found themselves terrorized by the family. Ruth Rau told the *Spokane-Review* that their ten-year relationship with the Weavers was "filled with gunfire, threats, vandalism and racist diatribes that made life a living hell."

By only the faint light of the moon, the team left the Rau residence at 4:15 a.m. and slowly navigated the dark rough-hewn trail leading to the Weaver property. All were dressed in camouflage, with weapons slung around their necks, and hats and face masks to conceal themselves after daylight.

The six deputy marshals proceeded in single file up the mountain until they reached a fork in the road, a point referred to by the team as the "Y." The right fork led to Weaver's driveway and the residential compound; the left to a meadow of ferns. Here the two surveillance teams divided, and proceeded in separate directions. Hunt, Norris, and Thomas took the left fork through the ferns and headed up the hill to an observation post. This point, which is located an estimated nine hundred feet above elevation, was situated about a half to three quarters of a mile from the Weaver compound, and gave the team an unobstructed panoramic view of the Weaver property. The fork was about a hundred yards from the Weaver's driveway.

The second team, consisting of Cooper, Roderick, and Degan, stealthily crept in the cover of darkness along the right fork toward the edge of Weaver's property to a thick fold of trees about two hundred fifty to three hundred yards from Weaver's driveway. As daylight broke, they took careful note of activity on the Weaver compound. The morning air and cool breeze off the mountains were peaceful and quiet, almost relaxing, until a sudden movement in the woods caused the dog to bark. On cue, Randy Weaver, his son Sammy, and Kevin Harris ran from the house and took positions among the rocks outside. After quietly surveying the still forest for several minutes, they slowly retreated into the house. Did the Weaver's know the marshals were there? Had someone tipped them off?

The bark of the dog echoed through the mountains and made it difficult to pinpoint its exact location. Monitoring the dog's movement would be critical to the final arrest plan. Any exposure could be deadly.

When Weaver and company returned to the house, Cooper, Roderick, and Degan worked their way back to the "Y" and joined the other team members at the observation post to their left. It was about 8:30 a.m. The team took a few minutes to decompress and assess the situation. But there was no time to waste. There were too many other potential surveillance positions to be checked out.

Roderick, Cooper, and Degan moved on to another observation point, a large rock embedded in a hillside about two hundred fifty yards from the Weaver residence. They continued to watch and listen, with the rock and surrounding trees providing a veil of cover. They saw no movement, so Roderick and Cooper decided to advance even closer to the cabin, to another large rock about a hundred yards from the property edge. After noticing that three windows on the side of the house facing them were open, they slowed their pace to reduce noise. Occasionally they could see unidentifiable figures moving about inside, and hear unintelligible dialogue.

To test the safety of their position, which would be ideal for surveillance during the actual execution of the arrest plan, Roderick tossed two large stones in the direction of the front driveway to see if the dog would bark. There was no response. Roderick made a mental note.

Cooper and Roderick then backtracked, reunited with Degan, and prepared to wrap up for the morning. Meticulous by nature, Roderick decided to take one final look at the lower end of the Weaver driveway. Cooper and Degan positioned themselves along the road to watch for any movement. All was clear and, when Roderick returned, the team slowly began the cautious trek to join the other three deputy marshals. Every few steps, the team would stop at a strategic point to take stock of their surroundings.

They had not advanced far when the spotters concealed on the elevated observation point warned them to get down. A car was coming up the road and the Weaver clan was bailing out of the house. Hearts were pounding fast and, suddenly, Roderick heard something coming their way in the woods.

# XX

# Shoot-Out at the "Y"

Even though they were gaining speed with each step, the three deputy marshals could sense that their pursuers were gaining ground. The foliage was thick and the exodus became increasingly disorderly. Roderick and his team wanted to avoid an armed confrontation at all reasonable cost.

Roderick was concealed in the trees about a hundred yards from Weaver's driveway when he first saw Harris and the dog "making a beeline right toward me." He radioed his colleagues to haul ass and head for the Y-fork in the path. The team united on the run.

About a half mile below the Weaver compound, the fleeing deputies reached a small clearing on the edge of the "Y." So did their pursuers. The events that ensued are hotly disputed, and will forever haunt those who survived.

Weaver's neighbor Ruth Rau was preparing to leave for the laundromat about ten-thirty that morning when she heard "kind of an explosive echo." She recalled hearing a lot of sporadic volleys of gunfire, and called the Boundary County Sheriff's Office. Of course, there was nothing out of the ordinary about the sound of gunfire in that neck of the woods.

Cooper and Roderick arrived at the clearing first, and saw Randy Weaver approaching from a distance. Cooper yelled, "Back off. U.S. Marshals." Weaver turned, began yelling to the others and ran toward the cabin. Within minutes, Kevin Harris and Sam Weaver stepped from the wood line, rifles in hand, with Striker, the dog. It was obvious to Roderick that Striker would remain on their trail and continue to alert Harris and Sam Weaver of their position. Roderick next heard a heavy-caliber weapon fired to his left. Striker stopped in his tracks and "froze." There was no chance of a peaceful escape with the dog on their heels. Roderick felt he had no other choice, and shot the dog. Sam Weaver screamed, "You son of a bitch."

The pace of events quickened. The participants' recollections differ widely. According to the deputy marshals, Inspector Bill Degan apparently identified himself to Harris and ordered him to stop and put down his rifle. The deputies recall Harris opening fire on Degan without warning. A later examination of Degan's weapon revealed that seven shots had been fired from its magazine. In the resulting exchange, Roderick was grazed by a bullet that tore his shirt pocket. Bill Degan was hit and fell to the ground. Cooper returned fire after Degan was shot and believed he had struck Harris who, according to Cooper, went down "like a sack of potatoes." Cooper next saw someone he initially thought was Sam Weaver running up the hillside, away from the "Y."

Suddenly all was quiet—like the eye of a storm—but Cooper and Roderick took no chances. They crawled cautiously toward Degan, assuming their adversaries were waiting for a clear shot. When they reached Bill Degan, the two combat veterans couldn't hold back the tears. Their colleague was dead. What they did not know was that sixty yards away, Randy Weaver was sobbing as well. His teen-aged son, Sam, had also been killed. Weaver carried the boy's limp body back to the cabin.

Harris recalled the morning's events differently. As he recounted it, Sam yelled, "You son of a bitch. You killed my dog," after witnessing Roderick shoot Striker. According to Harris, it was Degan who fired the first shot. Harris swore he returned fire in self-defense. During the ensuing volley, Sam was struck by a round fired by one of the marshals, most likely Cooper.

Cooper and Roderick were soon joined by the other three deputies, who crawled in from the observation point. They remained huddled around Degan's body for several hours, not knowing if conspicuous movement would draw additional fire. Early that afternoon, Hunt and Thomas quietly crept back to the Rau residence and called the Boundary County sheriff and USMS headquarters. They reported that the team was "pinned down"—and Degan was dead. They needed help quick. Within an hour the Idaho State Police Crisis Response Team had been mobilized and was en route, but traveling to Boundary County was a long haul.

This was the posture of things when my cell phone rang on the afternoon of August 21, 1992, as my family and I proceeded down U.S. Route 1 headed toward the mountains of North Carolina. The caller was John Twomey, Deputy Director of the USMS. A twenty-year veteran of the Marshals Service, Twomey had superb judgment and an unparalleled grip of the inner workings of the agency. He calmly explained that he had tragic news to report from Ruby Ridge. Bill Degan was dead and our arrest team was still "pinned down" on the mountainside. The Idaho State Police were en route to assist and our Special Operations Group was preparing for immediate deployment. I told Twomey to contact Doug Gow, executive associate director of the FBI, to enlist the aid of the Hostage Rescue Team if the situation did not improve. I told Twomey to hang on. I'd be there in an hour.

With my wife, son, and mother-in-law screaming, I whipped an illegal U-turn in fifty-five-mile-an-hour traffic and headed back to the Prince William County Police station on Cardinal Drive, about a quarter of a mile down the road. Within five minutes a detective was driving me to my home in south Fairfax County to change clothes. I threw on a suit and tie and arrived at USMS headquarters less than an hour after Twomey's call. I phoned the attorney general's staff to let them know what was happening and what we planned to do.

Members of my staff passionately counseled against bringing in the FBI, frequently considered a rival agency. Some feared we'd lose control and be perceived as incapable of handling a tough task. Others argued it was a vote of no confidence in our Special Operations Group. Neither argument dissuaded me. I wanted all the help I could get to prevent the situation from deteriorating further.

As we raced across Memorial Bridge in route to the J. Edgar Hoover Building, Twomey and Associate Director of Operations Duke Smith recounted what little we knew about the day's events. There were a lot of unanswered questions.

I remember that it was during that conversation that I was advised that Kevin Harris had also been shot. My thoughts turned to what I would say to Mrs. Degan when I called later that evening. She'd been notified of her husband's death by the U.S. marshal in Boston, but I owed her a personal call. Bill Degan's death devastated his family, but no one suffered more than his teenaged son, who suffered years with the loss of his dad.

My blood pressure was probably off the chart. Men's lives and the welfare of their families depended on the decisions I would make in the next few hours. Nothing in my training or experience prepared me to handle a crisis of this magnitude, but I was determined to maintain control and radiate self-confidence.

I enjoyed an excellent relationship with the top brass at the FBI, but I was a little apprehensive going into our meeting. The FBI perceived itself as the premier law enforcement agency in America. The Marshals Service was a small underfunded agency with limited duties, which often struggled to maintain its existence.

Would the FBI view this situation as an example of ineptitude, perhaps bolstering their frequent contention that they should take over our coveted fugitive-hunting duties? Or would they perceive it as an unavoidable crisis? Would the attorney general relieve me of command? In government, particularly at this level, every miscue is followed by some form of cover-your-ass faultfinding. And to mollify the public, press, and Congress, it often results in the sacrifice of a public official. That's the American way! And that's why the government, as an institution, is slow to react and at times indecisive.

We were greeted by a host of FBI officials when we walked into Deputy Director Larry Pott's office, including my official liaison with the FBI, Doug Gow. Gow had already notified the Hostage Rescue Team to prepare for immediate deployment. Their interest and apparent sympathy for our situation placed me at ease.

I gave a brief overview of the situation, using photographs to illustrate the tough terrain. Relaying the scant information I had, I described the circumstances of Degan's death and explained that our deputy marshals were "pinned down." They were unable to remove Degan's body without exposing themselves to gunfire. We needed immediate help. My staff provided all the intelligence information we had gathered concerning Weaver. In closing, I cautioned them that Weaver was a heavily armed survivalist who detested the government and was extremely dangerous.

When the dust eventually settled and the faultfinding began, some FBI officials would claim that I had overstated the urgency of our situation and the danger posed by Weaver. The facts confirm my opinion.

I left FBI Headquarters that evening relieved to know that the FBI would now take command of the operation. Since a federal law enforcement officer had been killed in the line of duty, the FBI, according to Department of Justice regulations, assumed primary jurisdiction and would call the shots from there on. I was still to send our Special Operations Group to Ruby Ridge to provide support. Our team would provide perimeter security. The FBI would go in to get Weaver and the others. I directed USMS headquarters to radio Roderick and Cooper that help was on the way, but it could be a while.

You would have a better chance of stumbling across a black bear in the wilds of Idaho than spotting a state trooper on the highway, particularly in the northern panhandle. Operating on a shoestring budget, on a typical day the Idaho State Police patrol almost a thousand miles of highway with only a few dozen troopers. In 1992, if a trooper's assigned vehicle broke down, he or she was grounded until it was repaired. There was no money for a reserve fleet. Despite their incredible dedication, asking the Idaho State Police to muster a team to assist our men on a mountain ridge on the Canadian border was a tall request, especially considering the volatile environment they'd be operating in.

When I returned to my office at Marshals Service headquarters, I collapsed in my chair. Marshal Mike Johnson called from Idaho to report that he was standing on the road below Ruby Ridge, awaiting the state police. Members of the news media, who monitored the radio communications of the state police and local sheriff's office, were already beginning to assemble. It would be at least another hour before the state police arrived. Since we no longer had primary jurisdiction, I told Mike to make no comments to the press, even off the record.

My next call was from Bill Sessions, director of the FBI. Sessions said the Hostage Rescue Team was assembled and ready, but they were having trouble arranging a flight. To our amazement the Department of Defense was demanding the outrageous sum of twenty-seven thousand dollars to fly the FBI Special Operations Team to Idaho. Bill and I simultaneously asked if we were all part of the same government.

Only one band of brothers bonds tighter than cops—the U.S. Marine Corps. Doug Gow, a former Marine, contacted an old Marine Corps buddy, Fred Smith, for help. Fred was the right guy to call. He had several hundred jet aircraft at his disposal as president and CEO of FedEx Corporation. Years later, I had the pleasure of representing Mr. Smith in a personal legal matter. He is a true patriot, as his actions on the evening of August 21, 1992, exemplified.

Shortly after Sessions and I disconnected, Doug Gow called with the news that FedEx would be transporting the FBI Hostage Rescue Team and USMS personnel to Idaho for four thousand dollars—roughly the cost of the jet fuel. FedEx employees would load all the FBI equipment, including robots, tractors, and sophisticated communications gear—a task the military had declined to even assist in doing. The FBI obtained the necessary FAA clearances and the plane was on the runway in just over an hour—wheels up at 6:30 p.m.

As our team from headquarters prepared for departure, I designated Tony Perez, chief of Enforcement and one of my most trusted aides, to oversee our end of the mission. John Twomey, in his typical polite but persuasive manner, calmly interjected and counseled me to send Duke Smith, associate director for Operations. Duke was higher in rank and could better deal with the FBI on-site supervisors. Twomey was one of the most experienced leaders in the USMS. I greatly respected his judgment, so I acceded to his request. Later, I would regret the decision.

After a brief dinner, Tony Perez and I parked ourselves in the Command Center and impatiently waited. It was buzzing with activity. The Center, situated in a secure area, was configured as a large horseshoe-shaped work station, with chairs and telephones at intervals. The structure faced a huge screen for viewing film or projecting television coverage. Perez had direct access from his office. From his window, we could see the sun beginning to set. Information was slow in coming. The only thing we knew was that the deputy marshals were still concealed in thick brush with the body of Bill Degan. The Deputy Attorney General's Office kept calling for an update, but there was nothing to report. As I sat there hour after hour, smoking an occasional cigar to relieve tension, I kept asking myself what else I should be doing.

The Idaho State Police began arriving around 7:00 p.m. Ruby Ridge time, followed by an entourage of national news satellite trucks. They decided to wait for the cover of nightfall before proceeding up the mountain. The FBI asked them to delay the rescue operation until an FBI SWAT team from Seattle arrived to assess the situation. At 8:30 p.m. the team headed into the dark of night. By this time, events were being covered live by every cable news network. On the east coast it was nearly midnight. Tony and I sat at the Command Center talking to Marshal Johnson on the speaker phone and watching the coverage on CNN. The outside temperature in Washington was a steamy eighty-five degrees. The temperature in the Idaho panhandle was expected to dip into the twenties that night, with the possibility of freezing rain and snow.

At about 12:30 a.m. our time, Johnson called to report that the Crisis Response Team was heading down the mountain with Degan's body and that no gunfire had been encountered. Sixteen minutes later I learned—not from our guys at Ruby Ridge but from CNN News—that Roderick and Cooper were safely on the ground with the body of Deputy U.S. Marshal Degan. We called the command post in Idaho to confirm. It was news to them. Everyone was relieved, but the elation was short lived. The fire of hell was just starting to burn.

Meanwhile, the FBI Hostage Rescue Team was en route to Idaho. During this flight, one of the most controversial operational decisions of the entire Ruby Ridge incident was made, crafting the so-called rules of engagement. The rules were refined many times before actual implementation, but at core, they directed law enforcement personnel to shoot any armed adult observed on the Weaver compound, as long as no child was endangered.

From my perspective, the most troublesome aspect was that Duke Smith initially believed that he had called me at the USMS headquarters from the aircraft and received my concurrence with the proposed rules. This was incorrect. I never received a call from Smith that night. This was confirmed by the phone logs on the aircraft and the USMS Command Center. In fact, around midnight I began asking why we hadn't heard from him. The first call I received from Duke was the next evening when Twomey called me into his office and said Smith was on the phone.

Duke Smith had a distinguished career with the Marshals Service. I believe he is a man of integrity who, in my opinion, had a serious failure of memory. It was a tense time for all of us. However, the resulting confusion later caused me to be the subject of a protracted lawsuit and required me to spend five hours in front of a federal grand jury defending myself. But it's all history now.

Because of the time difference, there was no need for me to get into the office early the next morning. I took a leisurely run along the George Washington Parkway, bordering the scenic Potomac River, and called my wife to assure her that I would be joining the family on vacation in the next day or two. I rolled into the USMS headquarters about 11:00 a.m. The next crisis developed around noon.

The FBI, which was responsible for investigating the death of Degan, was anxious to interview the five surviving deputy marshals. The arrest team was physically and emotionally spent. Duke Smith wanted to delay any questioning until they had been examined by a psychologist on site. It made sense and I agreed. These guys needed time to decompress. Tony Perez relayed my decision to Duke. The FBI protested, but the tension was short lived. We made the deputies available later that day.

As the sun rose in the chilly sky in Ruby Ridge, FBI observers detected no significant movement at the Weaver residence. Members of the FBI special weapons team were surreptitiously placed at strategic, well-camouflaged positions around Weaver's property. I called the FBI for an update; nothing new to report. They'd call me when a game plan was finalized. It became increasingly improbable that the situation would be resolved in the next day or so.

Around three o'clock that afternoon things were still quiet, so I decided to leave the office to buy some food. With my family on vacation, there was nothing in the refrigerator. When I returned in an hour and a half, there was a fax on my desk from the FBI discussing proposed strategy at Ruby Ridge. Before I could even scan the document, another fax came in telling me to disregard the first one because the proposed plan had been rejected by the DOJ. It apparently failed to include a satisfactory negotiation strategy. The memo said that a revised version would be forthcoming. I routed both documents to the Enforcement Division to be filed, and waited for the final plan. I received no other memoranda from the FBI that day.

The events of that afternoon are important because I was later accused of having acquiesced in the proposed shoot-on-sight directive outlined in the first memo, which I never read—I saw no need to ponder a policy directive that had been countermanded. Moreover, the policy statement pertained to the FBI Hostage Rescue personnel positioned on the ridge. Our personnel were located at the foot of the mountain and would have no contact with the Weaver family. Finally, the FBI did not consult with me on the operational strategy they intended to employ in apprehending Randy Weaver, and they had no obligation to do so. They were in charge. My orders were to follow directions.

The next call from the FBI came later that evening. Danny Coulson, deputy assistant director of the Criminal Section, said that they had decided to establish communication with Weaver and attempt to negotiate his surrender. Agents would drive up the rocky logging trail to the cabin in an armored vehicle and release a robot that would drop a portable telephone on the porch of the cabin. Although the plan seemed appropriate to me, Coulson never sought my opinion or advice. He said they'd keep me posted.

Shortly after the call from Coulson, Duke Smith called John Twomey. I came into Twomey's office and we put the call on speaker. Duke seemed upbeat, chatted about how good the hunting and fishing must be up there, and told us that they were getting ready to begin negotiations with Weaver and that the rules of engagement were now in place. Perhaps it was my ignorance, but I thought Duke was referring to the negotiating strategy. I politely cut him off in mid-sentence and told him that Danny Coulson had just gone over that with me. As I recall, Duke closed by telling us that he was going up in a helicopter for an aerial view of the compound. In a matter of minutes, one of the most controversial events in the history of the FBI would unfold. It would result in the most intensive internal investigation in FBI history, and unprecedented disciplinary action against twelve special agents. In the end, an agent would be charged with unlawfully killing someone in the line of duty—a first in the eighty-nine-year history of the FBI.

FBI Special Agent Lon T. Horiuchi heard the powerful turbo engines of the helicopter beginning to rotate as he looked down from his observation perch about seven hundred feet from the Weaver cabin. Horiuchi, a West Point graduate and thirteen-year veteran of the FBI, and two other agents, carried high-powered .308-caliber rifles equipped with ten-power magnification scopes. All three were trained to shoot with surgical precision, if necessary to protect other federal agents. They didn't move a muscle as the cold rain dripped from the trees above.

As the throb of the rotors vibrated off the mountainside, Horiuchi saw two people: first, a young girl running from the cabin to a rock formation; next, a young man standing on the porch. Neither appeared armed, so Horiuchi calmly watched their movements in his scope. Both eventually reentered the house. Minutes later, the copter carrying Duke Smith, the head of the FBI Hostage Rescue Team, and the Commander of the USMS Special Operations Group, lifted off. It was approximately 6:00 p.m., Idaho time.

Seconds later, Horiuchi saw three people run from the house to a structure called the birthing shed, a distance of about a hundred feet. The group consisted of the same young girl Horiuchi had seen earlier and two men. One man, who appeared to be carrying a rifle or shotgun, tried to conceal himself behind the shed. Horiuchi concentrated his attention on the armed man, who he believed was Kevin Harris. Harris seemed to be peering in the direction of the copter from the corner of the birthing shed. We later learned that the body of young Sam Weaver had been placed in the shed, and that Weaver's daughter was trying to view her brother's body.

When the copter advancing toward the compound swung behind Horiuchi, the armed man pointed the rifle in the agent's direction. From Horiuchi's perspective it looked as though he was preparing to take aim at the aircraft. The occupants of the copter reported that shots had been fired in their direction. Believing that his colleagues were in danger, Horiuchi carefully placed the crosshairs of his scope on the man with the rifle and fired. Although Horiuchi thought he had missed, the bullet struck the man in the arm or shoulder just as he ducked back behind the shed. The pace of things picked up significantly at that point.

Seconds later, all three people began running from the shed to the cabin. The last one in the cluster appeared to be the same guy Hoiuchi had fired at previously. As he took a final leap to the door, Horiuchi fired a second time. The shot grazed the man and penetrated a window on the front door of the cabin. Horiuchi heard a woman scream. Unbeknown to Horiuchi, the shot had struck Vicki Weaver in the head, killing her instantly. The bullet exited Vicki and seriously wounded Kevin Harris, later confirmed as the target of Horiuchi's second shot. But Randy Weaver was the man wounded in the arm near the shed. Weaver later said that his wife had been holding their eleven-month-old infant when the bullet shattered the door window.

About fifteen minutes later, the armored personnel carrier deposited the telephone on the front porch of the cabin. An FBI negotiator announced by megaphone that they had warrants for Weaver and Harris. He asked Weaver to retrieve the phone so that they could discuss their surrender. As the personnel carrier slowly descended the mountainside, the agents laid a hard cable to be used for telephone communications. They heard nothing from Weaver that evening.

The next six days were uneventful. To establish some rapport with the Weavers, the negotiator delivered food and bandages to their front door by robot. But Weaver gave no intention of surrendering. During the standoff, with increasing national news coverage, scores of Weaver sympathizers and white supremacy advocates arrived and tried to hike up the mountainside, keeping the USMS contingent busy twenty-four hours a day.

On August 28, as the FBI began making plans to forcibly enter the cabin and take custody of Harris and Weaver, a valuable intermediary showed up to assist. Bo Grietz, a retired U.S. Army colonel who had served with the Special Forces, offered to negotiate with Weaver. Weaver was a long-time admirer of Colonel Grietz, who was able for the first time to establish a substantive dialogue with the occupants of the cabin.

Two days later, Grietz was able to persuade Kevin Harris to surrender. He was promptly airlifted by helicopter to a hospital for treatment of his gunshot wound. Weaver and his daughters remained steadfast.

The most difficult hurdle the colonel faced was convincing Weaver that he'd be dealt with fairly if he and his daughters submitted to arrest. Weaver was convinced that he would be shot if he stepped out of cabin.

The following day, on August 31, the FBI turned up the pressure on Grietz, informing him that they intended to the end the standoff by employing whatever reasonable force was necessary. At 10:00 a.m., Grietz offered Weaver an incentive he couldn't resist. The colonel had arranged for one of the top criminal defense lawyers in the West, Gerry Spence, to represent Weaver, free of charge. Minutes later, Randy Weaver and his daughters walked out with their hands up. For some, the crisis was over. For others, things just got worse.

The aftermath proceeded on two discrete tracks: Weaver and Harris were indicted on a battery of federal charges that ended in a colossal disaster; and the FBI was designated to investigate the shootings of Inspector Bill Degan, Sam Weaver, and Vicki Weaver. At first, I was skeptical of the FBI conducting an investigation involving its own people. The USMS was a convenient scapegoat. The agents who interviewed me were clearly hoping to lay as much fault as possible on the Marshals Service. However, I was pleasantly surprised that the final report was thorough, fair, objective, and well-balanced.

In early September, I stood alongside my old friend Governor Bill Weld of Massachusetts and the bishop of the Roman Catholic Archdiocese of Boston at Degan's funeral. I delivered the eulogy, extolling his bravery and distinguished public service. The church was packed, with almost a thousand people present: a fitting sendoff to a fallen hero. I'd soon become accustomed to the sad office of presenting eulogies. I gave four my first year as director, more than any of my predecessors.

Problems with the prosecution of Harris and Weaver first surfaced when the two assistant U.S. attorneys assigned to the case visited the USMS headquarters one Saturday afternoon to explain that the centerpiece of the ten-count indictment would be a conspiracy charge extending back to 1983, when the Weavers moved to Idaho. The essence of the prosecution's case was that Randy Weaver, Vicki Weaver, and Kevin Harris conspired over a nine-year period to provoke an armed confrontation with the government. Elements of the unprecedentedly sweeping conspiracy included their alleged participation in white supremacy activities. The theory may have been correct, but it missed the mark.

I voiced my strong dissent to the form of the indictment. I am from the old school of prosecution: The easier to prove, the better. This was a murder case, pure and simple. There would be enough problems trying to reconstruct the events of August 21. Why create needless evidentiary hurdles? This was an invitation to a circus! The Idaho prosecutors rejected my suggestions out of hand.

The following Monday I called Bill Sessions, director of the FBI and a former federal judge. Sessions was equally perplexed and said he would call Attorney General Bill Barr. If he did it had no effect, because the indictment was returned by the grand jury with the conspiracy count included.

There were even darker days ahead. In the weeks directly preceding the trial of Weaver and Harris, a festering feud between the Idaho U.S. Attorney's Office and the FBI escalated into a full-scale confrontation. The agents took strident issue with the prosecutors' apparent obsession with Weaver's white-supremacy leanings and antigovernment sentiments. The prosecutors almost appeared infected with a tincture of fanaticism. As Director Sessions and I had pointed out earlier, dwelling on these peripheral issues diluted the significance of the murder charge and needlessly diverted the jury's attention. Strategically, it was a formula for disaster. Aside from being marginally relevant, if the prosecutors failed to prove these extraneous elements of the conspiracy, the jury might tend to disbelieve the evidence pertaining to the killing of Bill Degan.

The U.S. Attorney's Office encountered continuing resistance from the FBI in producing reports and documents required by the court's discovery order, a source of considerable embarrassment during the trial.

Another area of discord involved interviewing out-of-state witnesses, whose testimony pertained principally to Weaver's comments and conduct years before

August 1992. The FBI logically concluded that these were secondary witnesses and decided to have agents based in those other states conduct the interviews. This did not sit well with the U.S. Attorney's Office, which insisted that the case agents from Idaho travel to the other states to question the witnesses.

With the disagreement over conducting the interviews escalating, the FBI drew the proverbial line in the sand during the critical final months of trial preparation. The U.S. attorney for Idaho called me and asked that I assign several investigators to assist with final trial preparation. He said that help was needed to wrap up an assortment of crucial tasks. He had already recruited two agents from the Bureau of Alcohol, Tobacco and Firearms. Ordinarily, I would not have hesitated, but this was sure to cause tension with the FBI, an agency we enjoyed a close working relationship with. We were willing to grant their request only if our investigators were working in league with the FBI; not at cross purposes.

For me personally, things got even worse. The upstart governor of Arkansas, Bill Clinton, clobbered President George H. W. Bush, and my days as director were inevitably numbered. All my Republican colleagues bailed out of the Department of Justice and I was drifting on my own. I was not anxious to return to private practice. No level of compensation could compare to the thrill and challenge of running the Marshals Service, so I decided to hold out till the last minute, hoping a miracle would happen.

## A Little Help from My Friends

Thanks to the good offices of a few influential Democratic senators and a couple of well-known entertainers I had met during the production of movies featuring our agency, the Clinton administration asked me to remain in place for an undefined period. I literally received the notification at the eleventh hour. Clinton's transition team had hand-delivered a letter advising me in stark terms to vacate my office by midnight on the eve of inauguration day. I had packed up my books, papers, and memorabilia. The walls of my office were bare. My family and I decided we'd take a five-day Caribbean cruise before I launched a job search. At 12:15 a.m. on the morning we were to sail, I received a call from Clinton's DOJ transition coordinator asking that I continue as director. Of course I was pleased. A man on death row is always pleased when he learns his execution has been stayed.

Serving under Attorney General Janet Reno was extremely frustrating. Although I enjoyed a good rapport with President Clinton and a few key members of his staff, relations with Reno were strained from the moment we met. During the final run-up to the trial, Weaver and Harris's lawyers, particularly the flamboyant Gerry Spence, made appearances on every major TV talk show. Understandably, Spence told only his client's side of the story. Reno forbade me or anyone from the Marshals Service or the FBI to rebut their spin. In the weeks preceding the trial in April 1993, the media was tearing us apart, and fomenting increasing sympathy for the Weaver family. Members of congress who were considered friends of law enforcement were clamoring for public hearings on the Ruby Ridge debacle. As an untenured holdover, I was not sleeping well.

The trial of Harris and Weaver exceeded our worst expectations. It resembled a wobbling race car peeling off the starting line with parts falling in its path. Many government witnesses contradicted each other. The defense learned that some of the crucial crime-scene photos had been staged after the fact, which was not revealed until they were in evidence. Documents and physical exhibits were misplaced, mishandled, or disclosed in late stages of the trial, contrary to the court's discovery orders. These types of slipups tend to tarnish a prosecution's white hat. The judge repeatedly had to chastise counsel to stop bickering. The crowning blow occurred on the twenty-first day of the trial, when the U.S. district judge commented in open court that, "about seventy-five percent of the witnesses called by the government have been favorable to the defense." Not a good sign!

At the close of the government's case, the court dismissed two counts of the indictment. The judge found the prosecution's evidence lacking on the charges of assaulting federal officers in the helicopter on August 22 and possession of a firearm by a fugitive. With respect to the latter charge, the court concluded that there was no evidence that Weaver had traveled across state lines, as required to prove that federal crime.

Despite the prosecution's elaborate conspiracy theory, the trial distilled to one pivotal issue. Who fired the first shot—Harris or Degan? Mounds of evidence were introduced to recreate a fifteen-second snapshot in time. People saw and heard things differently. People always do. Compounding the confusion was the number of interviews conducted by the FBI in its parallel investigations—the criminal investigation of the death of Degan and the internal investigation of the rules of engagement. Multiple layers of inconsistency, even those dealing with minutia, tend to foster doubt.

I was later criticized by the Senate Judiciary Committee for not doing our own Marshals Service internal investigation of the events at Ruby Ridge. As I explained to the committee, if I had done so, there would have been a third set of interviews of the same people, with enough subtle nuances in recollection to provide even more ammunition for cross-examination. Besides, it did not make economic sense to duplicate the FBI investigation, particularly with our budget still hovering in the red zone.

But even with all the setbacks, no one seriously doubted that in the final analysis the jury would brush aside the smoke, credit the testimony of the arrest team, and convict Harris and Weaver of their respective roles in the killing of Degan. In the end, it came down to who you believed. In a criminal case, a tie goes to the defendant, because the government's burden is proof beyond a reasonable doubt. However, in the legal context, the boundaries of "reasonable doubt" have never been clearly staked out.

The morale of the Marshals Service on the day the verdict was returned was like Wall Street when the stock market takes a thousand-point dive. Harris was acquitted on all charges. Weaver was convicted only of bond jumping. Postverdict interviews with jurors revealed their shocking conclusion that Harris shot Degan in self-defense. Setting aside passion, prejudice, and frustration, I must concede that Gerry Spence did a remarkable job. Unfortunately, that was not the end. In the months following the verdict, Weaver and Harris filed a federal civil rights action against every law enforcement person, including me, even remotely involved in the death of his wife and son. The Senate Judiciary Committee held three days of intense hearings on all aspects of the events at Ruby Ridge, where Mike Johnson and I spent almost four hours explaining the decisions we made in preparation for the arrest of Weaver, and the steps we took to avoid an armed confrontation. Fortunately, I knew a majority of the senators who participated. They focused closely on the formulation of the rules of engagement. With one isolated exception, the senators on the panel appeared convinced that I had no role in their drafting.

The committee's final report made a number of well-taken suggestions as to how some aspects of the mission could have been handled better. Overall, they found no fault with any of my decisions or the tactical approach we adopted. They reserved their ire for the FBI and ATF. The committee referred the case to the Department of Justice for criminal investigation.

Six months later, after I had left the Marshals Service and returned to the private practice of law, I was called to testify before a federal grand jury in the District of Columbia. This required me to hire a lawyer, which the DOJ paid for. In five hours of testimony, I racked my brain recalling everything that had happened on August 21 and 22, 1992. The assistant U.S. attorney, who had assured me that I was not a target of the investigation, read me my rights before I answered any questions. She appeared skeptical of many of my answers. Evidently, she couldn't understand that as an agency administrator and not an operations person, I had no background in devising arrest strategy, particularly in cases as sensitive as this one. I delegated the details to those who did.

The prosecutor, whose work experience paralleled mine and who claimed no knowledge of operational law enforcement tactics herself, theatrically professed amazement that I had not insisted on having input into FBI operational plans at Ruby Ridge. She persisted even after I explained that the directives in question did not pertain to the Marshals Service. At times, her antics bordered on the ridiculous. Despite her demurrer, I got the inescapable impression that perhaps I was the focus of the investigation, particularly when she called me back for a second day. In retrospect, I'm certain that she was only doing her job, and was building a record that could withstand even the closest scrutiny. I suppose in the end she was satisfied with my answers.

The civil suit filed by Harris and Weaver loomed like a black cloud for almost six years. Both the U.S. District Court for Idaho and the Ninth Circuit Court of Appeals rejected my motion to dismiss. The district court found, and the appellate court agreed, that Duke Smith's claim that I had approved the rules of engagement was a factual issue for a jury to resolve. Federal lawsuits are rarely thrown out pretrial when critical factual disputes exist. Weaver and his three surviving children settled their claim against the government for $3.1 million dollars. However, the government refused to pay Harris any money. It was during preparation for the trial of Harris's case that Duke Smith finally acknowledged doubt that he had ever consulted with me on the rules of engagement. Based on Duke's affidavit, the claim against me personally was dismissed.

The timing was propitious. My name was under consideration for a federal judgeship at the time. If the allegations against me had not been dropped, irrespective of their lack of merit, I would have been neither appointed by the president nor confirmed by the Senate as a United States district judge. The government finally settled with Harris for three hundred eighty thousand dollars. As for the Degan family, they continued to grieve.

The aftermath of Ruby Ridge was dispiriting for all law enforcement officials involved, but their misery paled by comparison to the consequences for Special Agent Lon Horiuchi. Horiuchi was subjected to the same congressional and Department of Justice inquiries that I experienced, except that in his precarious situation, he wisely invoked his Fifth Amendment right to decline to testify. Considering the level of scrutiny he was under, any question pertaining to the shots he fired or the tactical decisions he made on August 22, 1992, was a potential landmine. In the end, the Department of Justice concluded that Horiuchi had done nothing that warranted criminal prosecution. However, the investigation did yield one casualty: One high-level FBI official pled guilty to obstruction of justice.

The results of the DOJ investigation had no deterrent effect or influence on state authorities. A coalition of Weaver sympathizers and antigovernment activists continued to clamor for Horiuchi to stand trial for murder. The din of their protests eventually succeeded. On August 22, 1997, five years to the day after Vicki Weaver was shot, Horiuchi was charged with manslaughter in Boundary County. The prosecution alleged that the charge, which carried a maximum penalty of ten years in prison, was based on Horiuchi's negligent firing of his rifle at the front door of the Weaver cabin without first ascertaining whether anyone other than his intended target was behind the door.

The county prosecutor demanded that Horiuchi immediately turn himself in. The FBI, however, was not going to allow an agent to be subjected to a lynch mob. The DOJ set the stage for a major constitutional battle by insisting that a federal agent acting within the scope of his or her duties was immune from state prosecution.

On the same day, charges were handed down against Kevin Harris for first degree murder, which carried the death penalty. The prosecutor announced that her investigation had concluded that Deputy Marshal Degan was in fact retreating when he was deliberately gunned down by Harris. Interestingly, her theory was directly contrary to the findings of the previous jury—that Harris had fired in self-defense. Because Harris was being prosecuted at that point for murder under state law, and the first trial had been brought under a different federal statute, the second case was not barred by the constitutional ban on double jeopardy.

The distinction was lost on Harris's supporters. The day he surrendered on new charges there was a near riot at the courthouse. More than two hundred people assembled to protest his prosecution—and they had a long memory. At the next election, three years later, the county prosecutor was ousted by a three-to-one margin.

Meanwhile, militant groups began plastering wanted posters on the streets of Boundary County. They featured a picture of Agent Horiuchi and offered a twenty-five thousand dollar reward for him "dead or alive." Rather than allow Horiuchi to submit to the jurisdiction of the Boundary County court, the Department of Justice filed a motion to dismiss in the U.S. District Court in Boise, Idaho.

After extensive briefing, including friend-of-the-court briefs by four former attorneys general of the United States and oral argument, the court ruled that Horiuchi could not be tried by the state for involuntary manslaughter. U.S. District Judge Edward J. Lodge concluded that under the Supremacy clause of the United States Constitution, a federal law enforcement officer could not be ordered into a crisis situation and then have the reasonableness of his actions decided by a different governmental authority. Judge Lodge further found that under the prevailing conditions, Horiuchi's actions were objectively reasonable and that he was consequently immune from prosecution.

The State of Idaho appealed the decision to the notoriously liberal U.S. Court of Appeals for the Ninth Circuit. A three-judge panel affirmed Judge Lodge's decision. The State of Idaho, with the passion of a pack of crazed wild dogs, was not satisfied. The state asked the full court to rehear the case. On June 5, 2001, with a split of six to five, the Ninth Circuit reversed Judge Lodge and the original panel's decision. A slim majority found that Horiuchi could be tried by the state if he acted illegally in his capacity as a federal official. As is frequently the case with the Ninth Circuit, the decision had little basis in recognized precedent. The turn of events was startling, but not as surprising as what occurred next.

The federal appeals court sent Horiuchi's case back to Boundary County for trial. A week later, the county prosecutor dismissed the charges against Agent Horiuchi. This ignited a political firestorm, but it was too late to recharge him. The statute of limitations had run out. With the charges dismissed, there was no active case, and therefore, no justification for an appeal of the Ninth Circuit decision to the U.S. Supreme Court.

## XXI
# INCREASED VISIBILITY

Marshals Service recruitment soared the day the film *The Fugitive* hit the theaters.

Starring Harrison Ford and Tommy Lee Jones, and filmed with the assistance of our Chicago office, the movie portrayed U.S. Marshals as the nation's premier fugitive hunters. In addition to exciting interest in becoming deputy marshals, the movie had three other significant effects. First, it sent an unprecedented jolt of pride throughout the Marshals Service. Next, it reacquainted the nation with who we are and what we do. Finally, it gave Hollywood some new ideas. I was determined to ride the wave as far as possible.

Up to then, the Marshals Service had a reactive public affairs unit that responded to press inquiries and coordinated the occasional films and television productions that featured our agency or cases. Unlike the FBI, which had scores of agents assigned to massage the media, the USMS had only two or three non-law-enforcement employees to perform those duties. I beefed up the section with several new people who approached the job with the zeal of telemarketers. Their mission was to promote the Marshals Service and to inspire as much media coverage as possible.

In the wake of *The Fugitive,* at least one movie or television producer visited our headquarters every month to discuss a production idea. To capitalize on every opportunity, I designated Chief Inspector Bob Leschorn as my personal media representative. Leschorn was enthusiastic and well liked, and spoke the PR language. His extensive experience in tracking criminals, especially organized crime figures, also qualified him to serve as the technical advisor on all works in production.

Bob Leschorn and I cultivated a close working relationship with John Walsh, host of "America's Most Wanted." Walsh was delighted to feature our fugitives on his weekly broadcast, and allowed me to narrate some of our profiles.

John and I became fast friends and later worked together on two television movie productions.

Our aggressive fugitive profiling was contagious. Several Washington television channels began regularly broadcasting segments on our most wanted criminals in the D.C. area, and follow-up features on their capture. I found myself giving interviews to radio and television stations around the country on a daily basis.

On a parallel front, I placed increased emphasis on our relations with Congress. I spent at least a half day each week visiting key congressmen and senators. Following the lead of the FBI and other more prominent federal law enforcement agencies, we passed out mugs, hats, and tee shirts. When influential members of our oversight committees traveled, we often made deputy marshals available to assist with transportation and security. It paid great dividends.

Perhaps the most entertaining call on a member of Congress was my meeting with Congressman Barney Frank of Massachusetts. A member of the powerful House Judiciary Committee, Congressman Frank was a force to be reckoned with. One of my deputy directors, a former U.S. marshal for the District of Massachusetts, and I sat patiently in Frank's reception area for about twenty minutes. Periodically, the door to the congressman's office would open a narrow crack and two eyes could be seen peering around the edge. Finally, his aide walked out and said the congressman would meet with us only if I assured him that we did not have a warrant for his arrest. I thought it was a joke, but I later learned that the congressman was serious.

No matter how much spin I put on our mission, the Marshals Service still needed some "bling." Thanks to a supplemental appropriation engineered by Congressman Frank Wolf, we launched a series of national fugitive roundup projects. Working in league with state and local law enforcement agencies, we targeted violent criminals wanted in those jurisdictions.

Dubbed Operation Gunsmoke, the first phase, nabbed 3,313 wanted felons nationwide—262 for murder. Gunsmoke II resulted in 1,024 arrests, 779 for violent sexual assaults. Each operation was closely coordinated with the local media. The goodwill with state and local law enforcement agencies was priceless. The print and broadcast coverage was phenomenal. U.S. Marshals became a household word, not just a forgotten relic of the Old West. It had the added effect of instilling an unprecedented spirit of pride in the men and women who carried the silver star of a deputy U.S. marshal. Their families loved it, too.

Congress took note of the results. The next time I appeared before the Budget Committee, it threw in a couple of additional million dollars more than I requested.

*Recognizing Northern Virginia Sheriff's Offices in 1993 for their participation in Operation Gunsmoke, a national fugitive roundup, which netted over 3,000 violent felons. Sheriff Tom Faust of Arlington County is to my right, Sheriff Carl Peed of Fairfax on the left. (Courtesy of the U.S. Marshals Service.)*

As one of the last remaining Republicans in the Clinton Department of Justice, a bevy of handlers went with me to Congress. The Clinton folks were astounded by the warm reception I received from Committee Chairman Jim Moran, an old acquaintance. Before being elected to Congress, Moran had been mayor of Alexandria, Virginia, and he and I had worked together on several regional projects during my years as United States attorney. I am convinced that the courtesies Congressman Moran extended to me that day persuaded the Clinton Administration to retain me as director of the USMS. But still, I knew my days were numbered.

In early January 1993, as the transition in presidential administrations loomed, another media opportunity materialized. Don Johnson, the star of the "Miami Vice" TV series and numerous films, was coming by to visit. Johnson,

Bob Leschorn, and I spent the morning chatting in my office, and had lunch with his production team. They wanted to develop a reality-based series involving fugitive cases investigated by actual deputy marshals. We loved the idea and spent the next six months working with his executive producer refining the concept. Don Johnson and I became friends and kept in close touch. However, despite our best efforts, Attorney General Reno vetoed our participation in the series.

Johnson was a delightful fellow to work with, and very loyal to his friends. During the inaugural festivities for Bill Clinton, Don and his then wife, actress Melanie Griffith, held a star-studded reception for the president. Both Don and Melanie used the one-on-one opportunity to urge President Clinton to keep me on as the head marshal.

Not long after I left as director of the Marshals Service, Johnson called me with another production idea—a television adventure series portraying a fugitive-hunting deputy marshal. He invited me to assist with the production and serve as technical advisor for the series. I jumped at the opportunity.

We kicked around a number of names for the show, but eventually decided on "The Marshal," a joint venture produced by Paramount Pictures and the Don Johnson Company. The ABC network initially purchased thirteen weeks of the series with an option for follow-on seasons, all subject to their approval of the pilot. The central character was a young deputy marshal named Winston MacBride based in Los Angeles, with an eye-catching wife and two boisterous kids. MacBride tracked fugitives using his brains. He was sharp and resourceful, employing logic, common sense, a variety of high-tech gadgets, and a dash of chicanery to collar his prey. To play MacBride, Don Johnson recruited Jeff Fahey, riding high after costarring with Kevin Costner in *Wyatt Earp*.

*Talking with actor and television producer Don Johnson about a television series featuring the U.S. Marshals Service.*

Weekly episodes of "The Marshal" featured some tease and innuendo, but scant sex and minimal violence. Some were slightly "si-fi." MacBride rarely fired his gun. The result was suspenseful, but perhaps a little bland for the average viewer. The production was a calculated gamble, pitting suspense and intrigue against the modern viewer's seemingly insatiable appetite for the course and crude.

My role was two-fold. I supplied story line ideas based on actual cases handled by the USMS, wrote them up, and sent them to the script writers. The writers, Western Sandblast, were independent contractors affiliated with Paramount.

After sending a number of proposed story lines to Western Sandblast, I finally realized that script writing was a closed shop. If the idea was not hatched by a member of the guild, it stunk. All my ideas were quickly trashed.

My second task was reviewing scripts prepared by the writers. As technical advisor, I had to square the script with reality—a tall order. Their concept of reality bore little resemblance to anything the Marshals Service had ever experienced. To them, reality was measured in terms of the outer perimeter of possibility. Once I got acclimated, I kind of enjoyed it.

The filming of the pilot was a revelation. To reduce production costs, Paramount shoots in Canada, thereby avoiding exorbitant union wages while gaining expansive open space, and pleasing the Canadian government in the bargain. When I arrived in Vancouver to observe the filming of the pilot and confer with the script writers, Canadian Customs asked me the purpose of my visit. When I disclosed that I was a consultant for Paramount, they escorted me to a private area for questioning. I thought they had mistaken me for a fast-lane type—perhaps wishful thinking. After quizzing me in great detail about exactly what I intended to do at the Paramount studio, it turned out that I would need a work permit to enter the country, and would have to pay a fee of $100.

*Hanging out on the film set with Jeff Fahey, who played Inspector Winston McBride in the television series "The Marshal." On his left is Diane Sillan, the executive director of the production.*

Work begins early on a television set. Despite carousing with us until almost midnight, Fahey was in the hotel gym by 5:00 a.m., tightening up and going over his lines. After a light breakfast, the van left the Fairmont Hotel for the studio a little after seven. Filming began at eight o'clock. It reminded me of a boot camp. The director stood calmly on the sidelines, while his minions yelled and screamed instructions. About fifty employees worked around the set, including cooks and a cigarette girl. The cigarette girl poured pack after pack of smokes into a huge bowl all day long. They went fast.

The marquee actors, Fahey and his costar, had fancy recreation vehicles to relax in. The others sat unceremoniously on the curb of the 7-Eleven store where the scene was being shot, waiting for an assistant director to wave them into play.

Bob Leschorn and I stood around with the director, or sat around Fahey's RV chatting with the writers. I spent some curb time, too, talking with the secondary actors, an entertaining group with a carefree attitude.

The pilot was well-received by Paramount, the network, and the viewers, and got superb reviews. Rival networks responded by beefing up their offerings for the time slot. Originally scheduled for Monday night, "The Marshal" was eventually shifted to Saturday, up against a Chuck Norris production. Over time, our numbers declined. After two seasons, we got the ax, and Don Johnson's attention shifted to his new role as Nash Bridges, a San Francisco detective.

At first, I was enamored with the seductive and seemingly romantic lifestyle of the film business. It was fun to have lunch with Don Johnson and Melanie Griffith at Planet Hollywood, or dinner at a posh restaurant. As a result of working on "The Marshal," Paramount and others hired me to consult on several production concepts in development. However, life in Hollywood is tough for all but the top-tiered actors. For Jeff Fahey, it was feast or famine. One year he was living in a beachfront cottage at Malibu and driving a new Jaguar convertible. The next, he was temporarily living with friends, and struggling to make ends meet. He and I have stayed in touch. Today, he operates his own production company and we've collaborated on another television series we hope to have in production in the future.

Heading the Marshals Service frayed the nerves, but the daily thrill and challenge were unparalleled. It was readily apparent that turning the agency around would take at least five years, provided that a larger one didn't absorb us out of existence. The FBI was constantly trying to chip away at our more exciting functions, such as chasing fugitives and pursuing prison escapees. Without these duties, the daily routine of a Marshal would be fairly mundane, tempting the more energetic deputies to look at other law enforcement opportunities. Films like *The Fugitive* and shows like "The Marshal" injected unprecedented life and spirit into the men and women of the Marshals Service. But reality is often a cruel reminder that danger strikes when it is least expected.

## The Ultimate Sacrifice

Jack Gary McKnight was a thirty-seven-year-old accountant for Santa Fe Railroad. He had been convicted of growing large quantities of pot in the back yard of his two-acre farm, about twenty miles northwest of Topeka, Kansas. The state police seized one hundred four marijuana plants, obviously cultivated for distribution. McKnight's wife, Cynthia Marie, was also involved in selling their homegrown product, and eventually pled guilty to drug charges and was sentenced to thirty months.

McKnight was due back in court for sentencing at 1:30 p.m. on August 5, 1993. Because of the volume of marijuana plants seized from his cultivation plot and the presence of firearms, he was facing a mandatory minimum of ten years in prison.

The trial judge had decided to leave McKnight on bond pending sentencing. That proved to be a serious mistake. However, predicting a defendant's behavior is tough, but a task U.S. Marshals must undertake daily in performing their primary statutory mission of protecting the federal judiciary.

McKnight began preparing for court early on August 5. At eight-thirty he parked his red pickup truck in the main square of Oskaloosa, a small town just outside of Topeka. He strolled to his waiting Subaru and headed for the federal courthouse, just as his truck was propelled off the ground by a huge explosion.

The shock waves of the blast ripped through the small annex of the Jefferson County Sheriff's Office, just off the town square. McKnight's truck erupted in a ball of flame as sheriff's deputies scattered onto the street. Within minutes, they had identified the owner of the smoldering truck. It was a name they knew well. Suspecting revenge as his motivation, a deputy familiar with his case immediately placed a call to the federal prosecutor's office, but it was too late.

Special Deputy U.S. Marshal Gene Goldsberry had recently retired from the Kansas Highway Patrol. During his twenty-five years as a trooper, he had served as a patrol-plane pilot, a member of the governor's security detail, and a supervisor. Goldsberry, who had been diagnosed with terminal cancer, was also a black belt in karate who taught martial arts to other troopers.

On August 5, Goldsberry was working a security checkpoint adjacent to the elevator on the fourth floor of the Frank Carlson Federal Building—not his regular assignment. That floor housed several federal courtrooms, as well as chambers for three federal judges and their staff. The clerk of the court and U.S. marshal also had their offices there.

At 9:30 a.m., McKnight parked the Subaru at the federal building, grabbed a black briefcase, and walked to the glass doors leading to the bank of elevators. He punched the button for the fourth floor.

When the elevator door opened, McKnight moved with lightening speed. He whipped out one of his four pistols and, without warning, began blasting. The first rounds struck Goldsberry in the thigh and wounded a bystander in the elbow, wrist, and abdomen. Before Goldsberry could pull his weapon, McKnight fired again, this time at point-blank range, striking Goldsberry in the head. Another court visitor was hit in the arm. As McKnight pushed his way through the metal detector, he lit the wicks of small pipe bombs filled with gun powder.

McKnight ran toward the Clerk's Office with pipe bombs exploding in his path. He burst in with pistols blazing, firing at least sixty rounds. Pandemonium erupted. Employees ducked under desks, climbed up into the ceiling, or locked themselves into closets, as they had been trained. The judges and their staff did the same. McKnight kept shouting to the deputy clerks that he was not after them.

By 9:36 a.m., more than a hundred law enforcement officers were converging on the federal building—the FBI, ATF, U.S. Marshals, Topeka Police, Kansas Highway Patrol, Kansas Bureau of Investigation, and Shawnee County Sheriff's Deputies. Within seconds of the arrival of the first few units, McKnight's Subaru exploded, sending a burst of flames twenty-five feet in the air. Members of police special weapons and tactical teams were deployed around the building, which was surrounded by police as hundreds of employees were evacuated from the lower floors. Troopers and federal agents, weapons in hand, slowly made their way up the stairs to the fourth floor to confront McKnight. Scores of heavily armed officers gingerly scoured the building in search of McKnight. A trained hostage negotiator was available, if needed. Restless, terrified employees were encouraged to remain concealed until McKnight was found.

It took almost seven hours to locate McKnight, lying dead on the floor at the far end of the Clerk's Office. Officers approached carefully because pipe bombs were still attached to his body. Several had detonated, shredding his legs and hands. However, the cause of death was a self-inflicted penetrating gunshot wound to the roof of the mouth. Investigators were unable to determine if the pipe bombs had been detonated before or after the lethal shot, or whether the explosions were deliberate or accidental.

In the weeks that followed, speculation abounded. Who was the intended victim? Was it the prosecutor or the judge? Our concern at the Marshals Service was the actual, and perhaps unintended, victim, Gene Goldsberry, placed by chance in McKnight's path of destruction. Jefferson County Sheriff Roy Dunnaway described McKnight as angry and upset with the entire law enforcement community. Anyone connected with his case was a potential target, even the deputy marshal screening people who entered the court area. That's one of the greatest dangers court security officers face. They are the most publicly accessible court representatives.

The loss of Gene Goldsberry hit home a second time the next day, when he had arranged to formally adopt his stepdaughter, who still wears his U.S. Marshal lapel pin in his memory. To her the loss was immeasurable, and was compounded by the death of her mother the following year.

The Goldsberry family asked me to give the eulogy at Gene's funeral. Hundreds of law enforcement officers and court officials were present to pay tribute to a fallen hero. I was honored to add my words of appreciation.

Although I spoke at the funerals of more deputy marshals killed in the line of duty than any director in U.S. Marshals Service history, not every crisis that crossed my desk had tragic consequences. Some were humorous in strange ways.

### Hoodwinked

All ninety-four U.S. Marshals offices nationwide have responsibility for maintaining custody of seized property, mainly cars, currency, and real estate. Offices along the United States border may seize as many as two hundred cars a week. Most are sold as scrap; those with resale value are sold at auction. Because the storage fees mount rapidly, every office is under pressure to keep the inventory low.

One morning, a deputy marshal in a midwestern office received a telephone called from a detective with the city police department. The detective needed to look in the glove compartment of a seized Ferrari for a document of potential value as evidence. No problem. The deputy told the detective to come on by and he'd take him over to the lot. The detective arrived an hour or so later, however, the deputy was booking a prisoner and couldn't leave, so he called the storage lot and told the person on duty to give the detective access to the car.

A few minutes later, the detective returned. They wouldn't let him in. He'd left his credentials at police headquarters. The deputy, who was still processing the prisoner, was apologetic for being unavailable to assist. He handed the detective his deputy marshal credentials and suggested that he simply show them to the guard on duty. Perfect passport.

The shiny red Ferrari was recovered about six months later in a remote seaside village in California. The credentials turned up on the street eventually. The detective was never identified, but one thing is for sure—he was no detective.

Everyone at Marshals Service headquarters got a laugh out of it but, of course, I had to take some disciplinary action. The deputy could have been terminated, but his intentions were good and his record was blemish free, so I let him off with a reprimand. I figured that the ostracism he would receive was probably worse than anything I could dish out.

## Good Deeds Never Go Unpunished

The rationale of Congress in adopting asset forfeiture laws was to enable the government to seize the cash and property of drug dealers and racketeers, liquidate it, and funnel it back into law enforcement programs. A subsidiary goal was social restitution, repaying the community for the impact of the criminal activity. In the latter vein, I devised a plan in concert with the United States attorney for a Pennsylvania district, to use some of our forfeited real estate as temporary

*Announcing to the press a U.S. Marshals Service program in Philadelphia to allow the homeless to temporarily reside in forfeited properties during winter months. I was forced to cancel the program several weeks later when the City required that all of the homes dedicated to this project strictly comply with City building code.*

residences for homeless people during the bitter cold winter months. The folks at the DOJ loved the idea.

Early one chilly morning, I flew to Pennsylvania to unveil the program at a major news conference. Every politician in the city was there, pushing for a spot in front of the TV cameras. The mayor, chairman of the city council, director of housing, the U.S. attorney, and I all gave speeches as the news cameras rolled. The print media was ecstatic with glowing editorials the following day. The Marshals Office for that district arranged for more than a dozen families to move into these winter shelters, and even got the utilities turned on. I fully expected the mayor to give us the key to the City.

Several weeks later, the U.S. marshal for the district received a letter from the city. It was not the anticipated commendation. It was an official notice that some of our occupied seized houses violated the city building code. Unless we corrected the violations by a designated date, we would be summoned into court. Our housing assistance program came to an abrupt halt.

## Diverse Duties

Throughout the history of our country, U.S. marshals have been called on to restore order during times of civil unrest. I dispatched several waves of deputy marshals to Los Angeles to regain control of the community during the riots sparked by the Rodney King incident. When looting occurred in the wake of Hurricane Andrew, the U.S. attorney general ordered U.S. marshals to South Florida to maintain order in the tent cities erected to house the hundreds of displaced residents—not only to provide security, but also to assist in the distribution of food and water. In the aftermath of the hurricane I visited South Florida and toured the coastline by helicopter. Miles of buildings were leveled or damaged beyond reconstruction.

U.S. marshals have always had a broader portfolio of duties than other law enforcement agencies. That's because throughout their history they have always willingly assumed duties and responsibilities others didn't want. They have traditionally envisioned their peacekeeping role as including humanitarian assistance and, when necessary, population stabilization. It's an integral part of cooling the embers of social unrest, which can easily rekindle into resurgent violence.

Enforcing the nation's laws, bringing a semblance of order to the shattered world of victims of crime or natural disaster, and lending a helping hand to those in need is really what being a deputy U.S. marshal is all about.

One of my secret goals as director was to convince Congress to allow the USMS to absorb the Federal Emergency Management Administration (FEMA) into our agency. At that time, FEMA was under intense congressional attack for perceived mismanagement. The missions of the two agencies were compatible and the expansion would have given the USMS a new dimension of responsibility that would secure its long-term existence. Unfortunately, the time was never right to pursue the idea.

This same mind-set translated into other public service programs developed by Marshals Service personnel. Long before I became director, some of our big city offices had initiated programs to help young people in inner city schools, particularly in the lower income neighborhoods, who needed tutoring, or merely adult time and attention. Many of these kids had parents who were crack addicts and brothers and sisters who either hustled the streets or were in prison. In these families, education was not a priority.

Participating deputy marshals had diverse backgrounds, training, and experience to share with these attention-starved kids. As volunteers, these men and women visited public schools, usually at the elementary level, and provided tutoring in math, reading, and other subjects. And more: They devoted personal time to take these youngsters to athletic events, movies, and concerts. This was real grassroots crime prevention.

Eventually, the Marshals Service adopted the project as a nationwide program, "Partners in Education." Every office was encouraged to adopt a school, and most did.

## Housing Inmates and Other Budget Headaches

My greatest daily headache as director was trying to find bed space for the more than twenty thousand inmates in my custody each day. Today the number approaches sixty thousand. Attorney General Bill Barr, and later Janet Reno, chewed me out regularly for overspending my detention budget, which was around four hundred million dollars a year. We had no control over the number of inmates judges placed in our custody. The more the Department of Justice ratcheted up the intensity of its prosecutions, the more prisoners we had to contend with. The federal government operated only a handful of facilities for pretrial detainees. Consequently, each day we were forced to find and rent bed space from state and local detention centers, most of which were trying to squeeze us for every dime possible.

A continuing source of problems was New York City. Kristine Marcy, associate director for Operations Support, conceived the idea of leasing a prison barge. Tied up in New York Harbor, the barge would accommodate about four hundred inmates. It was an excellent idea. We were desperate for space. With the DOJ's

*Visiting the prison barge in the New York Harbor which housed almost 400 U.S. Marshals' prisoners awaiting trial. To my right, Associate Director Kris Marcy and U.S. Marshal for the Southern District of New York, Romolo J. Imundi.*

approval and a supplemental appropriation from Congress, we signed the contact. Several weeks later, Marcy and I visited the barge.

It was moored at a dock that fronted a public-housing area in the shadow of the Statute of Liberty. The road leading in resembled a war zone, with stripped-down cars, probably stolen, propped on blocks littering the path. The perimeter surrounding the barge and adjacent parking area was bordered by two rows of high fence topped with razor wire. At least it appeared secure.

As Marcy and I approached the entrance, we were greeted by the warden and the director of corrections for the City of New York, which was staffing the facility as part of the deal. I could not resist commenting on how secure the facility appeared with the multiple rows of razor wire. I speculated that they had never had an escape. The warden, a jovial guy, laughed and replied that the fencing was not intended to keep the inmates in, but to keep the car thieves out. Staff members did not relish losing their cars while on duty.

We were impressed with the physical facility, which included a fully equipped music department and indoor and outdoor basketball courts, but we were shocked by the staffing requirements. The barge had a physician and a dentist on duty sixteen hours a day, seven days a week. This added up to six full-time doctors! They said the union required it.

Even more disturbing was the need for a full-time pilot, drawing a salary of about one hundred twenty-five thousand dollars a year. This was a barge. It had no motor and couldn't move without being towed. Again, this was required by the union contract. The total operating cost was about thirteen hundred dollars per day per prisoner. Boy, did the federal government take a royal screwing, but we had no alternative. Ironically, most of the people we had in custody were being prosecuted by the feds to help reduce crime in the city.

While we were in New York that day, Associate Director Marcy and I also stopped by the U.S. District Court in Brooklyn, where the jury was deliberating the fate of John Gotti, the infamous mobster. Gotti, head of one of New York's most powerful organized-crime families, was on trial for a series of racketeering-related murders. En route to the courtroom being used for the trial, the bailiff walked us by "mobster row," where spiffily dressed mob bosses lined the stairway. As we passed, many tipped their hats and greeted "Ms. Mary," the sixty-three-year-old, four-foot-eleven, tough-as-nails deputy marshal who ran U.S. District Judge Ira Glasser's courtroom. When she gave directions, people jumped.

We had just sat down to talk with Judge Glasser when the deputy came in to report that the jury had reached a verdict—guilty. Gotti was immediately placed in custody and transported to the Metropolitan Correctional Center, a detention facility operated by the U.S. Bureau of Prisons. We arrived just before he did, and I had a chance to spend a few minutes with him. When the transporting deputies removed Gotti's handcuffs, I placed them in my pocket.

Attorney General Bill Barr and I later had the handcuffs mounted on an engraved plaque and presented them to President George H. W. Bush to commemorate his successful organized-crime-fighting programs.

The cost of housing inmates was only one aspect of our budget problems. Most presidentially appointed U.S. marshals were responsible people who handled their budgets well. But a few resisted all direction. One or two of them were total jackasses. As presidential appointees, they professed independence and claimed to take direction only from the White House. Some even believed they could spend their allotted budget as they saw fit.

The line of authority between the director and the ninety-four U.S. Marshals is somewhat blurred. Although it is generally understood that the director is in charge, nowhere will you find it in writing. In those rare instances when U.S. marshals were totally out of control, I had two options: I could ask the selecting U.S. senator to intervene, or I could request that the deputy attorney general of the United States order them to comply. I used both approaches, but frankly, most feared the wrath of the appointing senator more than the bark of the deputy attorney general.

I am a strong proponent of selecting U.S. marshals from within the ranks of the Marshals Service. Appointment on the basis of political patronage is a vestige of the past, and results in an eclectic lot. The spectrum can span from former career law-enforcement officials to farmers, clowns, TV weathermen, and professional athletes. One of the best U.S. marshals during my tenure was a Montana sheep rancher with no prior police training. He was smart enough to set office policy and delegate operational responsibility to the chief deputy, a career employee. When a crisis occurred on the street, he had the good judgment to stay out of the way.

Under the current structure, the top jobs in the Marshals Service are all reserved for political appointees. There are obvious hazards associated with placing a person with no law-enforcement experience in charge of a platoon of federal officers, and it makes no sense that a career deputy marshal can never rise to the rank of U.S. marshal, unless he's lucky enough along the way to develop some political clout. Continuing efforts to depoliticize the job have been unsuccessful. The Senate is reluctant to give up this political plum.

Our relentless budget containment efforts encountered hemorrhages in unexpected places. For example, about twenty-nine detainees in our custody were committed to St. Elizabeth's Hospital, a facility in D.C. that housed criminal defendants with mental problems. But nobody had an exact count or had reviewed their status. No head count had been taken in years. The USMS was being billed about two hundred dollars a day per person, plus other expenses associated with treatment. It amounted to well over a million dollars a year.

Our twenty-nine or so residents had been committed to the hospital, which was run by the D.C. government, after being found not guilty by reason of insanity by a federal court in the Capital City. One of them was John Hinckly, who had attempted to assassinate President Reagan.

Some of these people had been at St. Elizabeth's for three to five years, or more. I assigned an investigator to determine the status of each one. Sure enough, about half of them could not be found. So Kris Marcy and I visited "St. E's," and I asked the superintendent to show us the twenty-nine people that I was paying over $1.5 million a year to keep there. Only about fifteen could be found. The others were dead or had been released. Significant billing adjustments ensued.

On the other side of the ledger, the Marshals Service was the only agency that provided the DOJ with a steady and handsome annual income stream. From the liquidation of seized assets—houses, businesses, cars, boats, planes, jewelry, art, race horses, and an occasional reptile—the proceeds approached a hundred million dollars. Much of this money was returned to the state and local law-enforcement agencies participating in the joint investigation with federal agents that had resulted in the forfeiture of the property.

"Asset sharing," the transfer of asset forfeiture proceeds back to state and local police departments, created a tremendous incentive to involve the feds in otherwise local investigations, and could be quite lucrative. If assets are seized and forfeited as part of the combined effort, the proceeds are doled out according to the percentage of overall participation by each state and local agency. In the early 1990s, few states had asset forfeiture laws that allowed the money to be returned directly to the seizing agencies. Most state laws at that time turned the cash over to the state for general use.

## The Chase for Cash

The Comprehensive Crime Control Act of 1984, which enacted the present asset forfeiture laws, created a new theater in the war on crime—an unprecedented emphasis on disgorging the profits. Trace the money became the mantra. Police departments everywhere joined the chase for cash.

Small five-person police departments in sleepy one-traffic-light towns were no longer just looking to ensnare the unwitting speeder. Their sights were set higher—on the suspicious vehicle that met the profile of a drug courier. Sometimes they'd hit the jackpot. An officer would by chance stop a drug courier passing through town, and stumble upon contraband and a wad of cash in the car. The small department would turn the money over to the feds for "adoptive forfeiture" and eventually walk away with a fat check representing about eighty-five percent of the cash seized. A large jackpot might yield several hundred thousand dollars. For some, the return could be twice their annual operating budget.

Once word got around, cops began asking more questions of suspicious traffic violators, and pressed many for permission to search their car. Surprisingly, the majority of drug couriers confronted on the highway, knowing they were dirty and would probably be busted, gave the officer permission to search their car.

As U.S. attorney, I put the skids on the questionable practice of accepting adoptive forfeiture cases where local police had agreed to totally drop criminal charges against a person in exchange for their consent to forfeit cash or property. Some of these isolated cases were no doubt legitimate bona fide agreements, but I thought the deals might not fare well in the eyes of the public, particularly since a major chunk of the cash went directly to the police department.

One seized asset in our custody was a true cash gusher, pumping more than thirty million dollars a year directly into the national treasury. The Bicycle Club was the second largest gambling casino in California. Located on the outskirts of Los Angeles, the club had a staff of more than nineteen hundred and fifty people, and daily revenue exceeding two hundred fifty thousand dollars. But what made it unique was that it was operated by the U.S. Marshals Service.

We became the legal custodian of a one-third controlling interest following the conviction of two high-rolling Miami marijuana smugglers. Federal agents traced the paper trail of a portion of the drug kingpins' sixty-two million dollars in profits through several offshore banks and mortgage companies. The path eventually led to the Bicycle Club. Because illegal drug proceeds had been used to buy the club, the one-third interest was declared forfeited by the federal court. That's when we got involved.

The Bicycle Club was the economic engine of the small California community of Bell Gardens. The popular casino generated about ten million dollars in annual tax revenue. It also employed a sizeable part of the population. With one hundred seventy-five felt-covered blackjack tables, roulette tables, and baccarat wheels, the ornate casino raked in between ninety and a hundred million dollars a year. The stakes in some games were in the six figures. If the club went under, it would take the town with it.

We figured that our one-third interest, when eventually sold, would yield between thirty-five and forty-five million dollars to the Department of Justice asset forfeiture fund. Therefore, we had a strong financial incentive to operate the casino at peak efficiency. On the other hand, we felt uncomfortable dealing with the shady characters in the gambling business, some of whom were "known to law enforcement." They felt uneasy dealing with us, too. Some thought it must be some kind of sting operation. The pressure from antigambling and religious groups to divest the government's interest as soon as possible was relentless. But, it wasn't quite that easy.

In order to purchase our one-third interest, a prospective buyer needed big bucks, all cash. We couldn't hold any notes. Most important, the buyer had to have a clean criminal record, with no known connections to organized crime. That requirement cost us a number of prospective purchasers.

In time, the Marshals Service found a buyer, but not on my watch. No seized asset in the USMS custody ever received greater attention. We had our own representative on the premises daily to ensure that everything remained aboveboard. Books were audited regularly. And of course, the media had great fun—at my expense.

### Witness Protection

I got tired of all the bitching and moaning from people living under the protective veil of the Witness Security Program. There's no doubt about it. It's a tough life. But it's designed to be a life boat, a safe sanctuary for people in imminent danger, those targeted for death. Most applicants have agreed to testify as government witnesses in violent crime cases.

The induction process is extensive and involves psychological testing to ensure that prospective participants can endure its rigors, both the protectee and any immediate family in need of a secure environment.

There are no surprises. The ground rules are explained up front. Applicants receive a new identity, including driver's license and diplomas comparable to their actual educational attainments. Then they are relocated to a safe area. The program also does everything possible to link the protectee up with suitable job opportunities. However, it is often impossible to match the person's prior employment in either challenge or salary, particularly for those who were licensed professionals. Protectees must often suffer a considerable reduction in social status. And that's when the complaining begins.

The most difficult adjustment is coping with the total break from the past. No direct contact of any kind is permitted with anyone aware of the protectee's prior identity, except the assigned witness security inspector. To communicate with family members not residing in the household, participants must use an untraceable telephone system operated by the USMS. Protectees and participating family members must clear all travel with their inspector. Heavily armed deputy marshals accompany protectees to court appearances or to required meetings in the danger zone.

So what's the gripe? To someone facing an assassin's bullet, the program is an oasis in the desert. However, after a few months the desperation wears off and they get antsy for their old life. It's particularly hard for kids. Federal prosecutors or agents, in an attempt to gain a person's cooperation, may paint a rosy picture of witness protection—a mountainside cabin, a resort home, a nice suburban bungalow. Not quite. The program can't afford it. Agents and prosecutors also convince prospective participants that they'll receive a generous government stipend. Yes, they will receive a monthly payment, but few would consider it generous. It's more like basic subsistence, and for a limited time. After a reasonable period for transition, the protectee is expected to be financially self-sufficient.

These are the types of complaints I confronted each week. A couple of disgruntled participants vented their spleen to the media. Some even filed lawsuits claiming breach of contract or violation of their civil rights. None were successful. They had applied for the program, and we documented every step. Witness protection offers security first and reasonable comfort second, but no frills.

The witness protection program has been successful. No person in the program who followed instructions has ever been killed or seriously injured. In ninety-nine percent of the cases where security has been breached, it has been the participant's own fault. Perhaps a child or spouse contacted a friend or relative and revealed their location, or worse yet, slipped away for a secret meeting. Sometimes these inadvertent indiscretions are harmless; other times they're deadly. In most highly publicized cases of successful hits against program participants, the injured victim had voluntarily walked away from the program.

The Witness Security Program is the flagship of the Marshals Service fleet. Its members are specially selected and highly trained. It has a track record unparalleled in the world. Other countries seek advice and counsel from its elite staff of inspectors. For every protectee who has groused about the program's inadequacy, a hundred would swear that they could not have survived without it.

## Final Call

As one of the last surviving Republicans in the nascent Clinton Administration, it was inevitable that the dreaded call would come. Tara and I were in Salt Lake City, Utah, on June 20, 1993, attending the annual conference of the National Sheriff's Association. That morning, Senator Orrin Hatch presented me with the President's Award, conferred by the president of the association for promoting cooperation between the Marshals Service and the nation's sheriffs. When we returned to the room, there was a message to call Attorney General Reno. Janet Reno never called just to inquire how things were going.

To say that she and I never bonded is putting it mildly. However, our conversation that day was pleasant. She explained that the White House was close to finalizing its selection of my successor, and that I should pick a date to move on,

*Dedicating the United States Marshals Service tactical operations center at Fort Beauregard, Louisiana to Inspector Billy Degan, who was killed at Ruby Ridge. With me are Deputy Director James Roche and Chief Inspector John Haynes, head of the special operations group. (Courtesy of the U.S. Marshals Service.)*

any reasonable date. The offer was generous and I'll never forget the courtesy. I arbitrarily said October, which was fine with her. I ended up extending a month, to November, to assist my successor, Eduardo Gonzalez with his transition.

As one of my final acts as director of the Marshals Service, I named our Special Operations headquarters at Fort Beauregard, Louisiana, after Bill Degan. No other person in the agency's history better epitomized the mission or guiding principles of that elite unit.

I tell friends who are seeking presidential appointments to be equally prepared for the emotional high of accepting the mantle of office and the painful passing of the torch to another. With few exceptions, public service is finite in duration. You are a temporary steward of the public trust—as a commentator once put it, "your name is simply penciled in." I received a harsh reminder of how soon memory fades. About six weeks after leaving the Marshals Service, I called the new director, Eddie Gonzalez, and the receptionist asked me if I would kindly spell my last name.

# XXII
# Moving On

Life was agonizingly slow after I left the Marshals Service. With President Bill Clinton and the Democrats firmly entrenched, there was little likelihood that I'd be returning to government service in the foreseeable future.

Aside from income, there wasn't much about the private practice of law to excite me. No daily phone calls from senators, the attorney general, or the White House. My firm, Mays & Valentine (now Troutman Sanders), was a wonderful place to work, with a great group of people. I had a window overlooking the Potomac River, where I could watch sailboats with their brightly colored spinnakers dotting the waterfront.

The firm had great expectations that I would develop a booming white-collar defense practice. It never happened. I did take on a few criminal cases, but never felt comfortable litigating against my former colleagues in the U.S. Attorney's Office. They treated me with the utmost courtesy, but I always felt that I was trespassing on friendship.

I have the deepest respect for my friends who gave up the prosecution side to develop lucrative criminal defense practices. I was never able to make the transition. For me, the missing ingredients were enthusiasm and commitment. I was never able to summon the passion to be truly effective as a criminal defense lawyer. So I concentrated on cultivating a civil practice, mainly in the area of commercial litigation. It was challenging and sufficiently interesting to fill the day, but it lacked that vital element of adventure. The chase for billable hours just didn't cut it.

The only way to keep my spirit afloat was to develop some outside interests. Fortunately, the folks at Mays & Valentine were quite flexible as long as I produced a reasonable amount of business.

I devoted about an hour a day to working on scripts and story lines for "The Marshal." As much as I missed those weekly phone calls from movie stars and

Hollywood producers, even more deflating was their refusal to return my calls. Slipping back into the crowd was depressing, but I came up with an escape plan.

During my last week at the Marshals Service, I had appeared on two syndicated radio programs—one was "Larry King Live." I was fascinated, and with the right syndication, the money appeared to be fantastic. I began using every contact I had in the broadcasting industry to find a station willing to take a chance with a talk show devoted to crime and justice. At the time, there was nothing even close in the Washington market. When questioned if there was a true market for a narrow genre of programming, I pointed out that seventy-five percent of the evening news was rape, robbery, and mayhem. Some stations expressed interest, but no one would commit air time.

A few months later, fortune struck. My friend and client Bob Longwell, who had just left a job as general manager of WXTR, an oldies-format station, took over as manager of the largest talk radio station in the Washington market—WWRC, "Stimulating Talk Radio." Its fifty thousand watt signal extended to Richmond, Virginia, and from southern Pennsylvania to the Eastern Shore. The station was what those in the business would call a big boomer. Best of all, Bob had a two-hour slot on Sunday afternoon and was willing to give me a shot.

Preparing for two hours on the air was incredibly labor intensive, requiring about ten hours a week, and I had no staff. So I invited my friend Craig Floyd, director of the National Law Enforcement Officer's Memorial, to join the team as my broadcast partner. This gave us a tremendous advantage in recruiting guests since everyone in the law enforcement world knew Floyd. We were a hell of a team. The chemistry was there from our first moment on the air.

Fortunately, my old friend Ollie North also broadcast from WWRC. He and his staff spent countless hours tutoring us on how to put together our program. Another friend, disc-jockey legend Dave Kellog, critiqued our shows and helped burnish the quality of our on-air presentation. It took some work!

Filling two continuous hours on the air presents an enormous challenge. From the opening moment, you have to be prepared to leap from the starting gate with entertaining comments and penetrating questions. There is little time for reflection. You must train your voice to pronounce each syllable of every word clearly and precisely. However, the greatest source of continuing anxiety is hoping the scheduled guests show up. I learned always to have a backup plan.

Station management named the show "America Under Siege." The title was a little dramatic, but we could deal with it. Our shows were divided into two segments: the top criminal justice stories or issues of the week, and a related edu-

*With radio broadcast partner Craig Floyd, Director of the National Law Enforcement Officers' Memorial, at the memorial in Washington, DC*

cational or informational discussion. The educational segments dealt with such topics as lessons learned from autopsies, the quirks of forensic science, how drug lords build their dynasties, an undercover agent's inside view of the Mafia, a dialogue between rival street gangs, how inmates escape from prison, how a homicide investigator connects the dots, the insanity defense, and the art of defending the accused. Two of our most popular programs covered sports memorabilia fraud—how to determine if an autograph is real, and sexual assaults behind prison walls.

Although the show fit comfortably into the conventional talk radio mold, it had more of a news-magazine format than bare-knuckled debate. During a portion of each segment, we took calls from listeners, which was a hoot. Some were crazy, some were clever, but most were entertaining.

As our listenership gradually increased, so did the caliber of our guests. Before long we were booking the news makers themselves—top law-enforcement officials from around the country, the governors of Maryland and Virginia, dozens of congressmen and senators, best-selling authors such as Patricia Cornwell, and great lawyers such as John Roberts, now Chief Justice Roberts.

Police departments around the Washington area were champing at the bit to get a story on our show. The D.C. Police Department detailed two detectives each week to help with production, and we found a top-notch producer, Lee Caudell. After the first year, our listenership was among the highest of any show broadcast from the WWRC studios.

This was the life for me, but I only earned a hundred and twenty dollars a week. Quitting my day job was not an option. Union dues alone were almost a thousand dollars. Because Maryland was not a right-to-work state, the union contract covering broadcasters at the station barred you from the workplace unless you forked over the mandatory annual dues.

My stock climbed a bit when my friend Greta Van Susteren was tapped to cohost a show on CNN dedicated exclusively to crime and justice. "Burden of Proof" was a trendsetter spawned by the national obsession with the play-by-play media analysis of the O. J. Simpson trial. Other networks have attempted to replicate the format with limited success. I was a weekly guest on "Burden of Proof" and, in time, became one of the regular legal commentators on CNN, appearing on two or three programs a week. This resulted in a proliferation of invitations from other networks to comment on the legal issues of the day. I was one of the rare commentators at that time who took a conservative, pro-law-enforcement position. Since law schools almost uniformly inculcate a liberal twist on the law, most lawyers see the world a little left of center.

Soon, things got a bit out of hand. I was doing four or five programs a week on Fox News, CNN, MSNBC, CBS, and Court TV, as well as sound bites for the local stations. This required me to read three or four newspapers a day, in addition to preparing for my own radio show, which I plugged every chance I got. The exposure certainly enhanced my public visibility, but I'm not sure it did much for my law practice. Clients do, however, love to see their lawyer on TV. The real lure was my hope of a full-time gig as a network legal commentator.

### Weighing My Options

In 1996, I returned to my former firm, Reed Smith, after Mays & Valentine decided to close its Old Town Alexandria office. There, my practice focused on employment law, defending civil rights claims, and assorted commercial litigation. I am grateful that Reed Smith was tolerant of my love for broadcasting, which continued to overshadow my interest in practicing law. I was also able to remain active in the public policy arena. Another political ally, George F. Allen, had been elected governor of Virginia. I served on his transition team and was appointed to his Commission to Abolish Parole and Reform Sentencing, established to achieve two of his main campaign promises. We accomplished both goals. Based on our recommendations, the Virginia General Assembly abolished the flawed system that allowed criminals, even those committing violent crimes, to be released after serving as little as one sixth of their sentence. Under the new law, convicted felons were required to serve at least eighty-five percent of their sentence.

In response to the commission's report, the legislature also adopted voluntary sentencing guidelines to aid the discretion of judges and promote uniformity. The governor also appointed me to the Virginia Criminal Sentencing Commission, tasked with developing and implementing the guidelines. The governor's generosity extended even further. He put me in charge of overseeing the awarding of federal and state criminal justice grant money, and I became a very popular guy.

The Virginia Criminal Justice Services Board doled out big bucks, millions of dollars annually to law enforcement and to state and local government agencies in the Commonwealth, for criminal-justice-related programs and projects. It also developed training standards for certification of all sworn law enforcement officers in the state and people licensed in the field of private security. Each year, hundreds of police departments, sheriff's offices, and government agencies lobbied hard for grant money. You can be sure my friends in law enforcement kept in close touch with me as chairman. Needless to say, the time required to field my daily phone calls did little to nurture my law practice.

Unless you're a superstar, job security in the radio field rarely extends beyond today's broadcast. Craig Floyd and I learned that one afternoon after our show. The WWRC program director told me she needed to have lunch with me the following week. I took it as a positive sign. Maybe we were moving to prime time.

Over a sandwich, she casually revealed that the new general manager had decided to sell my air time to a minor league baseball franchise. Unfortunately, my advocate Bob Longwell had left to run a network of stations in Hawaii. My show was not being cancelled, just placed on "hold," indefinitely. It was like someone being wait-listed for college. The next week I learned the station was being sold to an all sports network. When the network offered to shift our broadcast base to a station in Baltimore, we declined. Too far to commute. Although slow in coming, the obvious finally clicked. I was never going to make it big in the broadcasting field, and it was time to get over it—and move on.

## Another Adventure

Briefly, I explored a new venture—banking. A long-time political ally, George Shafron, invited me to join the Board of Directors of the Heritage Bank, a small locally owned bank in McLean, Virginia. Soon I was totally engaged. I even began angling for a full-time executive position, as the bank expanded and diversified in services.

In the meantime, for several years I had been eyeing the possibility of becoming a state circuit court judge. The ambition had probably been inspired by my early days as a court clerk. Unfortunately, there were political barriers.

In Virginia, judges are selected by the General Assembly, which was dominated by Democrats; the process was extremely partisan. Consequently, there were only a half dozen or so Republican judges in the entire Commonwealth of Virginia; less than three percent. In the preceding one hundred years, only one Republican had been elected to a circuit court judgeship north of Fredericksburg, about fifty miles south of Fairfax County where I lived.

Although judges were formally elected by all one hundred forty members of the General Assembly, comprising one hundred delegates and forty senators, tradition dictated that the body as a whole defer to the local delegation. In rural areas, this made the single delegate and senator representing a county or city the judicial kingmakers. In counties with multiple delegates and senators, the selection process was more difficult and contentious. If a deadlock resulted, the governor filled the vacancy temporarily.

In Fairfax, the most populous county in Virginia, the delegation numbered twenty-seven fairly evenly split along party lines, with a slight Democratic tilt. Unlike other areas of Virginia, Fairfax used a merit process to select its judicial nominees, but there was always a political undercurrent. The best evidence was the record itself. There were no Republicans on the court. All fifteen circuit judges were Democrats.

Although I had been a high-visibility Republican for two decades, I always maintained a good relationship with the Democrats. Within the Fairfax delegation, I enjoyed an excellent relationship with a number of them, particularly Dick Saslaw, the Senate Majority Leader. Saslaw may have been liberal on some issues, but when it came to law enforcement, he was probably more of a hard liner than I was.

When I told Dick that I was interested in a position on the Fairfax County Circuit Court, he promptly volunteered, "Count me in." When Dick spoke, Democrats listened. State Senator Janet Howell, also a Democrat with whom I had a good rapport, pledged her immediate support. Almost all of the Republican delegates and senators were on board. But over the years, I've learned to run scared until the very end.

The balance of power in the Virginia Senate tipped in the Democrats' favor by one seat. Republicans were clearly gaining momentum, and Democrats could hear Republican footsteps close behind. I had even toyed with the idea of running for the Senate seat for the Mount Vernon area of Fairfax. It was a part-time position that would have allowed me to continue with my other interests. The incumbent, who despised me, had a strong Democratic base but a surprisingly low name identification. Mount Vernon, Virginia, was a "swing district"—sometimes it voted Democratic, sometimes Republican. Among the benefits of my frequent TV appearances and prior public service was significant name recognition. Of course, you never know if it's positive!

Several of my Republican buddies, without my urging, began quietly spreading the rumor that if I was not selected to be a circuit court judge, I would probably run for the Mount Vernon Senate seat. Whether or not I could have defeated the incumbent, several Democrats chose not to call my hand. Of the ten candidates competing for two vacancies, I got the most votes at the Fairfax delegation caucus.

I did not know what to expect when I arrived at Fairfax County Circuit Court on December 7, 1998. I knew several of the judges casually, but none well. From the first moment, everyone offered assistance, especially the judge sharing the neighboring office, Mike McWheeny, who spent hours each day teaching me how to be a judge. Judge Dennis Smith patiently spoon-fed me the law of domestic relations. Even though as a lawyer I had tried more than two hundred cases before juries, walking out into the courtroom and sitting down on the bench for the first time was a little intimidating. I was terrified of making a mistake or, worse yet, a fool of myself.

I have worked with thousands of people in my lifetime, but never has a group of men and women exhibited the warmth and friendship of my colleagues in Fairfax. The fact that I was a Republican was hardly ever mentioned, at least not until Chief Judge F. Bruce Bach gave his State of Judiciary address the following year.

Bach told the Fairfax Bar Association that at a recent meeting of all the chief circuit court judges in Northern Virginia, some verbal jousting broke out about diversity on the various courts. Bach said that he topped them all. In addition to women and blacks on his court, he even had a Republican. Bach, with his puckish sense of humor, told me my first day on the job that success on the bench requires only two things: gray hair to make you look distinguished, and hemorrhoids to make you look serious.

The crushing volume of cases in the Fairfax Circuit Court, the busiest in Virginia, forced you to master the art of judging quickly. Each judge handled almost seven hundred cases a year and averaged at least one jury trial per week, in addition to daily nonjury trials and at least fifty miscellaneous matters every Friday. A day to work quietly in the office, reading law or writing opinions, was a rare occurrence. The docket consisted of a mixture of civil, criminal, and, most dreaded, domestic relations cases. Domestic cases brought out the worst in both litigants and lawyers. Shouting matches and four-letter words were not uncommon. Custody battles often hinged more on revenge than the best interests of the child. Four years on that court prepared me for anything you could throw at me.

I lied to the General Assembly and the Fairfax County Bar Association when I told them unequivocally that I had no intention of seeking a federal judgeship.

### End of the Quest

Perhaps lied is too strong a term. I did not seek the Fairfax job only as a stepping stone to the federal bench. The political landscape had changed drastically in the intervening years. Chuck Robb had suffered a humiliating defeat by George Allen. As long as Robb was serving in the Senate, I had had no chance of being appointed to the federal bench.

When Congress created a new federal judgeship for Eastern Virginia in 2001, I called Susan Magill, Senator John Warner's chief of staff, to express my interest even before she was aware the position existed. Since the White House rarely selects people over fifty-five for federal judgeships, at age fifty-four I knew it was then or never. What made it especially inviting was that the new position was in Richmond, a hundred miles south of Fairfax, in a comparatively less-populated slower-paced area without gridlocked traffic.

Federal judgeships are sometimes jokingly called the last vestige of aristocracy in the United States. Because they are a lifetime appointment with full pay and benefits until the day you die, the competition can be tough. Although appointees must have good legal credentials, political pedigree is essential. After all, these are still, in essence, political appointments. Even though I enjoyed a good personal relationship with both the Virginia senators, John Warner and George Allen, so did the others in the chase. Federal judgeships at the U.S. District Court or trial level, while technically appointed by the president, are actually selected by the senators from that state who have the same political party affiliation as the president. Since President George W. Bush, Senator Warner and Senator Allen were all Republicans, the Virginia senators would prevail.

Campaigning for a federal judgeship is almost as challenging as running for political office. Rather than court voters, aspirants solicit endorsements from influential political activists with close ties to the senators, particularly the activists who raise the big money. That is where twenty years of active service to the Republican party, and helping in the various campaigns of each senator, paid dividends and gave me the edge. Two people, however, were instrumental in helping me pull this off: Susan Magill and George Shafron. Shafron was one of Warner's closest political advisors, and chairman of his finance committee. Magill had been Warner's closest aide for twenty years. I am eternally grateful to both, as well as to Senator Warner and Senator Allen. However, getting their nod was just the first hurdle. Rocky shoals lay ahead.

The next step was the interview with the Office of the White House Counsel, designed to explore the legal philosophy and analytical depth of the prospective nominee. Routinely asked areas of questioning include interpretation of federal statutes, the Federal Sentencing Guidelines, fidelity to legal precedent, and what traits make a good judge. The interview panel also delves into any matters that potentially could be embarrassing, such as arrests or sexual harassment complaints.

I interviewed first with the deputy counsel and then with Alberto Gonzales, the main guy. The White House counsel then makes his recommendation to the President's Judicial Selection Committee, which makes the final call. My only opposition was a delegation of Richmond lawyers who took umbrage with the appointment of someone from Northern Virginia. People who live down state don't really consider people from Northern Virginia to be *real* Virginians.

After I cleared this hurdle, the Department of Justice conducted its own competency and suitability review: telephone interviews with a dozen or so lawyers and judges who were able to attest firsthand to my legal ability and work ethic. The White House then referred the matter to the FBI for a background check. Because this is a lifetime appointment with removal only by impeachment, the Bureau digs pretty deep, sometimes all the way back to childhood years. The nominee receives a five-inch mound of paperwork to complete. The exhaustive forms trace your life from infancy: every address, school, and employer, with names and phone numbers. Because I had filled them out before, and fortunately retained copies, my law clerk Julie Gossman and I were able to accomplish the task relatively easily, in about two days.

Background investigations sometimes take months. In my case, it was completed in a little over a week. First, I'd had three prior FBI backgrounds done and many of the agents in the Washington FBI Office had known me for years. But more important, the agent assigned to my investigation wasted no time. Special Agent Mary Dolan was all business.

Once the background check clears, the president makes the formal appointment and sends it to the Senate for "advice and consent"—confirmation. This is when politics becomes a live-fire exercise. The Senate Judiciary Committee sends the nominee a thick questionnaire laden with land-mine questions to probe the inner workings of the mind.

On a parallel front, the American Bar Association (ABA) Standing Committee on the Judiciary does its own independent assessment of the nominee's qualifications. The lawyer who reviewed my background, Ossie Askew of North Carolina, was pleasant and fair minded. I will never forget his concluding comment as he wrapped up our extensive interview. He said that he had spoken to dozens of lawyers and read nearly six hundred newspaper articles about my career. He politely remarked that, "If I may say so," my image and reputation had matured over time, a little less brash and maybe a little more even handed. On reflection, I was flattered. After some introspection, I chalked it up to lessons life had taught me.

The historically liberal ABA granted me a "well qualified" rating, with one dissenting vote. The dissenting lawyer would have preferred a "qualified" rating; he doubted that anyone who had spent eighteen years as a prosecutor could be impartial. He apparently preferred those who devoted their entire career to defending criminals.

Once the Senate Judiciary Committee receives the ABA report, nominations are scheduled for a hearing, unless a member of the committee has a serious objection. Nominees for U.S. District Court are seldom formally rejected by the Senate. However, out of deference to the selecting senator if there is opposition, the nominee is passed over indefinitely for a hearing. Consequently, as months passed, I grew concerned that someone on the committee had flagged my nomination.

Finally, Senator Warner tracked down Committee Chairman Patrick Leahy of Vermont and asked about the delay. Senator Leahy, who owned a home in Virginia, apparently had followed my career, and professed great concern about my nomination. He found my background as an outspoken, tough-talking prosecutor unsettling. However, "as a favor to Senator Warner" he would reluctantly calendar my nomination for a hearing.

Given the politically charged tenor of the times, and the Democratic practice of blocking judicial nominees with conservative records, I thought my nomination was headed for interment. After several sleepless nights, I learned that Leahy pulled this stunt with almost everybody. The intent was to give the impression that Leahy was doing the other senator a favor.

I was apprehensive on the morning of my hearing before the Senate Judiciary Committee. It was the last hearing before the August recess; four other nominees had hearings at the same time. Both Senators Warner and Allen spoke on my behalf, as did Senator Jeff Sessions of Alabama. Sessions and I had served together as U.S. attorneys. Chairman Leahy asked the other nominees one of two soft-ball questions: Why do you want the job? or Do you think that pro bono work is important?

For me, Leahy pulled out a stack of news clips and fired away for at least forty-five minutes, citing comments I'd made over the years. Knowing that he held all the cards, I gave short, polite, unprovocative answers, sometimes spiced with a little disarming self-deprecating humor.

The underlying theme was obvious: How in the world can someone who has spent the majority of his adult life in law enforcement, and made all these zealous public comments, have a balanced perspective? I was prepared for the question, and knew that the fate of my nomination could turn on the answer.

I responded that my background was an asset that made me uniquely qualified. First, my government service, in many capacities and at many levels, had exposed me to a side of life few will ever face, not just as a spectator, but as someone responsible for finding solutions to people's problems. Life experience is a critical element of judicial problem solving—and I had it.

Second, my experiences as a United States attorney and head of the Marshals Service taught me to make decisions—tough decisions—in crisis situations. I had called the shots when lives were on the line. Even the brightest judge is ineffective who can't make a decision. Here, my record spoke for itself.

Last, because I had experienced law enforcement up close, I could separate the good from the bad and the real from the contrived. Sure, I have an appreciation for a well-investigated and prosecuted criminal case, but I also have little tolerance for the misuse of police power, abuse of constitutional rights, or prosecutorial misconduct. The law enforcement officer's mantle of authority is emblematic of trust placed by the people served—any breach is intolerable.

Without tipping his hand, Leahy reached for another newspaper article, this one a 1998 profile from the *Washington Post,* written just after I became a Fairfax Circuit Court judge. He focused on a quote in which I told the reporter that I was making a slow transition—I still occasionally sustained my own objections to lawyers' questions. Leahy spent a full minute remarking how he thought such judicial meddling was improper, then gave a cold stare, expecting to evoke a testy response.

My initial reaction was to tell him that it was a time-honored and accepted practice in Virginia, and the only way to keep some lawyers in check. But why cross swords needlessly? Instead, I smiled and replied that the reporter was a friend, and my comment was meant to be purely humorous. Leahy pursed his lips and said he had no further questions.

Leahy then came down from the podium and shook hands with the nominees, addressing each formally, some by title.

When he got to me, Leahy smiled and said, "Henry, good to see you in front of the committee again. You're gonna' be fine, but as you know, we need to make a record."

I was relieved that it was over, but a bit annoyed that I was wringing wet and a nervous wreck. That's the way they do it on the Hill.

*At my official swearing in as U.S. District Judge for the Eastern District of Virginia by Associate Justice of the U.S. Supreme Court, Antonin Scalia. (Photo courtesy of Robert Scott.)*

# Index

## A



## B



## C

## D



## E



## F



## G



## H

## I



## J



## K



## L

## M



## N



## O



## P



## R



## S